Praise for
To Light the Way

"Bringing to life characters you can't help but fall in love with, Nancy Naigle goes straight to the heart with this story of tragedy turned to triumph. A poignant reminder to never give up hope."

—SHEILA ROBERTS, author of *The Best Life Book Club*

"An emotional and uplifting story about surviving—no, make that thriving—after great loss, thanks to connection, friendship, and love (of all kinds!). Nancy Naigle truly understands the human heart and its incredible capacity for resilience. I came away wishing all the wonderful characters from Whelk's Island were my friends too!"

—MIRANDA LIASSON, Amazon bestselling author
and author of *Sea Glass Summer*

"A beautiful, tender, uplifting novel about love, loss, and the courage to embrace new beginnings. Nancy Naigle crafts a story that will touch your heart and inspire your soul."

—RAEANNE THAYNE, *New York Times* bestselling author

"Naigle returns to Whelk's Island in this charming tale of loss, love, and taking chances. *To Light the Way Forward* shines hope on the strength of family and friendship—and the power of coming together. Well-paced with rich detail, this story will delight readers."

—RACHEL HAUCK, *New York Times* bestselling author of
The Wedding Dress

"Nancy Naigle creates characters who are so multidimensional and real that it's like you are walking along the beach with them. It's a joy to go on their journey of miracles and weathering the storms of life.

To Light the Way Forward beautifully illuminates how resilient the human spirit is. Naigle splendidly captures the journey of love and loss through laughter, tears, and all the feelings. This book is an uplifting story of miracles and human connection. I want to live in the world of Whelk's Island!"

—ERIN CAHILL, actress, Hallmark

Praise for
The Shell Collector

"This is a beautiful story full of love, loss, and second chances. A collection of vivid characters, an inspiring setting, and heart-held hope for a better tomorrow."
—DEBBIE MACOMBER, #1 *New York Times* bestselling author

"As an avid shell seeker, I enjoyed this tale of surprises deposited among the tides, with its underlying message of finding just the shells we are meant to discover. A tender story of faith, love, and friendship that will warm the hearts of beachgoers and lovers of the sea."
—LISA WINGATE, #1 *New York Times* bestselling author of *Before We Were Yours* and *The Book of Lost Friends*

"A touching story of hope and renewal—proof that you can find more at the beach than shells."
—SHEILA ROBERTS, *USA Today* bestselling author

"An amazing emotional story of putting one foot in front of the other, of overcoming heartache, and of learning to live— and love—again. You'll cry—and smile—and you'll close the book with a very full heart."
—LORI FOSTER, *New York Times* bestselling author

"Nancy Naigle is at the top of her game with *The Shell Collector*. A compelling cast of characters—all acting in accord with their best lights—tackles the issues of loss and grief with wit and grace. 'The Wife' is my favorite new character. An uplifting, hopeful page-turner that shouldn't be missed!"
—BARBARA HINSKE, author of the Rosemont series and *Guiding Emily*

"A touching story about love, loss, and healing, *The Shell Collector* gives you all the feels. I enjoyed spending time at the beach collecting seashells—and pondering the encouraging messages inside them—right along with the characters. Don't miss this uplifting, faith-affirming read!"

—Brenda Novak, *New York Times* bestselling author

"*The Shell Collector* is a beautiful, emotional story about the glorious sunrise that can come after a dark night, about surviving loss and finding hope and joy again. Amanda, Maeve, and the entire cast will break your heart and then heal it all over again. I loved every word."

—RaeAnne Thayne, *New York Times* bestselling author

"In *The Shell Collector,* Naigle takes readers on a hopeful journey of healing after unimaginable loss. A tragic past, lovable characters, and a charming small-town setting align for a meaningful beach read. Don't miss this tender tale full of wisdom and insight!"

—Denise Hunter, bestselling author of *Bookshop by the Sea*

"*The Shell Collector* is utterly charming. Naigle's story of restoration, love, and hope is a perfect read any time of the year. The characters are fun if not a bit quirky, and the setting evokes so much peace. Well done. I loved it."

—Rachel Hauck, *New York Times* bestselling author

"*The Shell Collector* is an unforgettable story of love, hope, and healing. This inspiring novel has found a place in my heart."

—Jane Porter, *New York Times* bestselling author

"*The Shell Collector* gives voice to the profound truth of grieving and learning to come alive again. Nancy Naigle beautifully shows how love can come in so many different forms, as long as you're open to the unexpected miracles life has to offer. In her own words, 'Life is rarely predictable if we're doing it right.'"

—Erin Cahill, actress, Hallmark

Other Novels by Nancy Naigle

To Light the Way Forward

To Light the Way Forward

A Novel

NANCY NAIGLE

WATERBROOK

WaterBrook

An imprint of the Penguin Random House Christian Publishing
Group, a division of Penguin Random House LLC
1745 Broadway, New York, NY 10019

waterbrookmultnomah.com
penguinrandomhouse.com

A WaterBrook Trade Paperback Original

LIBRARY OF CONGRESS CATALOGING-IN-PUBLICATION DATA
Names: Naigle, Nancy, author.
Title: To light the way forward: a novel / Nancy Naigle. Description:
[Colorado Springs] : WaterBrook, 2025.
Identifiers: LCCN 2024043177 | ISBN 9780593601044 (trade paper-
back) | ISBN 9780593601051 (ebook)
Subjects: LCGFT: Romance fiction. | Christian fiction. | Novels.
Classification: LCC PS3614.A545 T6 2025 | DDC 813/.6—dc23/
eng/20240920
LC record available at https://lccn.loc.gov/2024043177

Printed in Canada on acid-free paper

2 4 6 8 9 7 5 3 1

Title page art from stock.adobe.com/eyetronic

The authorized representative in the EU for product safety and
compliance is Penguin Random House Ireland, Morrison Chambers,
32 Nassau Street, Dublin D02 YH68, Ireland.
https://eu-contact.penguin.ie

Wishing you a grateful heart that will allow disappointment and worries to drift out with the tide, and welcome love and light to surround and comfort you every day going forward.

To Light the Way Forward

Prologue

TUG BASNIGHT STOOD AT THE COUNTER OF HIS DINER, holding the latest issue of *The Scout Guide for the Outer Banks*. His fingers grazed the soft pink ribbon tied around it. Maeve would've loved the delicate ribbon—the color of her favorite sea glass—the ocean blue cover, and the gold foil lettering shimmering like sunlight on the waves. She had an eye for details and this—this was the kind of thing she made a fuss over. Her memory washed over him, and the weight of her absence pressed down on him again.

With a quick pull, the ribbon came undone, slipping through his fingers like a memory he couldn't hold on to. He set the delicate ribbon aside, too pretty to throw away. Maeve might be gone, but he still found himself saving pretty things, as if there'd be someone to wrap a fancy gift for someday again.

He glanced toward the booth where Maeve used to sit, expecting to catch a glimpse of her sandy flip-flops peeking out from the hem of her long skirt under the table. An old man with old habits, ones he wasn't ready to let go of just yet.

Tug flipped open the glossy book, the pages thick and luxurious. It looked totally out of place in his simple oceanfront diner.

Paul had convinced him to be a part of this—insisting on funding a spread to highlight Whelk's Island. Paul's business, Paws Town Square, had gained positive exposure in the northern Virginia edition, with a glowing story about Paul's work with military dogs. He was a true American hero. The book was designed to connect small businesses, show the people behind them, and serve as a vacation and community guide. And here he was flipping through it, trying to feel connected to a world that seemed to move on without him.

Tug looked through the beautiful photographs, searching for a familiar face.

There it was. Paul's. And his. "I'm a star, and they must've airbrushed me," he managed to say through laughter. "I look right good there." He straightened and pulled his glasses to reading position.

"Talking to yourself again?" The Wife called from the deck.

"Not talking to you," Tug replied without even a glance. His parrot, lovingly named The Wife, kept him company and sane most days, but she lived up to her name with all the unsolicited commentary. Still, he loved that old bird. Maybe he'd use that ribbon on a nice present for her someday. "I'm reading something. You can't read," he hollered back.

A series of smooching sounds came from The Wife's direction.

He shook his head and read on. There were snippets about each of the businesses and a summary about Whelk's Island.

> Whelk's Island isn't your typical tourist beach destination. No, this small town in North Carolina with beautiful sandy beaches and an abundance of shells has somehow remained a best-kept secret. It's a tight-knit community steeped in tradition, and if you do happen to veer off the highly traveled paths down the coast into this town and stop in at Tug's Diner, you're likely to notice a town secret hanging right there on the wall in plain sight.

Framed are shells along with the letters people have written to Tug about the special gifts they found while visiting. The shells are all different shapes and sizes, but they have one thing in common. Anonymous messages profoundly perfect for the moment in which they were discovered.

How the shells with the messages came to be, how they landed in the right hands at the right time, is a mystery, and for some, it's impossible to comprehend. But to those who've experienced it firsthand, Whelk's Island will forever hold a special place in their hearts.

Tug's heart swelled with love for Whelk's Island. They'd captured her perfectly.

Nostalgic tears blurred the words.

He'd been blessed with plenty of customers during every season. He loved serving this community, and a good meal at a reasonable price was getting harder to find with inflation.

But did he have the energy for an influx of customers? Tables were tight as it was. He'd have to hire more help if this ad did what it promised.

Just the thought made him tired. *I'll cross that bridge if we get there.*

The company that created the booklets was holding a launch party for the promotion of the guide in every new city. He glanced at the calendar, where he'd circled the date in red so he wouldn't forget.

If the storm swirling in the Caribbean ever got its act together and started moving this way, it might rain out the *Scout* shindig next week.

Tug never trusted early-August storms, and this one looked like it might actually hit hurricane status. He shook off the tingle that chased up his spine.

Chapter One

AFTER A WEEK OF WEATHER WATCHING AND PREDICTIONS, the storm reached hurricane status and hit a couple of smaller islands in the Caribbean. Following a few bobbles, Hurricane Edwina gathered strength, and now the models were predicting she would follow the coastline right through the Carolinas.

Whelk's Island hummed with anticipation as residents prepared for the approaching hurricane. Locals were no strangers to the routine.

Messages to past tempests peppered sheets of plywood all around town, reused each year. The spray-painted messages carried a confidence that leaned toward arrogance, almost daring the storms to do their worst. *GO AWAY, HUGO. TURN AROUND, THOMAS, OR ELSE!* and *FORGET YOU, FREDA* were some leftover warnings from the past.

No matter how bad the hurricane predictions got, there were always some residents who stayed put, defying evacuation orders with the same stubborn resolve as surfers who refuse to abandon the waves as a storm churns the ocean, threatening to rip them to no tomorrow in a blink.

Tug knew that attitude firsthand. He used to be one of those surfers riding the trickier waves the storm blew in. But with eight decades of experience, he'd grown less cocky. Tug had never evacuated before, but he would at least give it a thought these days. He wasn't sure if the storms were getting worse or if he was getting wiser, finally.

A man laid a tip on the counter as his family of four left the diner.

Tug gave him a nod of appreciation and wiped down the counter to make room for the next customers.

The aroma of freshly brewed coffee mingled with the anxious chatter coming from the line of people waiting to get in. The storm chugging out in the Atlantic was the topic of the day, and televisions on the wall caught everyone's attention with each update.

Tug couldn't shake the uneasiness gnawing at his gut.

Early-August hurricanes were a rarity, and the fiercest ones weren't usually until late September or October, but this one stirred disquiet in him.

He forced a smile through the ominous warnings, welcoming his customers like it was just another Monday.

In her cage, The Wife stretched her charcoal-gray wings to their full span of eighteen inches, then screeched.

Tug glanced toward her cage on the deck. Beyond the windows that overlooked the beach, the ocean was choppier than it had been earlier.

"Get your sea legs!" The Wife called.

Tug seated the customers, then walked out back to check on The Wife. "Are you okay?"

"Are you okay?" The bird cocked her head.

"I asked you first."

She jerked her head around. "No!"

He checked her food and water. "What's got you upset?"

"Get your sea legs. Time to go," The Wife said.

Tug laughed every time The Wife pulled that phrase out. The first time he'd ever heard her say it was to Willa, the woman he almost married a long, long time ago. Turned out The Wife knew Tug's taste better than he did, because she'd been telling Willa to go for months before Tug realized it wasn't going to work. The Wife had loved Maeve, though.

"It's getting antsy out there," he said to The Wife. He pointed to the water. "Do you recognize that angry-water dance? Don't worry. We'll get you moved to safety in due time."

She made water droplet sounds, one of her favorite noises, and then snapped her wings tight to her body.

Tug and Maeve had talked about this before.

How the ocean spoke its own language, warning of things to come.

This is my first big storm without you, Maeve. What do you think? Any communication from Maeve would be welcome, but all the wishing and talking to himself couldn't bring her back. *I'm always thinking about you.*

Sometimes it felt like Maeve was close by, but that would mean he believed in ghosts—and he didn't. He believed in angels, though, and Maeve had been the most angelic woman he'd ever known.

Life on Whelk's Island wasn't the same without her. He wasn't the same. He missed her. Every single day, sad moments snuck in. Life would never be the same, and that made it a little less appealing. He sighed.

"I'm just an old man talking to an old bird."

The Wife scooched close to the bars and lowered her head, insisting on a scratch. Tug slipped his fingers through and gently massaged her head. "Just like a woman, always wanting a shoulder rub." He reached down into the cabinet and pulled out a dried banana chip. "Here's a little something to sweeten your afternoon. We've still got a lot of work to do today."

"Heigh-ho, heigh-ho, it's off to work we go," she sang out.

"Talk to you in a little while."

"Goodbye. Talk to you later," The Wife said.

A couple of surfers paddled out along the pier. The restless ocean was producing good waves today. Tug could watch them all day, but he had a diner full of customers. "Keep an eye on the surfers," he said to The Wife.

She stood on one leg and stretched the other behind her. "Lifeguard on duty."

As he headed back to the kitchen, more surfers gathered next to the diner's fancy blue-and-white sign. It had become a traditional meetup spot for surfers when he started the place and was still surfing himself. Big and hand-sandblasted by a local guy, it was worth the years of breakfasts Tug had bartered for it. That sign had lasted all these years with only a few touch-ups. The only thing that had changed was the addition of a smaller swinging sign that read SURFERS ALWAYS WELCOME, which his surf buddies had given him when he officially hung up his board for good. The lifestyle of a surfer never goes away.

He stepped inside, doing a cha-cha as the servers whisked past him.

Tug washed his hands and plucked the next ticket off the clips. He dropped a basket of clam strips into the fryer just as the local news broke in again on the television show in progress.

The reporter was in a frenzy over the possibility of the hurricane making its way to their area. "And *now* it looks like this storm could threaten the Outer Banks of North Carolina," he said. "Residents need to prepare for the damaging winds and potential of a disastrous storm surge. If things keep going the way they are now, this tropical storm is expected to become a Category 2 hurricane by morning."

Tug looked up. The projections still looked like an enormous bowl of spaghetti. *We're overdue for another big storm.* They'd been lucky the last few years with the storms sort of bouncing off the Carolina coast before they got to Whelk's Island.

He tried to keep his mind on the orders. There was no sense getting worked up about the weather this early in the game. They had at least three days before that needed to happen.

As Tug pushed two orders of their popular octopus-shaped pancakes from the kids' menu into the pickup window, he noticed it was for the table where Amanda, the newest resident of Whelk's Island, and her kids usually sat.

He leaned over the counter. Indeed, it was them sitting there. He snatched one of the warm plates of pancakes back to swap with a fresh stack. The diner's famous octopus pancakes came with blueberry syrup to match the ocean, but Hailey was a strawberry fan. He quickly doctored up a custom version for her. This family was closer than real family to him, and he loved delighting them with the little things.

"I'll be right back," Tug called to the cook. "I'll deliver this order," he told the server, then carried all three plates over to their table.

"Tug!" Jesse squealed. "Hi! Mom said it was too busy for us to say hello."

"I'm never too busy for y'all." He gave Jesse a wink. "How's my man this morning?"

"Grrreat!"

"Glad to hear it." Tug set the plates on the table. "Traditional for Jesse with the Atlantic Ocean blueberry syrup, and the strawberry syrup for you, Hailey."

"Thank you for my special red sea octopus," Hailey said in appreciation of the strawberry substitution. At eight years old, she was quite confident in her preferences, not hesitating to inform Tug of hers the first time they ordered these pancakes.

"You are welcome, young lady." It was their special little something, and even though Amanda's family were still relative newcomers to Whelk's Island, having moved here a couple of years ago, this family had touched his heart in a way he never knew possible. He imagined this was what being a grandpa felt like. It was the best feeling in the world.

Jesse immediately stabbed his fork into his pancakes. "Mom says we have to leave town for a while because of the storm," he whined. "It's not even raining." He shoved a bite into his mouth.

From the way Amanda looked, the kid was wearing her out this morning.

"Well, Jesse, it's your mom's job to keep you safe." He leaned close enough to whisper. "What's so bad about leaving town if it's going to be raining here, anyway? Look."

The meteorologist on the local news dramatically swept his arm across the map, warning of possible high winds and rain.

Jesse rose from his chair to get a better look at the television, then plopped down and dropped his head into his hand. "It's sunny outside. I think the weatherman has gone cuckoo."

A loud whistle came from the deck. "People are more cuckoo than birds," The Wife squawked, ending with a high-pitched chirp.

"See? Even The Wife thinks so." Jesse looked pretty smug for a six-year-old.

Tug eyed the boy. "Did you teach her that?"

Jesse glanced around, trying not to look guilty, and then shrugged. "I might have said that to her a couple times."

"Mm-hmm. I know you." Tug settled his gaze on the young boy. "Can I expect her to be saying 'Jesse' soon too?"

"I wish." Jesse shrugged in disappointment. "She could say it if she wanted to. She just won't. I've been trying and trying to get her to say 'Jesse is the best.'"

Tug loved how Hailey and Jesse made a fuss over The Wife. If she outlived him, she'd be in great hands with these folks. He'd already written it into his will, not even bothering to ask, because if all else failed, Amanda's longtime friend Paul would take care of her since he had the perfect facility over at Paws

Town Square to house a wisecracking, opinionated old bird. Actually, Amanda and Paul were more than friends. Everyone else could see that plain as day, but they were taking their relationship slow.

Couldn't blame them. They'd both been through a rough patch. The kind some never figure their way through. But those two were better together, and everyone knew it. Tug just wished they'd make it official already, so people would quit gossiping about it behind their backs.

The volume in the restaurant softened, as folks' attention was captured by the weatherman's apprehension and the report about the potential weather risks.

"It's never ending. It's like this every fifteen minutes." Tug groaned. "Seems to me all the triple Dopplers, satellites, Nexrads, and quadruple-whatever predictions just get people worried way sooner than need be."

"We went to the grocery store, and there was no bread." Jesse's eyes were wide. "None." He made a big zero with his fingers. "I can't even have a sammich."

"I'll make sure you have bread," Tug said. "Don't you worry, little man."

Amanda brushed Jesse's hair back from his forehead. "We'll be traveling, anyway. We can stop and get some, and your grandmother has everything we need at her house."

"You're going to your folks' place?" Tug asked.

"That's the plan. I wanted to just go inland a little, but Paul insisted it was the perfect time to visit. He's right. It has been a while since we've been."

"I'll put together some snacks for your road trip," Tug said. "I pack a really good picnic."

"You don't have to do that," Amanda insisted.

"I want to. Besides, they love my cooking." He nodded toward the kids.

"We do!" Hailey and Jesse said.

"Jinx!" Hailey said it first, and Jesse should be used to it. She always beat him to the jinx.

"One of these days you're going to be faster than her," Tug teased Jesse.

Hailey put her fork down. "The lines were forever long at the store. I thought we'd never get here. It's almost lunchtime, and we're just having breakfast. I was starving. This hit the spot."

"Well, folks round here have been through a lot of hurricanes over the years. Some were false alarms, but it never hurts to be prepared."

"Now, wait a minute." Amanda lifted her coffee cup and cocked her head. "Maeve once told me you hosted the best hurricane parties on Whelk's Island back in the day."

Tug pressed a finger to his lips and slid into the booth next to Jesse. "I used to, but that was a long, long time ago. The storms weren't as brutal back then, or maybe we just weren't informed enough to know the difference. They seem to get worse every year."

"Don't let me find out y'all are planning a big old party and sending me out of town with these two. Else we're staying." Amanda giggled, and Tug loved how her smile could light up a room.

"Let's have a hurricane party," Jesse said. "Will there be cake?"

"No, I'm just teasing Tug," Amanda assured him. "We're leaving tomorrow." She turned to Tug. "They don't want to go. We're all dragging our feet a little."

"It's the right thing to do. Leave, I mean, not drag your feet."

"I don't feel good about going without Paul." Her lips trembled, and she pressed them together.

Amanda would probably always hold a fear in her heart about being separated from the ones she loved, since Jack was killed while deployed. It was a sensitive situation. Tug wondered if Paul had thought that through.

"Why don't you come with us?" Jesse begged.

"I'm not going anywhere. I'd rather go down with the ship!" He regretted the flippant remark when concern washed over Jesse's expression. "I'm teasing. Does this look like a ship? Paul and I will both be safe."

"Then we should be safe here too."

"How do you argue with that?" Amanda pulled her plate in front of her. "Maeve said her house had weathered every hurricane—"

"But Maeve was a stubborn old gal, and she didn't have these two precious hearts to protect. Enjoy the time with your folks. Seriously, even in the weaker storms, it's frightening. The houses creak and moan. The ocean is so angry you wouldn't recognize it, and when you get back, you'll have the best treasures the sea can wash up."

"I can't wait," Hailey said.

Chapter Two

THE FRONT DOOR OF THE DINER SWUNG OPEN, AND FOUR deeply suntanned men walked in. "There an old surfer in the house?" one of them bellowed.

"Excuse me." Tug slid from the booth. "We've got windows to board up." He patted the table twice and then pointed a playful finger at Jesse. "You be good for your mom." Tug leaned in toward Amanda. "Stay in touch. We're going to be fine."

Tug headed for the two men at the entrance of the diner. "Hey, boys." He'd known them since they were just shaggy-haired teens riding waves at the pier. They were men now, with families and real jobs. But they still often stashed their long-boards down here after a morning of surfing to come in and grab coffee and breakfast. "Thanks for coming over to help me get ready. We all know these storms have a mind of their own."

"That's for sure," Skip said. "I already boarded my place up and sent the family ahead to my in-laws'."

"You're staying?" Tug found it hard to hide his surprise.

"You know he's leaving." Skip's best friend, Bebe, elbowed Skip. "Missus wouldn't let him stay."

"I don't want to," Skip defended himself. "My family needs me, and I'm smart enough not to risk my fool neck on the waves in a hurricane now." Skip looked at Tug and thumbed toward Bebe. "You know where that guy will be."

"We have this talk every year." Tug ran a hand through his gray hair, but he understood. He really did. He'd been one of them a long, long time ago.

Bebe had wild hair, and his skin looked like leather from all the years in the sun. "I hope we can find the panel numbers on those old boards for all the graffiti on them. They got more paint than they got wood on 'em."

"Hey, they've done the trick for fifteen years. No reason to replace them now." Tug grabbed the storage door keys from the hook and led the way down to the storage area. "I even came up with a couple of new warnings for this storm."

"I don't think there's room to paint any more new sayings." Skip chuckled. "It's looking like abstract art as it is."

Tug wagged a finger in Skip's direction. "That's *my* abstract handiwork, and I'll find a spot. I take great pride in these paintings. It might just be hurricane warnings to you, but to me . . . it's art, and it works!" He twirled an imaginary paintbrush in the air.

"Yeah. Whatever. Don't quit your day job." Skip slapped Tug's back.

Tug shrugged, enjoying the ribbing.

"Since we added two-by-four frames around the boards after Dorian blew through and *tugged* the corners right off them, you should have some room to paint your warnings there." Skip laughed at his own joke. "See what I did there? *Tugged* at the corners."

Tug shook his head as he unlocked the door to the storage room. "Yeah, yeah. Get to work." The guys started pulling sheets of plywood out and leaning them against the building. For the first time, Tug was happy not to have to do it himself.

Before previous storms, he'd been the one to board up Maeve's house, too, but Paul was taking care of that for Amanda now that she lived there. The pretty blue beach house had weathered every storm that had hit this coast since it was built. That was back when craftsmen were so proud of their work they overbuilt rather than skirt even the code minimum to turn a dollar. They sure didn't build them like that these days. Not even the million-dollar homes.

His vision blurred as tears built, as they still often did when he thought of Maeve. Regrets had a way of tearing a man's heart at the edges like a weathered hurricane board.

Bebe slid out another sheet of plywood. "Can't even make out most of them." He stood back, trying to decipher the spray-painted words. "I can't even make this one out since there are so many names on top of each other."

"I think it was *Matthew*. That one goes on the front windows. F1, and there should be panels F2 and F3 right behind it if we put them back in the order we took them down. Oh, look." Tug gestured toward the board Skip was carrying out. It read, *DON'T GET ON SANTA'S NAUGHTY LIST.*

There were four names scratched out. ~~DORIAN~~. ~~FLORENCE~~. Then ~~FAY~~ and ~~IAN~~. The last scrawl wasn't a name at all. Just *HASTA LA VISTA, HURRICANE* in big letters.

Bebe hiked a sheet over his head with a grunt. "Remember the back-to-back storms that one year? Flooded the beach roads for weeks."

Tug recalled it well. "Who could forget? People were coming to the diner on floats and inner tubes. If I remember correctly, you and Bebe paddled around on your surfboards for the better part of a week."

"Guilty on both accounts," Bebe agreed. "But in my defense, I only used the inner tube to get back to my house, so I could get my surfboard. We'd all been at Skip's when that storm bounced back and hit us again. No one expected that."

Tug laughed at the explanation. When he was their age, he might've thought it was a pretty good excuse too. "Well, there's always you, Bebe. You never surprise me anymore."

"I'm taking that as a compliment." Bebe grinned, never apologizing for his love of surfing. He was more chill than all the rest of them put together, but when it came to these big weather events, he was always here to help.

"You're a good one, no matter what they say about you." Tug clapped Bebe's shoulder, then chuckled when the backhanded compliment registered on his face.

"Wait—what?" Bebe looked confused. "Who said what?"

"Kidding, Bebe. Thanks, boys. I've got a diner full of customers, but as soon as you get these in place, you've earned a free lunch."

Ladders rattled as they hit the side of the diner, followed by the hum of screw guns securing the discolored plywood. With two teams at it and everything prenumbered, it wouldn't take long.

"One last thing," Tug said before he turned to head back inside. "Can y'all bring the big coolers from storage up to the kitchen for me?"

"Sure thing," Skip answered. The guys had helped enough times to know the drill.

Tug probably didn't even need to be here supervising. "I'll meet you inside when you're done." He walked through the front door. "No hurry, no worries," he announced over the chatter. "We aren't closing early. We're just getting the windows boarded up so everyone will have a safe and dry place to come until the storm decides what it's going to do. Sorry to steal your view so soon. With any luck, it will have all been for nothing."

A rolling echo of thanks filled the space. There were a few appreciative shouts from the customers too. "You're always here for us, Tug."

"My pleasure," he said with a smile.

Tug cleaned a table for the guys and plopped a Reserved sign on it to hold it for them.

About half the people inside right now were probably scoffing at the warnings, while the other half were worried.

Tug refrained from comment, not wanting to sway anyone one way or the other, because the ugly truth was, people lost their lives in these natural catastrophes every year. The tropical storm was gaining strength, but her path was still uncertain, bouncing from east to west in a squiggly trail.

Amanda got up from the table, her children beside her.

"You know, Tug, you could come with us," Hailey said. "I asked Mom. It's okay."

"I can't leave The Wife."

"Paul will take care of her for you," Jesse said matter-of-factly. "He has to stay to work. You can come and take care of us."

"I'd like that very much, but I think I'm going to stay where I can be helpful to the folks who stay behind who are not prepared. I have food, water, and generators. People will need the basics."

Amanda rested her hand on Jesse's drooping shoulder. "We are going to be fine. And we will be back in no time."

Hailey bit her lip.

Tug stooped and leaned in. "Are you okay?"

She shrugged. Wise beyond her years. Losing her father at such a young age, she'd stepped into the big-sister role and been sensitive to the pain her mother experienced when Jack didn't come home from his tour of duty. Reuniting with Paul, Jack's best friend, had been a blessing for them all.

"Are you worried?" Tug whispered.

Her lips pressed into a thin line. She glanced over her shoulder, then turned her back toward her mother.

"You can tell me," he said.

"What if we come back and you and Paul aren't here anymore?" she whispered. "What do we do then?"

"Can I talk to you? Out there in the gazebo?"

Hailey nodded and allowed him to take her hand. Tug gave Amanda a wink. Amanda pressed her hand to her heart as he led Hailey outside.

"My mini-Maeve. You're smart just like she was. You're so much like Maeve I don't know how you aren't related."

"We love her like family," Hailey said.

"Me too." He nodded to one of the tables. "Sit with me for a minute." He held out the chair for her and then sat across from her.

"Mom says that makes us family."

"I guess it does, then." Tug reached over and squeezed her hand. "What can I do to help you?"

"It doesn't make sense to me. If it's so dangerous we have to leave, I don't know why you and Paul can stay."

"That's fair. So here's the thing. Every storm is different, but usually it's a lot of high winds, and they can cause power outages. Sometimes shingles fly off, and some signs will blow out, leaving shards of glass lying around. The buildings moan and groan against the high winds, which is pretty scary to hear, and the way we sit along the coast, we always experience some flooding."

"We could just stay inside and wear ear plugs, so we don't hear the scary sounds."

Tug couldn't hold back a smile. "You're right. You could. But with no power, it'll be hot and miserable and there's nothing you can do until the storm is over except sit there and wait. Sometimes the electricity goes out for days. I promise, you are going to be way more comfortable at your grandparents' house."

She twisted her foot nervously, then looked into his eyes. "Will you call me every day and let me know you're okay?"

"Sure. I can do that. Don't be afraid. We'll be okay."

"I'll pray every day. Every hour!"

"I know you will, Hailey. You are a sweet angel. I'll be praying for you, too, and we will be back together soon. You just wait and see."

"Thank you, Tug." She leapt up and raced to his side, wrapping her arms around his neck. "I love you."

"I love you, too, kiddo."

She released him, and he stood and reached for her hand.

"Will you do something for me while you're gone?"

"Anything," she said, hope dancing in her eyes.

"I've been thinking I need some new pictures to put up around here. Could you work on that for me?"

"Yes! I'm getting really good at drawing." Her face grew serious. "I can definitely do that for you."

"I still have the picture of the diner you drew for me. It's very special to me."

"I'll pack my markers to take with me. You just wait until you see what I make for you this time." She looked like her spirits had lifted.

"I think your mom is ready to leave. Why don't you get Jesse and y'all tell The Wife your plans so she won't worry about you two while you're away?"

Hailey ran off and grabbed Jesse, who was resistant until she explained what they needed to do.

Amanda walked over to him. "What would I do without you, Tug?"

"You've got Paul. You'll always be fine."

"I like having both of you on my side."

"I like it too." He pointed to the line of customers still growing outside his diner. "I'm going to get these folks seated."

There was a constant flow of customers all day long, and the to-go orders were still piling up at closing time. Tug worked until they had every single one satisfied before calling it a night.

Chapter Three

UPDATES ABOUT THE HURRICANE IN THE ATLANTIC BUZZED on the television, leaving Rosemary grappling with her situation. Though there was no threat of the hurricane here in Pennsylvania, she'd planned this trip to Whelk's Island months ago and, depending on which of the models was right, it could be bad news for that area. It was unfortunate timing.

The storm was moving so slowly, she might be able to get to the island to visit her high school friend Kathleen and leave before it ever came ashore—or not.

Rosemary dreaded the conversation sure to arise about this with her daughter, Nina.

Since she'd moved in with Nina earlier this year, they'd had their share of differing opinions. They'd based the decision to live together on economics. Nina's divorce left her alone with a teenage daughter in their huge house. With interest rates through the roof, it made little sense for Rosemary to purchase her own home when Nina had all that room. One household payment, one yard to take care of, and they'd help each other.

But Rosemary hadn't considered how living under someone else's roof would stymie her. It was different when you were on your own turf.

This morning she'd gotten up extra early to prepare a nice breakfast for her daughter and granddaughter. The last time she'd done it, she hadn't taken into consideration that they were always in a hurry in the morning, and they'd left without touching it.

Rosemary peered through the glass window of the oven at the breakfast casserole. The cheese had blistered just right, and the smell of the salty breakfast meats peppered the air in the most delicious way.

She turned off the oven and grabbed the pot holders. Warm air wafted toward her as she took out the piping-hot casserole and set it on the counter.

"That smells amazing." Kendra breezed into the room. "Mom never cooks stuff like that."

Nina walked in right behind her. "I do. Sometimes. We just don't have a lot of time for that during the week."

"Which is why it's my pleasure to do this for the two of you." Rosemary grabbed three small plates and started serving the casserole. "And I know you're in a hurry—you always are—but it's just a few bites, and breakfast is the most important meal of the day."

"I'll be the size of a house if I eat like this, Mom," Nina said.

"You'll burn it off before lunch. Trust me." Rosemary watched Kendra take a bite, praying she'd like it.

"The best!" Kendra gave her a thumbs-up.

The teen shoveled the small portion in so fast Rosemary had to hold back from telling her to slow down. Nina had already voiced her aggravation about Rosemary cutting in too often with unsolicited advice.

Rosemary plastered a smile on her face. "I just want to be helpful."

"I know, Mom. Thank you." Nina walked over and gave her a hug. "I know you mean well." She released her, her smile drooping. "But mostly you just make me feel inadequate."

"Oh, honey. No. That wasn't my goal." Rosemary's heart

sank. It seemed no matter what she did, it was wrong, or not the way Nina wanted it.

"I know, I know. In my heart I know. I'm just . . ." Nina stopped and put her purse on the counter. "You know what? Let's take five minutes and sit down and eat."

"I'm done," Kendra said.

"Then have seconds," Nina said through a forced smile.

"Awesome." Kendra scooped another serving onto her plate and plopped down at the table.

Rosemary sighed. "You don't have to—"

"I know, Mom, but you're right. We should appreciate your help. It's just a few minutes. I'm sorry I kind of ruined the whole moment."

The moment had been ruined, but Rosemary appreciated the sentiment. It was so hard to live in the shadows. She'd always been the lady of the house, and she didn't know any other way to be, with or without Kai. *I miss him so much.*

They quickly ate breakfast in quiet with only the television in the background. Rosemary mentally kicked herself for not thinking to turn it off when they agreed to stay and eat. The meteorologist pointed out the various models and hurricane threats to the coast.

"Guess you'll have to reschedule your trip." Nina got up and put her plate in the dishwasher.

"Not necessarily," Rosemary said.

Nina slowly turned and pulled a hand to her hip. "You can't go with a storm on the way."

At seventy-two, Rosemary wasn't about to start taking orders from her daughter.

"Actually, I can." She checked her tone, trying to keep her words kind and even. "I don't need your permission, and with the storm moving so slowly, I can probably get there and come back before it ever makes a turn."

Nina huffed. "Don't be silly. There's a hurricane barreling up the coast. It's no time to go on a pleasure trip."

"There's nothing barreling." Rosemary cocked her head, resisting raising her voice. "That storm is days away, and they don't even know where it's going to land. Have you seen the cone of uncertainty? The only thing the weather reporter is certain of is that he's got our attention and bread sales are up."

"Stop downplaying the situation." Nina snatched her purse from the counter. "You haven't seen Kathleen in fifty years."

"And I don't have another fifty to wait. I've been looking forward to this."

"Why is it suddenly so important that you need to travel with a hurricane on the way?"

"It's still just a tropical storm."

Nina raised her hand. "I'm not arguing with you. This is ridiculous. I don't think you should go see Kathleen. This conversation is going to have to wait. I've got to get to the office." She motioned for Kendra to get up. "Come on. If you want me to drop you off, we have to go now."

Rosemary stood her ground, not wanting to make things worse but unwilling to give in. "This trip is more than just a meetup with an old friend. I need to feel the sand beneath my feet, the salty air in my hair. I miss that. I need to do this for me."

"You can. Just not during a storm. I love you, Mom," Nina said. "Your time is your own. It's not like you can't reschedule." She shrugged as if it were no big deal.

"I don't want to reschedule." It felt like a big deal. "Why can't you just be supportive of my decision?"

Nina closed her eyes, her jaw set. "You know what? Do whatever you want," she said. "I know you're going to anyway." She grabbed her things and stormed toward the door with Kendra chasing after her.

They left aggravated and in a hurry just like every other workday.

Rosemary grimaced. That was a horrible way to start the day, but there was nothing she could do about it. She'd tried, and all she did was make things worse.

She sat back down to finish her breakfast and then cleaned up the kitchen.

Rosemary pressed her lips together, trying not to be angry with Nina. She was under a lot of stress. The divorce had left her bitter and tired, but Rosemary didn't appreciate catching the brunt of her moods. It was a lot like when Nina was a brooding teenager—only at least back then, she had Kai to talk her down when it made her crazy.

The tension in the room lingered, a silent reminder of the unresolved conflict between them. Kai had always been the peacemaker.

"What was I thinking coming here, Kai?" If only he could answer.

She picked up her coffee cup and walked into the living room.

Nina was probably thinking the same thing right now. They'd always ruffled each other's feathers. Kai had always said it was because they were so much alike, but Rosemary was certain she'd never been as controlling as Nina.

Moving here was proving to be a huge adjustment. It had been six months already, and it still didn't feel like home.

Rosemary missed Hawaii, and she missed being outside on the macadamia farm. It was hard work, but it was a labor of love, and she and Kai had always been such a great team. The activity had kept them young.

She cherished those memories, but the farm was too much for her to handle on her own, and the offer had been too good to turn down. Selling the farm had been the right thing to do.

Moving in with Nina was the part she hadn't thought through, and getting out of this without hurting Nina's feelings wasn't going to be easy. She couldn't imagine what her life was supposed to be like, but it sure didn't seem to be this.

Rosemary was busy chauffeuring Kendra to after-school activities, but Nina didn't want her doing things around the house except in her own room. What a waste of idle time. Nina treated her like she was an old lady, and that was already wearing on her.

Rosemary had her own emotions to deal with after losing Kai and leaving Hawaii, and she was trying so hard to do the right thing by Nina and Kendra that it was making everything unenjoyable. *I'm sad. I have to change this.*

Restless, she picked up her phone and called her friend. "Hey, Kathleen. It's Rosemary. I was hoping I'd catch you at home. Are you busy?"

"Just tidying up before I head out to play some pickleball with friends." Kathleen's voice was full of energy.

"Are you worried about the storm?"

"Not really. We've been through tons of them. Might be nothing but a rain event. I've got enough groceries to last me no matter what, and a generator to last a few days if we lose power. Nothing to worry about at this point."

"You don't think it'll be a hurricane by the time it gets to North Carolina?"

"Who knows? They get everybody all hyped up, and half the time it's nothing."

"Then half the time they're right?"

"I suppose that would be true," Kathleen said. "Are you worried? If it looks like we're going to take a hit, we'll evacuate. We've done it before. Would you rather reschedule?"

"No. Not really. I've been looking forward to our visit. I just wanted to get your local perspective on the situation. You know how these weathermen can be."

"Don't I know it," Kathleen said.

"But if now isn't convenient, I can be flexible."

"It's the perfect time!" Kathleen seemed delighted. "Please come."

"Great! I can't wait to stroll along the shore and indulge in fresh seafood. If I eat one more frozen square piece of salmon, I'm going to turn into one." Since when did salmon grow in squares? "I'm not sure it's even real salmon. Doesn't have any taste."

"Tell me about it. We live in a generation that relies on frozen food and microwaving, air frying, and Instant Pots, which is just a fancy crockpot if you ask me. Give me old-style home cooking any day."

"I feel the same way. I'll make you my special macadamia-crusted mahi-mahi while I'm there. Everyone raves about it." She'd wanted to make it for Nina and Kendra, but they belly-ached so much, no matter what she offered to make, that she just let them order pizza on the nights she was supposed to cook.

"Around here, we usually grill mahi, but I'm open to trying your recipe. It sounds delicious. My neighbors keep my freezer full of fresh fish. We'll do a potluck so you can meet every-one."

"I can't wait to catch up." Even though they'd only recon-nected through social media once Rosemary moved back to the mainland, Kathleen had been to every reunion and they'd had fun reminiscing about old friends. She knew who had died, di-vorced, and dodged bullets, as she liked to say.

"Me, too, and this is the perfect time to come," Kathleen said. "The best shells always wash up after a storm. No matter what the weather does, we'll have fun. Come on. What's the worst thing that could happen?"

"It turns into a hurricane, and Nina will utter those words we hate to hear."

"I told you so," they said in unison.

"My girls are the same way," Kathleen said. "It's why I really like knowing they are three states away. They stay out of my business."

"You're smarter than I am."

"No. Your daughter just caught you while you were aching. It had to sound like a great idea to be surrounded by your daughter and granddaughter. When I lost Stu, I was a hot mess too. I'm thankful that we had the foresight to invest in this beach cottage all those years ago. It was so hard to be in our home without him. I packed up and moved here immediately. This was my sanctuary. I totally understand why you'd want to leave the home you'd spent nearly fifty years with Kai in. Everything is a memory, and that's painful."

"It was. Every repair that hadn't been done. Every project we did or didn't complete together. He was in every inch of that farm." Her throat tightened. "It seemed like such a great idea to move to Philadelphia, and since Nina was sort of grieving the end of her marriage, I had this fantasy that we were going to be on this uplifting journey together. You know, navigating through our emotions to move forward like one of those best-friend movies you see on television. But mostly we just bicker. It's exhausting."

"Don't give it another thought. We're old enough to do what we want, and wise enough to be safe about it. If that storm transforms into a hurricane and makes landfall on Whelk's Island, we can take shelter and enjoy canned beans and wine by candlelight until the electricity is restored. If it looks really threatening, we'll take a road trip inland. No big deal."

Of course they could pivot on a dime, and she needed some adventure in her life right now. "What do you think about me coming early?"

"I've already got your room made up. You can come right now. You've got my address. What's stopping you?"

Rosemary hesitated, but only for a moment. "Not a thing. I'm on my way." She hung up, slugged back the rest of her coffee, and raised her hands above her head, offering a little hula swish of her hips to the heavens. "I miss you like crazy, Kai. This would've been way more fun with you, but I can't wait to get on the road and share some laughs with my old friend."

She showered, got dressed in travel clothes, and packed a suitcase in less than an hour. She could almost feel the sand between her toes.

Acid churned in her gut at the thought of calling Nina to tell her the plan. Nina would blow a fuse, and she really had no appetite for dealing with that right now. In the kitchen, she took the dry-erase marker and scribbled a note on the message board.

> Gone to Kathleen's on Whelk's Island, then on to
> St. Augustine to see Patty. Weather permitting.
> See you in a few weeks.
> *Mom*

She swept away *in a few weeks* with her fingers and changed it to *soon*.

Soon gave her more wiggle room. Could be sooner or later.

Silently marking things off her mental packing list, she remembered James. He was just a red betta in a small bowl. He didn't eat much, and he required little oversight, but he did need some attention. Nina had brought the fish home as a surprise the week after Rosemary arrived. It was a welcome present, and he was beautiful. Nina thought the betta would be good company, but honestly, most days Rosemary felt like that fish looked pretty miserable all alone, and most days she did too. But that wasn't his fault.

She rustled through the entryway table drawer for an envelope. Twenty dollars should be enough for Kendra to remember to feed James and perhaps clean his water while she was away.

Rosemary jotted down the instructions and tucked the envelope safely beneath Kendra's pillow.

"That's it. I think I'm ready." Rosemary inhaled deeply, then blew out the anxiety she felt about making Nina mad . . . again. "This is my life. I need to live it."

She made her way toward the door, the wheels on her suitcase chugging along the hardwood floors. She locked up, stepped outside, and loaded her belongings into her car.

With Kathleen's address punched into her GPS, Rosemary backed out of the driveway, feeling like she'd just sprouted wings.

She donned her sunglasses and drove in silence for the initial hour.

It was a beautiful, clear summer day, and having missed the morning commute traffic, she enjoyed smooth sailing out of the city.

She found a comedy channel and settled in, laughing out loud at some of the jokes. It was just her, the radio, and the sunshine.

It was nearly a seven-hour drive to Whelk's Island, but if she limited her stops, she could still get to Kathleen's before dark.

Chapter Four

AMANDA HAD BEEN PRAYING THE STORM WOULD TURN back out to sea and held her breath with every update. Walking through the living room, she caught the tail end of the weather report on the television. The meteorologist announced the upgrade of the tropical storm to a hurricane. It now had a name—Edwina—and it was time to prepare for the possibility of it landing and affecting their area.

Her heart sank. She glanced around, so thankful for their home. Maeve's generosity in giving her family home to them when she passed, especially when they'd been friends for such a short time, had been a life-changing blessing for them.

Maeve's words echoed in her mind. *"This house has weathered many storms. It's sturdy and strong. You will be safe here."*

"You okay, Mom?" Hailey stood in the doorway.

Amanda pasted a smile on her face. "Yes, sweetie. They've upgraded the storm to a hurricane. It's time to pack. Looks like we'll be going to visit your grandparents in Ohio for sure."

"That seems really far to go just because the weather is bad here."

"I know, but what a great excuse to visit." She could feel herself overplaying it for Hailey. "You know they don't get out much anymore. They will be so excited to spend time with you."

"That's important too." Hailey seemed reconciled to the idea. "I'm packing my markers and stuff to work on some pictures for Tug while we're gone. Can I bring Maeve's favorite jar of sea glass with us to show Grandma?"

"Sure, honey. That's fine."

Hailey hugged Amanda's waist. "Thanks, Mom." She spun away and ran off, bounding up the stairs to her room on the third level.

Amanda had been gathering various items the last couple of days in case things got bad. She picked up the hurricane-preparedness list she'd torn out of the newspaper.

She packed her bag with necessities and tucked her most important papers inside an envelope to take, then tucked the rest in Ziploc bags and put them back in the safe to protect them in case water got into the house.

Everything here was about ready. It was still only midmorning, but there was no sense dawdling. The sooner they got ready, the easier it would be to get out of town. She'd heard horror stories of miles of backed-up traffic during storm evacuations.

"Kids, I have to run over to the shop to pack up the rest of my inventory. Do you want to come along?"

Salt of the Earth had started out with herbal salts she'd made for her home recipes. She'd dreamed of turning it into a business, but with two littles underfoot, it hadn't really been an option until last year. Now they were both in school, and Hailey and Jesse had turned out to be great little helpers.

She probably never would have gotten the business off the ground had it not been for Paul's encouragement. It still amazed her how the two of them were brought back together. They'd lost touch after her husband, Jack, was killed while on a six-month deployment. Jack and Paul had been best friends, promising to always have each other's back. But on that deployment, Paul was on a different assignment. He and Amanda hadn't spoken in a long time when they crossed paths on the beach on Whelk's Island. Her heart raced every time she thought of that day. Her life had changed—somersaulted in a way—because of it.

Paul had encouraged her to expand her offerings to include other herbal gifts like sachets and jellies. He'd been a patient mentor, helping her with the business side of things but remaining hands-off enough that she felt she'd done it on her own, and she appreciated that.

Her small business was growing at a steady rate, and people were now signing up for annual subscriptions to receive new products every quarter. The business model was solid, and she and the kids were having a ball creating social media posts about the products.

Jesse and Hailey raced down the stairs with Denali plodding along behind them.

"I'll take that as a yes." Amanda propped her hands on her hips.

"I call the front seat!" Hailey declared.

Jesse lurched to a stop. "She always calls it first."

"You can have it on the way home," Amanda said.

Hailey was relentless on that stuff, so Amanda tried to keep things fair without a fuss. She reached down and gave the bulldog a pat on the head. "Sorry, Denali. You know you're not allowed in the shop. County rules."

Denali plopped to the floor, stretching out on his belly, looking a bit put out.

"Sorry, buddy." Amanda grabbed her keys, and the kids followed her to the car. They piled into her white SUV and drove the few blocks over to the shop.

"Look, Mom." Jesse pointed to the pallet of sandbags piled high next to the building.

"Paul had those delivered. They are going to put those around the entryways to protect the shop from rising waters."

"Maybe we can use it in a sandbox afterward," Jesse reasoned.

"You have a whole beach of sand. Do you really need a sandbox too?"

He paused, and she could almost see the wheels turning in his little mind.

"I must be crazy." He laughed so hard his face turned pink. "We have the biggest sandbox ever already. What was I thinking?"

"Some people like to draw in the sand for relaxation," Hailey said softly, always the grown-up. "Maybe we could use it in the garden between the herbs."

Amanda glanced over at her daughter. "That might be really pretty in the herb garden. We could work on that next year."

"Mom, I'd love that. It would be so beautiful."

"I think so too. Come on. Let's get to work." She and the kids got out and went up to the shop. "Okay, guys," she said as she unlocked the front door. "I'll get all the containers down, and you put them in the boxes for me, okay?"

"Got it."

"One kind in each box." Amanda sat on the floor and started unloading the bottom cabinets. "The different-colored labels are the different flavors."

"We understand, Mom." Hailey picked up three boxes and positioned them beside her. "Jesse, I'll pass them to you, and you put them in the right box, okay?"

"Yep." He plopped onto the floor. "Ready."

Amanda started handing jars to Hailey, and soon they were moving faster than a robotic assembly line. "It shouldn't take long at this pace."

Less than an hour later, everything was boxed up. "That's it.

We'll slide each box into a trash bag to help make sure they don't get damp."

"The salt is in jars, Mom," her ever-so-practical little boy said.

"I know, but if the water comes up real high . . ." She sighed. "You're probably right. If that happens, we've got bigger problems."

Jesse's jaw dropped, as if the possibilities finally tumbled together. "Oh, that would be terrible," he murmured.

Amanda didn't like them worrying. "We'd make more," she said to lighten the mood. "No big deal, right?"

"Right, and if it doesn't even storm here, well, no problem." Hailey looked pleased. "But maybe the trash bags, just in case."

"This is a lot of work," Jesse said. "Especially if it's for no reason."

"It's better to be prepared," Hailey said.

"That's right, Hailey." Amanda knew those words had probably come from Hailey's chat with Tug earlier. "I appreciate having two such good workers to help me."

"I'm going to work for you forever, Mom," Jesse said. "Don't you worry."

It took another hour to put everything away. Satisfied that everything had been done and was secure, Amanda locked up and followed the kids to the car.

Before pulling away, she glanced at the cute little sign that read SALT OF THE EARTH, hanging on the metal gate into the yard. Only secured by two S-hooks, it was likely to blow away. "Hang on." She got out and retrieved the sign.

When she got back in the car, Jesse seemed distraught. "Mom, is Denali staying with Paul?"

"Yes. It's a long car ride. You know Denali doesn't enjoy riding in the car."

"It'll be good for Paul to have Denali with him since we won't be there," Hailey agreed.

"I'll miss him, though," Jesse said.

"It's best to consider what's best for him," Amanda said. "And we won't be gone that long." *Hopefully.*

He fell back against the seat, pouting.

She'd learned a long time ago not to give in to that. She ignored the little pity party, and it was over when they got home a few minutes later.

They pulled into the driveway. The beautiful sign Paul and the kids had made for the house when they christened it The Shell Collector always made her think of the day they presented it to her. A truly pivotal day in their lives.

It was hard to walk away from your home when you knew there was the possibility of damaging weather. She'd never really understood why people didn't want to leave. It seemed crazy, but now part of her was resistant to the idea too.

A horn honked from behind her in the driveway.

She jerked around to see Paul bounding out of his truck toward her. She got out of her car, and he pulled her into a hug.

"Missed you. Are y'all about ready?" he asked.

Hailey and Jesse bailed out of the car. "Hey, Paul!"

"What are you two up to? All packed?"

Jesse shrugged. "Pretty much. We finished up at Mom's shop. Hailey's been taking pictures everywhere all day long. She read on the internet that you should do that before a storm for insurance."

Paul nodded appreciatively. "That's very smart. I see who the brains of the operation is around here."

Hailey blushed.

"I've got a surprise for you before you leave." Paul clapped his hands.

Jesse gave a fist pump, but suddenly Hailey started crying. "I don't want to go. You might need us."

"Oh, bug. I always need you, but you can pray for me and send me funny texts, and we'll be back together before you know it. I promise."

Amanda flashed him a panicked look. She hated for him to make a promise he couldn't keep. There were no guarantees, and her children had already experienced their share of those kinds of promises.

"I'm going to miss you, but I think you're going to like my surprise," he said.

Tug drove up and walked over.

"Is Tug part of the surprise?" Hailey asked.

Jesse's mouth dropped. "Are we all going together? Awesome!"

"No. Sorry, no. That's not the surprise, but Tug is going to give us a hand. He and I will be here together, but I have a friend who needs to move his Hummer limousine to higher ground, and he's offered to give y'all a ride to Ohio."

Amanda laughed. "Seriously?"

"Yeah. That way, you don't have to drive. Y'all can play games or watch movies. It's super fancy. And then when the storm is all clear, he'll bring you back home if I don't beat him to it."

"A limousine?" Hailey shrieked. "I'll be like a princess. Can we play DVDs?"

"Sure."

Tug smiled. "I packed a picnic for your trip, and some snacks for while you're visiting your grandparents, so you'll think of me."

Amanda put her hand on Jesse's back. "Tug, we always think of you, and, Paul, you are always thinking of us. This sounds amazing, but what about my car?"

"We're going to park it inside Paws with us. There's room."

The wind was picking up. Amanda caught her hair and pulled it into a ponytail to keep it out of her face.

"Those outer bands are beginning to reach us," Tug said.

"What is that?" Jesse pointed toward the road and dropped into a sumo pose with his hands on his knees. "It's a whopper."

A bright lime-green Hummer that looked about two blocks long drove up to The Shell Collector.

Jesse let out a low "Whoa!" and Hailey squealed. "*That's* our limo?"

"Go get your things. Looks like your ride is here." The kids disappeared up the stairs in a fit of giggles, and Amanda leaned into Paul's chest. "I'm so not ready to leave you."

"I know. Don't worry. It'll fly by. We have to take care of family first. We've got a lot to do here to help the neighbors and small businesses get ready. It's going to be a twenty-four-seven effort. You wouldn't see me even if you were here."

"I appreciate you taking such good care of us. I love you for that." She looked at Tug. "Both of you."

Paul dropped a kiss on her forehead.

"It's what makes me happy."

"I'm going to get them moving," Amanda said.

"I'll bring everything down." Paul followed her up the stairs.

Tug was putting the picnic basket in the back of the limousine when they all walked out with their bags.

The driver, Travis, loaded their bags in the back, and Amanda put the craft tote bag and the game tote bag in the back seat. "Good thing this thing seats about a dozen with all the stuff we're bringing."

"Yeah, I was thinking there wouldn't be room even if I wanted to come with you," Paul said.

"We could make room for you," Hailey said.

Amanda kissed Paul, reminding herself it wasn't goodbye.

Still, since she'd lost Jack so suddenly, her heart lurched at every parting. Would she ever get over that feeling? She could see the same anxiety washing over her daughter's face, the way her chin set when she was hanging tough. Hailey had handled the past few years so bravely. Amanda prayed Hailey didn't feel as broken inside as she did some days.

Paul had been a blessing. God had most surely put all these things together, because there was no one else skilled enough to have made it all happen and all seem so right.

Jesse ran from behind the house, dirty and out of breath. He held out a handful of Spanish moss to Amanda.

"Oh, Jesse. I don't know if the limousine driver is going to appreciate you putting that in his truck. I mean, it might have little bugs in it."

"Mom. If that storm comes and it blows a hundred miles an hour, all of this might fly away. Maeve would be so sad. She knows we put it in the tree for her."

Paul hugged Amanda closer. "He has a point," he said. "Come on, sport. Let's put that in a plastic bag before we put it in the truck, okay?" He led Jesse to the house, turning to walk backward and mouthing, "Problem solved."

When Paul came back out with Jesse at his side, Amanda was talking to Travis, but Hailey was standing frozen next to the limo.

"What's wrong?" Paul asked.

"I don't want to leave you behind," Hailey said.

Jesse reached for Paul's hand. "None of us do."

"It's going to be a fun trip, and when you get back, it'll be all blue skies again. Come on. Be good sports about it, okay?"

Amanda straightened, sorry that the kids were whining, but they were echoing her exact sentiments.

"I know," she said. "We don't want to leave, but safety comes first. Tug and Paul will take good care of everything here. We'll have a nice visit with Grandma and Grandpa and be back before you know it."

Jesse's shoulders slumped. "Fine."

"Get on in there, sport. You take care of my girls while you're away, okay?"

"Yes, sir."

"Okay, everybody climb in. We've got to get on the road." Amanda ushered the kids into the limo.

Once all the goodbyes were said and done, she closed the door and turned to wave to Paul and Tug as they drove off in the Hummer.

Please be here when I get back.

Hailey put her hand on Amanda's arm, then rested her head on her shoulder.

Chapter Five

Tug watched Paul as he waved goodbye to Amanda and the kids. "Hard to say goodbye to something that special, isn't it?"

"Hardest thing I've had to do in a long time." Paul dropped his hand.

"When are you going to make it official and marry that girl? You can't just be the hero. You two should be married."

Paul gave Tug a look. "Is this really the time for that talk, Tug?"

"Feels like as good a time as any."

Paul sighed, then looked in the direction they'd just ridden off. "I know," he said. "I just don't want to push her too hard, or she might back off."

"It's been three years since Jack died. The longer you act like the family friend, the harder it's going to be to shake that role, and I know you want more."

"I do, absolutely, but—"

"But if something happened, you would regret it the rest of your life. She loves you. Those kids love you, and they deserve the stability of a father in the home."

"Amanda is a wonderful mother. They are just fine without me."

"I don't dispute that. But God made a family—a mother and a father—for a reason. And you love them."

"I do." Paul walked over and dropped the tailgate on his truck. He set a five-gallon bucket of tools on the ground and started pulling plywood from the back. "It's not like I haven't thought about it. In fact, I was thinking about talking to her father if I pick them up after the storm, get his approval for when the right timing comes along."

"Good idea."

"Thank you . . . and it's complicated. You know?"

"Things are never as complicated as we make them," Tug said. "Most of the complications are just what-ifs that couldn't even happen."

"Suddenly, you're a shrink."

"Eighty years of experience speaking here, Paul, and I'm only butting in because I think it's what you want and you're too chicken to do something about it. And I love you like a son. You two deserve to be together."

"Well, if this is the day for all things sappy and supportive"—Paul set down the board and balanced it against his leg—"I'm worried about you, Tug. You haven't been the same since Maeve died. We all miss her, but you've lost your spirit."

"I'm not the same," Tug admitted. "A piece of me died with her. I don't know if I'll ever get over it." He lowered his head, quiet for a long moment.

"We're here for you. You know that, right?"

"I know." He lifted his gaze to meet Paul's. "I'll be fine."

"I don't want you doing anything crazy during this storm. I want you to come stay with me."

"That's crazy."

"No, it's smart."

"Are you afraid I'm going to throw myself into the ocean like one of those shells that keep washing up with the messages in them?" He'd been low for a long time now, but he'd never do anything like that.

"Tug, some days, yeah, frankly. I've seen the signs and I'm worried."

"I'm sorry I worried you." The last thing he wanted was to cause his friends to worry. "The diner is all boarded and sandbagged. The only opening we've got is the front door and the back exit. I'm only doing to-go orders until the storm comes. Then I'll shut down. Promise."

"Then you'll come to Paws with me."

"I can stay at my house. Always have. Never have had a problem down there. That place is built for these storms."

"No." Paul shook his head. "Nuh-uh. We're manning this together. Don't fight me on this. I could use your help. Sheltering safely in place was part of the design when we rebuilt Paws Town Square. Take advantage of it. You know you're not going to leave The Wife in your house. One window breaks and freaks her out—no telling where she'll end up. New York City or Bermuda maybe? Please, man."

That was true. And The Wife was funny about storms. "Fine. I'll come to Paws."

"Good. Now, let's finish up this place and mark The Shell Collector off our list."

They lifted the last few boards into place and double-checked all the windows and doors.

Tug thought of the many times he'd done this for Maeve. "The way this place sits back off the beach on this dune, it's not likely to have any debris issues. It's made it through a lot of storms. I'd be surprised if she even wobbles," Tug said. "You know Jarvis was a shipwright. He worked on boats, and this thing is built like a battleship."

"Good. I'd like very much for it to be standing when this storm passes."

Chapter Six

AMANDA STARED OUT THE WINDOW OF THE TREE FROG–colored limousine, glad for the blacked-out windows. People were pointing and kids were waving frantically. She'd hate to dash all their Hollywood hopes that someone famous was sitting inside. Just a woman and her two kids.

She looked at her watch. They'd left an hour ago. They were still just about within hiking distance of her house, and the kids were already getting antsy.

"If the storm comes while we're still driving, can we just go back home?" Jesse asked.

Travis's eyes lifted to the rearview mirror. "That will not happen," Amanda reassured them. "Come on. Let's play some cards."

They started a game of crazy eights, which turned the complaining into giggles.

As usual, Hailey won four hands in a row. Amanda was pretty sure the girl had a photographic memory.

Traffic was finally moving. She'd never seen this many cars all going in one direction in her life.

Tired of cards, Hailey put a DVD in the player, and she and Jesse stretched out on their bellies on the long plush sofas to watch.

It was a relief not to have to entertain them. At least for a moment.

Travis lowered the window between them to speak to Amanda. "I'm going to stop and fuel up in about twenty minutes when we cross into Virginia if you'd like to get out and stretch or get a snack."

"Thank you. That'll be great."

Hailey and Jesse both popped up. "Are we almost there?" Jesse asked.

"No. Not even close, but we are going to stop and have time to stretch in a bit."

"He said snacks," Jesse said.

She looked at them both. They knew Tug had packed them more than enough food, but why deny them something so simple? "One snack each. We need to be mindful not to take too long. We don't want to hold him up."

The stretch Hummer pulled into the truck stop, taking up the whole lane at the fuel pump.

Jesse peered out the windows as the vehicle came to a stop. "Look. Everyone is looking at us."

"Because we're in a limo." Hailey was smiling and waving like a superstar.

Travis laughed. "It'll take a bit to fuel this thirsty beast up. Y'all can get out and stretch and move around."

"Thanks. Come on, kids." Amanda, Jesse, and Hailey hopped out of the limousine and headed inside.

Amanda balanced their selected snacks and perused the magazines for something to read.

Hailey walked over and hung on her arm. "The line is forever. Mom, can we go outside and wait for you?"

"All right, but stay right up here by the entrance, and keep Jesse close by. Do not go into the parking lot for any reason. Understood?"

"We'll be careful. I promise." Hailey turned to Jesse. "Come on."

They speed-walked to the door and, just as she asked, stopped to the left of the entrance. They were good kids. *Why do I even worry?*

She stood in the long line, not any more patient than they were.

Travis was still standing at the pump. That made her feel better until she noticed Hailey and Jesse having a very animated conversation with an older woman out front.

She quickly paid for the snacks, stepped outside, and called to them, but they were too deep in conversation to hear her over the rumbling big rigs at the pumps on this side of the building.

"Excuse me," Amanda said as she approached.

The woman turned to Amanda and curtseyed. "My goodness. These two are a delight. I'm afraid I've never met an actual princess." She leaned in. "Your secret is safe with me."

Amanda shot the kids a look.

"We were just explaining our predicament to this fine woman." Hailey spoke in a not-so-bad British accent and stared wide-eyed at her as if begging her to play along.

"Yes, Mum," Jesse chimed in.

"Oh my goodness." She ruffled Jesse's hair. "These two belong to me. Sorry—they could bend your ear for a week. I'm no princess."

Hailey gave the woman an exaggerated wink.

"Hailey, stop. We're just a regular family traveling—"

"In the longest limousine I've ever laid eyes on. It's fine. And these two are delightful."

Hailey placed a loving arm across Jesse's shoulders, still playacting and glowing as if she fully expected to win an Emmy. "It's our secret. It's been divine meeting you, ma'am."

Amanda lifted her gaze to the heavens. *Oh, Jack, they've got your flair for drama!* "I'm afraid these two are being mischievous and the long ride has just begun. We're evacuating for the storm. Headed to Ohio to spend some time with my folks." She leveled a stare at her little tricksters. "Fess up, you two. In your real voices."

"Sorry—we were just playing," Hailey said with a giggle. "You're really nice, and it was fun. Thanks for talking with us."

"You two had me completely fooled! I curtseyed, you little boogers." She was smiling, though. "What a wonderful accent, although I really like this southern lilt even better."

"Lilt?" Jesse's brows pulled together. "Like from the dryer?"

"Uh, that would be lint, Jess," Hailey said.

"Where in the world did you two learn how to talk like that?" The woman turned to Amanda. "They really had me going."

"*Peppa Pig,*" Jesse said matter-of-factly.

"And *Mary Poppins.* We watched it again last night."

"It is one of their favorites," Amanda said, nodding. "You two are a hot mess. Apologize for tricking this nice lady."

"We're sorry."

"I accept your apology, and it was all quite innocent. A welcome distraction, actually. I've been driving all day." The woman's blue eyes danced beneath her auburn bangs. "I'm on my way to visit with a high school friend. We haven't laid eyes on each other since graduation. Why, that's . . . I haven't even done the math."

"That had to be a really long time ago," Jesse said.

"Yes, for sure, but we reconnected on the internet. We've talked on the phone a few times the past few months, and we decided to get together."

Amanda smiled. "That's so exciting. Isn't it funny how some people you will just stay connected with forever?"

"Yes. It's like picking up where you left off, no matter how long it's been. I used to live in Hawaii and miss beach living. I'm just as excited to see the ocean as I am my old friend."

"Where are you headed?"

"To Whelk's Island."

"That's where we live!" Hailey said.

"Really? Well, isn't this a small world!"

Amanda frowned. "It is. Only, you know there's a hurricane coming up the East Coast, right?"

"I know. My daughter was having a fit about me traveling because of it."

"Well, there's still some uncertainty, but they've recommended an evacuation. If you're going to ride out the storm with your friend, go straight there because when the evacuation becomes mandatory, they will divert all roads to be westbound only."

"Oh dear. That could be a problem."

"Ready to roll when you are," Travis called out.

"We're on our way." Amanda pressed the bag of treats into Hailey's arms. "Here, you two walk—don't run—over to the car and get in."

"That's no car, Mum."

Amanda looked at the woman. "They are pretty good at that. I had no idea." She gestured to the limo. "Scoot, you two. I'll be right there."

"My name is Rosemary," the woman said. "This has honestly been the highlight of my day."

"I'm glad they weren't a bother."

"Are you kidding? I think most kids have forgotten how to use their imagination to entertain themselves. I'd say you're doing something right."

"Well, thank you. You don't know how much that means, because they've had a tough haul of it the last few years. They are my world."

"I have to ask. Is the prince, Paul, made up too?"

"Paul. He's not a prince, but he is . . . he is my knight in shining armor. No, that's too flashy of a description. He's humble and kind and giving. You know, he's like that perfect conch shell you find on the beach, intricately patterned and perfect despite being tossed in the surf for decades."

"That is special. I'm so happy for you." Rosemary's eyes lowered. "Do you think it's safe for me to go to Whelk's Island? My friend doesn't seem worried at all, but running into you like this and your evacuating makes me wonder. I don't want to be foolish."

Amanda glanced over at the fancy limo. "This is all Paul's doing. It's a very long story, but I lost my husband a few years back. I ran into Paul on the beach. I hadn't seen him since I'd lost Jack. He and Jack were best friends. He vowed to keep me safe. I think it'll be fine on Whelk's Island. Those locals have been through lots of these storms, but it was important to him, and I didn't want to take any chances with my children, so I appeased him."

"I understand completely."

"Let me give you this." She dug into her purse. "This is Paul's business card. If things get tricky, you call him. He owns a business in town, and they'll be weathering the storm there. Tell him you met me. He'll make room for you, and you couldn't be in better hands. Oh, and if you end up without electricity and need food, Tug over at Tug's Diner is your man. He's lived on that beach his whole life, and he'll be open no matter what. You couldn't meet two nicer people than Tug and Paul. Look them up if you need anything."

"This is so generous of you. Thank you." She waved the card. "It's nice how He makes sure we are on the right path, isn't it?"

"Yes, ma'am. I couldn't agree more."

"Why don't we exchange numbers? If you want to know

what's going on without worrying Paul, I've got nothing better to do than to chat with you. Heck, I'll entertain those two kids of yours on the phone if they are on your nerves."

"Be careful what you wish for."

Rosemary took out her phone. "Can I send you my number?"

"Yes. Absolutely." They exchanged phone numbers. "I'm going to take you up on checking in on the actual situation. Sometimes those newscasters make things out to be so much worse, and I don't want to worry if that's not the case. You really wouldn't mind?"

"I'd be honored. I'll be your personal on-the-ground reporter."

"Perfect." Amanda hated to leave the woman. She was so nice, Amanda was tempted to invite her to come with them, but that was crazy. "We have to get on the road. Be safe."

"You too."

Amanda walked over to the limousine and climbed in. She felt a familiar nudge, like on the day she'd met Maeve. She smiled, recalling the delight on Rosemary's face as she interacted with Jesse and Hailey. How crazy was it they'd crossed paths with this woman heading for Whelk's Island while they were going in the opposite direction?

She clutched her phone. *I'll be calling to check on you, Rosemary.*

"Mum, what's on your mind, dear?" Hailey's British accent was quite convincing.

"That you two are always full of surprises!" She leaned over and tickled them. "I love you two to pieces!"

Once they cleared all the evacuation traffic, the trip was a lot smoother, and Amanda helped the kids track where they were on the atlas she'd bought at the truck stop. They were having fun, and it seemed to do the trick on the "how much longer" questions she'd thought she would be fielding by now.

She wasn't even to her destination, and she was yearning for home. For Paul.

Chapter Seven

IT WAS JUST PAST FIVE O'CLOCK WHEN ROSEMARY CROSSED the North Carolina state line and pulled into the gas station and visitor's center at the border.

While she pumped the gas, she texted Kathleen.

Rosemary
About an hour out

Kathleen
Welcome to North Carolina! Can't wait. Don't speed. You'll get a ticket.

Rosemary laughed. *Okay, so not everything has changed since I was a teenager around here.* She'd gotten her very first speeding ticket on her way to Nags Head. Not even being young, tan, and in a tank top could get her out of that ticket—and she tried it all, right down to crying. She'd lost car privileges for an entire month because of it.

The closer she got to Kathleen's, the more excited she became. Kathleen said she'd dragged out all the old yearbooks. Rosemary had lost track of hers eons ago. It would be a hoot to look through them.

She passed the Kitty Hawk sign, trusting the GPS to get her

to where she was going. She could just as easily be in Florida, and she wouldn't know the difference.

"In one mile, turn left," the GPS said.

Up ahead, a small nondescript sign read **WHELK'S ISLAND 12 miles** in black letters with an arrow. If she hadn't been following the GPS instructions, she'd have cruised right past it.

There was absolutely no one on the road. It was a little eerie for a beach town to be this empty on a summer evening. Finally, she came upon a couple of small shopping centers and a go-kart track next to a gas station.

The speed limit dropped to twenty-five miles per hour, and Kathleen's warning about speeding caused her to tap the brakes.

So, this is Whelk's Island.

Each street sign had a little whelk shell decorating the corner and a beachy font for the street name.

Homes along this stretch were an array of muted pinks, blues, and greens, reminding her of one community back in Hawaii.

If it weren't for the boards covering many of the windows, it would probably look very welcoming.

As it was, it felt a bit daunting.

I sure hope I'm not setting myself up for a big old "I told you so" from Nina.

It wasn't much farther to Kathleen's, but she could see on the map that the ocean was just a couple of blocks over. Dying to even peek at the water, she took the next turn and parked at the end of the street.

She got out of her car, and emotion washed over her.

It had been months since she left behind the sun-kissed beaches of Hawaii. The rhythmic sound of crashing waves greeted her like an old friend, instantly transporting her back to the days of salty air and endless horizons.

The familiar sounds brought her comfort. When she saw the water, she couldn't hold back the joy that rose within her. She ran toward the shoreline. "Oh, it's so beautiful. I've missed this." She threw her arms in the air and breathed in. Each breath renewed her.

She stopped short of the water and slipped off her shoes. The wet sand shifted beneath her eager feet.

She kicked her toes through the warm water. A wave rolled in, swirling around her feet and causing her to sink into the sand. She laughed in sheer delight when the wave churned up around her ankles and splashed her high on her legs.

In that moment, all the stress back in Pennsylvania fell into the past, replaced by a sense of peace that only the ocean could provide.

Kathleen was waiting—and she could come back—so she headed to the car, brushed the damp sand from her legs and feet, and patted her clothes. Thank goodness her outfit was light and gauzy. It would dry quickly in the heat. She leaned against the car, fluffing her pant legs to let them air-dry.

"That was therapeutic. Oh my gosh, it's going to be so relaxing being here." It didn't look like a threatening storm was on the horizon.

She slipped on her shoes and started the car. "Best decision I ever made."

With a touch of her finger, the GPS showed she was only three miles from Kathleen's house.

Rosemary drove past a row of beach cottages and then over a four-lane highway. On the other side, a few big commercial buildings looked a little out of place, although they were beautifully landscaped. *Probably the city buildings.*

Typical beach houses up on stilts lined the next blocks.

She turned onto Kathleen's road and started checking house numbers.

The houses on this street were on big lots. When she pulled into the driveway, she felt as excited as a teenager going to her first sleepover.

Kathleen's house was inviting with its classic coastal style, showcasing a beautiful shade of seafoam green on its shiplap siding. It stood out from her neighbors', which were all pastel colors. Nautical navy-blue shutters complemented the siding, and her front porch had rocking chairs with playful navy-blue polka-dot cushions. It was bright and cheerful, and that didn't surprise Rosemary in the least. Kathleen had been a big personality back in school.

Three cars were parked in the driveway. She pulled in beside them to not block anyone in.

Rosemary grabbed the gift bag from the passenger seat, a simple hostess gift to thank Kathleen for inviting her to visit. The curling ribbons she'd tied to the handles of the bag were in their old school colors: black, gold, and white. That felt kind of silly now, but it was too late to change it.

As Rosemary walked toward the house, laughter drifted out from the patio. She hadn't expected there to be anyone else here. She hadn't really prepared herself to meet a group of people, just one old school pal from a long time ago. Why hadn't Kathleen mentioned she was entertaining?

She knocked on the front door and waited, feeling more nervous by the second.

A moment later, Kathleen swung open the front door. "Perfect timing. Come in. Come in."

Kathleen wore a cotton tank dress and sparkly flip-flops, and although it was clearly casual beachwear, she looked like a million bucks with her silver hair styled in a fashionable bob, flashy jewelry, manicured nails, and glasses with fancy crystals on the sides.

Rosemary felt underdressed, even in her gauzy outfit. She

tugged the loose ends of her linen blouse, shifting self-consciously.

Kathleen gave her a big hug, then gestured her inside. "This is one of my high school buddies," she announced to her friends. "Y'all, meet Rosemary Allen."

"Hi." Rosemary took in the faces of the men and women seated around the room—mostly couples. It was clear this was a group that got together often, which left her feeling a bit awkward. "Nice to meet you."

"Oh, I'm sorry. Allen was your name in high school. What's your married last name again?"

"Palakiko."

Kathleen let out a hearty laugh. "Pal-uh . . ."

"Kiko. Palakiko. You got it."

"Palakiko. Whew, well, give me some grace if I slip up and call you Rosemary Allen like when we were back in school."

"Fair enough." Rosemary handed Kathleen the hostess gift. "Just something small to say thank you."

"You always were the sweet one. Thank you." Kathleen set the gift on the counter and gave Rosemary a glass of wine. "Let me introduce you to everyone."

There was no way she'd remember a single name in five minutes. It was overwhelming and a little rowdy, with beach music playing and one couple doing the old Carolina shag in the middle of the living room.

Kathleen walked Rosemary out to the deck, where even more people were hanging out. "Y'all, this is my high school friend Rosemary. She's come to visit for a while."

"Nice to meet you" and "Hope you're hungry" were tossed around.

"This is Johnny." Kathleen gestured to the tall silver-haired man at the grill. "He can fix anything, and he's so much fun. A big flirt, but it's all in friendship."

"Nice to meet you, Rosemary. We got one heck of a deal on all this shrimp and a bushel of oysters, since everyone was heading out of town. You like your oysters raw or steamed?"

"Both," she said. "I haven't had oysters in a long time, though, and that was on the West Coast."

"If you liked those, you'll love these," Johnny explained. "Our oysters are a little more briny, I'd say. This area of the coast is known for the best oysters, and it isn't even an *R* month. You'll see. They'll be great."

"Living my whole adult life in Hawaii, I'm well versed in seafood."

Johnny's brows perked up, and he swung his gaze toward Kathleen. "You didn't tell me you were bringing hula dancers, Kathleen." Johnny swiveled his hips, his extended belly lobbing over his belt.

"Oh, Johnny. You're such a card. Get back to work. Everyone is starving."

Kathleen leaned in and whispered to Rosemary as they went back inside, "The way he drinks, there's no telling when he'll actually get around to cooking all that stuff. Doesn't matter, I don't guess. We have the whole storm to get it cooked and eaten."

"All these folks live right here in the neighborhood?"

"Yeah. Pretty much. One big happy family. Almost everybody is retired, so it's super easygoing. Nice people. You'll love them."

Rosemary tried to look enthusiastic, but she was tired from the long drive, and Kathleen hadn't even shown her where her room was yet. The evening of giggling over yearbooks together that she'd been looking forward to wouldn't happen tonight.

"I'll be right back." Kathleen squeezed her arm as she swept past her and headed outside.

Rosemary sipped her wine and took a seat at the end of the

couch. The people were nice enough, but no one seemed in a hurry about eating or getting the house prepared for the storm, despite the pile of plywood on the porch.

She got up and walked into the kitchen to see if any snacks were out. There were oodles of libation options, but no snacks.

Rosemary's stomach rumbled. She set her wineglass in the sink. The last thing she needed was to drink wine on an empty stomach. Just as she reached for her purse, ready to head back into town for something to eat, Kathleen burst through the door, laughing with her hair tousled. She looked breathless and wild-eyed, as if the outside world had chased her all the way back inside.

Chapter Eight

ROSEMARY WASN'T SURE WHETHER TO LAUGH OR WORRY as Kathleen stumbled into the middle of the room. "Man, the wind is picking up. We might actually get this storm after all. Where's Peggy?"

The statement made Rosemary's nerves jangle.

"Over here." Peggy jumped to her feet. "What do you need?"

"Do up one of those grid wager things like you do during football season but for the time the storm hits. Hurricane Edwina has been as fickle as a high school football player trying to pick a prom date. She doesn't know what she's going to do. Could be anytime from now to Friday the way things are going. Everybody get your dollars out!" Kathleen kept moving through the room, checking in with everyone.

"I'm on it," Peggy said, then disappeared into the kitchen.

"My money is on the storm not hitting us at all." Johnny walked into the room from the deck. "The sooner we board up, the more likely it won't hit, in my experience. We better get busy, or we might just jinx ourselves into a direct hit."

Rosemary almost choked.

Kathleen patted her on the back. "Don't listen to him. You okay?"

"Yeah. I just swallowed wrong." She caught her breath.

"Johnny, you're enough wind for all of us." Kathleen turned

to Rosemary. "Johnny's at least a Category 1 storm any day of the week. Don't you worry about Hurricane Edwina. She probably will look like a rain shower compared to Johnny." Everyone laughed. "Rosemary, we'll be on the beach in the sunshine before you know it. I can't wait to show you our beach."

Rosemary didn't want to take that from her, so she smiled and kept the fact she'd already dipped her toes in the Atlantic to herself.

"As I was driving in, I saw an enormous building on the right that was beautifully landscaped and had a big, towering entrance," Rosemary said, gently shifting the subject. "Was that the municipal center?"

"Ha, not hardly," Kathleen said. "Our municipal center is nothing to brag about. What you drove by is a dog park slash kennel place. This guy came in and resurrected the old grocery store building . . . or was it a department store? I don't remember—it shut down so long ago. A real eyesore. There were weeds the size of trees growing out of the asphalt parking lot."

"I hate it when companies leave buildings empty like that," Rosemary commiserated. "It's such a waste."

"Yeah, well, this guy has opened a few of these places across the country. He came in and gutted it, repurposed the place for retail, a fancy kennel with indoor and outdoor dog parks, pools and walking trails that people can use for a small fee even if they don't have a dog. I keep my cat there when I travel. It's amazing and really affordable. They do a lot of military-focused goodwill too."

"Plus, for the people kenneling their pets, they get a discount for each day they come visit and walk them." Peggy piped in. "It's really a cool model. Good for everyone."

"That sounds so neat. I've never heard of such a thing, and it sure isn't an eyesore now. It was beautiful."

"Well, it's sort of a combo business and foundation. He has

some heavy-hitter sponsors, I think." Kathleen shrugged. "He's a war hero, and he does all this rehabilitation and training for retired military working dogs, and employs veterans. I don't remember the whole story, but it's been great for the town. High-society types headed to the more touristy areas up the coast stop and drop their pets here, bringing more business for our small merchants. So far, that has only affected our sweet little town in positive ways."

"As long as city council and zoning don't take their thumb off the no-hotel policies we have in place," Peggy added, "I think Whelk's Island will stay just the way we are."

"That's a blessing," Rosemary said. She'd seen the effects of urban sprawl even near their farm in Hawaii, which had been really rural for a long, long time.

"I'll take you over to see it once we get past the storm, if it even happens. We can walk the trails inside. It's air-conditioned, which is great in August," Kathleen said. "The humidity here is about enough to take your breath away."

"It's hot in Hawaii, but thankfully the trade winds help balance it out."

"We don't have any trade winds around here. Maybe someone will put some of those giant windmills out in the ocean to cool things down."

"You never know," Johnny said. "Who's ready to help me get these boards up? We need to get this done before we play."

As folks gathered to start prepping the house, Rosemary asked Kathleen, "Is there somewhere quiet I can call my daughter to let her know I got here okay?"

"Of course," Kathleen said. "And you need to bring your bags and get settled in. Let me show you to your room."

Kathleen led her to the guest room at the end of the hall. "Your home away from home."

The guest room was blue and white, with soft touches of yellow. "It's so bright and cheerful."

"I'm glad you like it. I tried to re-create this picture out of a *Southern Living* magazine spread a few years back. I had to make the curtains, and I painted the dresser, but I really like how it turned out too."

"I had no idea you had so many talents. I bet that was a fun project."

"It was a little stressful. It took me a while to get it all pulled together. I tell everyone who attempts something like that to commit to the very end, because it looks way worse before it looks better."

They shared a laugh over that.

"I tried some faux painting once. It was the same way."

"Then you know. Well, thank you for the compliment. I really hope you're going to enjoy staying here."

"I know I will." Rosemary hugged her. "Thanks for opening your home to me. I hope some of your talents rub off on me."

"I love redecorating. It's my passion. Now, call your daughter. I could talk about this stuff all night long." Kathleen pulled the door closed behind her as she left.

Rosemary sat on the bed. She was excited to be here but a little sad about the circumstances. What had felt so nonnegotiable this morning now seemed a bit like a hissy fit on her part. She mustered the courage to dial Nina. Hopefully she'd cooled down by now.

The call went to voicemail.

Probably for the best.

"Hey, Nina. It's Mom. Just wanted to let you know I made it to Kathleen's. Sorry I didn't catch you. Things are fine here. There's a ton of activity going on for storm preparedness. You don't need to worry. The plan is to go inland if the storm does start to head this way. Honey, I'm sorry I snapped at you this morning. I was trying so hard to give you and Kendra a pleasant morning send-off. Anyway . . . you take care and know I love you."

She hung up and set her phone down, relieved there was no drama to deal with. Being here after that long ride was about all she had the energy for right now.

She kicked her shoes off and leaned back on the bed. If she closed her eyes right now, she could probably sleep until tomorrow, even with the party going on.

Her phone jingled out the song that was Nina's ringtone.

Rosemary put her hands over her face. Nina would know she rejected the call if she didn't answer, so she did. "Hi, Nina."

"Hi, Mom."

"I just left you a message. I was calling to let you know I arrived safely. I thought that was the polite thing to do."

"I can't believe you left."

Rosemary sat up on the bed and crossed her legs beneath her. "Look. I've been around for seventy-two years. I can make my own decisions. Yes, there's a possibility of a hurricane, but I can assess the situation. I will not put myself in unnecessary danger, but I won't let you treat me like I can't handle myself. I lost your dad, but I didn't lose my good sense."

"Some days I'm not so sure of that, Mom."

"Nina, I don't think you realize it, but when you insinuated I can't make a rational decision, that really hurt me. We've both been through a lot. Your divorce. Losing Dad. We are both grasping for things that we can control, and we are making each other miserable."

Nina didn't disagree.

"I need you to respect that I can still make choices for myself. And I'll admit, leaving this morning was probably more of a knee-jerk reaction to our argument than a well-thought-out decision, but I felt like you pushed me into a corner and I needed to get some space between us."

"I didn't mean to make you feel that way, but, Mom, I can't take care of everyone. Your—"

"You don't have to take care of me. That's just it. You have a daughter to raise, and you're a wonderful mother. Concentrate on that."

"I don't think you've ever said that to me before."

Rosemary froze. "Oh, honey, if I haven't, I am sorry. I think you are an amazing mother. You are taking on the whole world, and you don't need to. Let me decide what's best for me, okay?" She knew her daughter well enough to know she wouldn't give in this easily. "Let's plan to have a constructive conversation about this when I get back. A little time apart might help us come up with some fair ground rules."

"Fine." It was a slice of a word, followed by silence.

That one-word response could mean a million things. Aggravated by it, Rosemary said, "Well, it's been heavenly talking to you."

Nina growled. "I hate it when you say that. It's so sarcastic."

She withheld the comment that was on the tip of her tongue. "You get some rest. You sound tired."

"Now who's telling who what to do?"

"Take a breath, Nina. Good night. I love you."

"Good night, Mom. Thanks for letting me know you got there safely."

Rosemary dropped the phone and shook her head. *That didn't go as bad as it could have.*

Her stomach rumbled again.

She pulled herself together and eased back out into the hall like a teenager after midnight, snatched her purse off the hall table where she'd set it earlier, and casually headed for her car, trying not to draw attention to herself.

All the action seemed to have moved outside. A few boards had been put up, but there were more supervisors than workers.

While everyone focused on the workers, Rosemary hustled to her car, thankful no one stopped to ask her where she was going. She hopped inside and put her key in the ignition.

I'll just zip out, grab something to eat, and they'll never be the wiser.

Chapter Nine

VOLUNTARY EVACUATION HAD STARTED EARLY THAT MORNing, and the hotels in the more populated towns south of them had already closed their doors and canceled reservations. On Whelk's Island, renters had been required to evacuate, but the locals weren't mandatory, and most of them were headstrong.

Business at Tug's Diner was over capacity even as early as the afternoon, to where Tug had limited the menu to only take-out orders to keep up with the onslaught of residents wanting to grab something quick as they readied their homes for the possibility of a brush with Hurricane Edwina.

Tug was taking orders and serving out of the front doors when he caught sight of Paul and Chase in line.

He waved to them over the heads of the people in line. "I thought you'd be too busy for Hot Dog Tuesday today," Tug teased.

"Are you kidding me?" Paul looked at him like he'd lost his mind. "We live for Hot Dog Tuesday." They inched up to next in line. "Even if it had to wait until dinnertime."

"The usual for you two. Three each all the way." Tug grabbed tongs and a box. "Coming right up."

Tug made the hot dogs and passed the order out the door to Paul. "Hey, before you go, if this storm continues to chug up the coast so slowly, I think I should relocate Amanda's inventory. A slow mover means big flooding. With the timing of the tide, the storm surge could clear that dune and her place is going to be underwater. I've seen that place flood before."

"Really? We should pack her out of there, then." Paul looked at Chase. "I know you have things to do at home, too, but could you help me with Amanda's place after this?"

"Absolutely."

"Good. That's been bugging me. I just hadn't had a second to call you." Tug never stopped, quickly moving people through the line with their orders. "I'm going to bring The Wife over to Paws tonight if that's okay. The storm isn't supposed to impact us until overnight tomorrow at the earliest, so I'm going to spend tonight at my place."

"That works. Thanks for mentioning Amanda's place. We're going to pack up the inventory next."

"Probably all for nothing. I know you've got a hundred other things on your list."

"Nothing is more important than Amanda. Besides, sometimes intuition is twice as good as science." Paul and Chase left, and the line in front of the diner still snaked out to the street.

How many of these people were grabbing something to eat because they were getting ready to evacuate, and how many planned on riding out the storm?

It was after seven-thirty when the line of customers finally cleared out of Tug's Diner.

Tug had cleaned up, mostly. He'd put away the tables he'd set at the front doors as a makeshift counter and covered the electronics in plastic to weather the storm just in a case the boards gave way and a window broke. He walked out to check on The

Wife. She was a creature of habit. Leaving familiar surroundings wouldn't make her happy.

"You ready to go for a ride?" he said to The Wife.

"Time to go."

"Yes, it is." He opened the cage and let The Wife walk up his arm to his shoulder. "We're going to go visit Paul until the weather clears. That means you have to ride in your little cage."

The bird tilted her head and shook her feathers before bowing to him.

He rubbed his fingers through her feathers. "You're my best gal."

It only took a couple of minutes to pull the travel cage out of storage, and The Wife walked right inside without pause.

He set the cage on the table near the door out onto the deck. "I'm going to do one last walk through to be sure I turned everything off. I'll be right back."

Tug whistled while he checked the kitchen one last time. The Wife joined in when she felt like it, sometimes with the right song, sometimes with a random shout-out or whistle, but it was company just the same.

He boxed up the leftover hot dogs and hamburgers and then headed to get The Wife.

"We're going for a ride," Tug called out to The Wife as he made his way through the empty diner.

"On the road again!" The Wife sang out.

As Tug walked out to the deck, she bounced her head and repeated the chorus in a pretty good Willie Nelson impression.

"Hellooo," someone called from the doorway of the restaurant.

Tug stopped and turned.

The Wife paused and stretched up. "Come on in. Hello."

Tug gave her the stink eye. "Behave."

"Is anyone here?" the voice came again.

"Coming." The Wife mimicked Tug the way she was known to do.

"Troublemaker," Tug whispered.

The Wife laughed.

"Not funny." He pointed at her. "Not another word out of you."

She lowered her head and made a kissing sound.

He carried her cage inside and set it on the table of the booth just inside the door. Across the way, a short auburn-haired woman stood in the middle of his diner.

"Hello? Can I help you?" Tug asked.

She looked a little flummoxed. "Hi? Hello. I'm sorry. Are you still open?"

He walked over to her. "Well, I just packed everything up, but I can't turn away a hungry neighbor. What would you like?"

"I'm not picky. Most anything will do. I hate to bother you. It's not like missing a meal is going to kill me."

"Missing a meal might make you cranky, though, and cranky women can be dangerous. Could kill me!" He was only half teasing. He used to keep Nabs in the truck to ward off Maeve's cranky attitude if she went too long between meals.

The woman laughed at his joke. "Well, I've been known to get a little hangry, but I don't think you're in any danger at the moment," she teased.

"Good to know. We were just getting ready to leave, me and my friend here, and get ready for the storm. I thought I knew about everybody in this town, but we haven't met before, have we?"

"We haven't. It's my first time visiting Whelk's Island. My friend has a bunch of people securing her house, but who knows how long that will take? I didn't want to be a bother, so I thought I'd zip out and grab something to eat. I just didn't realize they would shut down everything so early."

"They issued an evacuation order earlier today," Tug said.

"Voluntary, though, right?"

"Yes. So far, anyway. Not that it matters to the locals."

"Oh, well, we're planning to stay. My friend says they aren't worried about it."

He lifted his brows, but he didn't remark.

"You look like you don't approve." Her lips pulled into a straight line. She must've read his body language.

"Not my place to judge either way," he said.

"You're still here," she said a little defensively, but there was a playful tilt to her lips.

"True enough." He shrugged. "But I'm just an old diner owner who has nothing to live for."

"You love The Wife," The Wife called out.

"Oh, is your wife here too?" The woman peered past him.

"No. I don't have a wife."

She didn't look convinced.

He raised a finger, then hooked it for her to follow him. He gestured toward the cage, where The Wife took up pretty much all the room. "Meet The Wife."

"That's meeeeee," the bird called out. "Tug loves The Wife."

The woman started laughing, her eyes dancing as if she were absolutely delighted. "Oh my goodness. Well, isn't she just full of herself?"

"That's one way to put it."

The bird tsk-tsked.

"Does she say a lot?"

"Too much most days. She's got a better vocabulary than me most of the time. Over four hundred words is what I was told when I got her, but that was a long, long time ago, and she's learned to say a lot of things and mimic sounds over the years. I have no idea how someone counts that, but she's got a sense of humor, and she knows good people when she sees them." He eyed The Wife. "She seems to like you . . . Er, did I get your name?"

"I'm Rosemary."

"Well, nice to meet you, Rosemary." He walked over to the counter. "I have both cheeseburgers and hot dogs already prepared. I was taking them to my buddy. Or I could quickly make you my personal favorite, pancakes."

"Pancakes are my favorite, too, but let's keep it simple. I'd be so thankful for one of those cheeseburgers. When all these boards come down and you're open, I'm holding you to those pancakes."

"My kind of girl," The Wife cried out and followed it with a wolf whistle.

Rosemary's eyes narrowed. "Are you sure that's an actual bird that's doing all that talking and you're not some kind of ventriloquist?"

That struck Tug in the funny bone. "Quite certain. I've got a monthly bird-feed bill to prove it. But I look forward to making you pancakes one day very soon."

Rosemary blushed.

"You ever been through a hurricane before?" Tug asked as he pulled out a cheeseburger and the fixings for her.

"I grew up in Virginia Beach, but I don't remember being scared about hurricanes. Then again, that's sort of the good part of being a kid. In Hawaii, hurricanes rarely make landfall, but I've been through a couple of monster storms over the years."

"I gather you know how destructive these storms can be, then."

"Yes, sir. I sure do, but it's so beautiful living on the water that it's a small price to pay, don't you think?"

"True. Only, the waves in Hawaii are way more treacherous

than around here. So big you can stand up and not touch the water in the curl."

Her eyes lit up. "A surfer, I take it."

"About a million years ago."

"The waves are enormous in some spots, but they can be calm too. Have you ever been to the islands?"

"Dreamed about it when I was a kid. You know, catching a clean line in the pipe, which would've been the ultimate rush, but no. Hawaii seemed about as far as any foreign land to a small-town guy like me."

She laughed. "I was going to say it's just an airplane ride away, and that's true if I were talking to your twentysomething self, but honestly, it's a brutal flight when you get to be our age. Five hours just from Honolulu to the mainland."

"Our age?" He shook his head. "We're nowhere near the same age."

"Don't be so sure," she said with a wink. "I think we're closer in age than you think. But you know, maybe it would still be worth going. The five-hour leg isn't so bad if it's not backed up to hours of layovers in the airport and more lengthy flights. I'd probably break it up and visit the different cities for a day or two before taking the next hop. Actually, that's a really good idea."

She looked like she was planning her next trip right here. He liked the way he could almost see the wheels turning as she thought out loud.

"I've always wanted to see Napa and the redwoods." She kept talking as he prepared the cheeseburger. "Maybe stop in Texas and see those longhorn cattle on the way. Vegas! I've never been to Vegas. You?"

"Nope. Whelk's Island is about the extent of my travels."

"What? Seriously?"

He spread his arms wide. "Why leave all this?"

"Why indeed! You have an excellent point."

Her quick and easy comebacks made him grin. "Need any condiments?"

"Just some ketchup. I thought I'd sit in my car and watch the ocean. Do you mind if I do that from your parking lot?"

"Suit yourself. It's an excellent view."

"Thank you." Their eyes locked for a nanosecond longer than was normal.

He looked away. "If that storm keeps picking up speed, you and your friends might want to head to the shelter. I've seen this island flooded to the point people were using pool floats to get around for over a week. You good with a paddle?"

"Excellent, actually. I was ready for an adventure."

"Well, you're likely to get one." He passed the styrofoam container over the counter to her. "I hope you enjoy the burger and come see me after the storm is over. I'll be open for business."

"What do I owe you?" She pulled her wallet from her purse.

He waved her off. "Not a dime. You take care. Come see me after the storm."

"I'll take you up on that." She gave him a finger wave as she walked out.

The Wife leaned into Tug's shoulder. "Bye, Maeve."

He watched her walk back to her car.

"That wasn't Maeve, you silly bird. Her name is Rosemary. She's just visiting."

The Wife gave a hearty laugh. "Storm's coming."

"Yes, it is. Shall we go see Paul?"

Bobbing her head in approval, she fluffed up and leaned in with rapid-fire kisses.

Tug smiled. "Well, that's a yes if I've ever seen one!"

Chapter Ten

TUG GOT UP THE NEXT MORNING AND DRANK HIS COFFEE on the deck. Closing the diner today had been the smart thing to do, but it left him with a little too much free time on his hands.

He wished he hadn't given in and promised Paul he'd shelter at Paws with him. He'd have been so much more comfortable at home. If he hadn't already taken The Wife to Paws last night, he'd have called Paul right now and said, "Thanks, but no thanks."

Staying at the diner might've been an even better option since Maeve wasn't around to keep him company, and he could've prepped food or done something productive until the storm passed.

But a promise was a promise. As he tossed a few things in a duffel bag to get ready to go over to Paws Town Square, the doorbell rang.

Maybe it was the county checking in on folks who hadn't evacuated yet. Sometimes they did that around here, especially if the evacuation had been upgraded from recommended to mandatory. Although he hadn't heard that to be the case.

He opened the door to Paul's smiling face.

"You weren't going to blow me off, were you?" Paul stepped inside, then nodded when he noted the duffel bag.

"Thought about it," Tug said. "But no, I was getting ready to come over."

"Cool. I'll save you the trip. I had to fuel up all the vehicles. Just topped off my truck, so I thought I'd shoot down here and get you."

"You mean, make sure I showed up?"

"You're not mincing words, are you?" Paul said with an impish grin. "Got anything you want me to carry down?"

"Just a couple of things I thought might come in handy." Tug pointed to a crate of things he'd gathered.

"Cool." Paul picked it up. "Meet you downstairs."

On the ride over to Paws, Paul told Tug he'd received word from Amanda and the kids, and they'd driven straight through to her parents' place. "I'm thankful to know they made it safely."

"That's good. I know they hated to leave you, though."

"Believe me, it's harder on me than it is on them," Paul said.

"That's your own fault."

"It was the right thing to do. You know that." He pulled in a breath. "Hey, did you catch the weather update?"

"Didn't even turn on the television. I'm going old school. The storm will get here when it gets here."

"Well, not going old school. I've been tracking it. The storm has picked up speed. Looks like it will probably hit around dinner."

"That's a good sign."

Paul had a questioning look on his face. "A good sign would've been Hurricane Edwina had turned and headed out to sea."

"Well, that's true, but in my experience," Tug said, "it seems the most damaging storms hit in the middle of the night. Like a sneak attack."

"Interesting."

"Don't know if there's any hard data on that—just this old man's recollection."

"That's worth something," Paul said. "We'll take all the good signs we can find."

By seven o'clock Hurricane Edwina teased the coastline again, bringing with her the heaviest rains. Inside the building, the sound of wind and rain battering against the metal storm panels created an eerie backdrop.

Paul paced in his office, which overlooked the entire ground floor of Paws. Four of his employees were sitting at a table in the middle of the agility training area, playing Scrabble. They had a few of the smaller dogs out with them. "None of them, the people or the dogs, seem too concerned," Paul said. "The noise is mind numbing."

"It's only just begun," Tug said. "But these metal buildings make it sound even worse."

"I'm worried about a few of the retired military working dogs. A couple experienced some pretty tough trauma on the front lines. Big noises can unsettle them."

"You've always said they are soldiers too."

"Yeah. I guess I do say that all the time, but it's true. Folks forget that these dogs have emotional baggage when they come home too."

"Probably more so, because they can't talk it out."

"Well, I do my best. I'm going to go check on my soldiers," he said to Tug. "We've got a long storm window ahead of us."

Tug saw the concern etched on his face. "Need help?"

"No. I just need to ease my mind." Paul went downstairs.

Those dogs weren't the only ones anxious because of this

storm. Paul might've been the one who insisted Amanda take the kids out of town, but neither one of them wanted to be apart.

Tug turned his attention back to the weather channel. A blonde wearing a big raincoat hung on to her hood with one hand as the rain pelted her. "The rain is really coming in down here on Atlantic Beach," she said, blinking. Poor girl had to shout over the gusting wind. She let out a squeal when a piece of paper flew against her body.

He felt a little bad for laughing. The woman slapped the soggy paper away like it was some sort of critter on the attack. "Things are really flying around here. I'm going to get inside. There's a parking garage across the way. We're going to stream some footage and check back in shortly."

The cameraman swooped away from the reporter and showed the ocean crashing against the sand, then panned to the street-light, where you could see the rain coming down heavy and at an angle that really accentuated the wind speed. A decorative flag on a pole in front of one merchant whipped in the air. About that time, a box blew down the street.

"How's it looking?"

"Like Mother Nature is throwing a tantrum," Tug said.

Paul leaned against the back of Tug's chair, watching as the meteorologist broke back in to give his update. Hurricane Edwina was still gaining strength. Winds were expected to be over one hundred and ten miles per hour. "I've never been through a storm this size before. Guess this will be the test to see if I got what I paid for," he mumbled.

"I imagine we'll lose power soon."

The lights flickered.

"Don't say things like that," Paul said.

"I think this storm is coming no matter what I say. Besides, you said you have a generator."

"I do, but the longer the power stays on, the less damage this storm is causing."

"Good point." Tug leaned back in his chair. "Thing about hurricanes, they aren't always very fast. Did you know there was once a hurricane that lasted twenty-eight days? The Great Bahamas Hurricane back in 1899. You might just want to settle in for the long haul."

A loud rumble reverberated through the building.

"Was that thunder?"

"I hope that's all it was," Tug said.

Time dragged on.

The power went out around ten o'clock that night, but the generator kicked right in, and the extra noise actually became more soothing than the sound of the storm.

Paul kept walking the perimeter inside the building, making sure all was okay. He was nervous, but Tug didn't know how to soothe his concerns.

As the hours passed, the atmosphere shifted between tense anticipation and weary resignation. People were getting tired, but they were too amped to sleep.

Time seemed to stretch endlessly, each rain-pounding moment feeling like an eternity as they waited for the worst of Hurricane Edwina to pass. Conversation ebbed and flowed, punctuated by the occasional ping of something slamming the building as if they needed a reminder of what was going on outside.

For two days, Hurricane Edwina parked over top of them, dropping inches of rain without a pause.

Finally, on the third day, the howling winds subsided and the first rays of dawn brightened the sky. Low and full, the clouds rolled by like a video on fast-forward. *Good riddance.*

Tug cooked breakfast for the thirty or so people, counting the employees and their families, who had sheltered here at Paws Town Square. Paul hadn't skimped on the kitchen space when designing this place, although most of the storage was filled with pet food.

But Paul, being a smart thinker, had stocked up on plenty of food to get them through the storm, and Tug was taking full advantage of having the quiet kitchen to himself. Everything was shiny and new, unlike his diner. The smell of fresh-made biscuits he'd slid into the oven a bit ago filled the air while he scrambled eggs and fried a huge pan of bacon.

Tug was pulling the biscuits out, golden and irresistible, just as Paul walked in.

"You, my friend, have impeccable timing," Tug said. "Every single time I have a meal ready, you show up out of nowhere."

"My mom used to say that about me too. Looks good." Paul smiled but then lifted his phone in frustration. "I lost my cell signal. I don't like that," he said. "But I could get used to waking up to home cooking."

"It's what I do best, but you have another option. A better one named Amanda and two delightful kids that would probably fight over who will pour your juice." Tug checked his phone. "I don't have a signal either."

"Well, that's not good." Paul turned on the television in the kitchen. "Somehow we still have cable, though."

"Thank goodness for that generator," Tug said.

"True. Let everyone know we can eat in my office upstairs and keep check on the storm updates. Hopefully, the worst of it is over."

Tug walked out of the kitchen and called out to the others, "Breakfast is ready!"

The sound of people talking as they made their way to the food was soothing to Tug. "We can all eat up in Paul's office. It seems we have cable. Go figure."

Everyone made their plates, then went to Paul's office to eat and catch the most recent weather updates on the big-screen television.

The chatter was optimistic. There were no reports about Whelk's Island specifically, but for the most part, those south of them were reporting back, and it looked like the storm was finally rolling out to sea.

"Think we can open the storm panels?" Chase asked. "I'm going stir crazy in here."

"Yes. Looks like the worst is over. Let's eat, and we'll get to work on that." Paul scooped his eggs onto his biscuit and took a bite.

Everyone looked a little bleary eyed from lack of sleep, but it seemed like Paws had withstood the storm.

Paul, Tug, and Chase surveyed the situation while spending the next four hours opening and storing the storm panels. The trees Paul had planted when they opened Paws had blown over. They were young trees, so that didn't surprise any of them, but even Tug, who'd been through lots of storms, couldn't believe the enormous amount of sand that had washed in. A layer hid the dark pavement, piling around the tires of the vehicles.

"The storm hit right at high tide. This is what they were talking about, the storm surge being a game changer." Tug was eager to get home and check on his place. "The water was so high I bet we've got major flooding closer to the beach."

"I'll drive out and see," Paul said.

"I'm afraid that wet sand is going to be more like quicksand," Tug said.

"Good point. I'll get the guys to pull the skid steer out and clear a path to the road." The three of them crossed the parking lot to the street to get a feel for how the roads were. From here they could see several trees down, and across the highway an entire row of power lines was down.

"That's going to take some time to repair," Tug commented.

"Holy cow." Paul nudged Tug's arm, pointing to the other side of the building. "Is that what I think it is?"

Tug turned to where Paul was looking. Parked as if it belonged there, a fishing boat now sat up against the right side of Paws Town Square. "If you think it's a boat, yeah, it's what you think it is. Pretty nice one too."

"How the heck—"

"The marina is a long way off. I have no earthly idea. I'd say it's probably a good thing we couldn't see what was going on out here from in there."

"For sure." Paul reached for his phone. "I wish I could call Amanda." He lifted it, hoping for a signal.

Until they got this parking lot partially cleared, it was doubtful they could get to anywhere with a signal, even in Paul's big four-wheel drive.

The ditches overflowed across the street.

A police siren caught their attention.

The SUV pulled up and rolled down the window. "Everything okay over here?"

"Think so," Paul said. "I own Paws Town Square."

"I recognize you from the town council meetings," the officer said. "Hey, Tug. You stayed down here?"

"I got talked into it."

"Probably a good thing. The beach roads down your way are still completely underwater."

"We can't get down there?" Paul asked. "Not even with my four-by-four?"

"No. We blocked off the roads to keep anyone from trying until we can make sure it's safe. There are a ton of guidelines we have to follow. Power lines, all that, to be sure it's safe. Until the tide goes out, we won't even be able to start that."

Tug let out a groan.

"I'll keep you posted, Tug," the officer said.

"Yeah, thanks. I appreciate that. How about at the point? Maeve's old place," Tug asked.

"Things are in pretty good shape out that way."

"That's good news." Paul stepped closer to the vehicle. "You have cell service?"

"No, but I have an update on it. They think it'll be back up by tomorrow. The tower out here had some damage, but some people are getting out intermittently. So, you might just keep trying. I think it's a combination of the tower down and just a lot of people trying to call at once."

"Maybe," Tug said. "Some old-school ways are just more dependable. I bet my landline at the house is working."

"Well, you can't get down there to check." The officer gave Tug a look that said he suspected Tug would try.

Tug just grinned. If he had his truck here, he'd be there by now.

"We're still following up on folks we couldn't get to during the storm," the officer said. "Live power lines down, a few roofs pulled off in the wind. The shelter is pretty full."

"Remind anyone displaced that Paws is open to the public, free of charge, and I have a generator and space available for their pets. It's not a hotel, but it's comfortable. Plenty of benches to stretch out on."

"And Tug's cooking," Chase added.

"I might come and take a nap here later myself," the officer said.

"You're welcome to. Not kidding."

"Well, y'all stay out of trouble. We've got our hands full with people getting out here before the water subsides. Had some dude wading in chest-high water with a cooler of beer waving me down for help earlier. Drunk as a skunk and as shriveled as a prune. He was out in the storm the whole time, and he has a house here. What was he thinking?"

"Seriously?" Paul and Chase looked horrified.

"I could venture a guess from a short list who it was," Tug said. "Crazies in every generation."

The officer's radio crackled with a muffled announcement. "That's me. Gotta go." He pulled off, hit the siren in a short whoop-whoop, and did a U-turn toward the oceanfront.

Paul draped his arm across Tug's shoulders. "Guess we're going to have to wait to see how much water we're dealing with down in your neck o' the shore."

"Guess so." The one thing Tug was never that good at? Waiting.

Chapter Eleven

HURRICANE EDWINA'S POUNDING ON NORTH CAROLINA was all over the news, even up in Ohio, and Amanda couldn't pull herself away from it. The storm made landfall and bounced offshore and bumped back into the coast like a ball at the hands of a pinball wizard. None of the models had predicted this. Edwina maintained power and kept battering the coast even after landfall, with mounting rainfall.

The meteorologists kept repeating that although the winds had lost strength, the prolonged rains could wreak just as much havoc with flooding and that could be more dangerous.

It was all Amanda could do to shield her children from the devastation and concern.

She didn't want them getting caught up in all the speculation. She and her parents had agreed there'd be no news on the television where the kids could see it until they received word from Paul that things were okay.

Amanda left the house under the guise of getting ice cream, to bring up the news and weather channel on her laptop and get the most recent updates. It was almost impossible for her to do that in the house. The kids were right at her side every moment.

She sat in her car in the supermarket parking lot and watched. National coverage flashed pictures from up and down the

East Coast, flipping so quickly between Florida, Georgia, and the Carolinas that at any given moment she wasn't sure where the images were coming from, only that she was searching for anything familiar but praying she wouldn't recognize a thing.

Images of rising water from unprecedented storm surge, roofs ripped from buildings, and people wading through waist-high water filled the screen. On one channel, they showed a sailboat parked lopsided in front of a strip mall. She didn't recognize the area, but one had to wonder just how far from the marina that boat had sailed through the storm. It seemed more like something you'd see in a movie than in reality. They also showed homes dangling over crashing waves, the water littered with household items.

That's someone's lifelong memories. Their safe home sweet home washing away in the tide. Being sucked out to sea. Maeve, you told me how angry and unforgiving a stormy sea could be. It's terrifying.

She tried to concentrate on the softer words Maeve had said too. *"These storms wash ashore all the best treasures. They bring items from the depths that have hidden in the sand for centuries."*

Posts about the storm filled social media. #HurricaneEdwina was trending, and it wasn't pretty.

Another home had lifted right from its foundation and settled over ten feet away. Amanda tried to remind herself that people on the internet often exaggerate updates. Surely there was good news too.

She prayed The Shell Collector had withstood this storm like it had so many others, according to Maeve.

She pressed redial on her phone. Each unanswered call to Paul added another layer of worry to her already-frazzled nerves. Her mind was fixated on her house, on Paul and Tug, and on the friends who called Whelk's Island home.

"Ring!" She glared at the phone. "Yes, I'm talking to my phone."

The phone buzzed. She snatched it up, but it was just an alert that she had an upcoming appointment.

"Seriously? It's like you're playing a game with me now. Buzzing like that and getting my hopes up."

Now I'm going crazy. I'm complaining to my phone. An inanimate object.

She stared at it, willing it to ring, but it didn't.

"Fine, be that way. But just so you know, if I find out you're the one not working and that is why you aren't ringing, I'm going to toss you in the ocean."

Her phone buzzed again.

"Is this a trick?" She picked it up. "Seriously. A reminder to water the plants? The last thing they need is water. They had a hurricane. Haven't you been listening to the news?"

The tiny number next to Paul's name showed how many times she'd tried to reach him, with no luck. Each attempt went straight to voicemail. She tried Tug again, but he didn't pick up, either, so she left him a message. The silence stretched, tightening the knot of anxiety in her chest.

She rested her face in her hands. Soft tears fell at first. Trying to act like she wasn't worried for Hailey and Jesse's sake was wearing her down. But it wasn't just for them. She felt a panic to her core that Paul wouldn't be there when she got back. She couldn't go through that again.

Tears streamed down her cheeks, and she allowed herself to let the emotion ride. When she finally lifted her head and took a breath, she felt calmer.

It was the top of the hour. She brought up the live feed from the local news affiliate near home.

The familiar face of Cindy Farmer in the station logo raincoat, her hair blowing in the wind, brought her a little comfort.

"Friends and neighbors are working to assess damages in this area. As you know, it's peak tourist season on the coast and seasonal increases in population and limited access on and off the barrier islands can be difficult even without a weather event. Over the last few days, there have been major traffic delays, as some locals evacuated. There was not a mandatory evacuation for most of our viewing area, and of course, many of the lifetime residents wouldn't have left even if there had been."

"Cindy, what is the situation? Power, water, phones—all the necessities," Amanda said to the screen, not caring that it was also an inanimate object.

"Tom, we're receiving reports that one of the cell towers sustained damage, and the entire county is without power. When nightfall comes, it'll be another long one for the folks that stayed to weather this storm. And while the few people that stayed are toughing it out, others are in a line, trying to get back to see if their homes are still there."

"Is there a lot of damage to homes?" Tom asked.

"We're still gathering reports of damage. You can see from our footage here, there are broken windows, gas station awnings twisted, and the entire roof on this beach house behind me was lifted off. Interestingly the storm surge has brought an unexpected amount of sand across the main roads. We've never seen anything like this, but the emergency teams turned us around so we couldn't get you any pictures of that. We're staying close to the situation. Reports are just beginning to come in. What I can say is, despite the devastation by the hurricane in our area, it is a miracle that we've had no reports of loss of life." She pressed her hand to her heart. "I just have to take a moment here to share what's on my heart. Where there are miracles, angels are around." She shook her head, clearly emotional.

"The storm is tracking east in the Atlantic now. Good news for the coast."

"It is, Tom. As the water subsides, the county is at the ready to plow the sand covering the roads. We've seen vehicles engulfed in sand. One had sand clear up to the dashboard. Digging out will not be quick in this state of disaster. We'll have further updates as we're able to gain access to more of the area, but I think we can be thankful that this community will come together to get through it."

Amanda let out a long breath. "Okay. Not good, but not horrible." Nothing really specific, either, but she felt at least more hopeful.

Suddenly, panic bubbled inside her. Paul must not have cell service. Worst-case scenarios played in her mind. What if he was hurt? What if Paws Town Square wasn't as hurricane-proof as he believed? The thoughts made her sick to her stomach.

She slapped down the cover on her laptop and went inside the store to buy the ice cream the kids would be expecting. Adding to the mix, she threw in a can of whipped cream and some chocolate sprinkles.

As she stood in line to check out, a woman with a British accent spoke to someone behind her.

Immediately, her mind went to their trip here when Hailey and Jesse were talking to Rosemary, pretending they were the children of a British princess. It made her smile, and the smile felt good.

The cashier rang up her purchase, and she couldn't get out of there quick enough. As soon as she stepped outside, she scrolled to Rosemary's cellphone number.

Please answer.

The phone rang twice before she got behind the wheel of her car. She started the car, then moved the phone to her shoulder so she could pull the seatbelt across her lap.

"Hello?" The voice was crystal clear.

"Oh my gosh. Hello?" Amanda could barely speak. She was so excited to have someone answer. "Rosemary? We met at the truck stop. I was the lady—"

"Amanda. Yes, I remember. I'm so glad you called. I wondered how you and the children were coping. I hoped you weren't worried."

"I've been so worried. I can't get through to Paul, and I'm not sure what to believe in the news. Plus, nothing is specifically Whelk's Island. We're such a tiny map dot in that area."

"Yes, it is a wonderful little town. I got to see some of it before the storm hit."

"How is everything there?"

"We don't have power, and we haven't gotten out yet, but spirits are good, and people are trying to stay connected and help one another. It's kind of a mess. I bet Paul doesn't have cell service. My friend's phone has been out. Someone said two towers nearby got damaged. Not sure how I got lucky to have service. I have one of those cheap networks."

"Well, I'm so glad you do." Amanda swallowed back the emotion. "I'm just so relieved to talk to someone back home. Are you safe?"

"My friend's house is fine. We had a lot of rain and crazy wind, but no damage at all here, but she's not right on the water. We're still getting rain, and some places are flooded. I hope we can get out tomorrow and really see what the state of affairs is. Paws is literally up the street from where I'm staying. If we can't drive, I can walk that far to check in on Paul."

"Oh my gosh, would you?"

"Of course," Rosemary said. "Honey, don't worry. There's cleanup—no question about it—but what we're hearing is there was no loss of life, and that's what is important."

"Yes. That brings me peace. Surely if something as huge as Paws Town Square had been damaged, that would have made the news."

"Definitely. My friend knows all about your guy's business. It sounds quite spectacular. I'm sure you're very proud of Paul."

"I can't even put into words how amazing he is."

"You relax. Everything is going to be okay. I'll call you tomorrow with an update."

Part of her wanted to beg Rosemary to go find Paul right then, but if the roads weren't passable, it was ridiculous to put Rosemary in danger just to soothe her concern.

Please, Lord, I know the seasons follow Your plan. The tides swell and release at Your predetermined touch. You are always with us. I place my concerns and anxiety over the damage brought by Hurricane Edwina to our hometown, our family, neighbors, and friends in Your hands. Please wrap them in Your care and keep them safe.

Bring me back home to Paul. Bring our little family safely back together. I am so thankful You brought Paul into my life. Help me know how to help others, to be Your hands and feet during the rebuilding and recovery, and to help others see the faith that will see us through this storm. I know You are in the boat with us, that the waters may be choppy but You will lead us to a safe landing always.

Chapter Twelve

ROSEMARY WAS SO HAPPY TO SEE THE SUN THAT SHE COULD barely contain herself. It looked like the rain might finally be gone. It wasn't easy to be cooped up in a house during a storm with someone you barely knew, and she didn't really know why she'd thought it was going to be like a slumber party, because she and Kathleen didn't really run in the same circles in high school. She hadn't even realized that until they went through the yearbooks together. She didn't remember half the people Kathleen did.

Kathleen carried a wilted plant into the kitchen and set it in the sink.

"In the dark, I didn't even really notice I'd forgotten to water this poor thing." She turned on the faucet and let it run. "Hopefully we can resuscitate it."

"It should spring back to life." Rosemary leaned against the counter. "I think I'm going to go take a walk over to Paws Town Square. I talked to that nice young lady I met on my way here. She hasn't heard from her guy, and she's worried. He owns Paws. Want to walk over there with me?"

"Oh, that sounds like heaven. I'm so tired of these four walls. Paws is not far. I'll come with you." Kathleen turned off the water. "Let me go put on my shoes. Wouldn't it be great if a restaurant was open? I'd give anything for a hot meal. There are a couple of little ones on the way."

"We might get lucky. I'll wait for you on the front porch." Rosemary was hungry for something good too. They'd lived on peanut butter and crackers and leftover charcuterie since the night she'd arrived. Kathleen might know how to host one heck of a party, but she hadn't planned any further out. No bottled water, no extra propane for the grill. They'd run through the whole tank cooking oysters the other night. She didn't even have a flashlight, but it had worked out fine.

Rosemary thought about her phone call with Nina. She felt bad about the rift between them. Somehow they had to figure out how to navigate their changing roles as mother and daughter. Family is family, and nothing else should ever get in the way of that. But she would think on that more later. It was time to get out of the house and breathe in the fresh ocean air.

Kathleen walked out in a vibrant peach jogging suit with navy-blue piping and matching tennis shoes and earrings.

Two different worlds. That pretty little outfit was going to come back with mud spatters, but she wasn't about to call Kathleen out on it.

Rosemary walked down the stairs. "Feels so good to get out."

"It's sticky." Kathleen plucked at her jacket.

They walked in silence to the end of the street.

"This way." Kathleen turned to the right. "There's a few shops up this way." She took a few steps forward. "Uck!" she shrieked, lifting her tennis shoe from where she'd just sunk in the sand almost to her ankle. "What the heck?"

"Careful." Rosemary stretched out her arm and helped Kathleen get her footing.

"It's like quicksand." She sloshed forward. "Oh great, and we can't get through this way. Look. It's flooded."

They turned and went down to the next block, which appeared to sit higher. Kathleen finally shed the matching jacket and tied it around her waist.

The roads were fine in this direction. A small shopping center with a deli, ice cream shop, bait shop, and convenience store was just ahead.

The entire canopy over the gas pumps had lifted and lay upside down on the other side of the parking lot. Each of the businesses still had their windows boarded up.

"Doesn't look like they are in any hurry to reopen," Kathleen said.

"I wonder if they know about the damage. I'm guessing a lot of these folks evacuated."

"Probably. I think next time they are calling for a storm, I will too." Kathleen brightened. "Look. People!"

She picked up the pace, and Rosemary was practically jogging to keep up with her friend's long strides.

"This is perfect," Rosemary said. "I was hoping we could get to Paws Town Square from your house."

"Yeah, it's right here."

"Looks like they fared well."

"Thank goodness. It's like a ghost town," Kathleen said.

They walked toward the guys standing near the front entrance.

Kathleen waved from fifty yards out. "Hello!"

The tallest of the three waved back. "Y'all okay?" he called out.

"Yes," Rosemary said as they got closer. "We're fine. Just needed to get out of the house. It's tough being cooped up for that long, but you have a generator. That's what I hear, right?"

"It is. You're welcome to come hang out. We've got the televisions on, water, snacks."

"Air-conditioning?" Kathleen asked.

"Yes, it's quite comfortable inside."

"It's so muggy out here," Kathleen complained.

"Make yourself at home." He reached out his hand. "I'm Paul."

The name struck Rosemary. "Paul, as in Amanda's Paul? Paul, who owns this place?"

His smile was toothpaste-commercial perfect. "Yeah. That's me."

"You're not even going to believe this. I know this is going to sound nuts, but I met Amanda and her kids when they were leaving town. They were at a truck stop in a lime-green stretch limousine truck."

Paul's eyes sort of bugged out. "Yes! That was her."

"I was on my way to visit a friend."

"You didn't exactly pick the best time to vacation here," he remarked.

"No, I did not, but is there really ever a bad time to rekindle a friendship?" Rosemary noticed Kathleen had stepped closer, as if on a stage cue. "This is my friend Kathleen."

"Hi." Kathleen shook Paul's hand. "We haven't officially met. I board my cat here, pretty often actually. I'm Kathleen Callahan."

"I'm sorry we hadn't met before."

"I love what you've done for this town. I've walked your trails a few times. Promised my friend here that I'd bring her over to check them out at some point." Kathleen turned to one of the other men and smiled. "I know this guy, though. Hi, Tug."

"Kathleen, it's good to see you."

"Tug?" Rosemary looked at him. "Oh my gosh. I feel like Dorothy in *The Wizard of Oz*, with the tin man and the scarecrow. Amanda mentioned you too. She said you'd keep us fed if the need arose. I didn't realize you were *you*!"

"That's me. It's good to see you again. I believe I owe you some pancakes."

"You remember. Yes, we've already met, and I didn't even realize it. Thank you, by the way, for the other night. That burger hit the spot."

"Good. I didn't catch your last name."

"Palakiko."

"Right. You mentioned you lived in Hawaii. Pau-pokey-kikkoman . . . Sorry—that's a pathetic attempt to say it. I'll practice."

"Well, I was married to it for fifty years. I'd like to think I've mastered it."

"I'm sure your husband will appreciate that."

"She's widowed," Kathleen blurted out.

Rosemary glared at her.

"I'm sorry," Tug said.

"Thank you." She shifted her attention to Paul. "When I met Amanda and the kids, we exchanged numbers. I talked to her last night. She said she'd lost contact with you. She was really worried."

"Your phone is working?" Paul looked shocked and then very excited. "None of our phones are working. Can I use your phone to call her?"

She handed him her phone. "Just press Send. I already brought up her number."

Relief flooded Paul's face. "I don't know how I can thank you."

"Press Send already. She's going crazy not knowing," Rosemary said. "I tried to assure her things seemed okay here. I'm so glad everyone is fine."

"Put her on speaker," Tug said.

"Yeah. Okay." Paul made the call, grinning as he shifted nervously. "Amanda. I'm standing here with your new best friend. I'm so glad to hear your voice, babe."

"Thank goodness. I've been so worried." Amanda's voice shook.

"Yes. I wish I could've called you. There's no cell service. Everyone is still surveying the damage. We couldn't get out of the parking lot. When the water subsided, we realized the tide had swept in tons of sand. We're digging out, but there's going to be a long cleanup ahead of us."

"It's hard to picture. I'm just thankful everyone is okay. You called from Rosemary's number! So she found you?"

"She sure did. I'm sorry you were worried."

"I was trying not to be," she said. "It's great to hear your voice. I don't want to ever be apart during something like that again."

"I'm here too," Tug said. "Don't go getting mushy. You're on speaker."

"Tug. Love you. We're all fine. I'm so glad to know y'all are okay too."

"The guys had to break out the skid steer to clear a path for us to get out of the lot," Paul said. "I'm getting ready to take Tug over to the diner, and it's the first time any of us are getting out. I can't wait to see you."

"I wish I'd driven myself. I don't want to wait on Travis to come pick us up."

"I'm anxious, too, babe, but there's no power, and we're not even really sure what all we're facing yet. We'll get a plan of action in place. Just relax. Enjoy the visit with your parents. There's nothing left to worry about. I promise."

"This is Rosemary, Amanda." She leaned in to the phone. "I'll keep you updated until the others get their phones going. My friend literally lives less than a mile from Paul's business. I still can't believe we crossed paths and it's worked out like this. It's certainly a Godwink, isn't it?"

"I'd say so. Thank you, Rosemary. I love you, Paul. Tug, we're all missing you and The Wife too."

"It's not the same around here without you and the kids,"

Tug said. "As soon as you get home, I'll fix all of you your favorite meals. Tell Jesse I'm going to throw him an after-the-hurricane party."

"He will love that. I'll tell him," Amanda said. "As soon as Paul can get me there, we're in!"

"I love you, babe. I am missing you like crazy. In case the phone issue doesn't get resolved, I'll get Rosemary's address and stay in contact with her so we stay in sync."

"That would be wonderful. I tried not to worry, but I—"

"It's okay. I never want to worry you, but love has a way of making us do that sometimes."

"Yes, it does." Her voice was soft. "And that's good in so many ways. I'll talk to you soon."

He handed the phone back to Rosemary. "We're going to let you go, Amanda," Rosemary said. "You've got my number. Call as you need to. Bye now." She tucked the phone in her back pocket.

"You're an angel just showing up like this," Paul said. "Thank you."

"I'm so glad I could help. It was so funny how we crossed paths that day. Hailey and Jesse are wonderful children. I enjoyed talking to them so much. I hope I'll get to see them again while I'm in town."

"You can count on it. You're invited to the party," Tug said.

"Why don't you ladies go inside? There are tables of snacks and water. Kathleen, you can show Rosemary the trails and take a load off. We're getting ready to run up the road and check on some things. Make yourselves at home. Chase here, he's my right-hand man. And the left, come to think of it. He can help y'all with anything you need."

Kathleen let out an exaggerated sigh. "Thank you. I feel so sticky and icky. A little AC sounds like heaven."

"Enjoy it. I'm going to take this guy to see if we can get down to the north end of the beach and see how things look at the diner and his house."

Rosemary raised her hand and crossed her fingers. "Good luck. It was so good to meet you, Paul and Tug. This is great. Who knew?"

A Godwink in so many ways.

Chapter Thirteen

TUG CLIMBED INTO PAUL'S PICKUP. "THANKS, MAN. I HOPE they've got the road open by now."

"Except for the sand, things don't look too bad."

"Never seen the sand wash up like this before, though. It's hard to tell if we're even on the road."

"I know." Paul pointed out damage as they slowly cruised through the area. A twisted canopy, toppled trees, and an overturned trailer.

Tug's heart pounded. The damage was more significant than he'd feared.

"Oh no. Hey, stop," Tug called out.

Paul jumped on the brakes, and Tug hopped out of the truck and ran over to the little bar called The Tackle Box.

The force of the sweeping tide had removed an entire wall, leaving the bar exposed. Bottles of liquor lay heaped in a pile between toppled barstools wedged against a stud.

"Is Fisher around?" Paul walked up behind Tug. "This is a mess."

"I hope he was well insured. I think he used every nickel he had to build this place. Kid refuses to take out a loan for anything. Don't see too many folks these days do that. He has a good head on his shoulders, despite the kick-back attitude, but this isn't good."

"I hope he evacuated," Paul said. "We'll check around and be sure he's not here, then see if we can't get someone to his house to check on him. Man, I wish I'd thought to touch base with him. You beach guys are hardheaded sometimes."

"Yep." Tug wasn't even going to argue the point. He was glad now that he'd let Paul talk him into weathering the storm at Paws.

"Fisher, can you hear me?" Tug called out. He leaned in, listening, then walked to the other side of the bar. "Are you here?"

They carefully picked through the debris. "Thank goodness there's no sign of him."

"I feel so bad for him," Tug said. "Come on. Let's get to the diner. Once folks come home, they're going to want a hot meal. Comfort food might not cure anything, but it helps. At least I can do that."

"I hope Fisher is okay," Paul said as they walked back to his truck. "He's going to be sick when he sees this."

"I didn't figure he'd evacuate. I'll be honest—I'm not sure he's living in the little place up near the church anymore. Ever since he opened the bar, I think he spends most of his time here." Tug's stomach sank at the thought. "I hope I'm wrong and someone talked him into leaving town."

"We'll drive by his old place. Maybe he's there."

"We'll track him down," Tug said. "And then we'll help him rebuild. Whelk's Island has been through way worse than this, and this small community always comes together."

"Absolutely," Paul said. "You know I'm right there with you."

Paul gunned the engine to get out of the soft sand. "Thank goodness for four-wheel drive." The sand crossed the beach road in drifts. "I hope we don't get stuck. I'm usually the one pulling everyone else out."

Tug reached for the pillar grab handle to steady himself

as they forged ahead, each bump jolting his tired bones. He couldn't wait to sleep in his own bed tonight.

Paul gripped the steering wheel, his knuckles white as he swung wide to go around a row of orange cones and his wheels spun into the sand.

"I don't know about this, Tug." He pointed to the right. "Is that the top of a fire hydrant?"

"It can't be." Tug peered out the window. "Slow down. Let me look." He got out of the truck and whisked the sand from the exposed red metal. Sure enough, it was the red nut on the top of a fire hydrant. He stood, barely able to believe it. "We've got to be driving on more than two feet of sand here."

"Are you sure?"

"Yeah." Tug dragged in a breath. He pulled on the bill of his ball cap and looked in both directions. "Come on. We better turn around before they run us off."

But it was too late. A county officer rode up on a four-wheeler.

Paul pulled off his sunglasses. "Good afternoon. Just out trying to assess the situation."

"Yeah. We're all still doing that. The water breached the dunes. Can't let you go any further. The cones are there for a reason."

Tug climbed back into the truck and stuck his head out the window. "I've never seen sand wash in like this before. We're headed to my diner."

"You're going to have to wait until we get clearance from the county that it's safe."

Tug lurched forward. "My diner is not even a mile down the road."

"I understand, but you're going to have to wait. We can't get our emergency vehicles down there to assess the situation to determine a timeline for safe reentry for residents yet. Until then, sorry."

Tug leaned back in the seat with a gnawing sense of dread. He wasn't sure if it was worry over The Tackle Box or concern that the diner hadn't fared as well as he'd expected her to.

Paul glanced over at Tug. "Do you have any idea how hard it's going to be to keep this man from his diner?"

The officer leaned in. "Sorry. If I had more information, I'd tell you. I can take your number and call as soon as I get the all clear. It's for everyone's safety. You understand."

"I do, but I don't like it," Tug said.

"Many people are eager to get back to check on their homes."

"Can I go back up that way?" Paul asked. "I wanted to check on Maeve's old house. The Shell Collector. My girlfriend, Amanda, owns it now. She and the kids evacuated. I'd love to let her know things are okay."

"I'll have to see your identification. We're keeping track to be sure we don't run into any looting."

"Sure. Of course." He handed his license to the officer. "When things open up or if you see Fisher, the owner of The Tackle Box, could you let me know? We don't know if he evacuated or not. We think he still lives up at the little house past the church."

"I know Fisher." The officer shook his head. "I'll add him to the list. So far, no casualties. I'm praying to keep it that way."

"Amen," Paul said.

"Stay off the beach road, but if you turn around here and go up that way, you shouldn't have any problem. I drove by that way earlier. Didn't look like there was much damage at all in that area. And the sand didn't pile in at that end of the beach."

"Ten-four," Paul said. "We'll stay out of trouble." He handed the officer his business card. "Until cell service is up, it won't do you much good, but here's my information if you can let me know as soon as I can take Tug up to the diner. His house is farther down past that, but one thing at a time."

"Will do. Y'all take care." The four-wheeler sputtered off.

Tug let out a sigh and turned his body in the seat. "Well, I guess we wait."

"Guess so. Sorry. I know it's difficult. I'd be going crazy."

"I am. Inside. Let's check Maeve's place."

"Let's." Paul turned the truck around, leaving a significant indentation in the wet sand. "Guess we're lucky we didn't get stuck."

Tug had to agree. If they ignored the officer's order, they could end up in trouble. He'd have to be patient.

As they approached the big blue beach house, Tug's heart hammered. He missed Maeve so much. Thankfully, the house appeared to have withstood another pounding.

Paul pulled into the driveway and right up to the house. Tug got out and walked through the lower bays.

"Looks fine down here," he said.

They climbed the stairs to the entrance, and Paul used his key to enter.

Amanda had made the place her own, and there was so much life in the house now. Jesse's trucks and Hailey's artwork lay on the floor in the living room.

Tug walked back to Maeve's favorite room. The room full of windows where she showcased her trove of beach treasures.

Of course, with the windows boarded up for the storm, the usually bright and inviting room was dark, but it held all the treasures Maeve loved. Glass jars and bowls of shells and sea glass still lined the shelves.

"This place is as strong as you always said it was, my friend," Tug murmured. She'd always bragged about that.

He walked back out to the living room with a smile in his heart.

Paul came down the stairs. "Everything is a-okay on the third floor."

Tug pulled open the slider and rolled the storm shutter back, then stepped out onto the second-story deck overlooking the expanse of beach below. "You can see how far the water came up."

"Yeah, and it's still way higher than it usually is."

Piles of tangled seaweed, debris, and foamy residue left behind by the receding tide created a winding trail along the beach.

Ever restless, the ocean mirrored the turmoil in Tug's heart and mind.

The waves crashed so loudly he couldn't make out what Paul was saying. "Didn't catch that."

Paul continued the inspection. "There are a couple limbs down on the big tree, but there's even some Spanish moss still clinging to it. Jesse will be so happy. He was worried to death about that."

"Yeah. I see. Those kids sure loved Maeve."

"They did. They do. She's very much in everyone's thoughts here. Yours, too, I know."

"Oh, yeah." He patted his heart. Maeve would forever hold the key.

"Too bad the kids aren't here to see all this sea-foam. It looks like snow," Paul remarked.

"It does." But the sea-foam wasn't unusual after a big storm like this. It was a reaction to the churn of the waves and breakdown of organic matter, and it always carried the pungent aroma of seaweed mingled with musty old crab and oyster shells. Not totally unpleasant to him, after all those years working as a commercial fisherman.

Paul pulled out his phone and took a video and some pictures.

Tug could imagine Maeve walking over the dune toward the

house. A hand on her head trying to hold on to one of those huge floppy hats she loved so much, and her skirt swirling and lifting around her ankles. She was always a colorful sight.

Tug bowed his head and closed his eyes.

Please let everything be shipshape at the diner too. Lord, You've already taken Maeve. The diner is all I have. I'm feeling very alone right now.

He opened his eyes and stepped back from the railing.

Paul stood nearby, quiet, probably a million of his own worries racing through his mind, and missing Amanda. At least he'd learned from Tug's mistake. He'd been smart enough to get the girl and hang on to her.

The foreboding feeling taunted Tug.

The raw power of a stormy ocean was dangerous, but he couldn't imagine living anywhere else. A storm or two a year was a small price to pay to be on Whelk's Island.

"Ready to go?" Paul asked.

Tug nodded and led the way back down to the truck.

They headed south. A few shingles were loose here and there, and a shed had drifted off its foundation and landed in the driveway of one of the beach houses, but all in all, it seemed like this part of the coast had been spared.

By the time Paul and Tug got back to the turnoff toward Paws Town Square, there was a line of utility bucket trucks from the power company setting up along the area where all the power lines had toppled like dominoes.

"Are you okay, Tug?"

Tug brushed his hand across his forehead as he nodded, not wanting to worry Paul. He was sweating, and his heart was racing. Honestly, he wasn't sure if he was having a heart attack or panic attack, but the wave of depression left him with only one thought in his mind.

Who cares?

They made their way back, and the Paws lobby became a hub of activity as people gathered to partake in a spaghetti lunch for anyone who could make it. The aroma of garlic filled the air, emanating from the large basket of knots lovingly prepared by Tug to accompany the meal.

Paul had done a good job spreading the word. Everyone shared what they knew with neighbors, from the police chief to guys still wearing their safety vests after pushing back sand with the big loaders.

That was the thing about a natural disaster—it brought people to the same level, no matter where they started out. Laughter and conversation flowed as everyone settled in, savoring the food and the company and a sense of relief that things might soon get back to normal.

The chatter subsided as folks' appetites took priority. Then suddenly the room filled with a chorus of beeps, buzzes, chirps, and rings as cell service was restored, sparking excitement and anticipation as everyone grabbed for their phone, eager to reconnect with concerned family and friends.

Chairs screeched as people clamored to contact loved ones. The table sat nearly empty of people and full of half-eaten plates of spaghetti. In that moment, Tug felt alone. No one to call. Every single message to his phone had been a missed call from Amanda, and she'd surely been trying to reach Paul.

Paul stood over by the tables of food, a toothy grin on his face as he spoke on his phone. Tug could imagine the chatter of Amanda's kids and the excitement they must feel after being out of touch for a couple of days.

Chase jogged over, waving his arms to get Paul's attention. "Sorry, man. Someone's up front looking for you. I think it's important."

Paul nodded, lifting a hand to show he'd be right there.

Tug got up to cover the serving plates. No sense in the food getting dried out. He'd just wiped down one table when Paul walked over, looking worried.

"Everything okay?" Tug asked.

"Chase will finish this up," Paul said. "We need to go."

"Where are we going? Is everything okay with Amanda and the kids?"

"They're fine. Look, the road to the diner is still closed, but there's a city worker here to take us down there."

Sure, Tug knew a lot of people on Whelk's Island—even considered them good friends—but this was more than just someone being helpful. His thoughts swirled as if he was being pulled under by them, halting his ability to speak. He simply nodded and fell in step behind Paul.

At the entrance stood the same young officer who'd stopped them on the beach road earlier.

"Hello. Y'all ready?" It was rhetorical. He didn't even wait for an answer, just turned and led the way to the city vehicle, which was a weathered Jeep that had seen better days.

Rust crunched under Tug's shoe as he stepped up to get into the back seat next to Paul. Despite the warm temperature, he suddenly felt chilled and queasy.

The officer pulled out of the parking lot. "When I told the chief that I spoke to you two earlier, he told me this road won't be open for general use for another day or so, but he gave me special permission to take you down."

"The chief and I go way back," Tug said.

"Apparently everyone knows you but me. I'm new to Whelk's Island. My name's Jason. I just transferred up here from down on the Georgia coast. They took a beating too."

"This storm couldn't make up her mind," Paul said. "I really thought when she made landfall down there in Georgia, she'd fizzle out. I was surprised when she turned around and came back ashore up here."

"Yeah. It was ridiculous. It surprised a lot of folks. I think fewer people evacuated for that same reason. They thought it would die out or head out."

Tug swallowed hard when they drove by The Tackle Box. They still hadn't made contact with Fisher. Now that the phones were working, he'd try to call him.

Jason drove past the cones where he'd stopped Tug and Paul earlier.

Tug glanced at the fire hydrant, which someone had now exposed completely, as were the next ones they passed.

One thing at a time. The fire department must have had their teams out with the road workers all day.

As they approached the familiar stretch of road that led to the diner, Tug's heart sank like a stone in his chest. The expanse that had once been full of sea oats and a well-established dune was nearly leveled. Debris littered the area, and Tug was pretty sure the bright blue hunk of metal was from his roof, still a quarter mile up the road.

"Oh no," Paul said.

It was like a punch to the gut. Tug's once-thriving diner, the very heart and soul of his existence for the past forty years, now lay in ruins.

"I'm sorry. Chief said the pier probably went first, and that's what slammed into the diner. Between the pier debris and the tide . . ."

Tug held up a hand. He couldn't even listen. He got out of the Jeep and walked toward what used to be the side entrance to the gazebo and outdoor dining.

The storm had been merciless, leaving nothing unscathed.

The building he'd poured his blood, sweat, and tears into was now little more than a pile of rubble that needed to be hauled away before it littered the ocean.

Its walls splintered and its roof torn away, the diner looked like a giant had peeled it back in search of a snack. Decor, old surfboards, and those plywood sheets with the storm warnings were strewn in pieces. The barstools, which had been mounted to the floor, lay like dead soldiers.

Chapter Fourteen

FOR A LONG MOMENT, TUG SIMPLY STOOD THERE, UNABLE to tear his gaze from the destruction scattered across the dunes where the diner had once thrived. He couldn't manage a step, unable to walk given the heaviness of his heart.

A warm tear traced his cheek, followed by another.

Emotions churned inside him like a storm raging in his own heart—grief, anger, despair. Forty years of memories, of hard work and dedication, reduced to nothing in the blink of an eye.

The sign, proudly displaying TUG'S DINER to the world, was the only part that had remained intact. The smell of home cooking would no longer fill the air here.

The right side, the dirty side of the storm—that was the wrong side to be on. He'd had a feeling that's where they were in the scheme of things, but no one on the weather channel, for all the hype and excitement, had said that outright.

Hurricane Edwina was barely a Category 1 by the time she straddled Whelk's Island, but the backside of that storm had leveled her power all right here, and the heavy rains swept things away as quickly as she could loosen them.

Paul walked over and stood beside him. "Thank goodness you weren't in the building."

Tug would've at least shrugged, but a lifetime of work gone without a kiss goodbye burdened his slumped shoulders.

He'd thought about retirement a hundred times over the last ten years. It was supposed to be his choice, but now the decision had been made for him.

No, he couldn't have prevented it from happening, and yes, he probably would've been washed out to sea if he'd been here.

Finally, with a heavy sigh, Tug trudged forward, stepping over pots, boards, and siding toward his sign.

He rested his hand on it to steady himself, then looked toward the pier, which had its own troubles. Approximately one-third of the end was completely missing, and the beach entrance was too.

He'd always felt like this location was perfect, being up on the dune.

But there was no taming an angry ocean.

Bright blue and white boards mingled and collided under the pier.

"Which came first?" Paul said. "The diner or the pier?"

"The pier was here first. I fished off that pier as a boy. Caught my first flounder there. Dad and I carved a *B* in the bench we used to fish from."

He clutched his chest.

"You okay?" Paul put a hand on his back. "Tug?"

Jason ran over. "Do we need a medic?"

Tug shook it off. "No. I just need a minute."

"Are you sure?"

He nodded.

"We'll rebuild, Tug. I'll help. It's okay—this is all just stuff. We're safe. That is the most important thing."

Tug bit down, hoping to temper the anger and sadness swelling inside him. He knew Paul was trying to help, and he knew it was material, but this was his life. His whole life, and it was gone.

"I didn't expect this." Tug turned his back to them, trying to keep his emotions in check. "I had a feeling. This afternoon, I just kind of knew something was wrong. After seeing the damage to The Tackle Box."

"I didn't expect this either."

Tug moved forward.

"Careful," Paul said. "You're not in the right shoes for this. We don't want any injuries."

But Tug didn't care about that. He was numb. He picked his way through the debris, memories flooding back to him with every step—the countless hours spent behind the counter, the laughter of loyal customers, the camaraderie shared with his employees. It was all gone now, down to the special keepsakes that had once hung on the walls—lost to the fury of the storm.

The freezer stood in one piece behind the cement-block walls.

"I don't even know if anything in there will be salvageable," Tug said, pointing to the freezer. "But it looks like the equipment room is standing. We should check while the food is still good."

"We will," Paul said. "We'll figure it all out."

The road ahead would be long and uncertain.

Tug squared his shoulders. "I don't know if I've got it in me to start all over, Paul."

"You don't have to figure anything out right now. But I'm here to help . . ."

Tug turned and walked to the Jeep, passing Jason.

Paul gave him some space, and Tug appreciated that. He broke down, but only for a moment, or else he might never snap out of it.

First Maeve. Now this? Why would You take everything from me?

Tug stood between the door and the back seat.

"It's overwhelming. I get it." Paul's voice came from behind him.

Tug nodded. "Nothing we can do here that can't wait."

Jason climbed behind the wheel. "Want me to take you back? Chief said I could take you down to check on your house."

"Yeah, let's see the house. Do you know where it is?" Tug could read the thoughts running through Paul's mind.

"Chief told me how to get there. I think I know the place."

Jason started the engine and drove up the road.

"Can we check on Fisher on the way? I'm worried about him. The Tackle Box has a ton of damage."

"Absolutely," Jason said. "Where's he live?"

Tug leaned over the seat, pointing out the way. The water was still high in some areas over here, but the Jeep trucked right through it, sending up wild rooster tails of water behind them.

"Turn here," Tug said.

Jason had to stop where one of the sand fences had pulled from its place along the dunes and lay blocking the road. Paul jumped out and helped Jason pull it back so they could get by.

"It's the third little bungalow up here on the right."

"There's a lot of water back here," Jason stated.

"That one." The water was up about a foot above the front door, splashing against the house from the wake the Jeep had pushed its way.

Jason whistled through his teeth. "Tree down."

A tall pine lay across the front of the house, right through the roof. It was at a precarious angle, almost like a ramp from the root ball to the top.

Paul pointed. "His bicycle is here. He rides it everywhere."

"He's got to be in there."

Jason hit the siren.

Paul grabbed the handle. "I'll go check out the house."

"I'm coming too," Tug said.

"Let me check first," Paul said. "No sense in everyone getting wet if he's not even here." He dropped to the ground, the water up to his knees, but as he walked toward the house, it was deeper. He cupped his hands over his mouth. "Fisher?"

Paul stood still, listening for a reply. He took a few steps and then stopped and called out Fisher's name again.

"I heard something," Tug said.

"Fisher? I'm coming. Are you in there?" Paul lifted his knees and high-stepped to the house. "He's in here!" he called back to the Jeep.

Jason turned to Tug. "Radio is right here. You sit tight. I'm going to help Paul. We may need you to call for help."

"Got it."

Jason raced through the water, and Tug sat watching as he and Paul tried to get the door open. But the way the tree had fallen, the door wouldn't budge. They seemed to be talking to Fisher from the outside, but Tug couldn't make out anything from where he sat.

Paul and Jason sloshed through the water toward the back of the house.

It felt like a long time with nothing happening, and Tug's mind raced. Should he call for help? He glanced at the clock, making a note of the time. He'd give them four minutes to shout or show up.

"We got him!" Paul shouted. Tug let out the breath he didn't know he was holding. Jason and Paul came around the side of the house with Fisher propped between them.

"Fisher! Are you okay? Man, I was so worried when I couldn't get in touch with you." He didn't mention The Tackle Box. There was clearly enough trouble already.

They helped Fisher into the front seat of the Jeep, and Jason pulled some supplies from the back.

He handed a bottle of water to Fisher. "Here, drink some water."

"Thanks for checking on me. Man, my phone wouldn't work."

"What happened?" The tree was on top of the house, but why couldn't Fisher have just gotten the heck out of there?

"When it fell, it sent stuff flying and the entertainment center fell right on top of me. I couldn't get out from under it. I've been laying there on that wet couch, watching the water rise. It was like a bad movie there for a while when the storm was still kicking."

Paul got into the back of the Jeep. "Had to be terrifying."

"Wasn't good, man. It wasn't good. I thought I had broken my leg, but I can feel my toes and everything."

"We'll get you checked out," Jason said.

"No. I'm fine. Just achy and waterlogged." He held up his hands, showing them his wrinkled fingers. Jason handed him a blanket. "Wrap up in this. I'll get you to the hospital."

"No. I don't need the hospital. The last thing I need is a hospital bill. I'm fine. I'll sign something that says you tried to get me to go, but I don't need to, man. I just need a change of clothes and somewhere dry to hang out."

"We'll take care of you. You can stay with me," Paul said. "And when we get to Paws, I've got clothes. We can get you dry and warmed up."

"And fed," Tug said.

"Thanks, man." Fisher chugged the rest of the water and crushed the thin bottle flat, blowing out a breath of relief.

Jason handed him another bottle of water. "We were going to check on Tug's house," he told Fisher. "He was the one who said we should check on you."

"Thanks, Tug."

"You okay for us to drive over there before we take you back to Paws?" Jason asked.

"Heck, yeah. It's just right up the road here, man. Be crazy not to." He turned to Tug. "Your house is on stilts, and you don't have trees there on the oceanfront. Hopefully, you fared better than I did."

Tug hoped so, too, but right now nothing would surprise him.

But as they made the last turn, he could see the top of his house in the distance. It looked fine. The roof was there, and it wasn't in the middle of the ocean. That was a good start.

Resting easier, he closed his eyes and said a quick prayer. When he opened his eyes, they were pulling into his driveway.

"That's a lot of sand," Fisher said.

"It is." So much sand had washed up that it gave his stilted beach house the look of a ranch-style. At his age, fewer stairs wasn't necessarily a bad thing. Only his truck's windshield was visible. Besides the truck being buried, the house looked fine.

"Fisher, you wait here." Jason handed him another bottle of water and a pack of Nabs. "Are you warm enough?"

"Yeah. Fine, man," Fisher said. "I'm feeling better already. I can help."

"No need," Paul said. "We're just going to give it a quick look. There'll be time for helping later."

Tug hopped out of the Jeep, with Jason and Paul following. He walked up the newly created dune, right on top of the hood of his truck and stopped. Then he turned to the others and started laughing. It was hysteria. Flat-out crazy coming out of him, because who could process any of this?

"Edwina turned my truck into a stepping stone." Tug rested his hands on his hips. "Never would have guessed that was even a possibility."

Paul took his phone from his pocket and started taking pictures. "I can't believe it—and I'm looking at it." He turned and took a selfie with Tug on top of the truck behind him. "Amanda will flip when she sees this. As soon as they let us, we'll get a crew over here to dig this stuff out, and you might as well put in the claim on your truck today. It's a goner. Salt water and sand. There's no recovering from that."

Tug walked over the truck to the stairs, only a few visible now. "It's a shorter walk to the front door. Maybe I'll leave it this way."

"I should have made you bring your truck to Paws and park it inside. I'm sorry, man."

"It's my fault. I've never seen this much sand come in during a storm. It's crazy."

They walked inside. A couple of boards had pulled away, but the storm didn't break any windows. There was some water in front of the upstairs sliding doors. They sopped that up with towels and hung them over the deck rails to dry before they left.

"Okay, well, this is a relief," Paul said as they got back into the Jeep.

"I never would have expected this place to outlive the diner," Tug said.

"Well, let's not write off the diner yet. There's insurance. There are options. We'll figure it out."

"And we're all here to talk about it," Jason said. "We haven't had one loss of life. So glad you are okay, Fisher. We're really blessed by that. Now, I know you're eager to get back home, Tug, but until they officially open the road, I can't let you stay."

Tug didn't have it in him to argue. "I understand. Do you think we could stop back by the diner? If the stuff in that freezer is still intact, we should distribute it to the people here in town. I'd hate for it all to go to waste."

"Sure." Jason looked a little sheepish. "We have to drive right by there anyway. Don't think I need to ask permission for that."

Paul slapped him on the back. "Sometimes it's better to just ask for forgiveness."

Jason nodded like he hoped he wouldn't have to.

They rode back down to the diner. Tug stared out the window, not even able to look toward what was left.

"No! Man," Fisher said. "Tug? What the . . ."

Tug's heart sank. He hated to tell this young man that his bar made out better than the diner but was still going to be a lot of work.

Jason parked on the far side of the diner this time. From here they could make it to where the freezer still stood, looking oddly out of place, rising from the broken boards and shattered fragments.

"Want me to go look?" Paul asked.

"Would you?" Tug felt too tired to move. It was a lot to take in.

"Yeah. Of course."

Tug pulled his key ring from his pocket and handed it to Paul. "Check the power meter. It's got battery backup. You'll be able to see the temperature readings and any outages and how long they've been. I lowered the temperature before I left. With any luck, it'll be fine. Give some things a squeeze too. I don't always trust those new gizmos."

"On it. We might just have one heck of a cookout in the parking lot."

"Don't tempt me with a good time now." Tug forced a smile. *These are things. Things do not make us happy or who we are. I know this.*

Fisher sat in the front seat, looking shell-shocked. "I can't believe this. When I was a kid, my dad would say a man couldn't do anything to withstand Mother Nature if she wanted to take it. Never thought I'd see that play out in our own backyard."

"I hear you," Tug said.

Paul and Jason walked away, and Tug counted back the hours to when the power went out, checking his math. He'd never take a chance on thawed food, but there was a thermometer in there that showed the temps over the last four days. It was worth a look, and he loved feeding these people.

He smiled at that thought.

This might be the last time I have the opportunity.

Chapter Fifteen

The next day, Rosemary walked down the street toward Paws Town Square by herself this time. She'd missed the routine of morning walks and the sand beneath her feet since she left Hawaii, and it was such a welcoming feeling now.

The power company had restored the power at Kathleen's house last night. Mostly, the houses on this block made it through the storm with minimal impact. All the folks Rosemary met the night she came to town had shown back up, and it seemed like Kathleen's was just one big continuous party. Bottles of liquor filled one countertop, and an assortment of food that had started to thaw filled another. It was cook it or toss it, so everyone had spent the day cooking everything they had.

Rosemary made herself useful in the kitchen, cleaning up after the get-together while Kathleen slept in. She'd spent the morning creating tasty treats fresh from the oven, using whatever she could find in Kathleen's pantry, but it was as bare as the grocery store when the hurricane was announced. Rosemary prided herself on being resourceful, and she was able to pull together a lovely plate of cookies from the meager ingredients, which she planned to take over to Paul and Tug at Paws Town Square.

Had Amanda and those delightful children come home yet? It would be nice to see them again.

It wasn't that far to walk, but carrying the plate of cookies was making her arm a little tired. She switched hands and shook out her other hand to get the blood flowing again.

Several cars filled the parking lot of Paws today. It looked like things were getting back to normal here too.

She went in the front entrance of Paws. Just across the way, she spotted Tug and Paul talking near a row of cute retail shops, including one that apparently made treats for pets called The Barkery. Just past that was a store called Yap—like Gap, only for dog clothes—Toy Town, and The Veterinarian and FarmAcy.

"This place is amazing. It's like a little pet city in here," Rosemary commented as she approached Paul. "I heard it was special, but in my wildest dreams I hadn't pictured this. You must be a very clever marketer to come up with all of this."

"I didn't do it alone. I'm smart enough to know to surround myself with smarter people."

"A sign of a brilliant mind," she said. "I could learn to like this place."

"Thank you," Paul said. "I particularly love the walking trails."

"Amazing. Hey, I brought y'all cookies. You remember me, right?"

"Couldn't forget you, Rosemary," Paul said. "You're kind of a hero around here right now."

She blushed.

"You're my telephone angel. Thank you again for helping me connect with Amanda."

"Did you get your service back yet?"

"We did. And the electricity just came back too. Things are looking up."

"Never thought I'd complain about the generator, but it sure is nice not having that humming in the background," Tug said.

"I can see how that could get monotonous." Rosemary handed

him the covered plate. "We got our electricity back last night. I thought you might enjoy something homemade. I only had one container, though, so you two have to share." She wagged a finger playfully. "I don't mean to brag, but these cookies have been known to start arguments over who gets the last one. So play nice and share, okay? I'd hate to see a friendship ruined over chocolate chips."

Tug lifted the lid. "Oh, these smell good." He hugged the plate to his chest. "He may have to fight for his share."

"I'll let you have first dibs," Paul said.

"Now I know he's just feeling sorry for me. He'd never let a cookie get away."

"Well, that might be true. He knows me pretty well," Paul admitted. "Under the circumstances, I think you might need them, and if that will make you feel better, it's a small price to pay."

"What is going on that you need cookies to get you through? I will say, I usually have pretty good timing on these things." It was true. People couldn't figure out how she had such impeccable timing, and neither could she. Call it intuition—whatever it was, she was thankful for it.

"You must," Tug muttered.

Paul turned to her. "The diner and the pier took the brunt of the storm." He flashed her a look of concern.

"Oh no. Tug. I was counting on being your best customer. I'm so sorry. What can I do to help?" She placed a hand on his arm. "I'm not just saying that. I'm quite capable. My late husband was a farmer. I've done just about everything you can imagine."

Tug cocked his head. "I could see that about you. I'm afraid none of us can do much except wait for the insurance appraiser, and even then, I don't think we can rebuild it. You know, running a business these days is hard enough. Missing an entire season to rebuild? Well, I can't imagine I'd ever get caught up. I'm not as young as I once was."

"You're perfectly fine, and with age comes wisdom. Don't sell yourself short. No, sir."

But Tug wasn't smiling, and the weight of the conversation hung over them.

Rosemary turned back to Paul. "How bad is it? Seriously, what are we talking about here?"

Paul lifted a brow, and Tug gave him a nod. "Half of Tug's Diner is in the ocean. Sticks of blue and white lumber are sloshing around like toothpicks beneath the pier, and the rest is pretty much in a heap."

"Except for the new walk-in freezer space, which is full of food, still frozen." Tug shrugged. "I guess that's the bright spot. We'll feed folks and see what we can do to help those that have something worth saving."

Rosemary hurt for him. "Oh my word. I'm so sorry, Tug. That diner was your livelihood. I can't believe you're coping as well as you seem to be."

"I'm a hurricane of emotion inside," he admitted.

"I bet, and you haven't had time to really process it." She caught the look on his face. "Okay, I know that didn't sound very positive, but it takes time to process tragedy. Believe me, I've had my share, but being prepared for it helps us deal with it. It's good you're here with Paul. I want to volunteer. I've got nothing but time on my hands, and frankly, Kathleen is a nice woman, but she's . . ." She searched for a polite word.

"Different."

"Yes, that. I want to help. Please put me to work."

"We can do that. Tug said he'd rather feed the people stuck here in the storm for free than let the food spoil and file an insurance claim, so we're talking about doing a huge We Survived

Hurricane Edwina feast for the town of Whelk's Island right here in the parking lot."

"That's a wonderful idea!" She clapped her hands. "That's really generous of you. Doesn't surprise me either. I knew you were good people the moment I met you. I can cook, scrub, sweep, chop, serve, take orders—whatever."

Tug seemed to appreciate her gusto. His smile was thoughtful, and she valued it, knowing what he was going through.

"I'm ready," she said, prodding for an invitation. "I don't have any hurricane cleanup to handle. I'm the perfect answer to helping you prepare all that food for the community."

"Tug, she doesn't seem the type to say no." Paul gave her a wink. "And Amanda and the kids won't be back until tomorrow. We could use the help."

"See?" Rosemary widened her eyes. "Thank you, Paul."

Tug took a cookie from the plate and bit into it. "Wow. This is good."

She pretended to look put out. "I wasn't bragging. There're years of experience in that recipe."

"Well, you were bragging, but rightly so. These are delicious."

"You're welcome." She folded her arms. "So, what are we cooking for this town? What's the priority? I'm guessing easily spoiled items first."

"She sounds just like you, Tug." Paul took a step back. "You know what? I'm going to get the wheels in motion to get all that food moved here so that you can work all your magic. You two can handle the menus and the itinerary. Once we know the what, when, and how, I'll get my staff handing out flyers all over town and we'll get the city workers informed. They cross more paths than we can on our own. Deal?" Paul didn't wait for an answer. He gave them an approving nod and set off to make it happen.

"I believe he just made you co-captain," Tug said to Rosemary.

"Excellent," she said. "You won't regret it. Do you know what was in the freezer?"

He eyed her like she was crazy. "Do I know? I know right down to the pound for most of it." He tapped his noggin. "I've been in business for forty years. That place ran like a well-oiled machine, and on any given day, I knew what was in that freezer and what needed to be reordered next."

"Then I'd say we're in good shape. Is there a table where we can sit and work out the menus and the list of what we'll need to borrow from neighbors to make this all happen?"

He motioned for her to follow him over to a wrought-iron bistro set outside the Veterinarian and FarmAcy.

"I'm guessing some grills, probably seasonings if everything in the diner went out with the tide," she said as they walked.

" 'Out with the tide' is putting it mildly, Rosemary. I've never seen such destruction. Other than the food, I don't think there's a thing we can salvage."

She stopped, touched his arm, and then reached up and hugged him. He didn't tense up, and she took that as a sign this guy needed a hug right now. "My new friend. My heart aches for your loss," she whispered into his neck.

He let her hold that hug. This man may look strong, but inside, this had broken him. "I am here," Rosemary said. "You let me be your sounding board, your helper, your soft place to land. When the reality of all this hits you, you might need that."

"How did you land here at this time?" He stared at her. The question was larger than the words spoken.

"You know, I am not so sure about that, either, but I'd say it was not an accident."

He nodded. "Thank you." His brows pulled together and he

took in a breath. "I look forward to working with you on this. Let me grab some paper and pens."

They got right to work and nibbled on cookies while she took notes. She listed the food, and they ran down it to prioritize everything.

"This is good," Rosemary said. She put a star next to the highest-priority items.

"We can cook up some things like the burgers and freeze them to use later," he said. "That will extend our serving time."

"Great. Do you think we have enough freezer space for all that?"

"Borrowing chest freezers should not be a problem this week since most people will have to dump everything that was in there."

"True, Tug." Rosemary smiled softly. "You need this light, this purpose in your life today."

"I do. You're right."

"We will have fun doing this for your community. You'll see. Okay, let's work on the menus."

For the next hour, they brainstormed the best menus to make with what they had. Then they started working on the details for the flyer. "If Paul will let me use his computer, I can make one that's pretty."

"He's got all that kind of stuff in the offices."

"Perfect." Just as she was sweeping her papers together, something bright green caught her eye.

She did a double take and then grabbed Tug's arm.

"They're back!" Rosemary jumped from her chair. "I'd recognize that crazy limousine anywhere. It just pulled to a stop in front of the doors. Come on."

Tug was already on his feet.

Hailey and Jesse bounded out of the limo first, nothing but energy, as Amanda dragged their things out.

The kids flung themselves into Tug's arms.

Rosemary looked on. Amanda had said Tug was a friend, but this was family. She waved, delighted that when Amanda saw her, she broke into a huge grin and hurried over.

Amanda gave her a hug. "Rosemary. You and I were meant to meet that day. You kept me from worrying myself sick. Thank you for being so kind and being there for me when I was so worried. I'm so thankful we met."

Rosemary felt the sincerity in the embrace. "I feel the same."

Jesse was the first of the two to realize who their mother was talking to. His jaw dropped. He nudged his sister with his elbow, then strolled over. "'Ello." He rolled out a cockney greeting. "Welcome to Whelk's Island, Miss Rosemary. It's lovely to see you again." He took a bow.

"Indeed," she said with an approving smile. "I'm so glad the princess could get you back to town so quickly."

"Oh no, not the kingdom again," Amanda said with a laugh. "Come on, let's go inside. I want to find Paul."

Hailey giggled, turning her attention back to Rosemary. "We are so glad to be home," she said without carrying on the British prank. "It's very nice to see you. I'm sorry we kind of tricked you. I think we were car crazy from being cooped up in all that evacuation traffic."

"I found it quite delightful."

"And you met Tug," Hailey said. "I hope he's made you his famous octopus pancakes. They're my favorite."

Rosemary nodded. "Not yet, but I look forward to trying them soon."

"He's the best," Jesse agreed.

"What?" someone called from across the building.

Everyone turned as Paul moved toward them with a huge smile. "You didn't tell me you were on your way back."

"Should we leave? Come on, kids." Amanda pretended to herd them up.

"No! I never want you to leave my sight again." He swept her into a hug and spin, lifting her off the ground, and gave her a kiss that had the kids oohing and giggling.

He set Amanda on her feet.

She smiled. "I'll remind you, Paul Grant, you were the one who sent me away."

"I was thinking from a protection standpoint, but being apart from you is miserable. I missed you like crazy. All of you. Come here, you two!"

"How windy was it? Did you take the kite out?" Jesse asked.

"That kite would have ended up in Australia," Tug said.

"We didn't even get rain at Grandma's."

"Well, we got enough for everyone," Paul said.

"It looks more like the Sahara Desert, with all the sand everywhere."

"Wait until you see my truck," Tug said.

"I haven't updated Amanda on any of that yet," Paul said. "Figured we'd tell her together."

"Good idea," Tug said. "They wouldn't have believed it, anyway."

"This seems like family business. I should probably excuse myself." Rosemary took a step back.

"No!" came from Paul, Tug, and Amanda all at once.

Rosemary froze, stiff as a statue. They all laughed.

"You're a special part of this family now," Paul said.

Rosemary's shoulders relaxed a bit.

"That might be the nicest thing anyone has said to me in a long time."

"Where's The Wife?" Hailey asked. "She's always with you."

Tug pointed to the stairs. "She's up in Paul's office."

"Can we?" Jesse and Hailey begged.

"Of course." Paul laughed as they raced up the stairs. Then he opened his eyes wide and took a flirty lunge at Amanda. "I missed you. I love you. Welcome home."

"Thank you." Amanda kissed him and then squeezed his hand. "So, what is going on? Looks like it's business as usual here, but I need all the updates."

"That's going to take a while, but sit," Paul said, and they all walked over to the table where Tug and Rosemary had been working. The four of them settled in.

Paul rested his hand on top of Amanda's. "Paws did fine during the storm. Nothing major. But we've had some big losses on Whelk's Island."

She looked at Tug, who was looking down at the table, then back at Paul. "The house? Maeve's? Is everything okay?"

"Yes, actually. It took the storm so well you might never have known it hit here."

She pressed her hand to her heart. "Thank God." She closed her eyes and tilted her head. "Maeve always said we'd be safe there. Why did I ever doubt her?"

Paul took a big breath. "The diner is completely gone."

"What? Gone?" She leaned in. "Tug?"

Tug didn't lift his head. With his elbows on the table, he pressed his fingers to his temples and nodded. "Nothing's left."

"Tug? No." Tears slipped down her cheeks. "You know we're here for you."

"And the bungalow was under feet of water. Thank goodness I took Tug's suggestion to move your inventory from the bungalow to his place, but all the plants are underwater."

"That's okay. I can grow new herbs. Oh, Tug, I'm so sorry. Tug's Diner is the heartbeat of this town. The shells?"

Tug still didn't look her in the eye. He just shook his head.

Rosemary wasn't sure what that was all about, but whatever

it was, it was special, because Tug couldn't hold back the emotion. The way his shoulders shook, he was breaking down. Amanda was sobbing too. Rosemary stretched her hand out to cover Tug's, hoping it would help even just a little.

"We've got each other," Amanda said. "We will all be fine. It's just stuff and we have each other."

"I don't think I can see myself going through all it takes to start over again," Tug said. "It's a different time. And, Paul, I'm sorry you wasted your money on including me in *The Scout Guide for the Outer Banks*."

"It wasn't a waste at all," Paul said. "Whether or not Tug's Diner is standing doesn't change its legacy in this town."

Tug looked up, his eyes rimmed in red, his face damp. "Amanda, I'll help you reestablish your business if you want my help. How about that?"

"I understand. We'll pick up the pieces. All of us, and this town, will no doubt change, but it will feel so different without Tug's Diner."

"This town will be just fine without my diner. It's probably time for a new generation to feed these people." He let out a sigh. "Besides, this past year I've been feeling old."

"Don't be silly. You're in great shape, and the only thing slowing us down this year has been grief, but that's only because there was such tremendous love in our hearts for Maeve and we all miss her so much. She'll be a part of every step as we rebuild. You know it's true."

Maeve? The Wife had said her name the day she was in the diner. Whoever Maeve was, whatever her relationship with this group, she must've been very special.

Chapter Sixteen

"WITH ALL THAT NEWS, I'M ALMOST AFRAID TO ASK WHAT you meant about the truck statement, Tug." Silence. Amanda felt like she was in the eye of a hurricane. Calm and eerily quiet, with a foreboding hanging overhead.

"It's hard to explain."

She and Rosemary shared a questioning glance.

"Let's put it this way. I walked over the truck as if it were steps."

"I don't get it."

Rosemary looked bewildered. "Me either."

He stood and, with great animation, explained how the sand had washed up, creating a dune that engulfed his truck and piled over half the stairs to the entrance. The way he told the story—him climbing over his truck with huge, exaggerated steps, lifting his legs high in an attempt to demonstrate just what it was like to get to the front door—was so funny they were all laughing.

Paul pulled out his phone. "You may have missed your calling as an actor, Tug, but I've got a picture. Here we go. Look." He passed the phone to them. "Now his mime makes more sense, right? It was actually a pretty good portrayal of the effort."

"Oh my! That is incredible!" Rosemary handed the phone

back, her jaw still slack. "Tug, I've got my car here. If you need me to cart you around or you want to borrow it, you just say the word."

"Thank you, Rosemary. That's very kind of you." Tug looked tired. "I'll just be happy when the road opens so I can go home and sleep in my bed. I talked to the insurance company a little while ago. Apparently they don't want me to stay there until someone comes and checks the structure."

"You will come sleep at The Shell Collector with us," Amanda said. "The kids will be so excited. Plus, my guest room is really comfortable and quiet since the kids are upstairs."

"Thanks, Amanda. I'll take you up on that. No offense, Paul, but I can't sleep on that sofa one more night. These old bones just can't take it."

"No problem, buddy. So, did you two get a plan for all that food we just loaded into the freezer?" Paul looked at Tug and Rosemary for an answer.

"We did," Tug said. "Still think it's a miracle the water didn't breach that one area."

"It's hard to believe, that's for sure," Rosemary agreed. "But I always say there are no accidents, and I think you are doing exactly what you should with all that. We have a great plan."

Rosemary summarized the plan she and Tug had worked on and what the menus were for the next four days as people started coming back into town and the community dug out from the mess Hurricane Edwina had left behind.

"Wow. This is a lot to do, but I'm ready to help," Amanda said. "Just tell me when I need to be where."

"Paws will be the gathering point," Paul said. "We have the biggest parking lot, and we're central. There's a tractor trailer of bottled water and other necessities coming in later this afternoon. They'll park at the far end of the lot for distribution. A couple of insurance companies have already asked for space to work. So we're letting them set up shop here too. I'm just going to keep all the outdoor equipment packed away until the town gets through these first hurdles so there's more room for everyone to operate."

"That makes perfect sense." Amanda leaned against Paul. "It sure feels good to be back." She loved how he smiled as he looked at her.

"I needed that smile and ray of hope," he said.

Amanda wrinkled her nose and jabbed a finger in Paul's direction. "Next time, you're coming with us, or I'm staying put."

Paul crossed his arms, a slow grin tugging at the corners of his mouth. "Not a chance. My job's making sure you and the kids are safe, even if it means I've got to be the bad guy."

"I'm not leaving you again," Amanda stated.

Rosemary smirked, leaning against the counter. "Sounds like you've got your work cut out for you, Paul."

Amanda tossed her hair over her shoulder with a playful huff. "Better get used to it. Now, put me to work before I start giving orders."

Tug and Rosemary scooched together and motioned for her to lean in to review the list, divvying up tasks among them.

For three days, the Paws Town Square parking lot was humming practically around the clock. The insurance teams had set up tents and were staying in campers on the lot to be on hand to help residents complete the paperwork for their claims and support the adjusters as they made their way through the long list of claims. Thank goodness most of them were small. Only a handful of people were displaced.

Tug had settled into the routine with Amanda and the kids

at the house, and he'd even taken over cooking breakfast. Amanda reminded the kids that it wasn't some kind of swanky resort. Being treated to Tug's cooking was something to be very grateful for. Amanda was grateful, too, because with Tug so uncertain about his future, he was spending a lot of time cooking, filling her nearly empty chest freezer with all kinds of family-sized meals.

"You're spoiling me, Tug."

"I love every second. I appreciate you taking me in."

"Trust me, you've made my life so much easier. I only have to entertain the kids' constant chatter half as much with you picking up the duty."

"They are great kids."

"They are." Amanda's eyes teared as she thought about the long journey they'd been through following the loss of Jack, to now, where things seemed so perfect.

"You know, even when they declare your house safe to return, we'd love it if you spent more time here. Don't know why we never really did that."

"I guess because you spent so much time coming to me in the diner, and face it—I was in the diner all the time."

"Yeah. You were a workaholic. About time you took a break."

"I've never been too good at sitting idle," he said.

Although Tug was going through the motions, he wasn't himself. If Rosemary hadn't inserted herself into the plan to help him cook for the town each day, Amanda wasn't even sure if he would have done it.

The two of them together were a force. The food was great, but what they were doing was so much more. A smiling face, a kind word of encouragement, no expectations. And since Tug knew everyone, he'd been instrumental in helping people find ways to barter with others, connecting neighbors as they started repairs.

But every time Amanda tried to mention the diner, Tug changed the subject.

Losing Maeve had been hard for all of them—for the entire town—but mostly for Tug. They were best friends for more years than Amanda had been alive, and he'd made no secret that he'd been in love with her.

Nearly a year had passed, and mostly folks were shedding their grief over the loss, gradually shifting from tearful sorrow at the mention of Maeve's name to a place where they could enjoy and cherish the memories. There were so many wonderful memories to cling to.

But the light in Tug's normally sparkling eyes had dimmed when Maeve left them, and now they seemed almost empty. He wasn't angry, or grumpy, or even lethargic. He just wasn't Tug. She couldn't put her finger on it, but she was worried.

"Mom, there's a volleyball game on the beach today for all the kids," Hailey hollered from the table. "Can we go?"

"I heard about that. Of course you can. Leave Denali here, though."

"But he loves the beach," Jesse whined.

"I know, but you'll be busy playing, and it's not responsible to just let him run around."

"Okay." Jesse patted the dog's head. "Sorry, man. You can't come."

Denali didn't even lift his head. Amanda could picture the thought bubble over the dog's head saying, *Thank you!* Denali was more of a lie-around kind of dog, completely happy lazing around the house, only getting up to find a cool spot on the floor.

"Plates in the dishwasher before you take off," Amanda called out.

The chairs screeched as they pushed them back and raced to

the sink, clanking the plates together as they each tried to get theirs in first.

Amanda resisted the urge to reprimand them, grinning instead. "Everything's a race at that age, I guess."

Tug smiled too. "I guess we all started out with that much energy."

Of course, those pancakes and syrup he'd just fed them didn't help, but they loved it, and Tug loved doing it for them. Her comment may have sounded like a complaint, but Tug knew she loved every crazy thing about those kids. Even the clomping of their feet running up the stairs at the moment.

"Love you, Mom!" Hailey called out as she ran by with her volleyball, a towel, and a bottle of water.

"Me too." Jesse slid to a stop to peck her on the cheek.

"Love you both more! Good luck."

"We'll be back for lunch," Hailey said.

The door slammed, and for the first time since Amanda got back in town, the house was quiet.

"Whew." She stood and grabbed two coffee cups. "Share a coffee with me?"

"Sure."

She poured and then carried the steaming mugs to the table. "Feels good in the quiet."

Tug lifted his cup to his lips and took a sip.

"Tug, can we talk about the diner?"

He took in a breath.

"I know it's horrible. I went down there yesterday. I sat next to the heap of stuff and just cried. It's hard to believe that a storm could have pulled that building right off its pilings. It's heartbreaking. I can't even imagine what you're feeling." She swept her hair behind her ear, trying not to tear up again.

He nodded. "Can't battle the weather. It wins every time."

"Not every time," Amanda whispered. "We still have a roof over our head, and Paul said he thought they'd clear your place for you to get back in there tomorrow, but I'm not saying that because I want you to leave. I love having you here. You know we all love you."

"I know, Amanda. I love all of you too."

"I'm worried about you. Please talk to me."

"What's there to say?"

"Well, for one, your diner has been a landmark in this town for years. People love it. They will come back no matter how long it takes to rebuild."

"People will move along to another place. They'll build new habits. Time changes things. It's okay."

"Is it? That diner is your everything. You could always hire people to run it. That's an option. Are you really sure you're ready to let it go completely?"

"Yeah, I am. It's a shock, but it's time."

She leaned back in her chair. "Because Maeve's gone?"

"That's part of it, and that building was part of what made it special for me. It will never be the same." Tug paused. "I'm an old man, Amanda. I'm getting tired."

"You're not that old."

"Not that young either. You know how much work goes into owning your own business."

She rested her arms on the table. "Boy, do I. I had no idea how much work there was. All I wanted to do was make some yummy salt rubs and sell them. The bookkeeping, inventory, marketing, shipping—oh my gosh, there's just so much to it all. More stuff than what I want to do. Just grow herbs and make aromatic salts."

"Exactly. It's overwhelming to start over."

"I understand how you're feeling," Amanda said. "I've been struggling with what to do too."

"That surprises me. I thought that business was your dream, and you've done an amazing job in the short time you've been at it. I've been so impressed by how quickly you've pulled it all together."

"Thank you, Tug. I couldn't have done that without your help."

"I love being the resident test chef," Tug admitted. "For me, it's the cooking that's fun. The new recipes we've created with your products are very popular."

"I know. It's kind of cool to see them on your menus. I love that you're always up to test out new recipes with me. It's fun, but doing it as a business takes the fun out of it a little."

"I guess that's why they tell people to be careful about turning their hobbies into jobs."

"I've been thinking—while you're figuring out what you want to do about the diner, I'd be so thankful if you'd help me reposition Salt of the Earth for its next changes. Your experience would be so helpful."

Tug said nothing for a moment. "I'd love to help you . . . on one condition. It's not a partnership. Not a job. Just two friends helping each other."

"Friendship. Isn't that what it's all about, anyway?" She shifted to cross her legs. "I mean, when I met Maeve, who would've ever thought some mopey young widow would become best friends with a woman in her eighties who was just walking the beach one day? We were generations apart, and I was a hot mess with two kids."

"Maeve had a way of seeing past the messiness of daily life to the heart of a person," Tug said.

"Yes, and she helped me through the hardest time in my life, and somehow I was helping her too. I didn't even realize it at the time. I remember that night when we were on our girls' trip in Charleston and we knew her end was nearing. She shared how much her time with us had meant to her. I honestly was taken aback. I didn't know, and when she confided in me how she'd written those messages in the shells but where they landed was in God's hands, it was like proof that our lives are all intertwined. We just can't see His plan when we're living in the moment."

"That's true. Maeve saw things clearly. She was special."

"You are, too, Tug."

He shook his head. "No."

"Yes. Maeve taught me that in just sharing our gifts, no matter how little they seem to us, we are uplifting one another. She was right. We all matter in this gigantic puzzle."

"Maeve always knew what to say, and the right time to say it."

"She was wise. And sneaky."

Tug belly-laughed. "Oh yes, she was sneaky and tenacious!"

"Yes!"

"I really miss her," he admitted.

"I know. I do too. It's okay to miss her." She placed her hand on top of his. "You know, if you want to sell the property and retire, we will be your biggest cheerleaders. We'll even watch The Wife while you go fishing or on the required cruise, but you will not relocate down to Florida. That I will fight you over."

"Don't take it personal if this old man retires, but I promise I won't head south."

"I'm writing that down and holding you to it. You hear me?" She pulled a notebook in front of her. "Okay, switching gears. I think we're almost done with all the food we rescued from the diner's freezer. Does that sound right?"

"Yes. Tonight will be the last food service."

"I'm going to kind of miss serving folks," Amanda said. "It's been really nice seeing so many familiar faces every day."

"It has been nice. We probably all need to remember to pitch in and volunteer now and again. Not just when there's an emergency."

"It feels good," she said. "Rosemary has been a tremendous help."

"She's a good woman. Really helpful. Hard to believe she came into this town a stranger."

"She won't be leaving here one. I don't know how we came to meet up like we did, but I'm so thankful for it."

"She's worked her butt off," he said. "She's a pistol."

"You don't find too many people like that these days. She hasn't asked for a single thing in return." Amanda got up. "You know, I think I'm going to offer to take her shelling this weekend. All the best finds are after a storm. It could be fun. The kids would love it too."

"I bet she'd like that," Tug said.

"I think so too." Amanda picked up her phone. "I'm going to text her right now to be sure she doesn't make other plans for tomorrow before we see her."

Chapter Seventeen

ROSEMARY BRUSHED HER HANDS ON HER APRON. "THANK you so much for coming. Enjoy." It was seven o'clock, and she'd just served the last helping of food rescued from the diner's freezer. She was so happy to have been a part of the project helping folks following the hurricane, and she was sad that it was over.

In the last few days, she'd been as busy as she was back home on the macadamia farm with Kai. Home. Would she ever consider Nina's house home? She felt like a visitor there. Like she needed to be somewhere else but she didn't know where she belonged. Here, on Whelk's Island, was the closest she'd felt to being at home since she lost Kai.

Not like a "pillow to lay your head on" home, but a part of a community that appreciated her help. She hadn't cooked for that many people in her whole life, so she followed Tug's lead, and it all worked out.

It reminded her of the times she and Kai would put on a big meal for everyone who was helping with the harvest. Tired and dusty from a long day, the group always looked forward to sharing a good meal—a well-deserved break. She cherished those days with Kai. Surprisingly, instead of sadness, the memory filled her with a joy she hadn't felt in a long time.

She helped clean up and then shook out her apron and folded it neatly on the table. Tug was stacking empty trays into a box for the trash.

She walked toward him. "I'm going to miss teaming up with you each day, Tug."

"It's been really nice. Thank you for your help and the tweaks for the recipes. You're a good cook."

"Thank you. You're not so bad yourself."

"I bet Kathleen will be happy to have you freed back up for your visit," he said.

"Oh, we've been catching up in the mornings and in the wee hours. We're like schoolgirls reminiscing about boys and cheerleading. Stuff high school girls' dreams were made of."

"Uh-oh. You're not going to put together a seniors' cheerleader group, are you?"

"Hardly."

Tug pretended he was relieved. "Kathleen is nice."

"She speaks rather highly of you too. And your pretty blue eyes. Oh gosh, she goes on and on about your blue eyes."

He blushed.

"Tug, I believe you're blushing. Never would've seen that coming."

He tugged on his ball cap and averted his eyes. "How long do you plan to stay?"

"No idea. Originally, I'd planned to come and stay with Kathleen for a few days and then head down to St. Augustine to visit another friend, Patty, for a week, but when the storm came through, Patty's daughter summoned her to California. I think they are doing a Napa wine tour or something. So I don't know what I'll do."

"Napa. I bet it's pretty."

"Supposed to be, but beauty is relative. I mean, I lived in Hawaii. It's hard to beat that, but every place I've ever been has its own kind of beauty. Its own story to tell if you just give it an ear and listen to it."

"Never really thought of that. I've lived here my whole life. Started out crabbing as a kid, then a commercial fisherman, then the diner, and, well, there really aren't any days off when you're in business for yourself."

"That is true, but you've never taken time to explore? To travel a little?"

"Never."

"Have you ever thought about it?"

Tug looked a little surprised by the question. "You know what? I'm not sure I ever slowed down long enough to think about it."

"Well, my friend, time doesn't wait for anyone. If there's something you want to see or do, don't put it off too long. Life has a way of sneaking up on you—and trust me, I've learned that the hard way."

"Yeah, I know."

"I'm going to leave you with some homework tonight. You sit back and think about where you'd like to go. You owe yourself a little journey. Doesn't have to be far. Doesn't even have to be expensive. How about the mountains? There are beautiful mountains just a few hours from here."

"You got a side hustle from the tourism department?"

"No, but wouldn't that be a fun job? I'll keep it in mind." She was teasing, though. At her age, she wasn't looking for a job. Not the nine-to-five kind anyway—just a purpose. "Well, it's been pretty wonderful helping you. I hope this won't be our last little get-together. I would love to just sit and talk one day while I'm here if you have the time."

"I think that might be nice."

"Can I expect a text or call from you, then? You still have my number, right?"

"I do."

"Good." She waited a moment, hoping for an invitation, but when one didn't come, she smiled and turned away.

"Hey, I've got a magnificent view of the ocean at my house," Tug said. "If they clear me to get back in, maybe we could sit outside and have that friendly chat. I can show off my ocean-front property, which is now smaller than it used to be."

"And those artsy truck stepping stones to the front door?"

"Yes. You definitely have to see that to believe it. Insurance company hasn't even called me back on that yet, but I figure the people that have no way to get around need priority over me right now."

"Maybe, but I wouldn't let them push you to the back of the line either. It needs to be taken care of. One less thing burdening you. You've been through a lot. It's quite a loss to lose your business. Don't underestimate the impact that will have on you, Tug. You'll grieve that loss. Heck, you had the business twice as long as the average marriage lasts these days."

They shared a laugh.

"Yeah, it's a disposable world these days," Tug said with a hint of regret. "I was still using some of the very first pots I ever bought for the diner."

"That does not surprise me at all." She walked over, stretching her arms out. "I'm a hugger. Always have been."

He allowed her to step close and wrap her arms around him. He held her tight, as if they'd known each other forever.

"A hui hou," she whispered and pressed a friendly kiss on his cheek.

"I know *aloha* is 'hello' or 'goodbye,' but I'm not familiar with that one."

She winked. "It means 'until we see each other again.'"

"I like that. A hui hou." It sounded more like a bird calling when he said it, but close enough.

She turned and left, hoping they would indeed see each other again. He was easy to be around, and she felt more like herself this week than she had, well, since Kai had died, and that was going on four years now.

The next morning, Rosemary was up with the sunrise as she usually was. Kathleen was more likely to lounge around until nine o'clock. So Rosemary busied herself in the kitchen making a quiche, which would serve up just as nicely later, whenever Kathleen rolled out of bed.

Rosemary poured a cup of coffee, then dropped a dash of cinnamon into it. A smidge of cinnamon carried a brightness that reminded her of the local coffee back in Hawaii. She carried her coffee out onto the porch and sat in one of the rocking chairs. Kathleen must've put the cushions away when the storm came. She wiggled until she found a comfortable way to sit.

The morning sun was bright. Seagulls flew above, occasionally calling out to one another in what sounded like laughter.

In the distance, heavy equipment rumbled, already at work redistributing sand from the roads back to the dunes, where it belonged.

She'd only caught a glimpse of the town before the storm. She felt bad for Tug. The reports about his diner were bad. That part of town was the last to get reopened, and from what she'd heard, they were still clearing sand.

She hadn't seen for herself what was left of the diner, and somehow it felt wrong to go and be a lookie-loo when it was such a terrible loss for Tug. She couldn't even imagine. Big storms had ruined the crop a few times over the years, forcing her and Kai to pick up the pieces and start again, but that was a seasonal impact. Apparently the diner was beyond repair.

Rosemary's cellphone buzzed, startling her. Seeing it was Nina again, she silenced it. Last night Nina had left a scathing voicemail telling her it was time for her to get home. It felt like a demand for compliance, and Rosemary had never been one to appreciate an ultimatum.

Did I make a mistake leaving Hawaii? No. Even with the profit she'd made on selling the farm, it would be a stretch to afford starting over there. She knew in her heart that location wasn't the issue.

She had no intention of talking to Nina until she figured out her next move. The problem was, she wasn't entirely sure who she was without Kai. For so long, they'd been a team—a solid, unshakable one.

Untangling herself from the perfect duo they'd been felt like trying to unbraid her very identity. Some days, it seemed like the best parts of her had vanished with him, leaving her adrift.

A faint rustling broke through her thoughts. She turned to see Kathleen stepping out the door, her turquoise-and-white beachy-patterned pajamas catching the porch light. Barefoot, Kathleen grinned and sniffed the air dramatically.

"Exactly how is a girl supposed to get her beauty rest with something that smells this delicious coming from my kitchen? It's like heaven's moved in."

"It's a quiche. I'm sorry. I didn't mean to wake you. I thought it would heat up nicely whenever you decided to get out of bed."

"I think it smells too good to even let it cool down," she said with a hearty laugh. "I'll grab a cup of coffee and join you."

"Great." Beeping sounded from inside. "Oh, that's the timer. It's done." Rosemary followed Kathleen back into the house and silenced the oven timer.

While Kathleen fixed her coffee, Rosemary served slices of the warm quiche on dessert plates.

"Looks like pie," Kathleen said. "Breakfast of champions."

"It's healthy."

"I wasn't complaining. I like pie."

"Who doesn't?" Rosemary commented as she took a seat.

"It's so fun spending time with you. Isn't it great how we can catch up just like that?" Kathleen said with a snap of her fingers.

"It is. Thank you for letting me come, with the hurricane and all. I really needed this time."

"Well, you haven't done much relaxing. You've done more work for my community this week than I have the past few years."

"You've been busy helping neighbors. I've enjoyed lending a hand up at Paws. It felt good to feel like I was needed again. It's been a while since I felt like that."

"I'm sure your daughter appreciates you. Kids just don't show it when it's their parents helping out. Mine are the same way. Why is that? We must've done something wrong raising them."

"No idea. I did the best I could at the time. I'd have done a lot of things different with a lifetime of lessons under my belt."

"Exactly. We have kids before we even know how to live our lives. We're hardly equipped to raise ourselves."

"Amen!" Rosemary lifted her coffee. "I think with losing Kai, I'm more sensitive now to it, ya know? He always made me feel appreciated. I think it's probably more me than Nina, and me missing Kai." She hadn't realized that until just now.

"Our grief comes out in a lot of ways," Kathleen said. "I'm sure a big part of me being on the go-go-go all the time is unresolved loneliness. Being a widow ain't easy."

"No, it's not, but I'm going to try to be more aware."

"All of this mess going on with the cleanup is a little overwhelming for some folks too." Kathleen shifted the topic.

"Of course. You got really lucky."

"For sure, but some neighbors you met from the party before the storm are talking about heading inland. No solid plan. Maybe a day or two. I might go if the insurance guy comes about the fence before they leave. You should come! There's shopping and we'll hit the casino—a chance to unwind and get away from all this mess until they clean it up."

Casinos weren't Rosemary's style, and since she was living in one little room, she had no room for frivolous shopping excursions. "I don't know. I barely know them."

"That didn't stop you from volunteering at Paws all week," Kathleen replied, a little annoyed.

"That's different." Rosemary wasn't quite sure how to say it without hurting Kathleen's feelings any further.

"Well, you think about it. If you don't want to go, we won't go. I'd have to kennel Prissy, anyway. I wonder if Paws is taking in new reservations yet."

"I didn't think people kenneled cats. Aren't they self-sufficient?"

"They are, but I would never leave her all alone. She'd be sad," Kathleen said. "By the way, I invited the neighbors over for dinner tonight. It's just five of us, plus you. We'll be discussing the trip, and you'll hear how much fun we'll have. You'll want to go."

Rosemary's insides sank. "Or you could go and I'll stay here to meet the insurance guy and take care of Prissy."

"That's no fun."

"Well, actually, it would give me some time to figure out my situation with Nina before I go back."

Kathleen made a noise like a cat throwing up a hair ball. "I can't believe she left you that message. I'd have blessed her out then and there. Who does she think she is?"

"I'm sure in her mind she's being helpful."

"Pisses me off, and she's not even my daughter," Kathleen said.

"That's why I need some time to think things through. How can I be mad, when I don't even know what I want?"

"You really haven't dealt with the loss of Kai," Kathleen said. "I mean, yes, you buried the sweet man, and you sold the farm, but you have to rediscover you, and let me tell you from my own experience losing my sweet Stu that I am still shocked who I turned out to be."

Rosemary almost blew coffee out of her nose. "Why would you say that? You seem just like the Kathleen I knew."

"Maybe, but that's not the Kathleen I was as a married woman. I'd grown and changed and in some cases sidelined things that used to be important to me, because they didn't fit into my married life. I'm not saying that was a problem. I didn't mind those compromises, but I found it to be a new opportunity. A thrilling one. You're right. You need some time."

Rosemary pressed her lips together.

Kathleen stood. "I'm going to go, and you are going to stay right here and do some self-examination. I've got some books." She marched inside, came out with a stack of four, and shoved them in Rosemary's direction.

"Oh my goodness." Rosemary flipped through the titles. "Apparently it takes a lot of reading to do that."

"Well, you might hate a couple of them. I did, but at least one will resonate. I'm sure of it, but don't just lock yourself in this house. It's been four years. We're old, but we ain't dead, and there is still plenty we can do. And should do! You need to get out and meet people. Make friends. Fall in love. I can get you on the dating app."

"No. No, thank you," Rosemary said, shrinking back. "One step at a time. I'm not ready for online dating. Kai has barely been gone . . ."

"He's been gone four years." Kathleen filled in the blank.

"Three years, eleven months, and—"

"Whatever." Kathleen waved a hand in the air. "Long enough. It's more than acceptable to go out by now. You have to move on, honey. Our time doesn't go on forever. I see your mouth opening. Don't argue. Just take what I said and let it sink in. Come on. We are going for a walk on the beach."

"I'm going to meet Amanda later today to do that."

"Well, you can do it twice. Come on. Whelk's Island has the best figuring-out-life sand in the world."

Probably not better than Hawaii. But Rosemary allowed herself to be pulled from the chair and ordered to change into something beach-worthy.

Kathleen, tall and willowy, walked out in a flowy skirt over a tank bathing suit." Come on. I'm driving. I've got a favorite spot."

Rosemary had forgotten how inadequate she felt next to Kathleen back in high school, but that feeling sprang forth as if they were both seventeen again. Rosemary, dressed in a loose cotton dress and water shoes, shoved the ridiculous thought aside.

Funny how old thoughts can pop up out of nowhere even though they hold no value any longer.

She was completely comfortable with herself, and at this age it wouldn't do any good not to be. She silently apologized to her seventeen-year-old self for not having been wiser back then and focused on how excited she was to go to Kathleen's favorite spot on the beach.

Chapter Eighteen

AMANDA HAD BEEN EAGERLY AWAITING ROSEMARY'S AR-
rival, peeking out the window every time she thought she heard
a car.

Finally, Rosemary pulled into the driveway.

Amanda stepped out on the porch and waved wildly from
the second-level front door of The Shell Collector. "Rosemary!
Hello. I'm so glad you could come."

"She's here!" Jesse scooted around Amanda and bounded
down the stairs with Hailey right on his heels.

Rosemary got out of her car to a bouncing hello. "Hi! Wow!
What a pleasant welcome! *I* feel like a princess."

Jesse and Hailey giggled over that reference to their first
meeting.

"We're going to teach you to collect shells," Hailey said. "I've
got an extra bag you can use." She thrust one of her mesh shell-
collecting bags toward Rosemary. The one with the seahorse
fabric trim and shoulder straps.

"Thank you, Hailey. This is so pretty."

"It's one of my favorites," Hailey said proudly. "I wanted you
to find pretty stuff, and this is a lucky collecting bag."

Rosemary cocked her head. "Do you think we might find a
shell with a message in it like people talk about?"

Hailey's eyes widened. "If we're lucky. The shells with messages are very special . . . You can ask Mom."

"I'm honored." Rosemary flashed a friendly smile toward Amanda.

"Do you want to come up and have some tea first?" Amanda asked.

"No. I'm dying to get on the beach. I can't believe how long it's been since I walked along the surf. I've missed it so."

"Then let's go." Amanda came downstairs, and the four of them headed for the sandy path to the beach.

"Thanks for coming," Amanda said again. Being around Rosemary was such a pleasure. She was positive and warm, like an old friend.

Hailey and Jesse raced ahead of them.

"My friend Kathleen said we were going to go walk on the beach this morning."

"You've already been?"

"Not actually. We got dressed and drove down to the other end of the beach. She said it was her favorite spot, but all we did was sit on top of the dune. No walking. We just sat there. Don't get me wrong. It's beautiful, and very different from my ocean in Hawaii, but I love to walk in the wet sand. Feel it under my feet."

"I know what you mean. It's so grounding."

"Exactly."

"Well, come on. The kids and I are so excited to share our little piece of Whelk's Island with you. We have some favorite spots where we seem to always find the best shells. You can walk, splash, dig—heck, we'll bury you if you want."

"Now, this is my kind of fun—well, except the burying part. Never understood that."

"Me either. It's so itchy!"

"I know. But all the rest, I feel lucky to be in on the family plan," Rosemary said.

They walked over the weathered dune and down to the water. There had been very little activity down here since the storm. The sand looked so smooth, and the shells shone like little neon signs saying "Pick me!"

Amanda couldn't stop smiling. It was so nice to walk on the beach. The kids' giggles hung in the wind, rising and falling with the break of each wave as they jumped and splashed ankle deep in the water.

She picked up a shell or two as they walked, and Rosemary already had a few little pieces of sea glass in her bag.

"This reminds me of walks with my husband, Kai. We could walk and enjoy the beauty, never having to speak a single word."

"It's special when you don't have to fill every moment with small talk. You just know what's going on in their head."

"You and Paul seem to have that."

Amanda nodded. "We do. We are very good together."

"Yet you aren't married?"

"No." The thought of being married again scared and excited her at the same time. "I lost my husband, Jack, three years ago. Paul was the best man in our wedding. He and Jack were in the Marines together." Jack's last goodbye echoed so clearly in her mind to this day. "Jack left just before Christmas. It was supposed to be a six-month deployment, but he didn't make it back."

"I'm so sorry." Rosemary sighed. "I didn't know."

Amanda lowered her voice. "It's been hard. It's hard to know what to do. I'd never want to dishonor Jack's memory."

"You're a young woman. No one expects you to never love or marry again."

"I know that in my mind, but inside it's just really hard to navigate."

"It's always easier when it's not your own problem. Experience speaking here," Rosemary said. "But is it more your concern over what other people will think? What do you think? This is your life, and you get to take the path that feels right for you."

"I guess I'm afraid to make a mistake," Amanda whispered. "It's not just me. It's the kids too. I never planned to make those big decisions alone."

"Honey, we all make mistakes. Luckily, we all have a reverse too. I understand what you're feeling. Even selling our farm after Kai died was very hard to qualify. . . . That's not the word I'm looking for, but you know what I mean. I felt like I owed everyone an explanation, but really it was all in my heart's timeline. If you ever need to talk, people say I'm a good listener. But first, talk to Paul. He may feel the same."

"That's so hard."

"No, it's not. Do it. You'll gain clarity, and it will all seem so much easier."

"Why do I keep meeting smart older ladies?" Amanda laughed. "I'm so grateful my kids spotted you at that gas station. I can't imagine going through life and never having got the chance to meet you. Thank you for being you."

"I feel quite the same. This is a special connection meant to be."

"My friend Maeve, she was too. She owned the house I live in now. I met her when I first moved to Whelk's Island. I was trying to figure out how I was going to raise my children alone. I was so broken. Maeve was walking the beach one day, and the kids talked to her. For some reason, Maeve took us under her wing. She really helped me understand and navigate the grief I was grappling with. She was a very special friend, and I carry so many lessons with me from her."

"I've heard her name several times. When did she pass?"

"We lost her last year. She was like the matriarch of this town. Kind and wise. I'm so grateful that our paths crossed. She had a profound impact on my life in the brief time we had."

"That kind of friendship doesn't come along often."

"No, it does not." Amanda knew how blessed she was, and how it had touched every corner of her life.

"I lost my Kai almost four years ago."

"I'm sorry for your loss," Amanda said.

"Thank you. I'm still figuring things out. Too bad Maeve isn't still around."

"I can do my best," Amanda said. "I'm no Maeve, but I've walked your path. Still walkin'." The wind whipped her hair forward. She chased it back over her shoulder and pulled a tie from her wrist to put it up. "Some things she made me aware of seem so simple now, but they were game changers."

"Look!" Hailey and Jesse came running up to them. Both had treasures to share.

Hailey held up a chunk of green sea glass, and Jesse cradled a huge whelk shell.

"Mom, this is like the one we found before, but with no message in it." Jesse put it to his ear. "Still pretty cool. It has stripes like a tiger."

"Does the ocean roar inside?" Rosemary prompted.

He put it back to his ear. "Yes!"

"Good finds, guys," Amanda said. She noticed how entertained Rosemary was by their excitement. "Maeve taught them about the treasures of the ocean. They are shell and sea glass maniacs now. Hailey can tell you which are the rarest from most to least, like it's the list of the presidents of the United States."

"Good, clean fun. Can't beat it." Rosemary stopped. "Was that thunder?"

"No. It's those bulldozers. They are still moving sand. I think that's going to be part of the background noise for a while."

"I don't really have my bearings. So, was Tug's Diner up that way?"

"Yeah, we will walk right behind where it once stood. The kids and I walk down there a few times a week. When we first moved here, it felt like such a hike, but now there's nothing to it. I'm still in shock that Tug's Diner is gone."

They walked on, and as they neared the pier, the sounds of reverse alarms on the trucks and equipment carried over the dunes.

Amanda shook her head slowly. "It's so hard to believe. That diner always felt so safe the way it was built against the dune. It seemed like nothing could take it away."

"I think Tug is still in shock," Rosemary said.

"I'm really worried about him." She trudged up the sand. "Losing Maeve was hard on him. They were best friends, but Tug was in love with Maeve. They had so much history."

"They both grew up here?"

"Yes, and he was in love with her, but his best friend got the girl. When Jarvis died, I think Tug assumed he and Maeve would eventually be together, but Maeve died with Jarvis still very much alive in her heart. Tug took care of her. Checked on her, made sure she was well fed."

"I don't doubt that," Rosemary said with a laugh. "I think I gained three pounds hanging out with him."

"Tug's a good man."

"So, he lost his soulmate. Married or not, the connection was there," Rosemary said. "And now the diner is gone."

"Yes. I hate that he lost the diner," Amanda said. "Tug *was* that diner! I can't imagine him not having it."

"Well, it's hard work to run a business every day, even when it's your life's work," Rosemary said. "It was a big decision for me to let go of the macadamia farm, but I know now that it was the right one."

"I know. I am trying to remember that he's older. He's agreed to help me with my business while he's deciding. I'm so thankful for that. Paul and I have chosen to relocate what's left of Salt of the Earth to a retail spot in Paws. It'll be a big change. I could really use Tug's help."

"I don't think I realized you had a business of your own. I just assumed you and Paul worked Paws together."

"No. I run a small herb salt business. It had been a dream of mine. I started it in the tiny bungalow where the kids and I lived when we first moved here. It was all I could afford. A real fixer-upper, but it was perfect right on the beach. We loved it."

"Home is a feeling and doesn't have a thing to do with how fancy a place is."

"Exactly. When Maeve got sicker, she offered me her beach house so I could use the bungalow for my business. It was very generous of her."

"It sure was. It's a beautiful home."

"It is. Memories of Maeve are so present in there. I think it's what has helped all of us get through losing her, because we still feel like we're keeping her love for the place alive. I'm sure Hailey will want to show you the shell room. It was Maeve's favorite room in the house." Amanda swept a tear away. "She's deeply missed."

"Yes. I know how that is. Only, I'm afraid to let anything else take up any space and chase Kai from my heart. It's so silly, but I feel like I'm protecting that space for him."

Amanda took Rosemary's hand. "Our hearts are so fragile, but nothing can take our memories."

"Thank goodness."

"Mom!"

The scream sent Amanda into a panic. She swung left and right, trying to track Hailey and Jesse. "What's wrong?"

"Look, Mom!"

"Y'all scared me to death! You can't scream like that." She didn't mean to yell at them, but what in the world caused them to screech like that?

"But look. It's impossible. It's a miracle," Hailey said with all the drama that convinced Amanda she was going to be in for one heck of a time when her little girl became a teenager.

"A miracle, huh?"

Hailey made a cocky "I told you so" face and held up a shell.

Amanda couldn't believe it. "No way." She took the shell from her daughter. "This is a miracle."

"What?" Rosemary asked.

Amanda leaned in, showing her the shell. "This shell used to be on the wall in Tug's Diner. I can't believe it. You're right, Hailey. It's a miracle you found this."

"I know. It's amazing." Hailey grabbed Jesse's hand. "Come on. Let's keep looking."

Amanda glanced from the stretch of beach where they found it back to where the diner used to be. "Wow. So, this town has a long history of shells with messages in them showing up for the right people at the right time. Over the years, some people who've found these special shells have sent them back to the town or directly to Tug to hang in the diner." Amanda was so tempted to tell Rosemary that Maeve had been the magic behind them, but that was a secret that she and Tug would hold forever.

"Really? Did you ever find one?"

"I did. I still have the first one I found on my nightstand. Actually, the kids found it on our hike back to the bungalow. It was a quote from Havelock Ellis that said, 'All the art of living lies in a fine mingling of letting go and holding on.'"

"Words to live by," Rosemary said. "I like that, and I feel like that is something I could work on."

"Honestly, it changed my life. I was in such a dark place. Grappling with the grief of losing Jack and how to be a good mother to these two without him."

"You know, maybe finding that shell will be enough to get Tug reengaged too. Might give him a little hope."

Amanda brightened. "Maybe. That would be wonderful."

"Maybe we should help the kids and see what else we might find." Rosemary hitched her treasure bag higher on her shoulder. "I'm armed and ready."

"I love that idea. I wish they'd let us get up closer to where the building is."

"I'm sure all we'd need is Tug's permission. It's his insurance that is covering the place should someone get hurt. I don't think the town really can do anything but try to keep people out for safety's sake, but they have a lot of other things on their plate."

"Let's see what we find out here. You take that way and I'll go this way."

"Divide and conquer. I like it."

Amanda was kicking through a pile of debris when something shiny caught her eye up in the sea oats. She tried to run, but this part of the beach was soft, and it was like running in place before she finally got any forward momentum. A big stockpot lay among the beaten-down grass.

She picked it up and hugged it. Tug's things, pieces of the diner's history, all tossed around like confetti.

When they got back together, they had some silverware and a big cast-iron pan that Amanda finally convinced Jesse to leave behind because it was so heavy. The stockpot, a barstool top, and a light fixture were also part of their collection.

Jesse squatted to inspect the pile. "Do you think he'd want any of this junk?"

"I don't know, Jess. It's kind of sad, isn't it?"

He squinched his nose and nodded. "Yeah. It makes me sad."

"Sorry, buddy. We'll feel better if we can help Tug feel better. What do you say we take the shell and the pot back to the house? We'll tuck them away and maybe find something special to make from them later when we figure out what's going to happen to the diner. For now, it can be our secret." Amanda looked at Hailey and Jesse. "What do you think?"

"I think that's a good idea. We don't want to make Tug sad," Hailey said. "Should we put this other stuff somewhere up on the dune, just in case he wants to find it?"

"Sure. I think that's a good idea. And we'll save this for the time being. Agreed?" Amanda put her hand in the middle, and the kids piled theirs on top. Rosemary did too. "The secret is tucked away for now."

They walked back toward Amanda's beach house.

Rosemary lifted her arms, letting the gentle breeze blow her dress as she walked. "It's so calm here today. I can only imagine what it was like during the storm. The trees were bending so far over I can't believe they didn't break. Thinking of this calm water making its way up over that dune is incredible. And now it's peaceful."

"It is. I guess it got all its aggravation out in the storm."

"My daughter and I have been going through some storms. I'm trying to figure out how we can find peace."

"What's going on?"

"She was going through her divorce when I lost Kai. I guess with both of us trying to find our new lives alone, it made sense that we would support each other. I got a wonderful offer on the farm. Hard to pass up. I was so sad and lonely, and I think I knew deep down it might not be a good solution to move in with Nina, but I just couldn't bear to be surrounded by nearly fifty years of memories. I felt like I couldn't breathe."

"You're living with your daughter now?"

"Yes, back in Philadelphia, which is part of the problem too. No beach. Nina opened her home to me, but we are not seeing eye to eye, and my grief just follows me wherever I go. Now I have the added burden of my daughter treating me like a teenager, and it's driving me crazy. 'Don't do this, Mom. Be careful. You can't do that. You're too old to do that.'" Rosemary blew out a breath that fluttered her bangs. "Oh Lord, I raised her. Doesn't she remember I'm the one that taught her all those sensible things?"

"Oh boy. I know my mom and I couldn't live together. She makes me nuts for the same reason," Amanda said with a laugh. "But I'm sure it's worse when you're the mom feeling smothered."

"I need to do something. I can't stay there."

"Are you thinking of going back to Hawaii?"

"No. I don't think that's the solution either. That's just it. I don't even know what I want. And I am sure it's not all Nina, although, in fairness to her, I've probably made her feel that way. I even sort of convinced myself she pushed me a bit to sell the farm, but I know that's not the case. It was an amazing deal. I don't have to worry about money. I am financially secure. I could do something, but I just don't know what. I'm sure I'm making her miserable too."

"Well, give yourself some time. I'm a good listener too. We'll help each other."

"Kathleen loaded me up with a bunch of self-help books from when she lost her husband."

"Good luck with that. You might have more problems after reading them," Amanda teased. "I must've gotten a dozen books from people when Jack died. Half of them made me feel worse."

"Kathleen thinks I just need to meet people and start dating.

She's so outgoing, though. Even in school, she was like that. The life of the party."

"I could see you as the life of the party," Amanda insisted. "Everyone fell in love with you the second they met you. You should stick around here. I'd love to have you as a neighbor."

"It feels good to be back on the sand. I didn't even realize how much I'd longed for the sound of the water and the feel of the sand between my toes. I've missed it. Maybe that's why I've been a little cranky with Nina too."

"I can't imagine living anywhere else. The walks on the beach sort of saved me after I lost Jack. You know, while you're in town, you are welcome to park at my house and walk on the beach whenever you like. It's my favorite stretch, and it's pretty quiet most of the time since there is no public access. We've got towels and anything you could need right there in the storage room at the stairs. You're welcome to grab a chair, towels, shell bag, a hat, sunscreen—whatever you need."

"I'll take you up on that. Maybe I'll bring one of those books and settle in for a day of reading out here."

They walked back up the path to the house. Jesse and Hailey were already running up the stairs to go inside when Amanda and Rosemary got to the sidewalk.

"And if you want company, we're just a shout away." Amanda stopped at the steps and brushed the sand from her feet. "You'll find your pace and your place, Rosemary. I moved after Jack died. It helps. Solves nothing, but it reframed things for me. Give yourself grace. Probably the best advice I have to give you came from one of those shells I found."

Rosemary was all ears. "I'm listening."

"Interrupt worry with gratitude."

"Oh gosh. That puts a different spin on things in my situation with Nina, doesn't it? I am grateful that she opened her home to me. I love her—it's just really hard living with her as adults. Actually, I think the two of you would be really good friends if you ever met."

Amanda shrugged. "The right thing will happen. Come on upstairs. I'd love to show you the house."

Rosemary paused. "I'm going to take a rain check on that. You have brought me so much joy today. Right now I'm feeling very motivated to do some thinking. Thank you for indulging an old woman. What you said has me feeling strong enough to take a hard look at my life. Maybe there's something I'm meant to do. I need a purpose."

"You'll find your gift for this season of your life. I'm excited for you."

"I'm sure I will. At least the last few days, I've felt useful and connected to others."

"You know," Amanda said, "I don't want to sound preachy, but if you're not busy Sunday, the kids and I would love you to join us for church. We walk down. It's a nice way to quiet the mind before the service. You could meet us here and we'll walk down together."

"It's been a while since I've been to church. I'd really like that."

"Good. Service is at eleven, so if you want to get here around ten-thirty, we'll have plenty of time to walk down. It's just a couple of blocks from my shop. Further now, but the kids still like the walk, and I like that it burns up some of their energy."

Rosemary remembered those days when tiring out the young ones was a priority. "I'm always up for a good walk. It's been invigorating to get moving again. Thank you for the invite."

"You're welcome. No pressure. Just know we'll be glad to have you if it suits you."

"Great. I'm going to head back to Kathleen's, but I'd love to come over and cook dinner for you and the kids one night. My treat, your kitchen."

"I can't turn that down."

"We could also invite Paul, and you could ask Tug if you like."

"I think that sounds like a great idea."

"We can pick a day next week," Rosemary said.

Amanda watched her new friend walk down the steps and get into her car. She waved. *Maeve, Rosemary might not know it, but I know you helped connect these dots. Thank you.*

Chapter Nineteen

ROSEMARY BLINKED IN SURPRISE AS KATHLEEN WHEELED her suitcase into the living room, dressed like she was ready to walk out the door. "Wait a second—did I miss something? You're leaving *now*? I thought you weren't leaving until tomorrow."

Kathleen gave an apologetic smile, brushing a strand of hair behind her ear. "Change of plans. We decided to get a jump on things, and, well, here I am. You don't mind, do you?"

"Well, no—"

"Thank you again for stepping in and watching over the house for me. I owe you. They'll be here in about fifteen minutes." She knelt to pick up Prissy who seemed a little miffed by the arrival of the suitcase. "You will be well taken care of while I'm gone."

The cat didn't seem to agree, leaping out of her arms and landing with a thud before zipping out of sight.

Rosemary raised a brow. "I was just having a cup of coffee. Have time for a cup before you go?"

"That'd be amazing, actually. I'm running on adrenaline right now, but it won't last." Kathleen glanced around the cozy room, then back at Rosemary with a flicker of guilt in her eyes. "Are you sure you don't want to come along? I hate the thought of you staying here alone while I'm off having fun."

"That is not the case. I'm grateful you are comfortable

enough to let me stay in your home and handle the insurance guy and Miss Prissy. Really, this works out for both of us. Don't give it a second thought."

"I am excited. I think we'll have a blast. There are shows at the casino and everything. What's your favorite number?"

"Um, gosh. Do I have one? I guess it's ten. That was my Kai's football jersey number."

"Let's see. I think that's a black number too. My favorite number is fifteen. I'll play both our favorite numbers and see if I can come home with more than I left with."

"Good luck with that. I've never been the betting kind."

"You might just never have given it a fair shake. You think about it. Who knows what you'll have planned by the time I get back?"

"We'll see." Rosemary could only hope she'd come up with some direction in that short period. She had a feeling it was going to take a lot more soul-searching than that to resolve her problems.

Kathleen sipped her coffee.

Rosemary got up and put a couple of cinnamon raisin bagels in the toaster. "Want some honey on yours?"

"Peanut butter," Kathleen said. "But you help yourself to the honey. It's local. It's supposed to be good for allergies."

She drizzled honey across hers and then carried Kathleen's over to her with the peanut butter. It was a quick breakfast, and good thing, because no sooner had Kathleen taken her last bite than there was a honk out front.

"My ride!" She jumped up. "Thank you again."

"You're welcome."

Kathleen grabbed her suitcase, purse, and sunglasses and raced out the door.

Rosemary was thankful she'd offered to stay back and look after the cat.

In the quiet wake of Kathleen's exit, Rosemary thought about how her mood had shifted after spending time with Amanda and her children. A new energy filled her, one that wasn't as judgmental about Nina's overbearing attempt at taking care of her. Grace—they both deserved grace to get through this.

Talking to Amanda about it had helped her step away from her own sensitivity to the situation. Kai always had said Rosemary and Nina were too much alike, both redheads and both strong-willed. Neither ever gave in. Maybe Rosemary had even been a little disobedient just because. *I know, Kai. You were right. I don't know what I was thinking moving in with her.*

Having the place to herself, Rosemary felt like she had wings. Cable was back on and just about everyone had power again. It was hard to believe just a few days ago floodwaters surrounded them.

She flipped through the television stations, but then decided to take full advantage of the quiet and lose herself in a novel all day instead.

The next morning, she got up early and went for a walk. There was activity in the Paws parking lot as she crossed the main road toward Amanda's house. It wasn't but a couple of blocks to the beach from here. A small market had its doors propped wide, and a neon sign flashed OPEN, so Rosemary stopped inside. It was one of those everything stores with groceries, sundries, and souvenirs. Probably wouldn't hurt to pick up a little peace offering for Nina and Kendra while she was here. The place was packed with Whelk's Island and North Carolina paraphernalia. She found a cute key chain of a blinged-out flip-flop for Kendra and bought Nina a travel mug with dolphins on it.

She left the shop and wandered down the street. The library was closed, but it had a cute little reading garden outside, really not much more than a series of raised flower beds, each containing a tree with flowers planted around it. Curved cement benches made it seem quite cozy, though, even if it was just a small space between a couple of buildings. She could picture whiling away a day here.

There was even one of those Little Free Libraries here in the garden, which was sort of ironic to have right next to the library. She giggled as she thought to ditch that self-help book for a romance novel. Kathleen had said she didn't need it back.

She dug the non-fiction book out of her tote bag and opened the door on the Little Free Library. Inside, the books were upside down, backward, and stacked whichaway. She grunted in disapproval and lined them up by genre, then size, until it was tidy. Then she slid the grief book onto the shelf and finger-walked the titles, finally deciding on a book called *The Magic of Sea Glass* in exchange. *I'm definitely getting the better end of this deal.*

She happy-danced her way over to a bench and flipped open to the prologue. Now, *this* was the type of book that would make her feel better. It immediately caught her attention, and she was delighted when she turned to chapter one and saw that the story was set in Rodanthe, North Carolina. She already felt completely connected to Lauren, the young widow in the story. The thought that the character was living through the same thing she was brought her comfort.

She was already on the second chapter when a woman walked past her to drop off books in the library night drop, then stopped at the Little Free Library box for a peek.

"Pretty day for reading outside, isn't it?"

"Perfect." Rosemary didn't even make eye contact. She didn't mean to be rude, but she was already being drawn into this story and didn't want to invite a conversation.

Thankfully, the woman walked away without another word.

She sat there reading until she got so thirsty she had to get up and find something to drink. She should've known better than to go for a walk without a bottle of water.

Across the way, an adorable yellow-and-white building with a flag out front had a sign stating it was a historic building. She stopped to read it. She hadn't even realized it was the post office. The little building looked more like one of those popular tiny houses. Rosemary could totally picture herself in there, crafting away in her own little she-shed.

She walked up to the pizza shop and ordered a slice of pepperoni and a bottle of water. They had outdoor seating with pretty umbrellas, so she settled in at a table for an early lunch and to get back to her book. This wasn't as cute as the library garden, but from here she could hear the ocean, and that was nice too.

It didn't take one page flip for her to drift back into the story, eager to see how Lauren was getting on.

Rosemary's phone pinged, startling her out of the fantasy world. She'd truly lost herself in that story. It had been a long time since that had happened. She looked at the message on her phone.

Nina

Mom, you've made your point. I'm sorry. You're right. I overstepped.

Her nose tickled, tears threatening over the apology.

Rosemary

Thank you, honey. I wasn't making it easy. I'm sorry too.

When are you coming home?

Rosemary's hand hovered above the text. Nina's house wasn't her home. She withheld comment on that and instead typed a safer response.

> Spending some time at Kathleen's house. I'm fine. I'll keep you posted.

She hesitated. *It's just a little white lie. Kathleen's not exactly here, but Prissy counts for something. If I tell her Kathleen is gone, she'll expect me to come home. I don't want to have that fight.*

Rosemary pressed Send.

Something inside nudged her. *A lie is never a good idea. Why would you lie about this?*

Nina
Stay in touch.

The three dots hovered and disappeared and showed up again. Finally Nina typed "Have fun."

Rosemary got up, the magic of getting lost in the book now gone. She stopped in the market again to grab cards to send to Nina and Kendra, since she knew where the post office was now. It would be an olive branch and a secret apology for the tiny white lie.

She picked out a couple of postcards and wandered over to the meat counter.

"Fresh catch every day," the man boasted. "I just put the tuna in the case."

"Really? Well, I'll take a small piece. It's just me."

"You're too pretty to be eating alone." He picked up a nice fillet and packaged it for her. "You know how to cook it?"

"Sure do, but thank you." She walked down the aisles for no other reason than she wasn't ready to go back to Kathleen's just yet, adding a spiral notebook and felt-tip markers to her basket.

She used to journal. Maybe picking up that habit again would help her figure out her next steps.

That and some prayers. I could use Your help on this one.

She twisted her fingers against the cross that hung from her neck. It was the gift Kai had given her on their first wedding anniversary. He'd said he knew she was a gift from God from the day he met her, and he still couldn't believe she'd said yes when he asked her to marry him. She treasured the dainty cross just as much today as she had when, through tearful eyes, he'd put it around her neck. He'd certainly been a gift to her too.

She checked out and distributed the bags for balance as she started her walk back to Kathleen's. She was crossing the main road when someone honked at her.

She hustled across the road, taking heed of the warning, but then noticed the truck slowing down. She'd gotten across as quickly as possible. She hoped she hadn't run right in front of them. She braced for someone to yell a warning, but when she turned, it was Tug in the driver's seat, wearing a big old smile.

"Hey there," she said with relief. "You scared me."

"Sorry. It was supposed to be a friendly hello honk. What are you doing?"

"Taking a walk. I was just heading back."

He bobbed his head, then leaned out the window a bit. "What are you doing tonight?"

"Finding myself" didn't seem like the right answer. "Kathleen went out of town, so nothing special."

"How about I pick you up? They said I can go back to my house. It's got the best view of the beach. We can do 'nothing special' together."

Her heart stuttered. It had been her idea in the first place, but now that he was actually asking, panic had run off with her verbal skills.

"I could pick you up at, say, six o'clock? I know where Kathleen's place is."

"Okay" was all that came out.

"Great." He reached his hand out the window and waved, then patted the door. "See you later." He turned the corner, and she stood there, clutching her bags. *Did that really just happen, or did I dream it up?*

"Ha!" She was excited, nervous, and a little dumbstruck all at once. Most of all, though, she was looking forward to spending time with Tug. No pressure. *It's not like it's a date. It'll be fine. Right?*

She stumbled, fortunately catching herself before she lost her balance. She turned back to see what had tripped her up.

Curious, she knelt to inspect the culprit.

A shell? I must be dreaming this. Wake up, Rosemary.

She closed her eyes, took a deep breath, and slowly let it go before opening her eyes.

Wishful thinking is all it is. I'm at the beach. There are millions of shells around here.

But she had to know. She picked up the large white shell. It wasn't anything special—well, not on the outside anyway—but when she turned it over, she almost dropped everything she was holding.

In red ink, as if scribbled with a ballpoint pen, thin and scrawling, someone had written,

> Life takes you to unexpected places.
> Trust the light to lead you home.

For a split second, she felt as if things were swirling.

She couldn't ascertain if she was spinning or the world around her. She stared at the shell.

The look on Hailey's face, serious and wide-eyed, when she'd explained, "The shells with messages are very special," flashed in her memory.

Rosemary's breathing came in heavy gulps, and a tear caught in her lashes as she reread the simple message.

"'Life takes you to unexpected places. Trust the light to lead you home.'"

What does that mean?

"Trust the light to lead you home," she repeated. Wrapping her fingers around the shell, she walked back to Kathleen's. *I've so desperately needed to feel at home.* A million things raced through her mind. How had the shell gotten there? Was it meant for her? And if it was, what was she supposed to get from it?

Prissy met her at the door, weaving through Rosemary's legs as she entered.

"Hey there, Prissy."

Prissy gave her tail a swish, then padded off into the other room.

Rosemary walked into the kitchen and put her things away. The fish would keep until tomorrow in the fridge. She sat at the kitchen table staring at the shell, trying to decipher the message.

It fit her situation. She had indeed been wondering where home was for her now. And was home a place or a feeling?

Her one true love was Kai, and their home in Hawaii. Was she making a mistake assuming she couldn't go back? Or was Nina's apology the light leading her back to Pennsylvania? Nina and Kendra were family, no matter how they frustrated each other.

The message was more confusing than helpful.

Prissy hopped up onto the kitchen table.

"Now, I'm not sure you're supposed to be up here," Rosemary scolded her but then held the shell up to her.

Prissy gave it a sniff.

"What do you think of this?" The cat pressed her face against the shell. "Perhaps this message wasn't meant for me," she said. "Could it have been one from Tug's Diner? If you find one that someone else had already found, does it apply to the new finder? That seems pretty technical." She sat there wondering. "I'm talking to a cat."

Prissy meowed.

"You seem to be listening. The diner is pretty far from where I found this shell. Probably unlikely it had been in the diner."

Prissy left in a single leap.

"Fine, then."

Rosemary carried the shell into the guest room and placed it on the nightstand, promising herself she wouldn't obsess over the message and what it meant. She could talk to Amanda about it later.

For now, she had just enough time to shower and change before Tug picked her up.

In the shower, though, the message replayed in her mind. Her brain didn't give two hoots that she was trying to set it aside. It was front and center.

It speaks to exactly what's weighing on my heart. Home.

Doesn't everyone need to feel at home somewhere? It couldn't have been meant for anyone else. What do I want my life to look like?

Every image that popped into her mind was old: life with Kai, life on the farm, in Hawaii. History she could envision just fine, but the future . . . it was blank. Things had changed, and she still wasn't sure how it had all changed her, but surely it had, because now she felt like she belonged nowhere.

Frustrated, she twisted the knobs to turn off the shower and wrapped herself in a big beachy towel.

She got dressed and went into the living room to turn on the local news. The big topic was, of course, the recovery from the storm. Pictures of devastation up and down the coast in towns she'd never heard of went by so fast they meant little, except there were a lot of people with a lot of extra to-dos to get done.

She glanced at the clock.

If Tug didn't show up, this was all just one big, wacky dream, and she'd wake up in the middle of the night hungry for popcorn. That would be okay too. All the fresh air had left her a little tired.

But at six o'clock on the dot, there was a knock at Kathleen's door.

Rosemary walked over and opened it.

Tug stood there. "Hey, you ready?"

"Yeah. Can I bring something? I should've asked you earlier. I don't know where my manners were."

"Just you."

"Then I'm ready." She joined him outside, and he held open the door of a white minivan with a Paws Town Square banner down the side.

"This isn't what you were driving earlier," she said.

"No. That was Paul's truck. He lent me this to use until the insurance pays me out for mine, assuming they will. I haven't been car shopping in years."

"Get ready for sticker shock," she warned. "I didn't ship my vehicle over, so one of the first things I had to do was buy a car. Ouch. We paid less for our first house than I did for that car, and it's not fancy."

"Yeah, I'm kind of worried about that. I'm a simple guy. It'll be hard for me to pull the trigger on a big ticket, even if the insurance is buying."

"I know what you mean."

They got into the minivan and buckled up. Then Tug eased out of the driveway.

He was a good driver, and he was taking roads she hadn't been down before. Probably the locals' back routes.

He turned down a road with high-dollar homes on both sides.

"Wow. Beautiful area."

"That's a long story." He turned down another road toward the water. In front of a stilted house there was a pretty cottage sign that read TUG'S SEASHELL HIDEAWAY, in a breezy script, with a colorful shell at the top. The blue-and-white sign was bright and welcoming, and the house was a soft watercolor shade of the same blue.

The color of his eyes.

A wraparound porch with white railings looked inviting.

Then she noticed Tug's truck. The roof of it, anyway.

"You weren't exaggerating about your truck being covered in sand. It's buried!" Rosemary pulled on the door handle and hopped out to investigate. "This is incredible."

She walked closer and peered inside. Her jaw dropped. "The sand is to the dashboard in there. How?"

He shrugged. "I would love to have had a video camera on all of it. It's hard to even imagine how that could've happened."

"You know that line about what doesn't break us strengthens us?"

He shook his head and chuckled. "Yeah, but it still hurts like hell."

"Tell me about it. And it takes time to get through it."

"If ever," he whispered.

"Oh, you'll get through this. I know we just met, but while I'm in town, it would be my pleasure to help. People come into our paths at just the right time or season. Maybe I'm yours."

"Oh. I've got people now?"

"Yeah. Lucky you." She pursed her lips and cocked her shoulder playfully. "You have your people call my people. Anytime."

Chapter Twenty

TUG WATCHED ROSEMARY TRYING TO FIGURE OUT HOW all that sand had ended up dumped on his doorstep.

"I swear, it seems more like a college frat joke than the remnants of a storm, doesn't it?"

"Not that I ever went to college, but yeah, I see what you mean."

"I didn't go, either, but I saw *Animal House,* and I guess we just hear about that stuff. I'd put my money on someone dumping sand here before I'd believe it was a storm, if I wasn't here to see it for myself."

"I don't have any enemies that I know of," Tug said.

"I wouldn't think you would."

"And now I have this one-of-a-kind walkway." He hooked his arm for her. "Shall we?"

"We shall!" She let him lead the way as they started climbing the newly formed dune entrance to his house.

"Maybe if I'm lucky," Tug said, "this will end up as famous as Carhenge, and I can charge admission."

"Carhenge?"

"In Nebraska. It's like Stonehenge in England, except this guy made it out of junk cars."

"I know of Stonehenge in England, but *Carhenge*?" She flashed him the stink eye. "You're pulling my leg."

"No. It's a real thing. I saw it on television one night. Some guy built a replica of Stonehenge out of junk cars. Spray-painted them all gray and stacked them. Went to the trouble to even space them out exactly like the real one."

"And he charges people to see it?"

"No, but there's a gift shop. So I suppose they make a little money off of it."

She shook her head. "Nebraska, huh? And here I thought they were only known for Cornhuskers, and frankly, I don't even know what a Cornhusker is. I mean, I know how to husk corn, but does that deserve a title?"

"It's the college football team," he said.

"Well, there you go. Cars stacked up like Stonehenge might actually be a sight worth seeing. I'm adding that to my traveling wish list."

Tug laughed out loud.

She spun around. "I'm not kidding. You don't have a traveling wish list?"

"I don't have a traveling list. No bucket list either."

"We're going to start you one. Today."

"We are, are we?"

She squeezed his biceps. "Yes."

"I'd heard redheads could be feisty."

"You haven't even seen me in action yet," she said with a lift of her brows.

With another hearty laugh, Tug stepped onto the hill of sand closest to the truck and extended his hand toward her. "It's safe. This is solid sand. I tried to poke a stick down in it. It's not going anywhere without help." He stomped twice, his shoe barely making an indentation.

"Convinced me." She grabbed his hand and hiked herself up. "Ah, here we go!"

"There used to be twelve steps to my front door. At my

age, I'm thinking maybe I ask them to leave this. What do you think?"

"I'd say we're about the same age, and I'm not old, so you aren't either. But I'd also say they'd be doing you a favor. Five steps is easier than twelve, no matter how you dice it."

"Was that a cooking joke?"

She tilted her head, then her eyes popped wide. "Oh, dice? Didn't even realize it. Yeah, I guess it was."

He shook his head with a playful smile. "Terrible joke, and you are *not* my age."

She raised an eyebrow, teasing. "How old *are* you, then?"

"I turned eighty on my last birthday."

"I'm not far behind," she said.

"I'm gonna need to see some proof of that, young lady."

"I've got a driver's license. I can prove it." She giggled like a schoolgirl as she stepped onto the hood of the truck behind Tug. "This seems so wrong." She raised her arms overhead as if she'd just stuck the landing on a perfect ten gymnastics routine.

"Sort of fun, though," he said. "We can't hurt it any worse than it is." He took her hand, and they made it to the steps together.

"I'm not a rule breaker usually," she said.

"Me either. I think that's what's so liberating about it." Tug opened his front door and held it for her to enter.

"Oh my. This is very nice." Rosemary walked inside. "Very comfortable."

"I like it. One of the best views in town, and the kitchen of my dreams." He led her into the kitchen and turned on the lights.

"Wow. That is the prettiest butcher-block island I've ever seen in my life." She ran her fingertips along the scarred dark wood. "I can only imagine how many meals have been prepared here. It's old, right? Not new pretending to be old."

"It's the real deal. It's made from reclaimed wood out of an old house that used to be on the point back in the early 1900s, and it has remained a butcher block ever since."

"How did you ever get your hands on it? It's gorgeous."

"I designed this kitchen around it. A guy who owned a huge restaurant up the coast used to buy fish from me for years back when I was a commercial fisherman. I was young. He fell on hard times, and he still owed me money when he was forced to close his restaurant, and he said he couldn't pay me."

"That's awful."

"Yeah, I'd worked hard to catch those fish. I wasn't going to just let him say sorry and move on. I told him I'd take the island and call it even."

"You didn't!"

"I did, and he told me if I could move it, I could have it. You can believe I enlisted about every friend I had to help me get that thing."

"Can't blame you."

"I don't think he thought I'd take it, but I did. It took a pickup truck full of my friends with a flatbed trailer behind it to move this thing out of there. Cost me a case of beer. I think I got the best end of the deal. Before I built this house, it sat in the garage, waiting for its time to shine."

"I could chop for hours here." She snuggled up close to it, pretending to chop and put things in a bowl. "It's exactly the right height. Let me know if you need a sous-chef while I'm in town."

"I could do that."

A squawk came from outside.

Rosemary clapped her hands in delight. "You already brought her home? Where is she?"

"I had her in the truck when I saw you earlier." He escorted

Rosemary out to the deck. "She loves being outdoors. She stayed out on the screened patio area in the diner all summer long."

"That's so neat," Rosemary said.

"There's The Wife," Tug said.

"I'm here! Honey, I'm home," The Wife called out like she was known to do when addressed.

"Say hello to my new friend," he said.

"Hello," The Wife squawked.

"Hi." Rosemary took a moment to admire the view. "Tug, you weren't exaggerating about this view. The Wife is very well kept."

"She is." But The Wife was going to be affected by the diner closing. "She's going to miss our customers. She loves attention."

"I'm sure you're already missing your customers too." Rosemary waved her fingers in The Wife's direction. "How are you? I'm Rosemary."

The Wife stepped from side to side on the perch and made a couple of clicking sounds.

"Today's been sort of rough. I'm glad I spotted you. With nothing to keep me busy, the reality is setting in. It's good to have some company to get my mind off of it. I miss the customers, the place—the business was my life. I don't quite know what to do with myself."

"There's got to be so much to figure out. Insurance. Timing. Makes me dizzy just thinking about it."

"That, and when I turned on the television to watch the midday news, they had aerial shots of the pier and what's left of the diner all over it. That was hard to see."

"They didn't have to ask you to air that?"

"No. They were just showing all the destruction. I guess that's public domain."

"Wouldn't hurt for them to maybe talk a little about the

other ninety percent of the area that was spared to sort of even out the perspective. Everyone wants to wallow in the bad news."

"I don't particularly."

"No. Of course not. I mean, it happened to you. You have to process it. It's personal. When the news focuses on only the bad stuff, people sitting at home only take that in. There isn't the balance of good and bad. That's problematic."

He grinned. "I like the way you think."

"I don't want to come across bossy, but—"

"You're going to anyway?"

"Well, yes, I guess I am. I was just going to suggest maybe not watching the news for a few days—you know, until things settle down or something new takes the spotlight."

"That's actually good advice. I'll tell you, it looks bad at ground level, but from above it's disastrous."

"Like a sucker punch?"

"By an enormous guy."

"Sorry. I hopped on my soapbox. I didn't mean to."

"I don't mind."

"I love the setup you have for The Wife out here. Was the one at the diner similar?"

"Pretty much. This one is twelve feet long and four feet wide. The same guy built them both for me. At the diner, the cage is . . . *was* square rather than rectangle. The first cage I built for her myself was out of wood. That was a mistake. Turns out she's quite the whittler."

"Oh yeah. That's funny. Her beak looks strong."

"It is."

"What's the story about you getting this million-dollar view? Are you a secret billionaire? Rich inventor with tons of patents? Or something even more spectacular like the real chef behind those famous frozen waffles?"

"Nothing so glamourous. I got lucky." He leaned forward, resting his forearms on the railing. "This part of the beach wasn't much when I bought the property. Everybody teased me about buying it, but I had a dream. There wasn't even a road down this far back then. I had an old International Scout four-wheel drive, rugged as all get-out and eaten up with cancer. Its fenders had more holes than a sponge from always being on the beach, but for a long time you couldn't get back here without a pretty rugged four-wheel drive."

"Really? It's so grown up now and with really ritzy stuff."

"It is. It was just me and the wild ponies back then. In fact, I lived in what is now the garage for almost ten years. One room. It was all I could afford to build. My best friend, Jarvis, and I built it one paycheck at a time. It wasn't much, but it was mine."

"Back then we had motivation to make our dreams come true."

"Right? Yeah, I knew someday I'd build this house. I had sketches and notes that I kept for years as I saved up. I lived lean for a long time to make it a reality."

"You had a good eye to snag this property. It's a beautiful area, and the neighboring houses are sort of amazing. That house is big enough to be a hotel." She pointed to the next house up the beach from him, which was about a quarter mile away.

"Nope. It's privately owned, and the extended family comes for two weeks every summer. The rest of the time it's rented out to wedding parties and fancy guests." He lowered his voice. "If I were a name-dropper, I could really impress you by the celebrities who have stayed there."

"But of course you wouldn't."

"Of course not." He pushed up his sleeves and shrugged. "However, I broke out a bottle of wine that one of those fancy visitors gave me. I have an entire case of the stuff, and I'm not much of a drinker. It would be nice to have someone to share it with. Do you care for a glass?"

"I'm not much of a drinker, either, but that sounds really nice."

They walked back inside, and he took a bottle down from the cabinet, along with two glasses, and started working the cork out. "I imagine it's supposed to be good, but I'm not knowledgeable about wine at all. If we don't like it, I won't even feel bad if we pour it down the sink." He laughed. "I'm fancy like that."

He gave her a wink, and finally the cork pulled free of the bottle.

She held the glasses by their stems while he poured.

He raised one. "A toast to my new friend. Rosemary, you are the one good thing that blew in with Hurricane Edwina. I'm thankful you crossed my path."

"Thank you. I'm grateful our paths crossed too."

They both took a sip. "It's not horrible," Tug said.

"No. Probably not to the people who know." She giggled. "Okay, so just how awful would it be for me to suggest we add some soda to this to make it more palatable?"

"I've got lemon-lime soda right here. I use it to make Amanda's kids sherbet freezes. That's why they love me so much."

"I'm sure it's the only reason."

"Yeah, pretty much."

"Well, I wouldn't be opposed to adding a scoop of lime sherbet to it either."

Tug whipped open the freezer door and slid the tub of sherbet across the island as if he were in a saloon.

"Ha!" she squealed. "All righty, then. I was joking, but I really will try it."

They started with a little splash of this and a scoop of that until they'd made quite a mess of it.

"This looks horrible," Rosemary said. "The red and green sort of looks like—"

"As bad as it tastes."

"Yes. And I had such high hopes."

"I don't think this is going to make it on a menu."

"Honestly, I think we just wasted your nice bottle of wine, because neither one of us could appreciate it, but our concoction of the sherbet-wine freeze might be a winner."

"I'm gonna let you believe that." He poured his glass into the sink. "How about some sweet tea?"

"Please!" She laughed all the way to the sink, where she washed out both wine glasses and dried them while he poured them some sweet tea.

He took a long swig. "Oh yeah. This is better."

She took a sip. "Oh gosh, so much better. You know, back in Hawaii, I used to make a sweet tea using pineapple juice as a sweetener."

"That sounds pretty tasty. Never heard of it. We do Arnold Palmers around here, ya know—mix lemonade and sweet tea—but never heard of mixing it with pineapple."

"I'll make some for you. If you like pineapple, then I think you'd like it." She smiled.

They nibbled on some sandwiches and veggies and dip that he'd put together for them. Nothing fancy, but that added to the fun.

"So, Tug, have you thought more about what's next for you?"

Had Paul or Amanda been talking to her? But she was new in town. He was probably being paranoid. "You mean with the diner being gone?"

She nodded.

"I've thought about it. Sometimes it's all I can think about, and sometimes it's all I don't want to think about."

"No one is going to judge you, no matter what you decide. Are you thinking about alternatives?"

"Trying to. I just don't have any good ideas. I can't sit around and do nothing. I enjoy being on the go. I love my customers, but I'm too old to rebuild. That's more than I'm willing to take on."

"You'll figure out a solution. There's always volunteer work. You could take up a new hobby. I don't know. It'll come to you. If you need to brainstorm, I'm around. Even if I'm gone, I'm a phone call away, and I got no horse in this race, so you will not get one moan, groan, or judgment on any of it."

"Thank you. That's very kind, and I may surprise you and take you up on that, but I'm not always that much of a talker."

"I think you're keeping your end of things just fine. I've loved our conversation tonight. It's fun getting to know you, and I feel quite blessed that you shared your million-dollar view and one-of-a-kind stair system with me," she teased.

"I don't have the patent on that stair system yet." He held his finger to his lips. "Top secret."

She leaned in. "It's safe with me."

"I know it is." His gaze traced the curve of her lips before meeting her eyes again. "I feel like we've known each other a long time. Is that strange?"

"I feel it too. It's easy. This has been such a nice visit."

"It really has. Thank you for coming over, and for being so understanding. It's hard."

"Oh? Yeah. I know." She sighed. "I mean, it's not the same at all, but it's sort of the same. Your diner. My husband. No matter what the loss, it's got to be processed."

"I suppose."

"I'm trying to figure things out in my life too," Rosemary said. "It's different when our life is upended at this age. When we're in our forties, even our sixties, it's like, whatever—we'll just pull ourselves up by our bootstraps . . . again. But now we're older, smarter, wiser about how fragile our lives are. I think it's important we really consider what matters to us. And let that lead the way."

"You've been thinking about this for a while."

"I have. For a couple of years now, and sadly, I don't have even a single bit of it figured out."

His gaze locked with hers, something unspoken passing between them.

"But I'm working on it."

They sat quietly for a long moment.

"You ready to take me home?" She finally broke the silence. "I think this is a poignant spot to end the evening."

"Certainly." Although he wasn't ready to say goodbye. He'd enjoyed having her here tonight more than he'd expected.

Chapter Twenty-One

TUG WALKED HER TO HER DOOR, WHICH ROSEMARY thought was really sweet. A complete gentleman.

That was the most fun she'd had in a long time. It was just her speed. Quiet and no expectations. Inside, she plopped down on the couch, enjoying feeling so good.

She'd almost forgotten this feeling.

It wasn't even eight o'clock yet, so she turned on the television to the game show channel. It was one of those trivia games, and she surprised herself at how many answers she guessed.

During the commercial, she got up and fed Prissy. Taking care of a cat was a piece of cake. Prissy barely came out from hiding except to eat. No sooner had Rosemary dropped the little scoop of food into the bowl than Prissy sashayed around the corner, tail in the air, like a performer taking the stage.

"It doesn't look all that appealing, Prissy. I believe if you were my cat, I'd make you something tastier, but this is what we've got."

Prissy dipped her face into the bowl and ate.

The insurance adjuster had taken pictures of the fence this morning, so all of Rosemary's responsibilities were done.

It was sort of nice being here alone with nothing hanging over her head.

Her phone pinged. It was Kathleen.

Kathleen
Are you home?

Rosemary
Yes.

We're having a ball. We are tempted to stay longer if you don't mind cat sitting.

Don't mind at all.

Prissy walked into the room, stared at Rosemary for a long moment, and then walked right over and curled up beside her on the couch.

Well, I think we've finally become friends. "It's you and me for a few more days." Was Prissy just sucking up for the promise of a home-cooked meal? Rosemary sank her fingers into the cat's soft fur. When Prissy started purring, Rosemary couldn't stop grinning. She'd heard nothing like it. And who knew cats vibrated like that?

"And all along I thought I was a dog person," she said.

Rosemary soon fell asleep on the couch, with Prissy at her side.

She dreamed of sunny days of walking the beach and woke up excited to relax in the sun. But the weather had taken a turn.

It was a drizzly gray morning again, and that put a damper on her good mood. A peek at the weather forecast didn't look too promising.

She wondered how Tug was doing. When he was driving her back last night, he'd glanced over to where the diner had once been. He didn't say a word, but she noticed the hitch in his breath and the set of his jaw. He had a lot on his mind.

Prissy jumped down and disappeared, probably to find another cozy spot to sleep.

That afternoon, being cooped up in the house was making her a little crazy, so she tucked the shell in her purse and went for a drive. She stopped at the library to see if they had the local newspapers available for research.

"Are you looking for anything in particular?" the librarian inquired.

"Um, well . . ." This woman probably knew everything there was to know about these shells, but Rosemary wasn't sure she wanted to share it with her. "Just looking up some of the town legends. I'd heard something about shells with messages in them."

The woman nodded. "That's true. People come in here all the time thinking it's just an old wives' tale, but I've seen some shells on display. I've never found one, but I know people who have."

"That must be pretty special."

"I'd say so." The librarian led Rosemary over to a small table in the corner. "Here, I'll get you set up. There are quite a few stories in the local paper about the findings. Some with pictures even. I'd have sent you down to the diner to talk to Tug. He's sort of the unofficial historian of them. He's been displaying them for years. Unfortunately, the diner didn't make it through the hurricane."

"That's terrible."

"It is. He built it from the ground up. It was the heartbeat of this town. The locals' favorite. It's heartbreaking, really."

Rosemary knew how hard it was to accept an unplanned change in your life. She said a silent prayer for Tug, then pored over the old-style microfiche articles until her eyes were weary. Some messages had been direct quotes from the Bible, others famous quotes, and a few were like a personal note someone might leave for a friend. Not fancy, but thought provoking and somehow promising at the same time.

In not one article was anyone speculating about how the shells appeared or the reasons behind who found them or where they were found.

Some had been found in the water. Amanda said she found hers near her house. One lady in an article said she found hers next to her mailbox, miles from the water. One thing they all had in common was that the words in those shells led those people in a positive direction during a challenging time.

"Did you find everything you needed?" The librarian approached her, smiling.

"Yes. It's so interesting. I was just finishing up."

"I'll put that away for you."

Rosemary got up and pushed her chair in. "Thank you so much for your help."

"Stop in anytime."

She walked outside and pulled her phone out. At least the rain had stopped, but it was still overcast. Rosemary scrolled through her phone, then tapped on Amanda's name to call her. She walked in a circle, relieved when Amanda answered.

"Hi? Amanda. It's Rosemary."

"Hello. It's good to hear from you."

"Are you busy?" Rosemary crossed her fingers.

"No. I'm just trying to keep these kids from bouncing off the walls. Rainy days are the pits around here."

"Want some company?"

"I'm dying for some adult conversation! Please come over."

"I'm on my way." Rosemary got back in her car. It was a quick trip to Amanda's, but if she remembered correctly, she'd go right past that little market.

Delighted when she spotted the market, she ran inside to pick up four Drumstick cones. Who didn't like ice cream? Hopefully, the extra sugar wouldn't make the kids any more ramped up than they already were.

With her little bag of treats, she drove to Amanda's and parked in front of The Shell Collector sign. The shell on the sign was much like the one on Tug's beach house sign. Probably designed and sandblasted by the same local artist.

Rosemary climbed the stairs. All these stilted beach houses had a ton of stairs, but it probably kept folks in shape. As soon as she knocked, there was a woof, followed by what sounded like a stampede toward the door.

The door swung open. Hailey, Jesse, and a huge black-and-white bulldog stood there staring at her.

"Miss Rosemary!" Hailey opened the screen door. "Mom didn't tell us you were coming."

"Mom! Miss Rosemary is here!" Jesse yelled at the top of his lungs, then turned to her. "You don't have to be scared of Denali. He's a marshmallow."

"Is that a fact? He looks like he might have eaten a lot of marshmallows." She held her hand flat in front of him. He lifted his nose, sniffing the surrounding air, then slowly lowered his head.

"Hi there, Denali. My name is Rosemary." She patted his solid head. "So nice to meet you, big boy."

Denali's nub of a tail started helicoptering.

"Oh, he likes you," Hailey said.

"I like him too. Only, I think he might like what he's smelling more than me." She bent down. "Sorry, sir. I didn't bring you one."

"Did you bring us something?" Jesse nudged Hailey in excitement.

"I did."

Amanda joined them at the door. "Come in, Rosemary. Welcome. I see you've met Denali."

"He's quite handsome. Looks like he could pull your car."

"I know, right? He's really sweet and so good with the kids."

"I brought a little treat for everyone. Hope you don't mind."

"Not at all."

Rosemary handed Hailey the bag, which she immediately opened. "Ice cream cones for everyone! Can we have them now, Mom?"

"Sure. I'm going to wait on mine. Rosemary, would you like yours now?"

"I'll wait and have mine later too."

"We're playing a game. Want to play?" Jesse asked.

"You two," Amanda said, "go play. Take Denali. Rosemary and I are going to have a grown-up visit. Mommy needs it."

"Oh gosh, when she says that, she means it." Hailey rolled her eyes. "It means she's just about to get stressed out."

Amanda seemed to force a grin. "If she doesn't grow up to be a psychologist or a mind reader, I'll be shocked."

"Going on thirty. Little girls are like that. I bet your mom said the same about you."

"Probably." Amanda led Rosemary inside. "Come on. I'll show you our favorite room in the house. I made some tea. I hope that's okay."

"It's lovely. You didn't have to do that. I did sort of invite myself over. But I'm glad you did, and I see why you wanted to wait on the ice cream."

Amanda had set out a shiny silver tea service, sugar cubes, and cream on the glass table between the chairs.

Rosemary stepped into the room, in awe of the color and beauty.

"Isn't it wonderful? It feels like walking into a warm hug to me," Amanda said.

"You're right. It sure does. Look at all the sea glass, and these shells are exotic."

"Those were mostly Maeve's collection. The kids have added a few things to it, but we've kept this sort of in appreciation of

Maeve. She brought so much to our lives. We want to preserve that."

"She must've really been something."

Amanda pressed her hands together. "I wish you could've known her. She was wise and kind and so generous."

"Sounds like you."

Amanda held her hand to her heart. "That is the nicest thing you could say to me. I really loved Maeve like family. I hope I can be even half the person she was."

Amanda poured the tea. They talked about the beach, and Amanda asked her about Hawaii and about Kai.

"Rosemary, you seem like you're doing really well, but I know no one can know what's in your heart. None of it's easy to navigate, losing a spouse."

"No. They can't."

"I used to think it was worse for me because losing Jack was so unexpected and we hadn't been married that long, but really it's heartbreaking no matter how or what the circumstances. I can't imagine watching my husband slowly die from a disease, or losing him after fifty years of marriage. Jack and I were like one person, and we'd only been married five years when he didn't come back. Hailey wasn't even in school yet."

"I don't know who I am without Kai. We were together my whole adult life," she said. "I don't know how to separate it—plus, I love all those memories. I think my imagination is too old to think of a new way to live."

"You're vibrant and so capable. And kind. I am glad we met. Crazy timing with the storm and all, and you were so helpful. It's like you've been a part of this community forever. I'm so glad you were still here when I got back. I would've hated to miss out on all this."

"Me too."

"I believe our paths crossed for a reason," Amanda said.

"Maeve was here for me. I hope I can be there for you. You know, sort of pay it forward. I don't know—I just feel like I've known you forever even though we've just met, and if I can help, I'd love that."

"Isn't it funny when that happens? I feel it too." Rosemary ran her hand through her hair. "If you can help me, you're some kind of magician or an angel, because I can't get myself figured out, and I've known me my whole life."

Amanda's laugh was light and genuine. "Maybe that's why we need help. We're too close to it. It sort of keeps us from seeing the entire picture when we're so hemmed in by this sad thing that has happened to us." She pressed her hand to Rosemary's arm. "It's different for everyone. I know that, but for me it was like . . . Well, it was like losing gravity. I couldn't grasp anything, no matter how hard I tried. Everything I reached for slipped through my fingers, like deciding what to feed the kids. It felt impossible. Jack had nothing to do with that, of course— it was just . . . without him, everything felt so much harder for a while."

"That is a brilliant analogy—like losing gravity. Yes. I totally relate. So, should we switch our tea for Tang? Oh gosh, you're probably too young to know Tang or that it's what the astronauts supposedly drank. Maybe if we drink that, we can manage gravity and make some progress," Rosemary teased.

"Like astronauts. If only it was that easy," Amanda said. "But really, whatever I can do, please let me be there for you."

That shell popped into her mind. Rosemary grabbed her purse, then leaned in. "Well, there is something I think you can help me with."

"Anything. What?"

Rosemary dipped her hand into her purse and withdrew the shell. "I found this—well, it sort of found me. I practically tripped over it walking home yesterday afternoon." She handed the shell to Amanda.

Amanda's jaw dropped. "Oh my gosh. You know I found shells too. I told you, right? Oh gosh, profound when it happens, isn't it?"

Rosemary nodded. "Do you think I was meant to find it?"

"Of course you were. Who else?"

"Well, I wondered if maybe it was one that had been at the diner or something. You know, sort of already claimed." It sounded stupid saying it out loud. "What does the message written in it even mean?"

Chapter Twenty-Two

AMANDA SET THE SHELL DOWN ON THE TABLE BETWEEN them. "No. If you found it, you were supposed to. The right people find the right message at the right time."

She picked the shell back up and turned it over. "'Life takes you to unexpected places. Trust the light to lead you home.' It could mean a lot of different things." Amanda pulled her feet up onto the chair. "The day I found my first shell, I'd been clinging to my memories of Jack. I was hurting so badly and it had been two years. I'd moved here for a fresh start, but still I had his old shirt hanging on the back of my dressing table chair." Her voice softened, her lashes lowering. Her hand gracefully recreated the back of the chair in the air. "I'd run my hand across that shirt so many times in a day. I couldn't let go. I couldn't move on. I was sad, and my heart felt like it weighed a ton in my chest. Every day was hard. Finding that shell and reading that quote opened my mind. I sort of pivoted for the first time."

"You told me about it. The Havelock Ellis quote. What was it?"

"'All the art of living lies in a fine mingling of letting go and holding on.'"

"It aligned with your struggle," Rosemary whispered.

"It did, but I wasn't familiar with Havelock or the quote, and I also wasn't sure what things I needed to hang on to or let go of. I mean, in hindsight, yeah, it was clear as a bell, but when you're in the middle of that stormy situation, it's messy."

Rosemary placed her teacup on the tray and took a deep breath. "You are wise beyond your years, Amanda."

"We've been through a lot, me and the kids. But we're wise from those battles, and I think we're finally stronger."

"I've been feeling lost," Rosemary said. "When I left Hawaii, after selling the farm, and moved in with Nina . . . it all seemed great on paper, but I don't feel at home there."

"Why not?"

"I don't know. I didn't feel at home in Hawaii once Kai was gone, so I don't know. I thought maybe it was because I was older, but some of the things you're saying are what I've been feeling."

"I don't think it matters how old you are. Love is love. If you're fully invested, when something separates that person from you, it results in a fracture. It'll mend, but it'll always be there."

"The loneliness follows you no matter where you go. Just like when you moved here to Whelk's Island," Rosemary said.

"Yes. Seems so."

"I don't want to sound ungrateful. My daughter has really gone to a lot of effort to make me comfortable, but she's managing me like another child."

"Yeah, I guess she's in mother mode. Sometimes that is hard to switch off. I can get a little bossy with Paul and Tug sometimes like that. Of course, they call me out on it."

"Well, we butt heads on it, but it isn't polite. I'd had my trip here planned for a while, and a day before I was going to leave to visit Kathleen, she actually forbid me to travel because of the storm, which was not even a storm yet."

"In all fairness, there *was* an evacuation going on," Amanda said, "but you are a grown woman. You can make those decisions, and you are fine. Everything happens for a reason, and we don't always know why we are being pulled in one direction or another. Think about that shell. If you hadn't made this trip, you never would have found it."

"True," Rosemary said.

"You came here. Life brought you to this unexpected place."

"It did, and now what?"

"Trust the light to lead you home."

"What's the light?" Rosemary asked, knowing Amanda couldn't really answer that. "Is it the sun? A place? A feeling?"

"Love?" Amanda shook her head. "I think only you can know how it fits into your future."

"I loved Kai so much."

"I never thought I could love again. I felt like what Jack and I had was the perfect love that nothing could ever compare to, but sometimes you have to live with the plan that has been designed for you. I put my trust in that, and I'm so thankful I did, because Paul is a perfect love too. Different from what I had with Jack, but just as special and perfect. I can't even explain how unreal it seems." Amanda paused. "Rosemary, don't be afraid. Trust what you're feeling. The questions in those moments that feel uncomfortable and wrong mean something, but so do the ones that feel right. We are meant to be joyful. I believe that."

Rosemary wiped a tear from her cheek, blinking back others. "You are so young to be so wise," she said, her voice soft with emotion.

"Not really. I'm echoing things Maeve helped me realize during those dark days following losing Jack. Probably not nearly as eloquently as she did, though." Amanda let out a hesitant giggle, but the warmth and admiration she felt for Maeve was clear.

"Maybe this shell and the light are like a lighthouse, guiding me," Rosemary said.

"A lighthouse *is* a beacon for guidance. That makes sense."

"And God's love is a guiding light." Rosemary sat quietly. "It could be about our friendship or the peace I feel when I'm on the beach here."

"I know that feeling," Amanda said. "I really started feeling safe and grounded when I came to Whelk's Island. But it could also mean romantic love. Maybe there's a Paul out there for you."

"No. I'm not looking for anything like that. Light is peace, hope." All of a sudden, Rosemary started laughing. Amanda must be wondering what was going through her mind. She could barely catch her breath.

"What?" Amanda looked completely confused. "What is so funny? Did I say something wrong?"

"No! No. I'm sorry. It just hit me. The light—it could be a train coming at me through a tunnel."

"Okay, not that! It is not something bad. It's good." Amanda slapped Rosemary's hand playfully. "You are crazy."

"Oh gosh, but I haven't laughed like that in . . ." She looked at her dear new friend. "Not in so, so, so long. Thank you for being my friend." She wasn't much closer to the meaning behind the shell or what the heck she should do, but she felt better.

"You don't think this was one of the shells in the diner?" Rosemary finally asked.

"No. Definitely not. I've never seen that shell."

Rosemary hadn't seen anything similar in the newspaper articles either. "I wondered, when I found it, if the whole thing was just tourist hype being perpetuated by the locals for business, but this seems very random."

"I promise you it is not hype. No one who has found one knows who or where they came from. And the messages are so poignant to the people that find them. It's very special."

Rosemary picked up the shell, turning it over in her hand. "How did it find me here?"

"I guess you were meant to be here."

"I guess so, but it hasn't been what I expected at all. This place is wonderful. I love the town, but I thought this visit with a high school friend was going to be a relaxing walk down memory lane. I realized when I got here that she is the same person she was in high school, but I'm very different from who I was back then, so the visit itself—not a home run."

"Oh. Sorry."

"No, don't be. She ended up going out of town with friends, so I've been at her house cat sitting. It all worked out, but when she returns, I guess I'll be going back, ready or not."

"You know you are welcome to stay here for a few days if you like," Amanda said. "We'd love to have you."

"No. Thank you. I can afford to rent a place if I wanted to stick around. But thank you. That is so sweet of you. I hadn't even considered that as an option. I feel like I need to find my place. Some of my best friends have passed, others . . . I have no idea where they are. I just need a start."

"I think you've made one. You just haven't realized it yet."

"Maybe I have. I need some friends."

"Um, you are quite easy to be friends with. I don't think you needed to leave Pennsylvania and drive all the way down here for that. You probably could've made friends right where you were."

Rosemary opened her mouth and then shut it. "I could have. Yes. So why did I drive how many hours with a storm in the forecast and worry my daughter? I was determined to get here."

"There was a purpose. Only you can figure that one out."

"Wow, what do I owe you for the therapy session?" Rosemary asked.

"I'd say it's about time for those Drumstick ice cream cones!" Amanda got up. "Come on."

They ripped into the ice cream with just as much excitement as Hailey and Jesse had, then relaxed in the chairs on the deck, watching the waves. They sat there, savoring each other's presence. No need for conversation.

Finally, Rosemary rocked forward in her chair. "Amanda, this has been truly a delightful day. I hope we can do this again before I leave."

"I'm counting on it. And I need some notice before you head out of town. I'm going to miss you. I think you really should think about staying. I can be like another daughter."

"Any mother would be lucky to call you hers."

"Can I get you to write my mom a note that says that? I think maybe she and Nina would get along better than she and I do."

They hugged, and Amanda called the kids down to say goodbye to Rosemary before she left.

Rosemary pulled away from Amanda's beach house, hopeful and feeling like she'd rolled back time. It was nice being around all that energy and positivity.

She was driving down the beach road, lost in her thoughts, when she spotted the minivan with the Paws logo painted on it near the little bar called The Tackle Box.

Rosemary parked next to the minivan and got out. There was a possibility it wasn't Tug at all. A few of these branded vans had been over at Paws, but it couldn't hurt to just see if he was around.

The slurry of sandy water and seaweed had left a line on the wall about her height and ran the whole length of the back side of the building.

"Wow." She stepped carefully around the debris into the paths that someone had swept clear. New landscape timbers created a path to the bar. It wasn't much bigger than a travel trailer—and not a big one at that. It reminded her of the ocean-side kiosks where vendors sold their wares on the island. Nina had worked in one of those for several summers, handing out snorkels, fins, and masks to visitors wanting to explore the reef, before she left for MIT to use that full-ride scholarship she'd earned. Nina was smart, and Rosemary loved how strong she was. A little bit of distance was helping her see things more positively, or at least try to.

When Rosemary rounded the corner, she saw that an entire wall was missing from the one-story building. There wasn't much more than a counter left. And yet a young tan man with hair that had been kissed by the sun and tousled as if maybe Edwina had blown him around a bit stood behind the bar drying glasses.

He had to be a surfer. He had that look.

The man gave her a Hollywood smile and set down the glass that he'd been drying. "Welcome to The Tackle Box, although it's more like a bait bucket right now."

"Thank you." She glanced toward the other end of the bar. There Tug sat upon a stool, slumped forward, hands cradling a glass. She turned back to the young man. "Are you the owner?"

"I am."

"I'm proud of you for pulling this together and reopening so quickly. It must be overwhelming to try to put things back together."

"Can't stop working. The bills come in no matter what. People need this place." He extended his hand across the counter. "My friends call me Fisher."

"Nice to meet you. I'm Rosemary." She glanced over at Tug,

who seemed to be in his own little world. "Has my friend been here long?"

"All day."

Two huge fans blew across the space, in an attempt to dry out the place, she suspected.

She mouthed "Excuse me" and walked over, then paused before placing her hand on Tug's back. "Hello, my friend," she said softly.

He turned his head. "Hello! What are you doing here?"

"Might ask you the same thing, but I'd guess that it's a colorful place that feels in need of a customer."

"Or two?" He eyed the stool next to him.

"Don't mind if I do," Rosemary said.

Fisher walked over. "What can I get you, Rosemary? On the house."

She looked at Tug and at the glass in front of him. "I'll have what he's having."

Fisher tossed his hair back. "Of course you will."

He walked away. Rosemary caught the movement at the other end of the bar—Fisher lifting a glass, adding ice, shaking, and pouring—but her eyes were on Tug. She resisted the urge to speak. Being here was enough, something told her.

Fisher slid a glass in front of her. "Here's to making waves in your glass and memories by the shore!"

"Poetic." Rosemary lifted the glass to her lips, hoping it wasn't so potent she'd choke and spew it across the bar like a fountain. Poor Fisher had enough to clean up. She took a teensy swallow and braced herself, but there was nothing warm or powerful about the concoction.

She took another sip.

Tug and Fisher exchanged a knowing glance.

"Is this what he's having?" she asked.

"Homemade cherry limeade," Fisher said proudly. "Half my chairs and inventory are floating somewhere around the Bermuda Triangle, I suspect, but I still know what my best customers drink. Lost my stuff, not my mind."

"I see."

"Not all of my customers come here for the libations. Bars aren't just for drinking, ma'am. They are for fellowship, sharing, a place to belong. You like the homemade cherry limeade?"

"It's perfect!" She lifted her glass toward him and then tapped hers to Tug's. "And here I thought you were wallowing in grief and too drunk to drive home. I'm not rescuing you at all."

Chapter Twenty-Three

TUG LOOKED AT ROSEMARY. *YOU MOST CERTAINLY DID RES-cue me.* As much as he was tempted, he refrained from saying it out loud. He'd thought what he was feeling was Maeve's familiar presence—well, the memory of it—until he heard Rosemary's voice.

Seeing her standing there surprised him. Pleasantly so. There was so much on his mind.

"When I saw the van, I wondered if you might need a ride home." She lifted her glass. "I guess you're quite able to drive."

He bobbed his head. "Yes. Quite."

"Come here often?"

"Fisher keeps me hydrated with my favorite tonic." Tug shook his glass, rattling the ice. "He says the lime juice has vitamin C and antioxidants."

"And the cherries?"

"No benefit whatsoever. Sugar mostly. I just like them, and he aims to please. I can't make his favorite meal anymore, but he's still holding up his end of the bargain."

Fisher tucked a bar towel into his belt. "Well, you were feeding me a good ten years before I ever opened this joint. I got you covered, old man." He turned to Rosemary. "How do you know this guy? Old girlfriend perhaps?"

"No. Hardly. I'm visiting a friend here in town. Tug and I met rather quickly right before the storm. But it was after that we sort of became friends instantly."

Fisher nodded, not looking completely convinced. "No surprise. He's a good guy. He's a legend around these parts."

"No." Tug rolled his eyes. "Don't listen to him."

"Won the East Coast Surfing Championships more than once." Fisher pointed to one of the longboards still affixed to the ceiling. "The hurricane couldn't steal his old board. He even signed it for me." He leaned back and pointed to the back quarter. "You can still see it."

"That was a long time ago." Tug felt silly admitting to something that was certainly not going to impress his new friend. "I signed it for him when he opened the place, but I won that championship when I was in my twenties."

Fisher stood straighter. "The East Coast Surfing Championships. It was a big deal."

"You weren't even born yet," Tug said.

"You were pretty big time, Tug," Rosemary said, looking impressed. "And here you told me you never traveled."

"Well, Virginia Beach isn't really that far. They come here. We go there." Tug shrugged it off. "Besides, it was a very long time ago before that event became renowned enough to pull in the best surfers. I haven't surfed in years."

"I bet you had a line of little Gidget girls in bikinis chasing you around," Rosemary teased.

He blushed. "I did okay." He wished he was sipping something stronger than cherry limeade right now.

"You seem to be a legend around these parts for lots of reasons." She turned her attention to Fisher. "I've heard praise of his pancakes from more than a few folks."

"Hailey and Jess? Paul probably."

She nodded.

"Add me to the list. I could live on his pancakes too," Fisher said.

"As I suspected. Legendary," she said. "He hasn't made them for me yet, but I loved his cheeseburger." Rosemary lifted her shoulder playfully as if she thought Tug was holding out on her.

"Whoa." Fisher leaned over the counter. "Tell me more." He tapped Tug on the arm. "Look at you two. I *knew* I felt a vibe."

Tug shook his head. "Down, boy. She came into the diner while I was closing down for the storm. It was a leftover cheeseburger."

"It's true." She raised her hand. "Girl Scout's honor. I did enjoy it, though."

"You two are in for some good times ahead. I'm gettin' a vibe here. Don't doubt me. I've got a sense about these things." He smirked and walked away, turning back only long enough to give them a thumbs-up.

"Sorry about that," Tug said. "He's a hoot."

"I'm flattered."

Tug leaned his arm on the bar. "What *are* you doing here?"

"Um, well. I really thought I was going to rescue you." She waved her hand as if pushing the comment aside. "I saw the minivan. I thought, as a good friend, I should stop. So, here I am."

"Why are you worried about me?"

"Because you are going through a trauma and you're not talking about it. I know how losing something precious feels, and I don't want you to feel that way. I don't know. I'm overstepping, aren't I?" She lifted her gaze to the ceiling. "I'm sorry. Sometimes I take action, and I don't really think about it first."

"No. It's okay. Thank you for thinking of me. I'm definitely feeling unanchored, but being with you is nice. It's grounding."

"It is?"

"Yeah, really nice. And you're right—I'm not talking about it, because I don't know what to think or do or where to begin."

"I know that feeling. When I lost Kai, it . . . I still can't even describe it."

"Exactly. I can't put it into words, so how do I talk about it?"

"I understand."

"Kathleen is lucky to have a friend like you. I wouldn't really have imagined the two of you being close friends."

"Can I tell you something, just between the two of us?"

"Anything."

"It's not exactly like I thought it was going to be, and we weren't even really that close in high school. She was all tall and model-like and popular, and I was, well, always in awe of her. And she was sort of the only person I knew how to contact. I was looking for something. I just didn't know what it was."

"Figured that out yet?"

"I'm not sure. My life with Kai was in Hawaii, and he wasn't there anymore. But moving in with my daughter? It's been stressful and a little unpleasant. I want to feel welcome and at home. Somewhere. Anywhere."

"And you don't feel that here?"

"I feel it here on Whelk's Island. Did I tell you Kathleen went off with her friends on a trip? I'm watching her cat."

Tug shook his head, laughing. "She left you? Sorry—I shouldn't laugh, but it sounds like something she'd do."

"Oh, it's fine. She invited me to join them, but it wasn't my kind of trip. I was happy to offer to watch the cat in exchange for the chance to breathe in this lovely beach air. She and her friends were exhausting. I just don't have that kind of energy."

"You have an abundance of energy."

"Well, not that kind."

"Kathleen is . . . She's a force. Best way to describe her."

"Well put."

"So, you're not spending your time visiting with Kathleen?"

"Nope, just her cat, Prissy, who has only as of yesterday become social, and I'm sort of enjoying her. I never thought of myself as a cat person, but cat tolerant maybe."

Tug laughed. "Well, thank you for stopping in to rescue me."

"I haven't, but while I'm here, if you wanted, I could help you sort of process some of this."

He liked her. She had an impish way about her that made him feel up, even when he didn't want to.

"And how would you see us getting started with that?"

"Well, how about we don't try at first? I'll bring a notebook and kind of jot ideas as we talk. Let's cook something together. We both love that, and it's a calming thing to do. We'll just trust that something brilliant will come out of it."

"We will?"

"Yes! Come on. Don't be a curmudgeon."

"A curmudgeon? I was just asking—"

"Just trust the process."

"The one you're going to make up? On the fly? While we're cooking?"

"Yes. In your kitchen on that really nice butcher block. I'm dying to chop on that. Please let me come sous-chef."

"How do I say no to that? Okay."

"Okay?" She danced in her seat. "Really?"

"Yes. What do you propose we make?"

"How about something that will fill the house with wonderful aromas? Lasagna? Can you make lasagna?"

"*Can he make lasagna?*" Fisher piped in. "Sorry—wasn't listening, just heard that last part."

"Sure, Fisher," they said together, which made all three of them laugh.

"Lasagna it is," Tug said.

"And buttery garlic bread," Rosemary added. "And I'll bring dessert. Fair enough?"

Tug stretched out his right hand. "Deal."

She pressed her hand into his and gave it a shake. "Can I push my luck and suggest one other thing?"

"You're going to anyway."

"You're right. Tomorrow is Sunday."

"All day long."

"Would you mind going to church with me tomorrow? Amanda invited me to come with them, but it might be nice if you joined us, too, and then we can go to your house from there."

Tug paused. "I haven't been to church in a long while."

"Oh?" She looked disappointed. "It's okay. I just thought I'd suggest—"

"I'll go with you," he quickly added.

She beamed. "Thank you. And for the record, it's been a long while since I've been too."

Paul walked in carrying a stack of tarps. As he handed them to Fisher, he glanced back and caught sight of them. "Hey, Tug, didn't expect to see you here. Hi, Rosemary."

"Thanks for lending me the tarps," Fisher said to Paul. "This will really help."

"I had a bunch. You're welcome to borrow them as long as you need them."

"You're a lifesaver." Fisher started unfolding one of them.

"Don't know about that, but happy to help." Paul walked over and stood next to Tug. "Y'all been here long? Everything okay?"

"Yeah, fine," Tug said.

"I was just leaving," Rosemary said. "Good to see you, Paul. Tug, I'll see you tomorrow."

Paul elbowed Tug in the side as Rosemary walked away. "To-morrow?"

"Stop it." Tug edged away from him.

Fisher raced down the bar toward them. "She was flirting with him. Tug, you like her, don't you?"

"I don't like anybody, or I like everybody," he said. "It's not like that."

Paul's smile was crooked. "Well, you sure seem flustered for a guy not interested. Just saying."

"You two are acting like teenagers. She's a nice lady in town for a short visit. End of story."

Paul had one of those condescending whatever-you-say looks on his face. "Okay, I'm just saying—"

"And, Paul, you are the last person who should be doling out relationship advice. When are you going to finally make things official with Amanda?"

"I love her. You know that."

"I mean marry the woman. Why not ask her to marry you? Those kids deserve to have a traditional family around them, and you two are committed to each other. I don't know what's holding you back."

"How did this suddenly become about me? You're projecting your stuff on me."

"Because Amanda is a fine woman and a wonderful mother and she loves you. Don't let that slip away."

"We're totally committed to each other."

"Well, technically, until you're married, you're not totally committed," Fisher said.

Paul dropped onto a stool. "Honestly, I bought a ring months ago. I want to ask her so badly, but I don't want to rush her."

"Don't want to lose her, either, do you?" Tug looked him right in the eye, no laughing or nudging. "She is not going to say no."

"How can you be so sure?"

"Because I know," Tug said. "I think especially after seeing how you two being apart because of the hurricane affected each of you and Hailey and Jesse, it's time to do something about it."

Paul looked nervous. "I hated being separated from her. I don't ever want to go through that again."

"Enough said." Tug tapped his hand on the bar. "So, why are you arguing with me?"

"Mostly because you're trying to keep the conversation off of you and the pretty new girl in town, I believe," Paul said. "But I'm going to let you get away with it, because you're right."

Tug patted him on the back. "And you are deflecting. We were talking about you."

"I've been worried about you," Paul said thoughtfully.

"Don't you worry about me. You need to quit pussyfooting around and take action."

"I know you're talking about Amanda again, but be careful. I might start with you."

Tug leaned back. "Oh, well, I don't need your help."

"Sure you do. Friends—and we're more like family—it's what we do. We lift each other up when the going gets tough, and that rubble up the road—well, it breaks my heart too." Paul's brows pulled together. "Losing Tug's Diner is a loss for the whole town."

Tug stood and hugged him. "Thank you." He clapped his hand against Paul's shoulder. "I've got some decisions to make."

Fisher tossed a bar towel over his shoulder and walked around the bar, inserting himself into the hug.

Tug looked at Paul and they laughed. Fisher was nothing if not driven by the mood of any given moment. That kid should've been born a few decades earlier, because peace, love, and beach waves were definitely Fisher's mojo.

"We will rise again," Fisher said with a fist in the air.

"Life will go on," Tug said. "I guess I should give up my stool. I haven't made much progress in any direction except for increasing my vitamin C from all the limeades I sipped on. I probably owe you a whole jar of maraschino cherries."

"Yeah, the garnish tray is looking pitiful," Fisher teased. "Kidding. It's pitiful because I didn't stock it. Wasn't sure anyone would even come with no walls, but there you were. Tug to the rescue. It gives me hope."

"I'll be honest. I kind of think the open-air vibe is working. You could always put up some of those drop-down sides for inclement weather with the insurance money instead of the rebuild."

"Dude, that's a great idea." Fisher looked around, framing his hands like a director might envision a scene. "I can see it."

"I'll see you soon." Tug walked out with Paul by his side.

"Why don't you come over and talk while I run the dogs through their trials tonight?"

Tug admired Paul's work with the retired military working dogs. And the way he'd taken a growing problem in America—abandoned box stores—and repurposed them was genius. Rather than try to expand on his own, he'd checked his ego at the door and created a franchise opportunity for veterans to help build them faster across the country.

"You've got plenty on your mind too. Why don't you think about what I already said to you tonight? And don't forget to ask the kids first and include them in the proposal. They'll love it. They love you, Paul. You are a good, strong anchor for them. It's time you lived as a family too."

"There you go deflecting again."

"Well, I had a kind offer from a pretty lady who seems to think she can help me figure out my next steps."

"Rosemary?"

"Yes, best thing that storm blew in."

Paul laughed. "I knew it. She's nice."

"She is."

"You like her."

"I won't lie. It's nice being around her." He caught the uptick of his heart, and that made him smile. "She's so effervescent."

"Effervescent?" Paul could hardly keep a straight face. "That's a vibrant Scrabble word. You're looking a little effervescent just talking about her."

"Oh, stop. I've got to get all the things together for my famous lasagna tomorrow. I'm meeting her at church. Then we're going to spend some time in my kitchen cooking it up, and, well, I suppose she'll be making me think about things. But at least in the kitchen, cooking, it won't feel so much like wallowing in pity."

"I'm glad you're coming to church. We've missed you there."

He hadn't been in a long time. When Maeve first left town, he'd still gone faithfully every Sunday, and even when she passed, he'd continued, but by the time Christmas came around, he was unable to keep his focus on the sermon. The many years he and Maeve sat in that church together were crushing in on him. It wouldn't be easy going back tomorrow, but it was time, and right now he needed to focus on what mattered.

"You said you already have a ring for Amanda?"

"I do."

"Might tuck it in your pocket and bring it over tomorrow night. I'll invite all of you to dinner. Could be a romantic way to propose on my deck overlooking the ocean, and no doubt the kids would remember it forever. And The Wife will probably say something charming, as she does."

"She's an unpredictable one, isn't she? I just hope she doesn't scream 'No' or 'Don't do it' before I get the words out. Or what if The Wife laughs like a nut? She does that."

"Ha! She does. I hadn't thought of that. It could happen, but hey, it would be a good icebreaker. Tell you what—I'll put a crisp hundred-dollar bill on The Wife saying something positive, like 'I love you,' or wolf-whistling."

"I'm not sure the wolf whistle equates to a yes."

"I guess you'll have to find out. Maybe come up with a comeback in case The Wife laughs. That is her go-to when she doesn't know what to say. Maybe something like 'See, even she thought we were already married. We're so perfect together.' I don't know—just do it already." He opened the door to the minivan. "And bring the kids into the loop. The sooner, the better. It's a big step for them. They deserve to be part of it."

"Yes, sir," Paul said.

Tug got in the van and started it up as Paul climbed into his truck.

Propose to her, my friend. Don't make the mistakes I've made, or you'll end up one lonely old man, and that ain't no picnic.

Chapter Twenty-Four

ROSEMARY WAS DELIGHTED BY HOW WELCOMING EVERY-
one was at church. Even after not having been to church in a
long while, not since she'd moved to Nina's house in Pennsylvania, she felt an immediate connection. She hadn't realized how
much she missed it until the service began, but she immediately felt the strength of His Word. In the joy of worshipping
with this close-knit group, the hymns came back to her, familiar and comforting.

The pastor's words carried the gentle urgency of a shepherd
guiding his flock. He had the pacing of a seasoned storyteller,
holding her attention with every detail, although she knew
them by heart.

How could it be that this pastor, whom she'd never met,
seemed to direct this sermon straight to her current situation?

She leaned in, absorbing the message.

Pastor Qualls's voice rose, pulling her in with the strength of
a tide. "In this season, I want to remind us all, if we see darkness
for long enough, we eventually adjust to it. We can lose awareness that there even *is* light anywhere around."

Paul reached for Amanda's hand. A gentle touch. Rosemary
missed how Kai would do that when they were in church. That
unspoken connection to the words of the day.

"As I look around the sanctuary today, I know that some of

you have experienced your turn recently. Hurricane Edwina brought in darkness." The pastor was compassionate. "You may be feeling that weighing on you at this very moment. The very best our faith can offer is indeed required in these times for us to trust in all the light we cannot see. But the light is there."

The light is always there. Something lifted in her heart. *I have choices.* She turned to Tug, who was listening intently. He was struggling now. He had harder choices to make. His problems made her own seem rather insignificant. He had tangible things to wrestle with, and the red tape of insurance and starting over made it that much harder.

"Maybe life has beaten you up lately," the pastor said.

Rosemary heard Tug catch his breath. He sure had it dished out to him. He looked as if he felt the pastor was addressing him directly too.

She'd never been a glass-half-empty kind of gal, and yet in this situation with Nina, she felt so negative and out of options. Stuck. And maybe she hadn't been entirely fair to Nina. *Help me see my options, Lord. Guide me in a way that will bring joy to Nina and to me. She's had a rough go of it too. I'm making things worse for her, and for that, I'm sorry.*

Pastor Qualls stood tall, lifting himself onto his toes as he addressed the congregation with fervor. "If you're struggling to grasp on to your faith in these trying times," he continued, his voice carrying a weight of empathy, "perhaps it's enough to hold on to the memory of a brighter moment, when you embraced God's light with unwavering conviction. Faith, you see, isn't always about seeing the light; it's about trusting that, even in the darkest of nights, there's a dawn waiting to break. It's about having faith in the unseen, believing in the presence of light beyond our immediate sight."

Rosemary nodded. *Faith.* She blinked back a tear. *I need to treasure every single day. Every moment.* She glanced over at Paul and Amanda—and Tug. *I believe these people came into my life for a reason.* The realization felt unbelievable but undebatable. *It's not so different from those shells. The right message for the right person at the right time.*

The image of the shell she'd found was so clear in her mind at that moment. *"Life takes you to unexpected places. Trust the light to lead you home."*

Tug whispered an amen.

Had she spoken out loud, or was he responding to the pastor? He must've had his own realizations too. Around the room, other heads were nodding.

This is a powerful moment. Her skin tingled with excitement as a flood of joy raced through her.

They stood for the next hymn. Everyone's voice lifted, strong and confident, following that sermon.

As the service concluded, Rosemary turned to Amanda. "I'm so grateful you invited me to join you. I needed this. Thank you."

Amanda squeezed her hand. "I'm so glad you came. And you, too, Tug."

"High time, wasn't it?" Tug looked a little sheepish, but he glanced at Rosemary. "Thank *you* for inviting *me.*"

"It was really good," Rosemary said as Paul, Amanda, Hailey, and Jesse rose and began edging out of the long pew.

Rosemary followed them and appreciated the kind touch of Tug's hand on her arm.

"You know how to rescue a man," he whispered into her ear.

She smiled. *Oh, honey, you haven't seen anything yet.* She kept the snarky remark to herself, because she believed she could help him. She felt it was her calling, the reason she'd landed in this little town. Not to renew a high school friendship.

Amanda and Paul stopped to chat with the pastor.

As Rosemary and Tug stood waiting, the feeling of community surrounded her like a warm blanket.

When she stepped in front of the pastor, his face pulled into a welcoming grin. "Thank you for coming. A new face. It's so nice to have you with us. You're a friend of Tug's?"

"A new friend," she said.

The pastor looked at Tug with compassion. "I'm so glad to see you here this morning. Welcome back, my friend."

"Thanks, Charles. I'll get with the girls and get back on the volunteer list. It's been too long."

"We are in the middle of planning a pancake night." The pastor truly looked delighted. "We'd love to have you at the helm of that."

"Write me in," Tug said. "You've got my number."

"I sure do." He patted Tug on the back as they walked out.

Tug waved to Paul across the parking lot, then held the van door for Rosemary to get in.

"Good way to start the day," he said, backing out. "It occurred to me while we were sitting there like old pals that you told me your last name, but I'm not sure I even know how to say it properly."

"It's Palakiko," she said, then spelled it out for him.

He repeated it perfectly.

"Very good," she said. "Were you ever married?"

"No, which is why I never had kids. I'm old-fashioned that way. I feel like a grandpa to Amanda's kids, though. I love having them in my life. They have been such a breath of fresh air for this old man."

"Wow. So, you're a confirmed bachelor?"

"I guess you could say that." He repositioned his hands on the steering wheel. "Not on purpose."

"I loved being married. Having someone to go through

things together. Uplifting each other when times got tough. And we had our share of tough times over the years, but I still believe marriage is wonderful."

"I'm sure it is with the right partner," he said softly.

"You just never found your person?"

"I did, but her heart was somewhere else." There was a lot of emotion in that statement.

Her heart ached for him. "I'm sorry."

"Don't be. It all happens as it's supposed to. I believe that, even though I don't always like it."

She nodded and looked out the window, enjoying the scenery on the short ride back to his house.

He pulled into the driveway and parked next to the pile of sand that led to his front door.

They got out of the van, and Rosemary kicked off her shoes. "I think it'll be easier to climb up with no shoes on."

Tug laughed. "Come on. I have another set of stairs over here. It'll be easier."

"What? You made me walk over your truck just to be funny last time, didn't you?"

"It was adventurous."

"I did sort of like it, but it wouldn't be a fun climb in heels, and especially not on grocery day."

"This way, my friend."

She gave him a playful look and caught up to him as they rounded the other side of the house. The stairs on this side were in perfect condition, and she noted the cute garage, which had a few old surfboards mounted to the side of it.

Inside, the house was bright and cheerful.

The aroma of sausage hung in the air.

"You started without me?" Rosemary asked. "It smells like heaven. Someone should make a candle that smells like that."

"I went ahead and cooked up a huge batch of sausage to save

us time with the lasagna. Plus, I wanted to have some to make sausage gravy this week. It's one of my favorites. Do you like sausage gravy over biscuits?"

"Sounds heavy."

"Southern. Comfort food. You've got to try it."

"Do you make good biscuits? I never mastered them."

"The best. Golden brown with a crispness to the top and soft as cotton in the middle. People love my biscuits."

"From what I've heard, they love everything you make."

"Good thing. Would've been hard to run a diner if I couldn't cook."

"True."

The two of them started laying out ingredients across the huge butcher block. Then Tug set her up with onions to chop while he got out huge casserole dishes.

"How much are we going to make?"

"It's my special recipe. Might as well treat others to some."

"And is it just me, or does lasagna taste even better when you take it out of the freezer and reheat it?" Rosemary kept chopping, hoping her homegrown skills were passable.

"So good. Hey, you're doing a good job there."

"I've had a few years of experience."

"Haven't we all, by now?"

The chatter was playful and easy as they talked about little things and worked on the lasagna together.

He asked her if she liked dessert, and she went on and on about her favorite spice cake recipe. "That came out really braggy. I did not mean it like that, but I know you'd love it. I'll make you one. Or my pound cake. It's amazing with the Hawaiian glaze."

"I'd like that. Or you can give me the recipe, and I'll make it for you."

"Wait a minute, mister. We have not known each other long

enough to share recipes. That's a very special honor. You know you can't just give a recipe to any old body. In fact, come to think of it, I'm not sure I've ever shared that recipe with anyone. Not even my daughter."

"Wow. You are serious about that."

"I am."

"Interesting. I'm not sure I've ever kept a recipe to myself. I always give all my secrets away, and people accuse me of not giving them the whole recipe, saying it doesn't taste the same. I think it's just all the years of seasoning in those old pots and pans I use. Or used."

"That's sneaky."

"No. I give them the recipe. Every ingredient," he said. "I'd never trick someone like that."

"No. I wouldn't expect that you would." And she liked that about him.

Rosemary started lining the pan with strips of lasagna noodles.

"I was told you used to have shells that people found on the beach in the diner. The ones with messages?"

He nodded. "True."

"That's so interesting." She wasn't sure if she should tell him about the shell she'd found, but why hold back? He might know something about it. "You know when you saw me on the street the other day? As soon as you pulled away, I found one of those special shells."

He laid down his spoon. "One with a message in it?"

"Yes."

"Really? What did it say?"

"It said, 'Life takes you to unexpected places. Trust the light to lead you home.' I asked Amanda about it, because I wondered if it might have been one of the shells that were in your diner, but she said she'd never seen it before."

"I don't recognize that saying either."

"How can I determine if it was intended for me and not misplaced by someone else?"

"You found it," Tug said. "Then it was meant for you."

"That's what Amanda said, too, but how?"

"Who knows?" Tug smiled. "It's just the way it always works."

"Funny it would be so far from the beach."

Tug didn't seem surprised. "They have been found all over this town over the years. So, what do you think? About the message?"

"I think it was timely."

"They always are."

Chapter Twenty-Five

ROSEMARY AND TUG FINISHED ASSEMBLING THE LASAGNA, and he carried the heavy casserole pans over to the oven and slid them inside.

They started tidying the kitchen, and Rosemary washed the pots, pans, and bowls while Tug dried them and set them on a towel on the counter.

"You're an excellent helper," he said.

"Thank you. It's nice being in the kitchen again."

"You don't cook at your daughter's?"

"No. They are really finicky and prefer to order in." She shrugged. "I think it's a waste of money, but it's not my household." She turned and folded the dish towels neatly on the counter as Tug made quick work of putting things away.

He dropped wooden spoons and other large utensils in a drawer and then paused. He lifted something from the drawer and turned toward her. "Did you put this in here?"

He held a shell in his hand. Puzzled, she stepped closer to look. "No. That's not the one I found. Mine is much larger. Is there a message in it?"

"I just opened the drawer and here it was."

"Interesting. May I?" She held out her hand, and he placed it in her palm. She pulled her glasses from the top of her head and eyed it closely. The message in his shell was specifically for him, by name.

Don't look back.
Tug, open and lift your heart in this final season.

"That's a timely message." She handed it back to him with aplomb.

"You really didn't bring this with you?"

"I most certainly did not. It would be inappropriate to imitate a shell like that. Wouldn't that be mocking something that is special to this town?"

"I don't know." His voice was quiet, his gaze locked on her. "I . . ."

"Are you okay?"

He sat on a stool. "Sort of blown away."

"Is that a hurricane joke?"

"No. Well, yes, but not on purpose." He smiled. "You see, only one other person knows this, but . . ."

She had to fight the urge to prompt him to go on.

"These shells, they have been a mystery on Whelk's Island for years. People swear they show up at the perfect time in their lives."

"Right. That's what Amanda told me too. That's very special."

"Like the one you found. Did it touch you in a special way?"

"Curiosity more at first, but yes, as I held on to it and the phrase rolled over in my mind, it resonated with me." It had taken hold of her, giving her the motivation to seek answers. "Deeply."

"Right. My friend Maeve. The last time I spoke to her, she admitted she'd been making them all those years. Now, she denied planting them. Some she'd thrown in the ocean, only for them to resurface at the appropriate time for the right person."

"Wow. I can't imagine how it must have felt to hear about their discovery. To be a tool, the hands and feet . . ."

"I'd wondered all along if she had a hand in it. She was a wise woman, so caring, so real. To the point, and a pistol for sure!"

"She was very dear to you."

He pressed a hand to his heart. "She was my everything."

Rosemary stepped over and hugged him. "Tug, I'm so sorry I didn't get to meet her. She touched a lot of people in this town."

"How could Maeve have left this for me? And how has it been here all along for me to find it today?"

She shrugged.

"I'm in and out of these drawers all the time. It doesn't make sense."

"Honey, there are a million things each day I can't figure out, but I'll say this: When it's something as special as that, you don't question it. Hold it dear, let it steer your path."

He sat there looking at her sort of blankly and then drew in a deep breath.

"This brings the pastor's words back to me," she continued. "Do you remember when he was talking about trusting there is light when things seem the darkest? We both sort of looked at each other at that moment."

"Yes, it was like he was talking to me," Tug said flatly.

She found that humorous. "Well, I thought he was talking to me."

"How do they do that?"

"I have no idea. Happens to me a lot. I guess I have a lot of lessons to learn."

"Or you're just very in tune," he said. "You are a wise woman. I gathered that pretty quickly when we first met."

"You did? Thanks. That's really nice of you to say."

"Not nice. Just an honest observation." He paused, looking down. "I hope you take this as a compliment, but you remind me of Maeve. Although, really, you're nothing like her. Well, not nothing like her. That doesn't even make sense. I meant it better than it came out." He glanced her way, the hesitation in his voice mirrored in his expression, as if he worried about her response to what he'd said.

"I'll take it as a compliment. Thank you." She wanted to ask him what he thought the words in the shell meant, but sometimes it was better to let things happen on their own rather than push. Something she wasn't all that good at.

Tug kept staring at the shell, then finally slid it back into the drawer where he'd found it.

The air was thick with the aroma of spices, but even the heavenly scent couldn't distract from the look on Tug's face. "Tug, you seem upset. Do you need some time? Would you like me to leave?"

"No. I'm okay. A little befuddled by it, but I'd really prefer you stayed."

"Good. I'm enjoying myself. So, change of subject?"

"Absolutely."

"Any word from the insurance carrier about the diner?"

"Yes. They started the assessment yesterday. Not sure how long it will take since they are working in disaster mode and all, but at least they are making progress."

"Well, that's good news."

"It is. Still don't know what I'm going to do, though."

"Well, you have some time. This is a lot to take in. You'll figure it out." Tug captivated Rosemary. The sadness in his blue eyes compelled her to draw closer, and she wanted to help him through this difficult time.

With no one in her life and no timetable, why not stay awhile and help a new friend in need? *Is this why I was meant to be here on Whelk's Island? Is this my purpose?*

There was no divine answer hanging in the air, but she knew one thing. She hadn't felt this alive in a long time. Not since Kai passed, and maybe it was because, for once, she wasn't the one with the biggest problem. Whatever it was, she liked the way it felt. Being near the water had brought her some peace that living inland hadn't.

Maybe helping Tug would help her find light to her own path. Do unto others and all that. It made sense.

"I was thinking," she said. "Our tomorrows may look nothing like our yesterdays, but God has a plan, and if we embrace each day for what it offers, we find that both are equally beautiful. I feel like even though things haven't been going well for me, I've been gathering these tiny glimmering moments of hope, memories so fond I never want to let go of them. Somehow I suppose it all braids together to increase our empathy, awareness, and understanding. We are wiser for each of those hard steps."

"Everything looks dark. I feel hopelessly lost," Tug said. "What Pastor Qualls was saying today, it really spoke to me."

"He lights our way, even in the dark. You are not lost. You just have to do your part."

"What's my part? There's nothing left. You've seen where the diner was. There's nothing."

"It's okay if you're too tired to reopen. You don't have to do what you've always done. You've had a good run, and I'm pretty sure you'll get enough money selling oceanfront property to see you well into your golden years."

"I've never thought of not owning the diner." He sat there contemplating. "You know we're *in* the golden years, right?"

"Guess we are, aren't we?"

"I've always worked. I don't know what I'd do if I didn't. I sure can't sit around here doing nothing."

"No one says you can't continue to have the diner. You can rebuild and do things as you always have. Or I can help you explore some ideas. I'm a wonderful planner. Remember that bucket list I was talking about? I told you I'd come in handy."

"The bucket list again. I'm not a material guy."

"Yes, but this should be right up your alley. A bucket list is not about things, it's about moments. I picked up some brochures from the travel agent. I've got them in my purse. We're gonna work on that together, because, Tug, that diner is just coordinates on a map." She lifted a hand. "I know it meant the world to you, but you are so much more than that building. There is so much light left in you, Tug. I see it in your eyes, and if there's one thing I'm confident in, it's that God will light the way."

"I don't know where you're seeing that." He held out his arms and looked at himself. "Doesn't feel like there's much left to me. I've been praying. I just don't see it."

She got up, pulled the brochures out of her purse, and laid them on the butcher block in front of him.

"Look at these. Just let your mind go."

Tug looked at her but didn't argue. He picked up a pair of readers and put them on. Leaning in, he shuffled through the brochures, pausing on a few before turning to the next. Some of them definitely intrigued him.

"You could do some of those things, you know."

He took in a breath. "Perhaps. Well, if I was just dreaming, this one looks appealing." His eyes remained trained on a picture of a man in a stream fly-fishing, surrounded by mountains and the most serene waters.

The way his smile curled at the corners of his lips sent a flutter through her chest. "I want someone to look at me the way you're looking at that travel brochure," she teased.

He lifted his chin in surprise. "I think I look at you with so much more than that. This brochure might give my hopes for adventure wings, but you? You bring out butterflies and feelings I haven't had in a long time. When I look at you, I see someone incredible."

"You do?"

"Yes, ma'am, I do. But things are a mess in my life right now. I've got nothing to offer." He took off his readers and set them aside. "I'm not as fun or as put together as you deserve."

"You are plenty fun, Tug. I love spending time with you."

"Maybe I just need time."

"I know, I know. I've been where you are. Sure, you may not have been married to Maeve, but losing her and that special bond you two had is like losing a spouse. It's impossible to prepare a heart for that. You don't even want to hear what a mess I was when I lost Kai, but I have a pretty good idea how you're feeling about losing her. And losing the diner, too, is right up there with it. You are a good man, Tug. There is so much ahead of you."

He sat quietly, but he wasn't arguing the point either.

Rosemary saw that as a win. "How about you walk me down this beach you know so well?" she suggested. "Let's just listen to nature. The waves, the wind, the rustling sea oats, and even those pesky seagulls The Wife seems to love to imitate, and I promise I won't say another word."

He sputtered, making that noise you hear when someone lets go of a balloon and it flies across the room. "You can't promise that."

"You're probably right. I can if you tape my mouth shut." She pressed her lips together. "I won't say anything until we get back. I can do that. It'll be nice and grounding."

"I think it'll be more fun to watch you try to stay quiet."

She playfully slugged him in the belly, which was surprisingly firm.

"I deserved that." Tug laughed. He stood and reached for her hand. "You are an absolute delight. Come on. I'd love to show you my beach, but there's not quite enough time left on the timer to go."

Had that much time already passed? "Only ten more minutes."

"Let's set the table, and then it should be done. Would you like to go out on the beach for a little bit and eat when we get back?"

"Sounds good."

"I hope you don't mind, but I invited Paul and Amanda and the kids to join us for supper."

"Mind? I'm thrilled. Lord knows we made enough to feed all of us and then some."

"I didn't think you'd mind."

"Get me started setting the table. Just tell me which plates, and I can handle the rest."

He steered her to a set of old china in the hutch. It was a sweet feminine pattern, stacked next to some lovely milk glass and a very ornate silver setting.

"You have some beautiful things in here."

"They were my mom's. She loved pretty things."

The love with which he spoke about his mother touched her.

The timer sounded from the kitchen. "I've got this under control," she said. "You get the lasagna."

She finished setting the table. "The aroma is mouthwatering," she called out.

"Comfort food."

"Can never have too much of that."

"You got that right. Come on. Let's take that walk," Tug said, entering the dining room.

"When are they supposed to be here?" she asked.

"I texted Paul. They'll let themselves in and entertain The Wife if we're not back when they get here. We can take our time, or not, if it's killing you to be quiet."

"I think I might surprise you." They left their shoes on the stairs, rolled up their pant legs, and walked over to the beach.

Chapter Twenty-Six

"HEY, TUG! WE'RE HERE." THE KIDS RACED PAST AMANDA straight to the deck to see The Wife.

"Doesn't look like he's here." Amanda turned to Paul. "That's weird."

"He texted me he and Rosemary were going for a walk on the beach. They'll probably be back shortly. Man, it smells great in here."

"It does. But hey, this little walk with Rosemary. Think there's some spark there?"

Paul shrugged. "Never know."

"That would be so great. I love her. And Tug needs someone right now."

"He's got us. Don't go playing matchmaker."

"I'm not. I'm just a little hopeful. It wouldn't break my heart for Rosemary to stick around."

"Well, the only one I'm worried about sticking around is you." He took both of her hands in his and kissed the tip of her nose. "I love you, Amanda. You mean the world to me."

"I love you too." The kids were singing on the balcony, no doubt trying to get The Wife to join in. "And Hailey and Jesse do too. I'm so thankful you are in our lives."

"Me too."

"They are so wound up tonight. What is wrong with them?" She headed to the back door. "What is going on out here?"

They burst into a fit of giggles. "We're trying to teach The Wife a song."

Hailey was out of breath from laughing. "She loves our singing. She won't sing with us, but she's dancing. Watch!" They started singing again, and sure enough, The Wife swung her head from side to side and stretched out her wings.

"Oh my goodness." Amanda looked at Paul with a grimace. "Tug is going to kill them."

"Naw, he'll think it's funny too. That bird has a mind of her own."

"True."

"Hey!" Rosemary was waving from the beach.

"Looks promising," Amanda whispered to Paul. Tug and Rosemary weren't holding hands, but they were both smiling and windblown. She waved. "I hope you're hungry, because it smells great in here."

They climbed the beach stairs to the deck. Tug threw his arms wide. "Hey, you two!" The kids ran into his arms.

Amanda loved the feeling of family they had with him. If only her parents were as warm and welcoming.

Jesse broke away from Tug and ran to Rosemary and hugged her, then stepped back and did a proper bow. "Madam. It is lovely to see you again." He must have been practicing his British accent with Hailey, because it was pretty convincing.

"Indeed," Rosemary said with a wink.

"Did y'all have a nice walk?" Amanda couldn't help feeling excited about these two spending time together, but Paul nudged her, clearly warning against pushing.

"It was so nice. This beach is like heaven. I feel like the old me again with sand beneath my feet. I guess you can take the girl out of Hawaii, but she needs sand under her feet!"

"Probably. I can't imagine not living at the beach now, and we've only been here a couple of years."

"Come on, folks. We set the table before we went for our walk. All I have to do is get the garlic bread broiled, and we're ready to eat."

"What are we having?" Jesse asked.

"Lasagna," Rosemary said. "And I helped make it."

"Good." He rubbed his stomach. "All of this space is ready to be filled up."

"He's so cute," Rosemary said as they walked inside. "I'm going to help Tug. What do y'all want to drink?"

"Water for my crew," Amanda said.

"I'm going to pour myself a glass of sweet tea," Paul said.

Hailey walked into the kitchen with her nose in the air. "I love garlic."

"My kind of gal," Rosemary said. "It's almost ready." She carried the lasagna to the table and started serving up healthy pieces of the meaty dish.

Tug came in with a long wooden bread bowl filled with the hot, buttery bread. "Who's ready to eat?"

"Me!" Jesse shot his hand in the air. "Mmm."

Tug flipped a piece onto his plate before setting the bowl on the table.

Hailey and Jesse sang the blessing, and everyone dug in. The conversation was easy and upbeat. Amanda was so glad to see Tug not looking worried for at least a moment.

"So, I've been thinking, Amanda," Tug said. "I'd like to make you a really sweet deal on the diner property to replace your shop."

"I don't need that kind of location for my little herbal salt business. Even if Salt of the Earth grew by leaps and bounds, I see it as more of an online business than a storefront. As long as the kids are in school, I wouldn't want to be tied to store hours."

"I'd rather it be a warehouse for you and the kids' future than end up a parking lot or something."

"Is that a possibility?"

He put his elbows on the table and sighed. "Well, I don't know. I was going through my mail and there was a letter. It was rather vague in content, but someone is interested in making an offer on my property."

"That's horrible. Vultures. The town doesn't even have all the power back on from the storm, and they are already circling, looking for easy pickings?" Amanda couldn't believe it.

"Well, don't be surprised if one comes to you as well," Tug said. "It was probably a mass mailing."

"Was it a decent offer?" Paul asked.

"It was more of an inquiry. I haven't called."

"Will you?" Paul asked.

"I don't know. Still thinking things through," Tug answered, but he was looking at Rosemary.

"Couldn't hurt to hear the offer," Paul said. "That property is probably worth more than you could spend in a lifetime." He glanced at Amanda, then focused on Tug. "I don't know if you aware that Amanda and I are moving and expanding her business into Paws. We've been talking about the possibility of you and Amanda partnering. She needs the help. You have the experience. Then you can sell your land and sit on a big pile of money for retirement. Roll in it if you want."

"Rolling in money." Jesse smacked his forehead. "I want to throw it in the air!"

"I guess that's something to think about," Tug said. "It would mean I wouldn't even have to clean up. They'd take it as is. Don't take this personal, Amanda. It's not that I don't want to partner with you. I'll be there to help you no matter how you decide to expand, but I just don't know that I'd want to be anything more than a silent partner."

"What will you do?" Amanda couldn't picture him sitting on the deck watching waves all day.

"I honestly have no idea at this point, but I have a new friend here who thinks she can help me figure it out." He grinned at Rosemary.

Amanda reached for Rosemary's hand and gave it a squeeze. "You know we're not going to want you to leave. You fit right in."

"I love it here, but Kathleen will be back soon, and as much fun as it was to reconnect with her, I don't want to take advantage of her. It's time for me to go."

"Well, you know I have two spare bedrooms," Amanda said. "Like I said before, you are welcome to come stay with us."

"Oh my gosh, it would be so fun to have you stay!" Hailey slid into the conversation. "Please?"

"That is a generous offer, but I'm sure the last thing you need is an old lady under your roof."

"Actually, it's exactly what we need," Hailey said. "You remind us of all the fun times with Maeve. We miss her, but with you around, it's better."

"It is, isn't it?" Amanda looked into her sweet daughter's eyes. "Well, the offer stands. You could stay for a weekend, a week, or a month."

"If you're good with plants, you can help us replant Mom's herbs for the salts," Hailey added. "They are very important to her business."

"I happen to be amazing with plants. I lived on a farm in Hawaii. I mean, macadamia tree farming isn't quite herbs, but I think I could manage."

Hailey clasped her hands under her chin. "Please come stay with us for a little while."

Tug tilted his head, looking as if he sort of liked the idea.

Rosemary got up to get something from the kitchen, and Amanda excused herself and followed her.

"I hope we didn't make you feel awkward, but we'd really enjoy having you stay with us for a while. You're like part of the family."

Rosemary blinked back the threat of a tear. "I really feel like family here. I'd love to come stay but not for too long."

"There's no such thing as too long for us. Now for you, my kids may have you running off in the middle of the night to get some peace!"

"I don't think so."

"We need you, and so does Tug. I'm so relieved Tug is talking to you about all of this. I've been so worried about him."

"He's a good man," Rosemary whispered, glancing toward the other room.

"He is, and it's been a hard year for all of us since Maeve passed, especially for him."

"He told me about that. He's really struggling with what to do about the diner. It's hard as we get older to keep up the pace. It's different when it's the familiar routine, but starting over? I get it. I understand his reservations."

"Well, thank you for caring enough to try to help him."

"Honestly, Amanda, I'm getting as much out of it as I'm giving. I've been having some reality checks too. It's been a real blessing for me ending up here."

"For us too." Amanda squeezed her hand.

Chapter Twenty-Seven

AFTER DINNER, AMANDA AND ROSEMARY CLEARED ALL THE dishes. "We've got this, Tug. Y'all go out on the deck with the kids. We'll be there in a heartbeat."

"Not going to argue with good help." Tug pushed his chair back from the table.

"I'll wash and you can dry," Amanda said to Rosemary as they walked to the kitchen.

They talked as the dishes clattered in the sink. "I can't wait to try your herb salts," Rosemary said. "You're going to have to put together a selection of them for me to try."

"Absolutely. Maybe you can help me put together some new recipes."

"Count me in."

When Amanda and Rosemary stepped onto the deck to join the others, the water shimmered under the moonlight.

"It looks beautiful," Rosemary said. "So peaceful."

"It's never peaceful with them around," Amanda teased as Hailey and Jesse talked back and forth with The Wife.

"Even that's nice. Children's laughter is soup for the soul. It's amazing to think I didn't know any of you before the storm." A gentle breeze pushed Rosemary's hair. "Being here reminds me of back home."

Hailey sidled up to them like one of the girls.

"In Hawaii?" Amanda could see that Rosemary missed it. "I've never been to the islands. Is it as beautiful as it looks in movies?"

"More so. It's the people, too, but you have that part here. The community and kindness."

"Wow. I like the big pretty flowers," Hailey said.

"Hibiscus."

"And coconuts. Did you ever drink out of one?"

"Many times, and the pineapples are so different there. It's so much better than the canned stuff."

Hailey was wild-eyed impressed. "So cool. Can you hula dance?" She wiggled her hips and waved her arms with exuberance.

"Well done, gal. Yes, I have practiced the art of hula for years. I was a young bride when I moved to Hawaii. You can't live fifty years on the islands and not become quite proficient at it."

"Now, I'd like to see that," Tug interjected.

"Eavesdropper." Rosemary popped a hip and flashed a flirty look in his direction. "Don't tempt me with a good time, sir."

Tug guffawed, and Hailey danced with excitement. "Please teach us!"

"Really?"

"Yes! Me too," Jesse said.

"Sure, I can absolutely teach you." Rosemary exuded confidence. "It's easy. Tug, can you help us with some music?"

"Probably not. Don't think I have many Hawaiian songs on my phone. Can you hula to Willie Nelson?"

"I can hula to anything, but why don't you do a search and play the hukilau? That's a fun dance."

He looked at her with his jaw slack and eyes wide.

She spelled it out for him.

"She's a mind reader too." He plunked the letters into his phone. "More vowels than consonants. Got it."

"Thanks, Tug. I'll let you know when to play it. Come on. Let's get down in the sand. It'll be easier to move your feet." They took the stairs from the balcony to the beach. "The hula tells a story."

Amanda leaned over the railing, watching as Rosemary, Hailey, and Jesse gathered in a circle in the sand below.

"Now, the hukilau is a special dance that celebrates the fishing traditions of Hawaii." Rosemary's voice was patient, and the kids leaned in, eager to learn. "We'll start by pretending to cast our nets into the ocean." She showed them the movement, and they followed.

Rosemary explained the significance of hula, not just as a dance but as a form of storytelling deeply rooted in Hawaiian culture. She spoke of the graceful movements symbolizing the natural elements—the swaying of the palms, the flowing of the ocean, and the gentle breeze that whispered through the air.

"Wait for me," Amanda said as she ran down the stairs. "I want to learn too."

She giggled at Paul and Tug gawking from above. Paul wolf-whistled, making her cheeks warm.

With a smile on her face and a twinkle in her eyes, Rosemary demonstrated the basic steps, her heels lifting and hips swaying.

"Perfect. You've got it. Okay, we'll try it with music." Rosemary lifted her hand in a thumbs-up gesture. "Music, Tug!"

Tug pressed the button and turned his phone toward them on the beach.

"Here we go." Rosemary danced in perfect rhythm with the music from Tug's iPhone. "Come on. Let go of your inhibitions and embrace the fluidity of the dance. You're telling a story. Be convincing."

With laughter filling the air, Rosemary guided them through the steps, patiently correcting their movements and encouraging them.

Amanda hadn't had this much fun dancing since she did line dancing years ago. "Follow along, Hailey and Jesse."

Despite their initial hesitations, soon they found themselves lost in the dance's rhythm, their movements becoming more proficient with each passing moment.

Hailey stretched out her arms as if perfectly casting an invisible fishing net, her feet moving in time with the music.

"Yes, Hailey!"

Jesse's face scrunched in determination.

"Jesse, you're moving just like the ocean waves," Rosemary told him. "Wonderful."

Tug put the song on replay and began clapping along as they danced again.

Jesse had a fit of the giggles. "Come dance, Paul!"

"Play it again, Tug. We're getting it."

Tug and Paul walked down to the beach.

The music swelled, and though their movements through the hukilau weren't completely synchronized, they were joyful. Laughter mingled with the ukulele music.

"That's enough." Rosemary waved frantically for Tug to stop. "Whew!"

"That's an intense workout," Amanda admitted. "I swear I don't get this good a workout in the gym."

"Oh, it's great for the body and the soul. I may have actually worked off that garlic bread," Rosemary said.

"Doubtful, but it's fun to think so."

"I could get used to watching you hula," Paul said. "I might request dinner and a show more often."

She swatted at him playfully.

"We'll put on a show," Jesse said.

"Not exactly what I was going for," Paul whispered to her.

Amanda delighted in the attention.

"Who is ready for dessert?" Rosemary asked. "I brought a

special dessert, and I didn't even know you were coming over. I think you'll like it."

The kids screamed out a big yes, and Rosemary started for the stairs.

"Hey, wait. Before we go up," Paul said, "I wanted to say something."

Rosemary stopped and turned, and Tug walked over to her.

Amanda noticed the kids clinging to Paul and acting goofy. The last thing they needed was more sugar. She'd never get them into bed.

Was something wrong?

"Amanda?" Paul almost choked on the word. He had the oddest look on his face.

"Paul?" She reflected his look.

Jesse started giggling.

The three of them stood with their hands in their pockets, looking at her. It reminded her of the see-no-evil monkeys lined up.

"What?" She checked her skirt to be sure she hadn't hiked it into her waistband or something.

"I'm wondering. Well, I already talked to these guys about it, and . . ." Paul moved closer to her. "Amanda, I never want to be apart again. I love you. I love Hailey and Jesse." He looked over at the beaming children, almost shaking with excitement. "Those two, they are every good thing about you and Jack. They are so special. I want to be important in their lives."

"You are. You were there when they were born."

"I want to be with you all every day. The good ones and . . . Well, we only have good ones, but we would make it through the bad ones too. We are so good together, and you know . . . I've always loved you. From that first dance, before you ever married Jack, I knew you were the one."

"You just liked twirling me," she teased.

"Still do." Paul slowly dropped to one knee and pulled the ring box from his pocket. "What I'm trying to say is, will you marry me, Amanda?"

"Marry?" Her chest heaved, and she stood there, stunned. "Um, I . . ." She tented her hands over her nose and mouth, her fingers redirecting the tears trickling from her eyes. Her heart wanted to scream yes, but she never thought she'd ever get married again. "Hailey? Jesse?"

"We said yes!" They pulled their hands out of their pockets. Each held up a shell. *YES* in bright pink with a flower on Hailey's, and Jesse's, a little less perfect but still legible, read *YES* in his favorite color, blue.

She knelt and pulled Hailey and Jesse into a hug. "You really think so?"

"Definitely," Hailey said. "We missed him so much when we went away. And when you get married, he can live with us like Daddy did, and we can be together always."

She looked at Tug. "You knew?"

He shrugged, neither confirming nor denying, but he knew.

She stood and turned to Paul, who was still down on one knee and looking not only awkward but a little worried. She sat on his knee and hugged his neck.

Paul swallowed hard. "Everyone here says yes, and I called and talked to your dad. He and your mom gave us their blessing."

"I love you, Paul. I would be honored to marry you." She kissed him on the cheek, then nodded toward the kids. "For us to be your family."

"Yes!" Hailey and Jesse shouted.

"Forever." She kissed Paul full on the lips like they never had in front of the kids, who let out a whoop before they burst into giggles.

"We're already family," Hailey insisted, "but now everyone will know."

Rosemary was crying, and Tug wrapped a comforting arm around her.

"Thank you." Paul patted his heart. "I'm the happiest man on earth."

"In the galaxy," Jesse added.

"Exactly, Jesse. You're so right! Happiest in the whole galaxy!" Paul took the ring from the box, and whether it was his shaking hand or hers, it was nearly impossible to get the ring on her finger.

Finally, she helped get it in place and splayed her fingers, flashing the ring in Rosemary's direction.

"Oh my gosh, Paul. Thank you. I'm so happy. Yes, yes, yes." She squeezed him tight. "My ring fits perfectly. It's beautiful. We're beautiful together. Thank you."

"I love you, Amanda. I plan to spend every day the rest of our lives making you all happy."

"And we're going to do the same."

The kids danced around and cheered. Jesse broke out into a hukilau solo that had everyone laughing. Her little life of the party loved being the center of attention.

"Well, I guess we're having celebratory dessert now!" Rosemary said.

"Kids, brush the sand from your feet before you go back in the house," Amanda reminded them. She wasn't ready to get up from Paul's knee just yet. "I can't believe this. I just want to sit here forever and hug you."

"I'd let you."

The kids raced up the stairs behind Tug and Rosemary.

"But I think we need to go up, or I'm going to be tempted to steal you all night," Paul said.

"Yeah, we'd better." She didn't care if the kids ate all the dessert now, because this was so exciting that no one was going to sleep.

"Why don't you let Hailey and Jesse stay here with me tonight?" Tug said while they ate dessert. "You two can have the rest of the evening to celebrate."

"Amanda?" Paul looked so hopeful.

"Heck, yeah." Amanda flashed Tug an "are you crazy" look. "You think you can handle them after all this excitement and sugar?"

"It'll be my pleasure." He turned to Rosemary and pointed to the upstairs. "I've got a real guest room if you want to stay and play cards all night with these two."

"How can I say no to that?" she said. "Besides, you're my ride."

"I'd be happy to take you home. You don't have to hang out with us."

"I haven't been to a slumber party in years," she said. "Oh, but I need to go check on the cat at Kathleen's."

"I think we can make that little road trip. You up for it?" Tug directed the question to the kids.

"We get to meet the cat?" Jesse asked.

"Sure, but she's kind of shy at first," Rosemary said.

"Let's get rid of the grown-ups. Then we will make our road trip." Tug looked over the moon.

"Wonderful," Rosemary said. "Hailey and I will do something girly. Count me in."

"Yes!" Hailey bounced to her feet. "More hula dancing."

"We might put on a show," Rosemary said.

"This is the best night." Amanda jumped up. "Quick, Paul. Let's escape before they realize what they're in for."

Hailey set her hands on her hips. "Mom, you know we'll be good. I'll be sure of it."

Amanda walked over and hugged her daughter's head to her

chest. "Honey, I know you will." She leaned down. "You're one hundred percent sure you're okay with this engagement?" She looked into Hailey's eyes.

Hailey smiled. "Two hundred percent, Mom," she whispered with her back to everyone else. "Daddy would be so happy for us."

"I think you're right, honey. You are so wise and wonderful. Do you have any idea how proud I am of you?"

"I love you, Mom. I'm proud of you too."

Amanda could barely see her way down the steps through the joyful tears streaming down her face. If it weren't for Paul's cautious hand guiding her, she would surely tumble. "I can't believe this."

"I've been wanting to ask for so long," he admitted. "After you left for the evacuation, I knew I couldn't wait any longer, but I was so afraid you would say no."

He stopped at the truck and kissed her, his thumb outlining her cheek.

Breathless, she said, "I could never say no to you."

Chapter Twenty-Eight

ROSEMARY WOKE TO THE SMELL OF BACON, AND AS NICE AS it was, it sent her straight to her feet, disoriented for a moment.

Laughter, the most precious and infectious sound, rose from downstairs.

She smiled and stretched, realizing where she was. Sunday had been a miraculously special day. Church, the time with Tug, Amanda and Paul's engagement, and playing with the children into the wee hours, including the wildest game of crazy eights followed by a talent show that went on for an hour. Tug had a job getting the kids to slow down enough to close their eyes. Exhausting but wonderful.

She didn't know what time it was, but she'd slept like a rock.

She stretched again, a little sore from the hula dancing, but a spark of vitality had fired up inside her.

The last twenty-four hours may have been the most fulfilling she'd experienced in years.

She quickly got dressed and went downstairs.

Everyone was there, including Amanda and Paul.

"Good morning," Rosemary said. "I'm sorry. I must've overslept."

"They'll wear ya out," Amanda said.

"Let me get you some coffee," Tug offered.

"Thanks." Rosemary walked over and hugged Jesse and Hailey. "I loved every single second of last night."

"Mom, we had so much fun," Hailey said.

"I'm sure you did. I'm glad," Amanda said. "Rosemary and Tug, thank you so much for your nice little engagement gift to Paul and me. We danced under the stars and talked about wedding plans." She blushed, leaning against Paul's chest. "I still feel like someone needs to pinch me."

Jesse leaped to her service.

Amanda wiggled away. "No. Jesse, I was joking." But it was too late because Hailey was in on it and now Paul was tickling her.

"Young love," Tug said, sliding a cup of coffee toward Rosemary.

"You read my mind," Rosemary said.

He winked. "They seem even closer. I don't even know how that's possible, but it will continue to grow and last forever, right in front of our eyes."

"It's so nice to be a teensy-weensy part of something so precious," she said.

"Hey, Tug. Amanda and I were talking about the space at Paws last night too. Why don't y'all come over later and check it out?"

"Why would you be talking about that when you had celebrating to do?" Tug looked at him like he was crazy.

"It's part of our future," Paul said, then seemed to realize what Tug was hinting at. "Well, it wasn't the *first* thing on our agenda." With a tilt of his head, he and Tug moved to the side to talk.

Rosemary's phone buzzed just as she took a sip of her coffee. She grabbed it from the table. It was Nina. She got up and slid out of the room so she could speak privately.

"Hello."

"Mom? Thank goodness. I was starting to get worried."

"I'm fine," Rosemary said.

"I know, I know. I just wanted to hear your voice."

"I'm on top of the world." She didn't even mind the interruption. "I'm doing great. It's been really nice to be busy and help others."

"You're not bored down there?"

"Bored. No. Oh gosh, far from it. It's a great little town full of wonderful people." Rosemary stood in front of the sliding doors overlooking the beach. The sun twinkled on the water, and the waves swept over the sand slowly this morning. It was so calming.

Tug and Paul walked through the room, talking, before they realized she was on the phone. "Sorry," Tug said as he led Paul out onto the deck.

"Who was that?" Nina asked.

"Friends."

"*Boy*friends?"

Rosemary didn't appreciate Nina's tone. "Uh, no. They are not boys. Those were men."

"Mother!"

"What?"

"Are you having some sort of midlife crisis?"

"No, I am not. I'm way past midlife, but I'm not dead either. I'm enjoying my time here at the beach with friends. Did you call for a reason?"

"I don't like this one bit. You have to be careful. Dating isn't like it was back when you were dating. Oh gosh, Mom, that was like fifty years ago. There are all kinds of scams a woman has to be careful of that didn't exist back then."

"I'm not dating," she shot back, her feathers ruffled. "But I certainly can if I want to." *Do I want to?*

"Mom, what if he's after you for your money?"

"Number one, I do not share my balance sheet with people. Please show me some respect. And number two, why are you all in a twist over this?"

"I don't know. Mom, I'm just worried about you. It's crazy out there."

"Well, I'm sure it's worse for you, but I'm pretty sure dating at my age isn't nearly as dangerous as you're making it out to be."

"I'm glad to know you keep your finances private. Maybe I'm overreacting, but it's hard to imagine you dating."

"It's hard for me to imagine as well."

"You have me so worried with leaving town and not knowing where you are." Nina let out a sigh. "Don't you think it's time you came back home? I could use your help. I think you need mine too. And you're a grandmother. You should be doing grandmother things."

"There is more to me than just being a grandmother. I can take care of myself. I recommend you remember that. You know, I'm the one who taught you every cautionary tale."

"Well, I'm not sure you're acting like that woman right now. Frankly, I'm not sure you are capable of being on your own. You're acting reckless."

"I'm not listening to this. Nina, you need to calm down. I'll call you later." Rosemary jammed her finger on the button and shook the phone, trying to hold back a growling grimace. There was absolutely zero release in hanging up on someone on a cellphone. She squeezed her eyes shut, trying to balance her emotions.

She let out a breath and opened her eyes. Tug stood there looking surprised.

"What was that?" he asked.

"I'm sorry."

"Are you okay?"

"Yes. It's my daughter."

Jesse ran into the room. "Want to play crazy—" He stopped in his tracks. "Maybe later." He darted back into the kitchen.

Amanda came out of the kitchen, looking concerned. "Is everything okay?"

Rosemary's face heated. "I'm sorry. It's my mess. I'm so sorry it nose-dived smack-dab in the middle of your celebratory morning. Please forgive me." But she wasn't okay, and tears were threatening to fall. "I'm just going to take a minute."

She rushed upstairs, trying with all her might not to cry in front of them. In the bathroom, she pressed a cold cloth to her face, but there was no stopping the hot tears.

A light tap came at the door.

"Just a minute." Rosemary tried to sound like she was fine.

"Can I come in?" Amanda asked softly.

There wasn't an ounce of holding back left in her. She turned the handle, and Amanda walked into the room and pulled her into her arms. "Oh, Rosemary. What happened? Tug and Paul didn't really catch what was going on. They just knew you were upset."

"My daughter. She's all in a twist about things."

"Why?"

"She thinks I'm an old fool, not capable of taking care of myself."

"Well, that is not true. I've been with you over several days here, and you are not only capable, but you're helpful and kind and smart. Is *she* crazy?"

They laughed, and Rosemary dabbed at the tears.

"Rosemary, I know you've been feeling a little lost. Maybe she's sensing that and is just worried about you."

"She's not worried. She's controlling. I'm so sorry. Her comments just struck me so wrong. She ordered me home." Rosemary started laughing again. "Who does she think she is?"

"Wow, yeah. Can't say my mom would take it too well if I gave her a what for like that either." They went into the bedroom, and Amanda sat on the edge of the bed. "Come sit. Let's just talk it out."

And they did. They talked and cried and laughed, and Amanda threatened to call Nina and give her a piece of her mind or write a note for her absence like she did for the kids' school.

Rosemary sighed. "I'm fine now. Embarrassed but fine. You are so sweet to come and talk me down. Thank you." She got to her feet. "I hope they aren't holding breakfast for us."

"Don't worry about that. Tug will keep ours warm for us."

Rosemary stopped at the door. "Maybe I should just go back to Kathleen's. I've already put a big damper on everything. I can walk back."

"No, you can*not* walk back. I mean, you're clearly capable—not saying you're not."

"Stop that. I know what you meant. I'm not that sensitive."

"I'm teasing, but it's too far to walk. Enjoy breakfast. We'll get you home afterward."

Rosemary ran her fingers through her hair. "I'm a mess, aren't I?"

"No, actually, I think you must be the only girlfriend I have who looks prettier after she cries. Your eyes look so blue right now."

"Well, that's something."

They went downstairs, and Paul and Tug acted like nothing happened. Amanda and Rosemary shared a thankful glance. Men would do anything, even give an Emmy Award-winning performance, not to have to deal with conflict and emotions.

Everyone finished eating, and Paul rounded up the clan to head back to Amanda's.

"Rosemary," Amanda asked, "would you like us to give you a ride back to your friend's house?"

"No," Tug said. "I'll take her back. I mean, is that okay with you?"

"Yes, that's fine. Thank you so much for the offer, Amanda, and for your friendship. Congratulations on the engagement."

Paul gave her a hug. "Well, I don't know how long you plan to be in town, but as soon as we set a date, you're going to have to get back down here. You can't be part of the proposal and not be part of the wedding. I think that's probably bad luck right up there with seeing my gal in her wedding dress."

"You can count on me. I'll even help! I'm a great coordinator."

"That would be awesome. I'm counting on you," Amanda said.

After they left, Tug walked over to the couch and collapsed. "Holy cow. Any time you think you're young, you should rent a set of kids to remind yourself you're old and tired."

"How early did they get you up?"

"Sunrise." He sat up. "They saw dolphins swimming on the coast here. I've lived here my whole life. I have names for those dolphins. I did not need to be woken up to see them again."

"What? I missed dolphins?"

"No, you got to sleep. I think that's a win."

"Yeah, it was nice, but *dolphins*?"

"They play along this stretch all the time. You'll see them soon enough." He rested his arms on his knees. "You going to tell me what's going on with that phone call?"

"My daughter."

"I sort of gathered that much."

"She didn't like the idea of *men* being in my presence."

"Oh? She heard us talking in the background. Sorry."

"No. You have nothing to be sorry about. I'm a grown woman. She's a grown woman. I don't know what's gotten into her."

"The thing is, we are getting older, and we need to use our time wisely. I've been thinking about what you said and what the pastor said in church too."

"Me too. It's a choice every day what we focus on," Rosemary said. "We can worry or not. We can be grateful or not."

"We can have fun or not," Tug said.

"Exactly. We can make that bucket list." She jumped up and grabbed the notebook out of her purse. "I meant to start this yesterday."

"Or not?" He was teasing.

"No! Because it will help you know what you want to be when you grow up."

"Oh goody! I've been meaning to do that."

"Grow up?"

"Yeah."

"Okay, it might not be that powerful, but it will help you kind of figure out what you want to focus on. Another diner or not. All that."

"Tell you what. Why don't I fix a picnic lunch and we work on that on the beach? It's gorgeous out there. It's only in the mid-seventies, and the humidity isn't even that bad today. We don't get days like this at the end of August often."

"Works for me. Take me back to Kathleen's so I can shower and change. Want me to make something for the picnic?"

"Not a single thing. I want to do this for you."

"Are you doing this to spite my daughter for me?"

"If that'll make you happy."

"Wow, you are a superhero."

"No, what is it you said to me yesterday? I liked it. Oh yeah. 'Don't tempt me with a good time.'"

"Ha. Kai used to say it all the time. I'm okay. You don't have to try to prop me up. Nina will get over it, and so will I. This is nothing compared to everything you've got on your plate."

"I want to. We're propping each other up."

"It was the best twenty-four hours I've had in I can't even tell you how long." She paused, hesitant to say the words, then blurted them out. "You were the light in my day yesterday."

"I like getting to know you. And the last twenty-four hours were pretty nice for me too. I'm not doing this just for you. It's for me too."

"That's so sweet of you to say."

"Okay, let's get you to your home base. I'll drop you off so you can change and visit with the cat. Then I'll come back and fix the picnic, and I can pick you back up if you want."

Rosemary found herself already nodding. "I want to. Definitely."

They walked down the stairs and across the truck stepping stone, then shuffled down the rest of the sand hill, which was becoming more of a slide than it was even just yesterday.

"I think the kids may have played on this while we weren't looking."

"I think you're right." She welcomed his arm, bracing to balance the last few steps down. "We could have taken the other stairs."

"I know, but this has been fun," Tug said. "I might have to forgo the Ford truck stepping stone idea, though."

They got into the Paws minivan and took off toward town. He slowed as they drove by the pier, eyeing the spot where the diner once stood.

"Stop here," she said. "Do you think you'd like to look

through that stuff and see if there is anything with any sentimental value you'd like to recover?"

Tugs lips puckered in thought. "I don't know," he admitted, his eyes still on the debris.

"Too soon?" she asked gently.

"I'll think about it."

"Fair enough. I'm game for whatever you decide."

"Okay." He shifted the minivan back into gear and pulled onto the road. They rode the rest of the way in silence to Kathleen's. "I'll see you back here in an hour."

"Sounds good," she said, unbuckling her seatbelt. "Should we synchronize our watches?"

"Only if that sounds fun." He lifted his arm, ready to do it.

"Just call me when you're ready to come back," she said, grinning. "If it's an hour, fine. If you take longer, just let me know."

"Okay. No need to sync the watches, then?"

"No." She was laughing. "You're a goofball."

"I kind of feel goofy when I'm with you," he admitted. "In a good way. It's nice."

She watched him leave. *Very nice.*

Chapter Twenty-Nine

TUG PULLED INTO THE DRIVEWAY AT KATHLEEN'S LESS than an hour later.

Rosemary opened the front door just as he was ready to knock. "Hi there. I was just coming out. Thanks for coming to the door."

"My mama raised me right."

"I see that."

They walked down to the van, and he held the door for her and shut it once she and her big beach bag were settled into the passenger seat.

It was such a pretty day for a drive that he took the long way, looping out near Amanda's and then heading back down the beach road toward his house.

They weren't far from Amanda's place when he noticed another For Sale sign in front of a house.

"Did you see that house for sale?" Rosemary asked.

"Yeah, I've noticed several go on the market lately. It's not unusual after a storm. Snowbirds and people who don't visit much themselves get tired of dealing with cleanup after these storms. I don't know why they buy houses instead of condos if they don't want any of the upkeep."

"A house can be a lot of work, especially if you're not living in it. That's a really cute house. It's close to Amanda too."

"About two blocks."

"That's what I was thinking." Rosemary shifted in her seat, getting another look at the house through the side mirror. "Know anything about it?"

"I know a doctor from Boston had it built. I can't remember if he was an orthopedic surgeon or a heart surgeon."

"Well, you don't want to get them confused when you need one or the other."

"Yeah, that could be disastrous." He repositioned his hands on the steering wheel. "I've never been inside, but I heard it has a lot of built-ins. Everything was custom. The wife came down to monitor things while they were building it, which is why it took so long to complete. She kept changing her mind on things."

Rosemary laughed. "I bet they hate it when that happens."

"Probably. I'm sure the contractors were paid handsomely for their time and the rework. They didn't come down often."

When they got back to his house, he headed straight for the beach path.

"Don't we need to get chairs and stuff?"

"I already took care of that. Come on." He extended his arm, and she ran the few steps to catch up and took his hand. They walked over the dune.

"You've been busy," she remarked when she saw the picnic sheet, chairs, and cooler. "This is so nice."

"I might be trying to impress you."

"You are." She took the seat on the left side of the cooler. "Ahh. It feels so good out here today." But she only sat still for about two minutes before hopping up and dragging her chair to the edge of the blanket. "I want to put my toes in the sand."

"Good thinking." He moved his chair up next to hers. "I was thinking too. Not about my toes in the sand, but more about all my stuff in it. About treasure hunting through the diner's rubble."

"What do you think?"

"We'd have to be careful. I don't want you to get hurt, and there's no telling what mess is all mixed in that rubble. Knives, broken glass—"

"We can be careful. There has got to be some stuff you wish you could find."

"A few things. Yeah."

"We can take it slow." She sucked in a breath. "Thanks for trusting me to help you with this. I think I'm going to accept Amanda's invitation to stay at her house for a couple of weeks. Do you think she meant it?"

"I know she did. It'll help her too. You'll give her a little break from the kids."

"Which I'd love. Yeah, Kathleen is coming back tomorrow. I was trying to decide what to do, but helping you go through the rubble is the best reason in the world to stay."

"Good."

She looked hesitant. "Do you mind if I take a sec and check in with Amanda really quick? I just want to make sure she's okay with me moving over there tomorrow."

"Sure, and if she's not, you could stay in my guest room. I promise I'd be a complete gentleman."

"I know you would be, but I think it would be better if I stayed with Amanda. It's a small town. People will talk."

"People will talk either way. Suit yourself." He leaned forward. "I'm a better cook."

"Right, but I'll be the best cook if I stay with her. Did I mention I can be a little competitive?"

"Well, there's that. It'll be interesting to see what I learn next."

Rosemary called Amanda.

Just from hearing Rosemary's side of the conversation, Tug could tell Amanda was excited to have her.

When Rosemary put her phone down, she was smiling. "I'm going to stay for at least two weeks."

"Great. We'll work fast."

"We will." She clapped her hands. "Isn't it crazy when things just sort of work out?"

"Let's eat while we get started on this bucket list thing you insist upon," he said.

"I'll admit I can be a little bossy, but in a good way...I think."

"I'll be the judge of that," he teased.

"I can't believe you've never traveled," she said.

"Never needed to." Tug opened his arms wide, gesturing toward the beach and the horizon. "Everything I ever needed was right here."

"Have you ever been just a little curious about other places?"

"I guess not. I thought about surfing in Australia or Hawaii in my younger years, but it seemed unattainable. I never considered what it would take to become a reality. I'm just a simple guy." He looked at her with interest. "So why do you think this bucket list exercise is so important?"

"Because you said you didn't know what you wanted to do. It's not about traveling. That's just something lots of people put on theirs, but you might not. I was just asking about that for me. It's a great starting point. Plus—wait. I've got some notes right here."

"You studied up on this?"

"Yes. Why are you so surprised?" She pulled a stack of folded papers from her beach bag and handed them to him.

"Is this something you were doing anyway, or did you just come up with this for me?"

"I already have a bucket list. So, yeah, I guess I did it to help you."

She'd put quite a bit of work into all this. There were a lot of printed pages, and she'd written notes on some of them too. "Why?"

"I don't know." Her gaze drifted out to the tranquil expanse of the ocean.

He sat silently beside her, the gentle lull of the waves filling the space between them.

"I care about your happiness," she admitted. "I know that might sound weird, since we barely know each other, but working so close through this disaster, I feel like I know you, and I thought it would help."

"It's not weird. I feel the connection too." His eyes met hers, and he was glad to see the hint of understanding in her gaze. "Can you give me the short version? Because I'm not reading all of this." He chuckled as he handed the stack of papers back to her.

"Fine." She summarized the documents. "Creating a bucket list of the things you've always wanted to do or see is a great way to ensure a life well lived. In some cases, yeah, it's travel or seeing something. Sometimes a bucket list item could be spending time with someone."

I like the sound of that. "Like you?"

"Or Hailey and Jesse. Or I don't know. Yes. It could be me." She giggled.

"Okay. I get it." He liked to see her laugh.

"You write them all down and check them off as you achieve them. You can add to it or take stuff off. There are really no rules, but it's a good way to see that you're giving those things that you hope to accomplish a priority in your life. You and I both know that we aren't promised tomorrow."

"So, how do I get started?"

"I'm so glad you asked that," she said. "There's actually an app for that."

He leaned back in his chair, feigning major dismay. "Oh no, not another app I won't know how to use."

"I'm kidding. We're not using an app. I don't know how to add an app to my phone, either, but living with a thirteen-year-old in the house, I swear it's all I hear. That's why we have this stack of paper to help us navigate the process."

"Thank goodness."

She dug into her big beach bag again. "Plus, I made good old-fashioned flash cards."

He laughed. "Well, as long as none of them require me to name state capitals, I think I can deal with flash cards."

"There are two things on each of these cards. It's a 'this or that' quiz. Tell me which you prefer. That will help me help you with your bucket list later."

"Shoot."

She flipped up the first card. "Beach or mountains?"

"I live at the beach, but I would like to go to the mountains one summer when it's unbearably hot here. Haven't been in years."

"Got it. How about hiking or driving?"

"I'm too old for hiking. Driving."

Noting his response, she flipped to the next card. "Vineyard or distillery?"

"Neither."

The list continued with airplane or train, cruise or tour, write a book or read one, music or musical, adventure trip or cultural explorations, learn a language or an instrument, and on and on. "That was the last one," she said, finishing the pile.

"That was a lot of questions. What's on my bucket list?"

"Nothing yet. I was just gathering information."

"This is going to be harder than I thought. At least tell me one thing from your bucket list."

"Okay. I'd like to walk up to the top of a lighthouse."

"I've done that," he said. "I can take you. There're a couple not far from here. I'll pack a lunch."

"Really?"

"Definitely," Tug said. "We'll make plans."

"I'd really like that, but don't get us sidetracked. We're working on *your* list."

"Well, put that on mine. Then we'll both check it off."

"I think that's cheating."

"You said there are no rules."

She pursed her lips, her eyes narrowing. "I did, but you can't just copy mine. At least give me a couple of things you think you might enjoy doing or seeing or making. Just wing it—money is no object on bucket lists. Like, there were a couple of things I wanted to see in Paris, but I didn't really want to go on the long flight or spend that kind of money, so I sort of did my own version. Ordered some fancy French wine and pastries. Went to a French restaurant with an authentic French chef to enjoy the cuisine and found books and movies about all those things. I dedicated four days to my Rosemary version of Paris. It was pure delight."

"Fine. I see. I like the way you think, lady. Then I've always wanted to see the northern lights. The pictures seem unbelievable. I'd like to see that for myself."

"Oh, yes. They say you can hear the air buzzing. That's a great start. Aurora borealis, here comes Tug. What else?"

"Maybe learn to paint with watercolors."

"Awesome. We can totally do that. We'll find you a class or maybe even videos online. You might be able to do that right from the deck."

"We could take the class together."

"We could." As the list grew, so did their laughter. The ideas became wilder and more whimsical. And Tug's initial hesitancy faded.

For two hours, they sat on the beach enjoying the day. They ate the lunch Tug had prepared, and then Rosemary finally started writing things on his bucket list.

"Come on," Tug said. "Let's pack up and head inside."

They carried everything back up to the house, then sat on the deck, watching the ocean. Tug looked over his list. "This is pretty good. Thank you for helping me with it. I don't know if it's going to be useful, but I've enjoyed working on it with you."

"Me too. Meeting you, and the unexpected friendships I've made here on Whelk's Island, have brought me a lot of joy."

"I might like this bucket list approach to life," Tug said.

"Dream it, wish it, do it."

"You are a piece of work, you know that? I love your relentless optimism." Tug looked at Rosemary. Her features softened in the setting sunlight. "I didn't realize how much I needed this. It's been a long time since I considered what I wanted to do rather than what I needed to get done."

A knowing smile spread across Rosemary's face. "Sometimes it takes a storm to clear the way for new beginnings."

"Poetic," he said in appreciation. It was true.

"And helping you see that . . . it's helping me in ways I never expected." She sighed. "When I lost Kai, I thought I'd lost my future too. But sitting here dreaming . . . it reminds me that there is still so much to live for. It's all in reach."

"Well, I don't know about that. There are some things out of reach on my list."

"Dreams are fun, though."

"They are. And thanks for not letting me give up. I will not reopen the diner, but I can see there are plenty of things that I could do by selling that property. And there are some local things I'd like to help with. The food bank, for example. Serving meals once in a while."

"I'd do that in a heartbeat. I loved working with you after the storm. It was very satisfying to help others."

"I know what you mean. I feel sort of amped up like I'm ten years younger all of a sudden. This bucket list is a testament to our resiliency. A declaration that, even in our seventies and eighties, life can, or should, still be an adventure."

She nodded as they watched the sunset. "It sure is."

Gratitude filled Tug's heart. Two friends bound by loss had united in hope. Maybe they really would get to have some of those adventures together.

He decided to take a chance. "I know you aren't in town much longer, but would I be monopolizing too much of your time if we spent tomorrow together, sifting through what's left of my diner?"

"Not at all. I'm here to help."

"Asking for help. It's not something I'm good at." He lowered his gaze, then looked up with a smile. "But I was hoping you would say yes."

"Thanks for letting me be there for you." There was a quiet moment of togetherness that spoke volumes. She shifted in her seat, her gaze flickering away before continuing. "We'll need to wear sturdy shoes to keep from getting cut. There's so much hidden debris. I'll pick up a first aid kit at the hardware store. I saw he was already reopened. I figure if we have one, we won't need it."

"Good planning either way," Tug said. "I can't wait to see what we recover. There are a lot of memories in that rubble." *Maybe we can replace lost ones with new, more precious ones.*

Chapter Thirty

A WEEK HAD GONE BY, AND ROSEMARY AND TUG HAD spent every sunny day working through the rubble at the diner. Once they'd cleared away some of the big stuff with the help of Paul and his equipment, they even let Amanda and the kids get in on it.

They recovered one of the framed shell letters, and it was even legible, which was a miracle in itself.

Then they uncovered The Wife's cage that had been out on the back deck in the gazebo. Made of wrought iron, it was fairly indestructible, but there were a few bent rods.

"What's that?" Rosemary asked.

"A pile of menus. They're laminated. Don't guess I'll be needing them."

"You should save at least one for a keepsake. We could frame it or something."

He placed one in the keep pile. They'd been at it for a couple of hours this morning.

Paul had brought over a pallet for anything they were going to keep so they could easily lift it with the skid steer and move it with the truck.

A dumpster was on site for the unsalvageable, and Paul had also brought a stack of cardboard boxes for whatever could be donated.

"Oh my gosh, is this what I think it is?" Rosemary held up a green soda shop–style milkshake mixer. An antique by now. "This is the old-fashioned kind. I love milkshakes."

"That was one of the first things I splurged on when I started my diner. I used to make the best milkshakes around."

"Then you still do, because Hurricane Edwina may have ruined the milk-shaker, but she didn't steal your recipes or your memories. Is *milk-shaker* a word? Probably not, but you know what I mean. I insist you treat me to a milkshake soon."

"Your wish is my command." He bowed.

"Joke all you want. All we have is just this very moment. We're not promised anything more. So we need to get what we want while we can."

"Milkshakes tonight, then."

"I can wait that long."

"Thank goodness."

He was teasing, and she knew it, but she couldn't help commenting further. "I guess if I made a comment like, 'Moments are comprised of either actions, thoughts, dreams, memories, or choices. It's up to you what you focus on,' you'd tell me you'd already heard that speech. Great . . . now I forgot the real point I was going to make. But yes. Milkshakes tonight."

"What are your priorities, besides milkshakes, at the moment?" he asked.

Love. Joy. Gratitude. Peace. "I want peace in my heart. I want to feel like what I'm doing makes a difference for the people around me. I want to feel like I belong."

"Do you think it's smart to let the diner go?"

"I believe you're making the right decision. This is your season to have some fun, and you can. You're in great health. Nothing is holding you back now but you."

"What about The Wife? I can't just abandon her. Birds aren't like cats. They need a lot of attention."

"I think you could count on friends to watch after her or board her over at Paul's. I'm sure he'd give you the family discount."

"True."

"Or if I'm around, I can help," she said. "The Wife seems to like me."

"You'd do that?"

"Absolutely. It would be my pleasure."

He seemed to like the idea. "I might take you up on that."

"Good. I hope you will."

"Actually, it's kind of nice timing to get that piece of information. Turns out I have to drive into Norfolk tomorrow for a meeting. Would you mind hanging out at my place? You don't actually have to do anything for her. She's pretty self-sufficient. She just needs some company throughout the day."

"Sure. I can do that. Is everything okay?"

"Yes. Fine. I was feeling kind of bad about leaving her all day. This will be better."

"What time do you need me there?"

"I'm going to leave early. I'll leave a key under the mat on the back stair entrance. Come on over whenever you get up and moving around."

"That works out pretty nicely. I traded out a novel at the Little Free Library. Now I can relax on your deck, listen to the ocean, and read. It'll be like a vacation. Oh, wait. Every day here is like a vacation."

"I love your sense of humor, and I appreciate your help. Thanks."

They worked a while longer, but the day was a scorcher. "How about we rest in the shade for a while?" he suggested.

"I'm not sure how much longer I can keep going." She brushed her bangs from her face. "I need to put some more sunscreen on."

They sipped cool water under the umbrella that Paul and his team had set up for them. "Was it ever this hot in Hawaii?"

"Oh, yeah. Definitely." She pressed her cold bottle of water against her neck.

"Do you miss it?"

"Sometimes. I lived there most of my life. Fifty years. But the farm was more than I wanted to handle without Kai. I know I did the right thing." She laughed. "I'll admit I kind of stalk the new owners on social media, though. They are doing a really good job. They're still doing the tours we used to do and starting some new traditions with community crafts and things like that. It's good."

"I bet it was hard to leave."

"It was. I stayed probably longer than I should have, but healing is a process. We can get discouraged and impatient with ourselves. We're so used to everything being a quick fix, and you can't fast-track grief."

"No, I don't suppose you can. I think you can make the mistake of not dealing with it right away."

"I think that happens a lot."

"What was it like? Your life in Hawaii."

"Oh gosh. There was never a dull moment. It was a pretty big macadamia farm. We employed a lot of people. We had some goats. It was a fairy-tale life. We worked that farm our whole married life together."

"Goats? Really?" Tug seemed amused. "I used to think I wanted some goats. My grandpa raised them."

"I can't picture you as a goat farmer." She considered it. "Like, not at all."

"Just a couple as pets. Gramps always had a few bottle babies. They followed me around like puppies. I got a huge kick out of them."

"It's hard not to fall in love with them," Rosemary agreed. "I have some good memories like that too."

"Did you ever work off the farm?" Tug asked.

"No. Never had to. We were really blessed with a good business, and I loved being a part of the entire process." It had been a wonderful life. She wouldn't have traded those days for anything. "I have some good macadamia recipes too. I'll have to make you some of them."

"I'd like that."

"You're making me do all the talking," she said. "I want to know more about you. Tell me about the diner. Were you always an expert in the kitchen? Was it your lifelong dream to own a restaurant?"

"No. Not at all. I was just a kid who grew up on the beach. Made money in my early years crabbing off the coast here. Later, I was a fishing guide for a little while. Then I worked with a commercial fisherman and eventually got my own boat and sold fresh catch to the restaurants right from the dock."

"How did the diner happen, then?"

"Mr. Carr used to own the pier. He was my dad's best friend. He never had kids of his own, but he always welcomed me to tag along with them. Back then, the diner building was a bait and tackle shop for the pier. He fronted me the money to start crabbing as a teen, then for my first boat too. Dad lived paycheck to paycheck. We didn't have much, and my mom died when I was only twelve. It was just me and Dad."

"I'm so sorry. That had to be hard."

"It didn't seem so bad, although when I see Jesse with Amanda, I wonder how it might have been to have a mom's influence too. But she raised me right while she was alive. She was a stickler for manners."

"That's sweet. You have excellent manners. It's something I noticed about you right away."

"When Mr. Carr died, he left me the bait and tackle shop. I had every intention of continuing to run it just like he had, but I was there all day and never had time to eat right, so I opened a lunch counter out of self-preservation, and it just sort of took off. Slowly, the bait and tackle area got smaller and smaller until I sold it off to a kid with a kiosk who sold it from the pier. Worked out for everyone."

"That's an incredible story. You didn't even know you wanted to cook."

"Nope. I'd cooked for my dad growing up, but I didn't even realize I was good at it. I was just doing what needed to be done. I loved having a meal for Dad when he got home from work. I guess that's where I first started enjoying cooking. Never really thought of that before."

"Tug, I think I need to call it a day. It's just getting hotter out here."

"I think that's a good plan. I'll leave that key under the mat for you for tomorrow."

"That'll be great, and I'll fix something so you'll have a nice meal when you get home."

"No one has ever done that for me before."

"Well, I'd say you're overdue for the special treatment, sir."

I don't mind one bit being the one to do that.

They parted ways, and Rosemary went back to Amanda's house. Amanda was working on some new herbal salt recipes when she got there, and the two of them decided to try them out on a new recipe in the kitchen.

"This smells so fresh." Rosemary held it to her nose again. "And it has a little zest to it. Maybe *zest* isn't the right word. . . . More like spicy hot?"

"It's got a little bit of bay leaf, savory, and chili pepper. I had to play with it a long time to get the right blend so it's not overpowering. I can't wait to try it out."

"It smells really nice. What are we going to try it on?"

"I was thinking chicken tonight."

"Let's do it," Rosemary said. "I'll make gravy and some stuffing to go along with it."

"The kids will love that, and how about we do some one-pan macaroni and cheese? Have you ever made it? It's so easy, and it's Jesse's absolute favorite."

"I've always made macaroni and cheese from a roux over cooked noodles and then bake it."

"You are in for a treat."

Rosemary and Amanda worked on dinner together, and the kids were a great test kitchen addition. They had clearly been put to the test before and didn't hesitate trying the new dishes.

"They eat so good," Rosemary said, surprised. "Most kids will complain about anything new."

"I'm so blessed," Amanda said. "They are the best."

Hailey held her hands up like a halo over her head, and then Jesse did too.

"And smarty pants. Did I mention they are smarty pants?" Amanda teased.

They giggled and gave Amanda the thumbs-up on the new product.

The next morning, Rosemary got up early and walked the beach with the kids and Denali, and then she went down to Tug's house. The key was under the mat, just as he'd promised. She walked inside and went into the kitchen to get a glass of water to take out on the porch with her.

A piece of paper lay on the counter. He'd left her a note. She could imagine his voice as she read it.

Rosemary,
I made a fresh batch of chicken salad for you. It's on the second shelf of the refrigerator. I hope you enjoy it. There are crackers in the pantry. That's the way I always eat it when I'm alone, but there's bread in there too. Make yourself at home.

Thank you again for giving The Wife some attention while I'm away. I appreciate it, and she will too.

Hope to see you tonight, but if you need to leave, just pull the door closed behind you and I'll talk to you soon.

Tug

"You are one sweet man."

She went out on the deck and struck up a conversation with The Wife about everything from Hawaii, to Nina, to how The Wife felt about watching the squawking seagulls dip in and out of the ocean. The Wife was a chatterbox today, and it was a lot more fun than she'd expected it to be.

"I'm going to be right over here reading my book. We'll talk in a little while."

Rosemary settled into one of the chairs to read. It was nice with just the sound of the ocean in the background.

The Wife would occasionally whistle over to Rosemary and say, "What are you doing?"

Rosemary felt obliged to answer, and no matter what her response was, The Wife would say, "Okay. That's nice."

Later, as Rosemary was eating lunch, she turned on some music. The Wife joined in, singing a couple of the songs.

Ever since Rosemary had found the shell, she'd thought about that Miranda Lambert song "Bluebird." She loved the lines "I'll keep a light on in my soul, keep a bluebird in my heart."

"This is one of my favorite songs," Rosemary said to The Wife, then pressed Play. The Wife seemed to like it, so Rosemary played it again, and when the music stopped, The Wife made a loud clucking sound.

"Do you want me to play it again?"

The Wife seemed to want an encore, so Rosemary said, "Play the song?" Of course, the bird didn't answer, but that's what she seemed to want, so Rosemary played it again. She repeated the process two or three times until, during the chorus, The Wife sang out, "I'll keep a light on in my soul!"

"You sang it!" Rosemary was so delighted she could hardly contain herself. And she didn't. She danced around, celebrating, while The Wife bobbed on her tree limb.

Rosemary later went inside and fixed pork chops and scalloped potatoes for Tug. She had no idea when he'd be getting home, but it would be a nice gesture that he'd appreciate.

If he called to let her know he was almost back, she could have it warm for him. She seasoned some green beans. "Got to have your veggies."

"Got to have your veggies," The Wife called from outside.

"Are you eavesdropping on me?" Rosemary teased as she put the finishing touches on the dinner. She covered it and wrote a note with reheating instructions for Tug. Not that he'd need them. Then she walked outside to say good night to The Wife before she left.

"Play the song. Wooo-oo-oo-oo-oo-ooo."

"You silly bird. You sound just like the intro to it. You are a trip. Okay, one more time, and then I have to go home."

Rosemary picked up her phone and found the song again,

then hit Play. As it began, The Wife echoed the "Wooo-oo-oo-oo-ooo" and swayed to the music. Rosemary raised her arms and glided around the deck, singing the chorus.

"I'll keep a light on in my soul!" The Wife sang her part too.

"Keep a bluebird in my heart," Rosemary sang out.

The song came to an end, and she felt a rush of joy. She had a bluebird in her heart today.

A slow clap came from behind her.

She jumped and spun around. "Tug? How long were you standing there?"

"Long enough to hear a nice duet. Well, I guess we should give the singer on the phone some credit. A trio."

She covered her mouth.

He shook his head. "Don't go shy on me now." He grabbed her hand and danced her around the deck.

Chapter Thirty-One

IT WAS A LITTLE LESS THAN TWO WEEKS SINCE ROSEMARY
had moved in with Amanda and the kids. Amanda and Rosemary were spending evenings at Salt of the Earth, preparing to
relocate her business to Paws Town Square. Despite its small
size, there were a lot of things to move. Thankfully some of her
herbs had survived the beating of the hurricane. It was a miracle, really, so they dug up those hardy plants and moved them
into containers. Having Rosemary by her side to help made it
fun.

That evening while repotting herbs, Amanda felt a rush of
anxiety at the thought of Rosemary leaving. "I can't believe the
time is flying by so quickly," Amanda said. "You need to stay
longer."

"I'd love that," Rosemary said, "but I don't want to wear out
my welcome either. I have something to tell you."

"Is everything okay?" Amanda recalled the day Maeve told
her that she was ill. *Please don't let anything happen to Rosemary.*
"Please tell me you are okay."

"I'm fine. Don't worry. It's nothing like that." Rosemary
seemed hesitant, though, and that scared Amanda.

A wry smile spread across Rosemary's face. "I looked at a
house this morning."

"Here? On Whelk's Island?"

She nodded slowly. "Yes."

Amanda screamed. "Really? We would love it if you moved here. Are you seriously considering it?"

"I think so. It was so exciting, and the house is really cute."

"Where is it?"

"Just a couple of blocks away. Apparently it's been a rental, and after this last hurricane, the owners have decided to sell rather than repair, but there wasn't much damage. The realtor knows a guy, so I've got someone going over there to do a full estimate tomorrow before I make an offer."

"An offer? This is real!" Amanda sat down. "I'm about to faint. I'm so excited."

"Well, don't do that."

"I'm fine. It's just, a lot is going on. The hurricane, this mess here at the bungalow, and now moving into Paws, getting engaged."

"Are you having second thoughts?" Rosemary asked.

"Rosemary, I love Paul. I do. I love him with all my heart. It was so easy to say yes to him."

"That's how it's supposed to be."

"But I never thought I'd ever marry again. I loved Jack. Our marriage was perfect. How do you even match that? But I trust Paul with my life, and my children. And I did with Jack, too, and this is the same but different. I know I'm not making any sense."

"You are making complete sense. You and Jack were wonderful together, but he's gone. You've been blessed with another love. A new season of love. It can happen twice, honey. Don't be afraid."

"I have no doubt, no hesitation. You could never convince me I'd marry again a year ago, though."

"That doesn't take anything away from this." Rosemary pulled Amanda into a side hug. "Honey, you're blessed to have two wonderful loves in your life. It's okay. Jack's not coming back. There's no recovering that marriage. You'll still miss him, but you'll have something fresh and alive in your heart. You're a young, beautiful woman, and Paul adores you. And I can see how much love you have for him too."

"I do," Amanda said.

"Even more importantly, he and the children have a wonderful and respectful relationship."

"I'm so grateful our paths crossed again." She let out a staggered breath, pausing for a long moment. "Why do I feel guilty about it sometimes?"

"I can't tell you how to feel, Amanda. I think it's natural. You don't have to let go of Jack's memory. That is safe in your heart, but it's the past. You are safe moving forward with Paul. He's a good man, and he will always protect you and the children and give you a good life. I believe that."

"I do too. I think I'm probably just tired and overthinking things."

"Probably. Let's call it a night here. A little time on the deck would do us both good."

Amanda nodded. "Good idea. We'll let the kids load up the plants tomorrow so we can nurse them back to health at the house. Paul is still working on getting the space built out with a new hydroponic system. I can't wait to see if I can get my herbs to thrive in that environment."

"I'm sure it will be great. No risk really. You could always grow and clip them at home."

"True." Amanda took solace in that.

"Have you and Paul set a date or talked about what kind of wedding you want to have?" Rosemary asked as they drove back home.

"Just something very small. I'd like to get married here at the house. I asked our pastor about it, and he thought that would be fine."

"I think it would be lovely." Rosemary clapped. "I'm ready to help you plan. Please let me. Whenever you decide, I'm here, and even if I'm not living here, I'll come back! Are you thinking you want a long engagement?"

"No. I'm ready to marry him now. I think I'm more worried about what other people will think, but I keep reminding myself that's really not their business."

"No, it's not, and Jack's been gone a long while now."

"Feels like yesterday."

"I know that feeling," Rosemary said. "It changes, but it's still there." She let out a heavy sigh. "How about we grill chicken and pineapple tonight? You can put your feet up, and I'll take care of everything. I love that fancy grill of yours."

Amanda pulled in front of the house and shut down the engine. "That sounds terrific. How am I going to go back to cooking all the meals again? It's been so nice having you around."

They got out and went up to check on the kids. Hailey and Jesse were so good about staying out of trouble so she could zip over to the bungalow when needed. They were lying on the floor, coloring, when Amanda and Rosemary walked in.

"Mom!" Hailey jumped up, carrying her masterpiece. "I made you something."

"I did too," Jesse said, sliding to a stop in her wake.

"I'm the luckiest mom in the world. Beautiful."

"We made something for you, too, Rosemary."

"You two are so sweet."

Hailey nudged Jesse in a "told you so" kind of way that made her wonder what all they'd been talking about while she was gone.

"Thank you both," Rosemary said. "I know I'm going to love it, but you save it until after dinner. I'm going to get that started right now."

"Good. I'm starving." Jesse clutched his belly.

"You're always hungry," Hailey said with a dramatic sigh as she turned and went back into the living room.

Amanda watched as Rosemary worked her magic at the grill. She'd just taken the chicken off when there was pounding on the front door. "Hailey, run and get that. Paul must have left his key."

"Mom?" Hailey called from the front door a few moments later. "We have company."

Amanda gave Rosemary a funny look, and Jesse ran around Amanda to see, but she caught him by the arm. "No, sir. You wait for me to see who it is." She wiped her hands on the hand towel stuck in the waistband of her jeans.

Rosemary followed her into the front room.

"Nina?" Rosemary looked shocked.

"This is your daughter?" Amanda recognized the name. "Oh my gosh! What a wonderful surprise."

"It is. Hey, Nina." Rosemary walked over and hugged the auburn-haired woman. "Amanda, this is my daughter. Nina, this is Amanda. And this is Hailey and Jesse. I'm so glad you are getting the chance to meet."

Amanda could see the resemblance between the women. Nina was taller by a few inches, but they could practically pass as sisters. "It is so nice to meet you." Amanda reached out to shake her hand, but Nina didn't accept it.

Rosemary suddenly looked confused. "What are you doing here, honey? This is a surprise. Why didn't you call?"

"I did. I called Kathleen."

"Why would you call her and not me? You drove all the way down here without calling me? It was a six-hour drive. Well, not that long the way you drive." Rosemary giggled. "She drives like a maniac," she said playfully to Amanda.

Nina didn't laugh. "It was a hike. I called Kathleen's, seeing if I could send anything since you'd been there so long. Being a responsible adult, I thought it was the polite thing to do. Only when I finally got her on the phone, she told me you're not staying there anymore. I felt like an idiot."

"Well, did it matter that I changed locations? I'm still on Whelk's Island. What's the difference?"

"The difference?" Nina threw up her hands. "Seriously?"

"Nina, I invited your mother to stay with us," Amanda quietly added. "We're so happy to have her here with us. My kids love her."

"I love her too." Nina spun toward Amanda. "You're a stranger. It was one thing for her to visit a friend from high school, but you? I don't even know why you're in the middle of all of this."

"We're friends." Amanda withdrew a step.

"Nina, what has gotten into you?" Rosemary's response was measured.

"Me? What's gotten into you?"

"I need this. The ocean. The beach. Friends. Adult conversation. All of it."

"You're living in the past."

"I promise you I am not. I'm making steps forward every day and learning who I am without your father. I'm finding out what I like to do. I'm making new friends, if you haven't scared them away."

"Never," Amanda said. "No. This is just a misunderstanding. Nina, come in. I'd be upset if I was in your situation too."

"Mom, we need to leave. Let's get your things." Nina was barely able to contain her agitation.

Rosemary stiffened. "I'm not going anywhere."

"Great. So now I've wasted my time coming here to get you, on top of it all." Nina's voice was sharp, her brow furrowed.

"To get me?" Rosemary's voice rose an octave. "I don't need a ride. I have a car."

"Well, you need someone to help you make good decisions, apparently."

"I'm quite capable, thank you."

"I don't even know why I care."

"No. Wait. Nina, you care," Amanda said, unable to stay out of it. "Or you wouldn't be here. But I promise you have nothing to worry about." Her heart ached for these women. Rosemary losing Kai—she knew what that was like, but she couldn't imagine how Nina must feel having lost her father and now feeling unable to help her mother through a difficult time, on top of her own divorce.

"Look, I'm sure you think you're helping, but you don't understand." Nina's jaw pulsed. "She's lying to me. I can't take care of her if I don't even know what's going on."

"I don't need you to take care of me, Nina."

"You do. You aren't making good decisions. I'm afraid you've lost your mind!" Tears spilled down her cheeks.

"Let's take a breath," Amanda said. "We can discuss this."

Nina glared at Amanda, her frustration now finding a new target. "And *you* are not helping."

Amanda couldn't imagine herself ever acting like this toward her own mother, and her mother had made her pretty crazy at times.

"I appreciate your concern, but it's unfounded. You will not talk to my friend like that. And I do not appreciate you showing up and creating a scene." Rosemary's calm demeanor wavered, a hint of steel in her tone. "Nina, I'm in my right mind, and I'm in perfect health. I am perfectly capable of deciding where I want to spend my time, and right now, I choose to be here on the beach with people who have shown me nothing but kindness. I love you, honey. And I don't know where all this is coming from, but I think we need a cooling-off period."

"A cooling-off period is a good idea." Amanda stepped between them. Both women were red in the face.

"I think you should leave," Rosemary said to Nina.

"And I can't worry about you like this, Mom. It's making me nuts. I don't have the patience for it."

Rosemary blinked twice, and Amanda wasn't quite sure what she was going to say.

"I think I already knew that. I think what had me hesitant on really believing I could stay was that I was struggling with how to do it without hurting *your* feelings. I guess that's not a problem now." Rosemary smiled, looking as if an anvil had been lifted from her. "I guess now is as good a time as any to mention I've been looking at beach houses down here."

"What?" Nina stared, her lips apart, but not another word came out. Finally, she lifted her hand in a wave and walked out.

Amanda stood there, not even looking at Rosemary until she heard the car start and pull away.

"I'm so embarrassed." Rosemary covered her face and cried.

"Don't be. I think she's just worried," Amanda said. "I could call her in a day or two and try to smooth things over."

"That won't be necessary. She's always had a temper, but she'll calm down. I'm sorry she was so ugly to you. I raised her better than that. She's not like this."

"She loves you. She's just in mama-bear mode. I know what that's all about."

"Only, I'm not a cub."

"No, you most certainly are not, but she's in protection mode because she loves you. We have to give her that. My guess is it's misplaced grief, her trying to help you because Kai is no longer around to help. Her own emotions raw from the divorce. There's grief to deal with in that too. Grief is hard on all of us."

Chapter Thirty-Two

TUG STOOD AT THE KITCHEN COUNTER, MAKING SAND-wiches for Paul, Amanda, and her crew. He loved feeding people, and these most of all. He hummed as he slathered peanut butter and jelly on bread for the kids and set them alongside the others—chicken salad topped with tomato, red onion, and romaine on kaiser rolls.

He stacked the sandwiches in the center of a platter, then sliced apples and added them, along with some clusters of red seedless grapes, for color around the edges.

That hukilau song was catchy. It had been on repeat in his head for a couple of weeks now, along with the wiggling hips that went with it. He danced over to the refrigerator to put the rest of the grapes back, throwing his arms out in the little net-casting motion on his way.

"Well, well," Amanda said from the doorway. "Is that the hukilau you're singing?"

"Not singing. Just humming."

"And casting your net."

"You make that sound naughty."

"I call 'em like I see 'em. Paul warned me not to play match-maker, but I guess you don't need my help."

"It's not like that."

"Isn't it?" Amanda hopped up on a stool at the butcher block. "Rosemary is very pretty."

"She is. I noticed." He grinned, refusing to look at Amanda. "Are you here to help or just give me a hard time?"

"I'm not giving you a hard time. I'm encouraging this!"

"Where is she?"

"She drove into town for something. She might stop by later. You're enjoying your time with her, aren't you?"

"She's nice, but she's also leaving town soon." He sounded disappointed.

"Don't be so sure," Amanda said. "It's not my place to say, but I think she's seriously entertaining the idea of moving here."

"And maybe not."

"She's welcome to stay longer at my place or as frequently as she likes," Amanda said. "And after Paul and I get married, Paul's place will be available. She's got somewhere to hang her hat if she wants to."

Tug hadn't considered Paul putting his place up for sale. It would be perfect for Rosemary, but how could he mention it without getting her hopes up that he might mean something serious? He'd never been married. *I might be too firmly established in my ways to ever promise anyone anything like that, but it sure would be nice for her to be around.*

Amanda was waiting for him to respond, but he could wait her out.

"Do you need any help carrying that stuff out?" she finally said.

"No. I've got it." He picked up the platter. "Amanda, maybe you should mention Paul's place to Rosemary or take her over to see it. Maybe she'll put two and two together on her own. It *would* be perfect for her."

"I like the way you think, Tug." Amanda snapped her fingers. "I can do that. And maybe you could at least tell her you like having her around." She hopped down, giving him a playful grin over her shoulder as she turned to leave. "Just sayin'."

Probably should. I sort of implied it already.

Lunch was quick. It always was when the kids were anxious to get down to the water to play.

"Tug and I are going to head down and help Fisher. Need any help getting anything down to the beach before we leave?" Paul asked.

"No. I'll let the kids haul their own stuff. I'm just going to carry one of those lightweight beach chairs down if that's okay, Tug."

"Sure. You know where everything is."

She went on tiptoe to kiss Paul on the neck. "Y'all have fun. We'll be here when you get back. Want me to start something for dinner?"

"No," Tug said. "I've already got hot dogs ready to roast over the firepit later. And s'mores." He stopped and turned back to the refrigerator. "Almost forgot to bring the sandwich I made for Fisher. He loves my chicken salad."

"We all do," Amanda said. "But, Tug, what is it with you sugaring up my kids? S'mores? Really? Now that I know you're capable of babysitting, I might make you pull duty when they get amped up over here by you."

"Uh-oh." Tug tucked his head and bolted for the door.

"You better run," Paul said. "She'll do it."

Tug stopped and turned around. "Maybe just marshmallows tonight."

"Good compromise." Paul and Tug high-fived.

"Better." Amanda gave him the okay sign.

Tug chuckled. "They were kind of hyper the other night," he

admitted as they walked out. "I guess the sugar could've been a factor."

"Oh, it's a real thing," Paul said. "I never knew that until I'd been around them for a while."

"Good to know." Tug climbed into Paul's truck, and they drove up to The Tackle Box. Fisher was already here. He'd been dedicated to keeping the bar open for his regular hours, even with slim inventory and no wall.

Tug went to pull the handle, but Paul stopped him. "Hey, I told Fisher that these temporary walls we're going to help him put up were some leftover inventory from my northern Virginia location."

"Why would you have temporary walls?"

"Just let him believe it, okay?" Paul looked sheepish. "You know he won't accept help, and he's a hard worker. I heard the insurance isn't covering the damage."

"None of it?"

"No, but it doesn't matter. I want to do this. I told him he could teach Hailey and Jesse to surf in exchange."

"That's still very generous," Tug said. "Not that I'm surprised. No worries. My lips are sealed."

He and Paul walked over and took a shortcut to the bar through where the wall used to be. "Hey, Fisher."

"Hey, guys. What can I get you?" Fisher grabbed two glasses and flipped them in the air.

"My usual," Tug said.

"I'm good for now," Paul said. "We just finished lunch."

Fisher's mouth dropped open.

Tug lifted a hand. "Don't fret, boy. I brought you a sandwich too." He tossed the tinfoil-wrapped sandwich, and Fisher caught it with one hand.

"Sweet. Thanks, man. I'm going to tuck this in the beer

cooler until we're done." Fisher hung up his apron and jogged out to catch up with them at Paul's truck.

It took all three of them to pull the huge boxes from the truck bed and lay them out.

The system was impressive. If he'd decided to reopen the diner, he might have opted for something similar on the gazebo for a more contemporary year-round solution. The hooking mechanism of the frames, which were made of lightweight aluminum, was well thought out. It was strong.

Paul jumped and did a pull-up from one of the frames. "Sturdy as it can be." He hopped down.

Fisher lifted one of the vinyl panels. "Paul, this is super high quality. I didn't expect it to be *this* nice. It looks brand new."

"I made them pack it up just like they found it when we were done. It's rated for high winds. I think the paper is in there. It should hold up even in a storm, but I'd clear everything out next hurricane and just open it up."

"Good idea. I was thinking of creating a storage area so I can actually lock everything down when storms are coming through."

"You could do that, or I bet you could get a utility trailer pretty cheap. You could park that in Paws or haul it inland super easy. Used ones they practically give away."

"I'll start keeping an eye out," Fisher said.

"Yeah, if I see any, I'll let you know. I'm forever running into them for sale. I just don't need any more." Paul started attaching the components to the rails so they could hang the vinyl.

The three of them worked quickly, but it still took the better part of three and a half hours to get the wall up. But when it was done, The Tackle Box had never looked better.

Fisher stood back. "This is incredible. Plus, I got a lot more space. I can put a couple of bistro tables there, or a dartboard. I owe you, man."

"It looks good," Tug said.

"It does, and it's a perfect fit. That sure worked out." Paul was playing it off like a pro. Had he not said anything to Tug, he might've believed it was old inventory too.

Fisher stepped over and shook Paul's hand. "I think I'm going to owe you more than surf lessons, but I'm good for it."

"Nope. We made a deal. A deal is a deal. I'm happy with it."

"Well, I appreciate this and helping me put it up."

"It would be hard to wrangle alone. It was like Twister with all three of us," Tug added.

Fisher couldn't look away from the new wall. "Looks like a whole new place. Sort of fancy even."

"This is really generous," Fisher said. "I'd like to do something to return the favor."

"You can pony up some engagement celebration drinks," Tug said. "Paul finally braved up and popped the question."

"What?" Fisher seemed excited to be in on the secret. "I hadn't heard."

"I asked Amanda to marry me."

"You did!" He smacked his hands together. "She's a great lady. Congratulations." Then he turned to Tug. "Speaking of ladies, what happened with that cute little redhead that came in trying to match you drink for drink without even knowing you only drink cherry limeade?"

Tug laughed.

"What is that?" Paul asked.

"Yeah, just before you dropped in that day, Rosemary showed up, and when Fisher asked what she wanted to drink, she said, 'I'll have what he's having.' She thought I was here drowning my sorrows and was going to rescue me."

"Hysterical."

"Should have seen her face when she took the first sip," Fisher said. "It was the teensiest taste, and this look of surprise came over her. It was funny."

"It was," Tug agreed.

"What about Rosemary, Tug?" Paul leaned on the counter. "You two get along pretty well." He turned to Fisher. "You know they fed the community from my parking lot."

"Everyone is talking about it. I heard they're a pretty good team. And she is the pretty part." Fisher grinned.

"Okay, you two young buckaroos," Tug said. "Lay off the old man. I don't need to be poked fun at."

"No one is poking fun," Paul said. "I think you and Rosemary make a nice couple."

"It was pretty clear she's interested in you," Fisher put in.

"They've been spending a lot of time together." Paul was eager to grease the wheels. "They worked on his bucket list together."

"You didn't already have a bucket list?" Fisher said. "Man. I thought everyone had one."

"Apparently I was the only one without one, but I've got one now."

"Well, when you're ready to do some traveling," Paul said, "I've got a girl working out of the northern Virginia location that handles all the travel for Paws Town. She can hook you up with the best deal around. If it didn't make your bucket list, one of my favorite places to visit is right up in the North Carolina mountains. That's driving distance."

"No, dude," Fisher interrupted. "You have to go out west. It's like the opposite of everything on this coast. The reds and browns. The mountains and huge rock structures will blow your mind."

Tug felt flustered by the conversation. "The stuff on my list was fairly simple—well, except seeing the northern lights—and I doubt I'll actually ever get to see them in my lifetime."

"Sure you can," Paul said. "Iceland, Alaska, Canada, even up in the northern United States. The trick is timing it just right to catch them."

"I'd love to see that too," Fisher said. "That would be amazing. Traveling to the national parks really gave me an appreciation for our beautiful country. Also confirmed I love the beach the most, which is why I came back. It was nice to visit those places but nicer to be home."

"I've got The Wife to think about, and I don't know. . . . At my age it just seems kind of crazy. I've never traveled before, so it's not like I'm missing it."

"Believe me. You are missing out," Fisher said.

"You need to experience the beauty of America," Paul chimed in. "Fisher is right. It'll open your eyes and lift your patriotism. Makes me proud to be an American when I see the beauty we're surrounded by."

"I'm just a simple man. I'm not made of money either. I don't even have a job, come to think of it." Tug had a tidy savings, and if he did sell the oceanfront property, he'd be set to do whatever he liked. Probably more than he could even dream of, but it still felt out of reach.

Fisher stepped forward and planted his feet. "You could rent your house out while you're traveling. I do that when I leave for a while. You'd be surprised how quickly houses on the beach get rented out. Even one like my little bungalow. Plus, I can help you manage it. I clean some rentals for a few of the big families down at our end of the beach. Been doing it for, like, five years now. You could get good money from your place. And I'd give you a deal on cleaning and readying it while you're away."

Tug never knew Fisher had anything else going on. "You do that in your spare time?"

"Yeah. My mom used to clean houses. I learned from the best. Doesn't take long to clean those up, and they pay pretty darn good for it. I'd do yours for next to nothing, though. Or you could get one of those RVs. A lot of older people do that."

Older? That struck him. It was different to refer to yourself as old. "Don't know if I really see myself hauling a house around. Not my thing."

"Yeah, and then you have to have somewhere to park it," Fisher said. "Probably a bigger pain to do that."

"Parking those monsters is probably a challenge," Paul agreed. "I'd love to take Amanda and the kids on an RV trip across the country. I'll need a big camper, though. Bunk beds for the kids. Bump-outs. I keep thinking maybe that would be a cool family honeymoon." He paused. "Is that cheesy?"

Tug shook his head. "Not cheesy at all, but how about making it a second honeymoon? I can look after those kids for a while. Your wife deserves a real romantic honeymoon with her husband. She's a mother every day. Make it special, then scoop up the whole family and do the second one. I think Amanda would love it, and I know the kids would."

"Would it be presumptuous to plan it without including her?" Paul thought out loud. "You know, to surprise her? Are there rules about that?"

"You're asking me? I've never been married," Tug said.

"Me either. Don't look at me for marriage advice," Fisher said. "I'm more likely to walk in Tug's footsteps and be a bachelor forever."

"Ask Rosemary," Tug said. "I bet she has great marriage advice. Or ask Google, or Siri, or Alexa. Lord, how many robots are telling us what's right and wrong these days?"

"And are they right?" Fisher said, looking doubtful. "That's the million dollar question. I don't trust anyone who doesn't have a face."

"You don't talk to Alexa?" Paul looked stunned.

"Nope." Fisher was adamant. "That stuff seems a little too

much like sci-fi to me. First, they tell you how to cook an egg. Fine. But then you ask for advice, and where are they getting that information? The internet is full of crazy stuff that is not true. And people believe it just because the robot says so." He shook his head. "Not this guy. Nope."

"I hadn't really thought about that," Tug said. "I gave in and put my lights on Alexa. I don't know what the big deal is. If you ask me, it's not that big of a step up from the Clapper light thing, and that was around in the eighties. This generation thinks they invented everything, but that two-clap light system was giving us automated lighting a long time ago."

Paul groaned. "Oh, Tug. Don't be telling people you had that cheesy clapper."

"I'm surprised you even know what it is," Tug said.

"I'm not that young. They were still popular in the nineties. My dad had one in his garage."

"I can see you don't really want to talk about the redhead," Fisher said.

"Her name is Rosemary."

"Beautiful name for a beautiful woman," Fisher said. "For what it's worth, she seemed really nice. If I were about forty years older, we might be fighting over her. I think she's the kind of lady a man dreams about having as a partner in life."

Oh, I've been thinking about it. Pretty much all I've been thinking about. And then darn if that hukilau song didn't start rolling through his head, and he could picture that little redhead hula dancer swiveling her hips.

Chapter Thirty-Three

THE LAST TWO DAYS HAD BEEN A LITTLE CRAZY FOR Rosemary—meeting the contractor to assess the cost of the repairs the beach house needed, calling Nina to tell her she was going to pull the trigger, and making the offer. Rosemary had been a bundle of nerves making that call and had braced herself for an ugly fight, but Nina reacted with kindness and understanding, even apologizing for her display at Amanda's. "How will I make that up to you?"

"You're my daughter, Nina. Nothing you can do will ever change my love for you."

"Well, you're a better person than I am. I'd replace me in a heartbeat after that scene I made."

"Nope. No one can replace you. I love you with all my heart. I have that redhead hot temper too. Just like your father always said, the red apple doesn't fall—"

"Far from the tree." They both laughed.

"I love you, Mom, and I'm so sorry. I know you're capable. I just wanted to protect you, fix the hurt, and, well, I just made things worse."

"You didn't. It was a blip. Honey, I'll still be closer than Hawaii, and you can zip down here and relax, maybe find some life balance. You know how much I worry about the hours you work."

"I know. And Kendra needs more time with me too. She's

really missing having the attention you gave her while you were here. That was great, but it also was only a Band-Aid for me not filling that void. I'm sorry, Mom."

"No more apologies about it. We're golden."

Rosemary hung up the phone, feeling completely confident in her decision.

She was on her way to tell Amanda when she decided to stop at the Little Free Library to swap out books. Again, the contents were all askew, but this time she found herself smiling and enjoying the chance to do a little housekeeping for the next visitor.

Her attitude about a lot of things had changed dramatically in her short time here. Living here was going to feel good.

She headed to Amanda's house, barely able to contain her excitement. When she confided that she'd made the offer, they celebrated with ice cream sundaes with the kids, although they didn't tell them that's what they were doing. They didn't want them to blabber about the details before the deal was done. Living within walking distance from them was going to be wonderful. They could even walk to church together.

"Would you like to go with me on a little ride? I'm dropping the kids and Denali off at Paws. I have a couple of errands to run," Amanda said as she cleaned up the ice cream dishes.

"That sounds great."

"Kids, go get Denali on his lead. We're going to head out." They didn't even pause and were back down with Denali a few minutes later.

With the kids' excitement, there was nonstop chatter on the ride over to Paws. Rosemary waited in the car while Amanda handed off the kids to Paul.

They drove to a flower distributor about forty-five minutes away to get an idea of what flowers Amanda would like for the wedding.

"Does this mean you two set the date?" Rosemary asked.

"No, and the more we talk about it, the more we just want to keep it very simple. I'm so ready to be married to him. I don't want to wait."

"Then don't." Rosemary pulled out her phone and looked at the calendar. "I'm assuming you'll want to do it on the weekend, because the kids will certainly need to be a part of it, or if you're keeping it small, you could probably get away with doing it on a school night. An evening wedding would be romantic."

"With lights in the trees?" Amanda perked up. "And candles in the paper bags with sand in them. Luminaries—that's what they are. The kids loved making them at Christmas."

"You could put them to work on those."

"Do you think it's tacky if we get married quickly?"

"Not at all. No one is going to question how perfect you two are together. And I think you're smart not to spend a ton of money on a one-hour wedding ceremony. People go nuts these days."

"I know. Neither one of us is into that. We just want our little family, a select few friends, like you and Tug, and if my parents don't come down, we can video them in. It's so hard for them to travel. But thanks to that storm, I just saw them. And my parents adore Paul. Always have. They have been waiting for this moment."

"Put your energy into the relationship, not the party. That's what I always tell young couples." Rosemary tapped some notes into her phone. "So, what would we need? Flowers? A cake?"

"Yes, but it doesn't even have to be a tiered wedding-type cake. Just a pretty one, because I think Hailey and Jesse will expect that. Maybe two round tiers with a little bride and groom on top."

"That's easy." Rosemary added it to the notes. "Any color themes?"

"It's going to be at my house. The house is already blue, so why not work with the natural colors of the beach and blue?"

"You'll need a dress."

Amanda smiled. "Yes. There's a cute dress I saw in a catalog. I'll have to find it and show it to you. It's soft and flowing, not too fancy."

Rosemary giggled. It was exciting to help Amanda plan the details. Nina hadn't let her do anything for hers. She and her sorority sisters handled everything except paying for it. "If you're not opposed to emailing or calling everyone, then the invitations aren't necessary. That's a huge time-saver."

"Don't need them."

"Got it."

"I think I can speak for Tug, but if not, I can do it myself. I'd love to cater the meal for the small group. I'm a good cook. I promise. I've done it a million times over the years."

"That would be perfect. I don't even care what you serve. It's about being together."

"I couldn't agree more." Rosemary squeezed Amanda's arm. "I'm so excited. Oh my gosh, it will be breathtaking. Twinkle lights all over the backyard and the ocean waves as the music. Wedding march?"

"I think Hailey and Jesse would like that. It's overkill, but I want them to love it."

"You are an amazing mother. This will be a very special day." Rosemary typed in a few more notes as they drove, then put her phone down. "I'm going to create a wedding plan for you with all this stuff we've been brainstorming. I think it'll help you decide on the earliest realistic date for what you really want. It doesn't have to take long to plan it. I'll help you. What do you think?"

"I think you're a genius."

"I think I'm as excited as you are!" Rosemary danced in her

seat. "I'll have to find a pretty beachy blue dress and some sparkly sandals."

"I have a pair of flip-flops with pretty rhinestones all over them. I think I'll wear those." Amanda flashed Rosemary a smile. "Is that too casual?"

"No, ma'am. This is your day and I think it'll be cute! Paul is absolutely going to shed tears when he sees how beautiful a bride you're going to be."

"Great. Then I'll cry for sure." Amanda swirled a finger in Rosemary's direction. "Put waterproof mascara on that list of yours."

"On it." She added it to the list.

They ended up spending almost two hours in the flower shop, looking at photo albums of previous weddings they'd serviced and talking to one of the floral designers.

When they left, Amanda looked overwhelmed.

"Are you okay?" Rosemary asked.

"Who knew there were so many kinds of bouquets?"

"Not me. That was way more information than I ever needed to know about flowers," Rosemary said. "We could tie a ribbon around a bundle of wildflowers or roses and call it a day."

"I kind of like that idea."

"I'll get this all in a document for you. Is the printer in the living room wireless?"

"It sure is."

"Great. I'll print it out for you and email you the file so you'll have it both ways."

"Thank you, Rosemary. You make a great wedding planner."

"I've seen the movie a time or two. Can't resist a young Matthew McConaughey. I still laugh when I think of his fiancée calling him Eddie. He does not look like an Eddie!"

"I love that movie. Seriously, though, I appreciate your help and you validating that what I really want is okay. Something simple and special."

"You deserve exactly what you want."

They got back to Amanda's, and Rosemary went to work on the wedding plan while Amanda started dinner. Paul was on his way with the kids. While she was working on her computer, her phone buzzed.

"Hello?"

"Rosemary. It's Tug."

"Hey, how are you?"

"Great. Was hoping we could get together for a little while and catch up."

"I've been running around with Amanda. We're talking wedding plans."

"The happiest day in a woman's life, I hear," Tug said.

"It is. Want to get together tomorrow? I have something I want to tell you."

"Is everything okay?" Tug's response held a hint of concern.

"Of course. Everything is great," she reassured him. "I've got some things to do with Amanda and the kids in the morning. How about we get together for lunch?"

"Sounds great. I'll make lunch for here at the house if that works for you. Any special requests?"

"Sounds perfect. Surprise me."

"That's becoming my new favorite pastime. Wait. Do I have to put that on my bucket list?"

"Now, you know that's a to-do."

"Ha! I'll see you tomorrow. Have a good night."

She hung up the phone, smiling. Life on Whelk's Island was a delight.

The next day, Rosemary showed up at Tug's at lunchtime. She was shocked to see the temporary dune cleared and his truck gone.

She climbed the stairs and stood at the front door for a moment with excitement flooding through her. She couldn't wait to tell him her news. She knocked, taking in a steadying breath.

"I'm coming," Tug's voice called from inside. "Hey, gal. Come on in."

"You've been busy."

"Oh. Yeah. I kind of miss the hill. Now I have car shopping to do. I've got to say, I'm tempted to build a slide down the other side of the porch."

"Sounds fun. I always loved the snake slide the best."

"You're a daredevil. I knew it!"

"Guilty." She followed him inside.

He stopped in the foyer and turned to face her. "I have something to say."

She almost bumped into him. "Oh? Okay."

"I don't want you to go," he said. "Maybe you picked up on how much I enjoy your company. I don't know, but I was talking to Amanda, and I realized I hadn't said that, so I want you to know that I don't want you to go back to your daughter's house yet."

"You don't?" She felt as light as a feather. *I guess no matter how old you get, it feels good to be wanted.*

"I've been dreading it," he admitted. "I can barely sleep for thinking about it."

"Don't lose another night's sleep over it, Tug." She couldn't help but grin. "I *want* to stay here on Whelk's Island."

He perked up. "You do? For more than just a little while?"

"Yes. I wanted to tell you before, but I didn't want you to think this was just because of you." Flustered, she took a breath and tried again. "No, wait. That's not coming out right, because it has a lot to do with you, in a really good way, but not only because of you."

"You're losing me." His brows pulled together.

She could almost see the thought bubble of question marks above his head.

"I really like you," he said.

Those words made her heart stop. "That's just it, Tug. I am so happy here. I don't want to lose you. And I'm okay if it's always this friendship between us, because I love spending time with you, and I love this place and the town and Amanda and Paul and The Wife—"

"I'm getting the picture. It's a great place to live."

"It is. And you're a great person to spend time with. I feel optimistic and hopeful around you." She clasped her hands, trying to pace herself but dying to just spit out the words. "I put in an offer on that house down from Amanda's."

"What?" He looked completely surprised. "I was not expecting that. This is great news!"

"I thought you had an idea that I was interested in that house the day we passed by it and you told me about when it was built and all."

"Everyone dreams of owning a beach house. I didn't think that meant you were going to put an offer on it."

"Not everyone dreams of owning a beach house. I didn't until right about that moment."

"Well, beach people dream about them all the time. The culture and tradition of living near the ocean is special. And this ain't no Hawaii, but it's beautiful, and I bet a lot of the activities aren't that different from when you lived on the islands. The seafood festivals, bonfires, surfing competitions, sandcastle-building contests, and collecting shells. It's a rich tapestry that shapes a beach community."

"Exactly, and I long for it, but not because I'm chasing yesterday." She was adamant she would never do that.

"Good. I think we're both learning there's nothing behind us worth focusing on," Tug said. "Memories are meant to be cherished, but today is where we need to focus—today and the hope of tomorrows."

"Right. My daughter was the only thing keeping me from moving forward, but I felt so strongly about it that I talked to her. Our conversation went much better than I expected, so I put in my offer, and this morning I got the call. They accepted it. I got the house."

"You're moving to Whelk's Island? Right up the street?"

"I am."

"Rosemary, you don't know how happy this makes me." He pulled her into a bear hug, swaying side to side. "I know you didn't move for me. But this old man has found a happiness like I've never experienced since meeting you. I've been dreading you leaving." He swept a hand through his hair and let out a breath. "This is fantastic news. Wow, so when will you be moving in?"

"The house was empty, and I negotiated the staged furniture in the deal. I also negotiated renting it until we close. So I'll be moving in immediately. I get the keys tomorrow."

"Wow. Well, when you decide to move, you really move. I'll do anything to help you get moved and settled in," Tug said with enthusiasm. "You can count on me. And what I can't do, I bet I know a guy who can."

"Oh, I'm sure you do. You know everybody!"

Tug looked proud of that. "And most of them owe me favors, which helps."

"For sure."

"Should I add getting you moved into your new house to my bucket list?"

"No. That is not a bucket list item. That's a to-do list item."

"I started one of those just today. Come with me." He had her follow him into the kitchen. He pointed toward the refrigerator.

On a magnetic grocery pad, he'd written *TO-DO LIST* across the top. Beneath that there was one item with a little checkbox next to it.

☐ *Surprise Rosemary every day.*

Rosemary blinked back tears. "That's the sweetest thing. Thank you."

"I guess I'll add 'Help Rosemary move in' to the list now."

She nodded. "I love the idea of being on your to-do list." No matter if they explored more of a relationship someday, it was good now, and it would all happen at the right time if it was meant to be.

"Helping you sounds a lot more fun than a to-do task to me, but I'll call it whatever you like as long as I get to have you around. You brighten my days."

"I'm so glad you think so."

"How about that lunch?" he asked.

"Yes, please. I'm starving."

"You're always hungry," he noted. "I love that about you."

Over lunch, he asked her when she was going to show him her bucket list.

"I've got mine written in my journal," she said. "I'll show it to you when Nina and Kendra bring my stuff down this weekend. Tug, I couldn't believe she was truly happy for me. She and Kendra are excited to see the place."

"I look forward to meeting them. Let me know what I can do to help."

"I will. I might even write it on your list," she said, tickled with the prospect.

"Have at it. And when you get your stuff, then we'll compare our bucket lists and plan a short road trip. I don't know if I'm the road-tripping kind, since I've never done it, but I'm willing to try it."

"I'm looking forward to that."

Tug's cellphone rang. "Hang on a second." He answered. "Yes, she's right here. Okay." He waved Rosemary over. "It's Paul and Amanda. They want me to put it on speaker."

"Hi, you two! You're on speaker," Rosemary said.

"Great," Amanda said. "We settled on a date for the wedding, thanks to your planning skills, Rosemary."

"You're very welcome," Rosemary replied.

"It's a short list of our closest friends—just twelve people, and you two are at the top! We're getting married in The Shell Collector's backyard, Saturday after next. I kept it simple, but two weeks is going to fly by."

Tug's jaw dropped. "What? This is great. Best news I've had all year."

"It's super fast!" Rosemary said.

"We just inked it in on the pastor's schedule," Paul said. "We'll be doing sunset vows. According to the internet, on September twentieth sunset will be just before seven. We will get started at six o'clock, so by the time we get all twelve cats herded and do all the 'I dos,' we can see the sun dip below the horizon."

"You'll both be there, right?" Amanda sounded worried. "Please don't tell me you have plans that night."

Rosemary glanced at Tug, her hand brushing his on the kitchen island as they exchanged a quick, knowing look.

"We wouldn't miss it," they said in unison, and Tug added with a grin, "No matter what!"

"Tug, I do need a favor." Amanda took a breath.

"What is it? I'm happy to do anything you need."

"Well, it's kind of a big ask. My mom and dad are not going to make it down. There are a few things I want to be traditional for the kids and for us. Would you walk me down the aisle? You and Jesse, of course?" she clarified.

"Yes! Yes! I'm honored. Absolutely. Anything for you two."

"I forgot to tell you, Tug." Rosemary shrank back. "I sort of committed us to cater the dinner for afterward. I could handle it, but I think we'd create something pretty fabulous together."

He pulled her close and kissed her on the cheek. "Thank you. I'd love to cook that meal with you. This is the smartest lady I've ever met," Tug said. "Y'all know how to make a man feel needed. It's a nice feeling." His eyes were misty.

That kiss hadn't gone unnoticed. Rosemary hadn't expected it, but her heart was pounding in response. His blue eyes twinkled as Paul and Amanda ran down all the details of their upcoming nuptials.

Finally, Tug hung up. "This is one good day. You're moving here. Paul's moving in with Amanda and the kids. They'll be a real family. Everything is right."

"I'm so thankful something brought me to Whelk's Island at just that time. I felt a strong calling to be here. I don't think that was an accident."

"Me either. There are no accidents. We're all just pieces to a much bigger puzzle." He sat there looking at her for an almost awkwardly long moment. "I can't wait to spend more time together. This is really happening, isn't it?"

"It is." She broke into a wide smile. "Butterflies just danced inside me!" *Did I just say that out loud?* She quickly changed the topic. "There are some short road trips I've been wanting to do. The Biltmore in Asheville isn't that far away, and I'd like to go on one of those whale-watching boats. I heard they do those right off the coast here certain times of the year."

"They do. I know the guy—"

"Of course you do!" She relaxed. "Let's do it together, then, since you know him and all."

"Yeah. Sure," Tug said. "I'm up for that."

"You have several things on your bucket list that sound fun." *I'd love to tag along.* She could easily picture spending a lot more time with him.

There was a hint of mischief in the lift of his brow.

She hoped that meant they might do those together too.

Chapter Thirty-Four

THE FOLLOWING WEEKEND, ROSEMARY STOOD AT THE door of her new home. This was a new start, and she felt like she'd been filled with vibrant light. Her smile hadn't left her face since she found this house and decided to buy it.

Her nerves were a mess about seeing Nina and Kendra, though. She prayed she and Nina would never have a blowup like that again.

Nina's car pulled into the driveway.

Rosemary ran out to greet them, waving like she was hailing a taxi. "Hello!" She and Nina had their moments, but it never changed her love for her daughter, and she had every intention of making that crystal clear on this visit, along with offering a long-overdue apology.

Kendra bailed out of the car before Nina even got the key out of the ignition.

"Grandma!" She ran over and flung herself into Rosemary's arms. "This is where you're going to live?"

Rosemary couldn't wait to share Whelk's Island with them. "I sure am. What do you think?"

Kendra danced with excitement, making a slow turn as she took it all in. "This house is like something out of a movie. The beach is right there. It's blowing my mind. Can you hear the waves? Is that really the ocean?"

"Sure can. That's the best part." Rosemary spread her arms wide. "Wait until you see the view from upstairs."

"I missed you. I took good care of James," Kendra said. "You didn't have to bribe me."

"I'm sure you earned it. Thank you, sweetie."

"I'm going to go get him out of the car." Kendra raced back to rescue the fish, passing her mother on the way. "Can we explore? I can't wait to check this place out."

"We can," Nina said. "But first we need to get your grandmother's stuff unpacked from the car."

"Fine." Kendra trudged back to the car.

Rosemary welcomed Nina, opening her arms for a hug.

"Hey, Mom. This is beautiful." Nina looked at the house. "I love the soft color and all the white accents. It's really welcoming."

"It feels right." Rosemary stepped back. "We're really okay, right?" She hated to sound desperate, but she felt a little that way. She loved her daughter, rocky relationship and all, and she'd never want to hurt her feelings.

"We are, Mom. I'm sorry I went off the rails like that on you. I don't know what to say except I love you and I guess I was trying to protect you, like you've always done for me."

"Someday I might need that level of help, but not yet, kiddo." Rosemary hugged her again. "I'm sorry too. I didn't help in the situation. I love you—don't you ever doubt that—and the next time we act like that, let's have a full stop and step away before it goes 'off the rails,' as you put it. Deal?"

"Deal."

"It's behind us. Forgotten." Rosemary pulled her daughter into her arms once more and held her for a long moment. Tears slipped down her cheeks. "I love you, baby girl. You will always be my baby girl."

"We love you, too, Mom." Nina swept a tear away and sniffled. "Stop making me cry. We are here to help you and have some fun."

"Yes, we are. Thank you for bringing my things, for understanding this decision and being so supportive."

Nina nodded, her eyes moist. "I'm still concerned, but I'll give you your space. You were right. I overreacted. I don't know why I equated losing Dad with you suddenly becoming helpless. Maybe I'm just projecting my own emotions from this divorce onto you. I've never felt so adrift."

Nina had definitely been struggling, but adrift? "Honey, I didn't know you were feeling that way. I'm sure losing your dad didn't help, but you've got this. You're doing all the right things. You are the smartest, most capable woman I've ever known."

"Mom, that's only because you raised me to be one. Just like you. If only I ever become the woman you have been."

"I'm sorry that ex of yours has been making things difficult for you."

"Me too. It's exhausting."

Kendra walked over, carrying two tote bags and balancing the fishbowl in the crook of her arm. "Here's James!" Kendra presented the bowl to Rosemary.

"He looks great. Hi, James. I've missed you." She took the bowl, and James seemed excited to see her. He immediately started blowing bubbles. "Welcome home, James," Rosemary said.

"Let's get this stuff upstairs," Nina said.

"Up there?" Kendra adjusted the boxes dramatically. "That's a lot of stairs."

Nina glanced at the stairs to the front door. "Mom, are you going to be able to do these stairs when you have groceries?"

Rosemary raised a finger. She could barely contain her excitement. "Follow me. There's a solution to every problem you can think of in this house. Lights even automatically come on under the lower cabinets in the kitchen when you walk in the room at night. It lights the way. Like magic, only it's all configured from a tablet in the kitchen that I have no plans to touch."

"Swanky," Nina remarked.

"A smart home, Grandma. That's what they call that."

"What I'm going to show you is even better than that." She walked toward a glossy white cottage-style door under the carport and swung it open. "I have my own elevator."

"Holy cow!" Kendra raced toward the door. "It's like a hotel. Mom? This is epic."

"Get in there," Rosemary said. "It's pretty cool, isn't it?"

"Like I said, you're the most capable woman I know." Nina shook her head. "You've thought of everything."

"Did I mention I negotiated all the staged furniture in my purchase?"

"You didn't. Is it nice?"

"Much nicer than what I'd have been willing to buy." Rosemary pressed the button, and the elevator rose to the first floor. "Check it out."

They walked into the house, and she gave them a quick tour, starting in the kitchen and ending with the best part, the deck overlooking the beach. The outdoor furniture was bright and welcoming. It had a white wood look but was made out of that new PVC stuff that required no maintenance. Ceiling fans turned lazily above them.

"This is like a resort," Nina said.

Kendra walked out and leaned over the rail. "It's louder than I thought it would be, but in a good way."

"She would've adored Hawaii," Rosemary whispered to Nina.

"I was always too busy to make the time to take her. Concessions I made for him. More mistakes."

"That's behind you now." Rosemary knew Nina was referring to her ex-husband. They were both workaholics. How they had time to make a child was still a mystery, because they sure didn't make time for much else.

"I'm working on a better life balance," Nina said. "I'm still a work in progress on that."

"You sure are," Rosemary said. "You'll get there."

"I'm gonna go get more of Grandma's stuff out of the car," Kendra announced. "I'll be right back." She hopped into the elevator, closed the metal safety grate, and hit the button. "Going down!" The elevator hummed into action.

"I hope you don't mind," Rosemary said. "I accepted an invitation for all of us to join Amanda for dinner. Paul and Tug will be there, and I think Kendra will get a kick out of Jesse and Hailey." She hoped she hadn't overstepped right out of the gate. "I want you two to get a do-over. She's really sweet. I think you would get along."

"I owe her a big fat apology." Nina visibly swallowed. "Guess I'll be eating crow."

"Or don't even mention it," Rosemary said. "Trust me, Amanda is not waiting on an apology. She understood where you were coming from more than I did. I think the two of you are going to get along just fine."

"Hey. I noticed almost all the houses have cool names on them," Kendra said, returning with some more boxes. "That's sort of fun. Are you going to name your house?"

"Of course. I was thinking about something with *Sanctuary* or *Tide* in it. I haven't gotten very far with it yet. What do you think we should name my new beach house?"

"Since this is sort of a new beginning for you . . ." Kendra pressed her finger to her lips. "How about *Rosemary's Thyme?* Like a play on the herb, but, you know, like it's your time too."

"Cute!" Rosemary said. "I like that." It fit Amanda better, but she didn't mention that, because it was so sweet that Kendra actually seemed engaged at the moment.

"Maybe. Or . . ." Nina shifted. "I don't know if you'd want to, but maybe work in *Palakiko.* Grandma always said it meant 'spark of existence' and that it was a blessed name. This place is a blessing for this time in your life, Mom. I know you need to be your own person. What about Palakiko Retreat?"

"Oh, Nina. I love that." Rosemary's eyes blurred with tears. "And it pays tribute to Kai. I miss him fiercely. You know that, right?"

"I know, Mom." Nina hugged her.

Kendra cocked her hip, but Rosemary gave her a stern warning look. Kendra picked up on it and nodded, pressing her lips together like it was killing her not to smart off to her mother.

Rosemary basked in the kind moment. "I love my girls." She gestured Kendra over into the hug.

"Mom, I hope you're happy here, and if you're not, you always have a place with me, or I'll help you get a cute little condo nearby." She squeezed her mom's hand. "Whatever you want."

"Thank you." Rosemary took a deep breath. "I think you'll quickly come to love Whelk's Island too. The community of it. It's so balancing." She let go of Nina's hand and motioned for them to follow. "Come. Listen to this amazing ocean. It'll chase the cobwebs right out of your brain. I feel so alive here."

They walked back out onto the porch.

"I hope you and Kendra enjoy Whelk's Island. It's perfect timing."

"It is. For you and me, and for Kendra and me. We need some no-drama fun. I've been working a lot, but I just hired another person for my team. I'm planning to off-load some responsibilities this year. This will be a good start on this balance I'm looking for."

"It will."

Kendra made another trip to the car and plopped a suitcase and a tote bag on the floor, then went straight down again.

A minute later, she stepped out of the elevator with the last of the bags. She placed them in the living room and went out on the deck. "Mom! You have to see this."

Nina rushed to see what the yelling was about.

Kendra stood pointing to the water with excitement. "I think I saw a dolphin!"

"Kendra, I doubt it," Nina said. "Probably just wishful thinking."

Rosemary joined them. "No. Look, there are three of them." It was the first time Rosemary had seen them, but Tug had told her about the frequent visits the dolphins made in these waters. She glanced at her watch, hoping they were on a schedule so she could see them often. "Look at them play."

Kendra was too busy watching to respond.

Rosemary took delight in Kendra's interest. "Wouldn't it be fun to come and spend long weekends here on summer break? I've collected some beautiful shells. You'd probably enjoy that."

"Life takes you to unexpected places. Trust the light to lead you home." Rosemary could hear the message in her mind as clear as if someone were reading it to her.

I am home.

"Can we go explore now?" Kendra spun around, looking to her mother for permission. "I can't wait to find some shells to take back with me."

"We don't have enough time right now," Rosemary said. "We're going to my friend Amanda's for dinner, but we definitely will tomorrow. I promise."

Rosemary loved how excited Nina and Kendra seemed about the new house. A feeling of strength and independence flooded through her. In helping Tug, she'd rediscovered her own gumption to give the rest of her life the best effort she could.

"I made a dessert. Let me get that and we'll head over there."

"Please tell me you made that pound cake you used to always make," Nina said.

"I did." Rosemary loved knowing that the simple things that were special in the past were still precious.

They made the short drive to Amanda's.

"It will be nice that they are so close to you," Nina remarked.

"I know. It really couldn't have worked out better. I can walk to the post office and the library from here."

They all got out of the car, and Hailey and Jesse must've been watching for them to arrive because they raced down the stairs to greet them.

Rosemary introduced everyone, and Kendra followed Hailey and Jesse into the backyard, while Rosemary and Nina went up to see Amanda.

"Aloha," Rosemary called out as they walked inside.

Amanda rounded the corner in a pretty pink apron. "Come in." She walked straight over to Nina. "I'm so glad to get to meet you again."

"I owe you a huge apology," Nina blurted out before she even said hello. "I'm really embarrassed, but I'd love to get another chance to get to know you."

"You've got it. Pretend it never happened. Come on in." Amanda looked at Rosemary. "Oh, Rosemary, please tell me that's the Hawaiian pound cake."

"It is."

"Mmm." Amanda took it and looked over her shoulder at Nina. "This stuff is addicting."

"I know!"

Amanda led them into the living room, where Paul and Tug were watching a golf tournament on the sports channel. "Guys, Rosemary and her family are here."

Tug stood. "It's nice to meet you, Nina. I've heard a lot about you. I'm Tug."

"It's good to meet you. And you must be Paul. Mom has talked about all of you."

"How do you like Whelk's Island so far?" Paul asked.

"Well, I haven't seen much of it, but Mom's house is great. I love knowing it's so close to such nice neighbors here in case she ever needs anything."

"We're here for her. There's a great support system in this community," Tug said.

"That's comforting."

Paul switched the television off. "Would y'all like to come sit outside?"

"Sure," Rosemary said. They followed Paul and Tug outside. From here, they could see the kids tossing a big playground ball around the yard. Kendra looked like she was having a good time.

Amanda walked out and kissed Paul on the cheek. "So, Nina, do you know how long you're going to stay yet?"

"I'm just going to stay a couple of days this time, but I'll be planning some extended weekends, for sure."

"We might even see more of each other if you come to visit than when I was living with you," Rosemary remarked.

Everyone laughed, thinking the comment referred to the beach location being so inviting.

Nina shrugged. "She's not kidding. I've been in a terrible overwork cycle. I'm recently divorced. I think at first it was a coping mechanism, but you know how that goes. The more you do—"

"The more they let you do it." Paul finished her sentence.

"Yes! Exactly, and I've got to find some life balance."

"Good luck with that," Paul said. "It's not an easy cycle to break. I'm a pretty good life balance coach. If you ever need to talk, give me a shout."

"That's really nice of you. I might take you up on that."

This visit was going better than Rosemary could've ever dreamed. Nina's good side was shining through, and everyone seemed to be enjoying the evening.

After dinner, the kids asked to be excused from the table early. Kendra, although much older than Hailey, had taken to her immediately, and the two of them let Jesse tag along as Hailey took Kendra to show off her treasured beach finds.

Rosemary got up from the table and helped Amanda clean up and prepare dessert and coffee.

"This has been so nice, Amanda. Thank you."

"You know you are always welcome in my home. How's the house feel?"

"Well, since it was completely furnished, I feel right at home. I've started a list of things I will need, but it's a short list."

Nina walked in with a few of the plates and loaded them into the dishwasher.

"Well, let me see the list before you buy anything," Amanda said. "I have all my stuff, and Maeve left me all of hers, and when Paul moves in, we'll have even more. I'm sure we can fill in some gaps for you. Believe me, you'd be doing us a favor."

"Great."

"And keep me posted," Nina said. "I've got to simplify. I think I have every gadget ever made. I don't even use half of it. If I ever had to pack and move, it would be a nightmare."

"Well, I may not be doing any shopping at all," Rosemary

said. "This is new news. Did I tell you, Nina, that Paul and Amanda are getting married here in the backyard next weekend?"

"No. Congratulations. How exciting," Nina said to Amanda. "He seems great. You two and the children, you make a beautiful family."

"Thank you." Amanda blushed. "I'm really excited. It's just going to be a real simple ceremony."

"That's all you need when it's the right thing," Nina said.

Amanda leaned in, nodding. "Right? People go crazy on weddings these days. We're only having like twelve people, including the pastor. If you're in town, you and Kendra are absolutely invited. We'd love to have you."

"That's very generous, but I don't know that we could swing back that quickly. Thank you, though."

Amanda's invitation to them touched Rosemary.

As the night wore on and they moved out to the deck, the sound of the ocean filled the air. What was it about the ocean air that made her sleepy?

Rosemary felt a contentment she hadn't known in years. She'd made her point, not just to her daughter but to herself. New doors were opening, and she was ready, more than ever, to step through them.

"I think we're going to head on home, Amanda. All this fresh air has me tired, and I'm sure Nina and Kendra would like to crawl in bed after their long drive today."

"Not me," Kendra said. "I'm fine."

"You can come back and visit with Hailey tomorrow," Nina said.

"Actually," Rosemary said, "Amanda, if it's okay, I wanted to ask if I could pick up Hailey to work on a project with me tomorrow. She and Kendra can spend the day at my house. I'm happy to take Jesse too. They all seem to get along so well."

"Can we, Mom?" Hailey and Kendra were flashing hopeful glances at each other.

Jesse marched over. "I want to go too."

"Great. This project is top secret and extra special," Rosemary said to Hailey, Jesse, and Kendra, twisting an imaginary key into a lock on her lips.

Amanda leaned into Paul's arms. "Lunch tomorrow? My place?"

Paul grinned. "Anywhere with you. Wouldn't miss it."

Chapter Thirty-Five

THE FOLLOWING SATURDAY, ROSEMARY BREEZED INTO Amanda's house with a singsongy *aloha*. "It's your big day!" Rosemary felt like a glass of champagne, bubbly and excited. "How are you feeling? Any wedding jitters?" The two weeks to Amanda and Paul's wedding had gone by in a blink, but everything had come together according to plan.

"None." Amanda appeared cool and ready. "I feel so blessed. No worries at all."

"Tug's bringing the food over in a little while. We have a beautiful dinner planned. After the ceremony, we will serve it. I picked up the cake this morning. I just put it in the kitchen. Where do you want to set that up?"

"I have a round table outside for it. Chase will carry it down just before we say our vows."

"Then you're all set."

Amanda's gown hung from a hanger over the door. A simple high-neck halter dress in an icy blue that complemented her eyes. Delicate rhinestones, no bigger than pinheads, shimmered at the neck and waist.

"Your dress is so feminine," Rosemary commented. "It's perfect. I love the way the fabric flows. It has a Greek-goddess look to it."

"You haven't seen Hailey's yet, have you? My friend from

church sewed it for us. She's a whiz of a seamstress. It's a perfect match. Go get your dress, baby."

Hailey hopped up and ran from the room. She came back carrying a hanger high in the air with a short sundress in the same soft blue material. "See! She even made me a matching hair ribbon with sparklies on it."

"You will both look so beautiful."

Hailey walked over to Rosemary. "Did you bring it?" she whispered.

Amanda looked curious. "What are you two up to now?"

Hailey rocked from side to side, looking a little guilty. She rocked nervously. "Nothing."

"It's probably perfect timing for you to ask, actually," Rosemary said. "We have something for you."

"A surprise!" Hailey looked ready to bust. "And Jesse helped, too, but he's with the boys."

"Oh, was this the project from your playdate with Kendra?"

Hailey nodded. "You're going to love it."

"I'm sure I will."

Rosemary excused herself to get her things from her car.

When she returned, she hung her dress on the back of the closet door and set her big beach bag on the floor beneath it.

Hailey bounced with excitement while Rosemary dug through the bag and pulled out two boxes. She handed a blue box with a sand-colored bow to Amanda.

"This is almost too pretty to open." Amanda shook it, listening for a hint.

"Wait till you see what's inside," Hailey said.

Amanda tugged one end of the ribbon. "You can use this ribbon in your hair too," she said, handing it to her daughter. She lifted the top of the box and swept back the delicate tissue paper. "Oh my goodness! Is this for my hair?"

"It is," Hailey said. "We decorated the hair comb with sea glass and tiny shells."

"It's perfect." Amanda lifted the beautiful comb. "I love it. It goes perfect with my dress too. Thank you. This is so precious."

"And there are blue sea glass pieces, Mom. For something blue and new. We even added a piece from Maeve's collection to make it a keepsake."

"You thought of everything." She squeezed Hailey's hand.

"And I have old and borrowed covered for you as well," Rosemary explained as she handed the second box to Amanda. "I had these cleaned at the jewelers. When I saw you in that dress, I knew these would be perfect for it. I hope you think so too. They were my thirtieth wedding anniversary earrings. If you don't want to wear them, that's fine. We'll put them in the lining of your dress or something to be sure you're covered."

Amanda flipped open the little velvet box that held the earrings. "You're right. I couldn't have shopped for something more perfect." She hugged Rosemary. "You being here is making everything so much more special. Thank you." She held an earring next to her ear and stood by the dress. "What do y'all think?"

"Mom, you're going to look so pretty." Hailey took her mom's hand and Rosemary's too. "We love you, Rosemary."

Rosemary sucked back a little squeal of delight. "I am so happy to be a part of this. Thank you." Tears slipped down her nose, and Hailey handed her a tissue.

"Here, Mom warned me we might cry happy tears."

"She's right."

The moments swept by, and before they knew it, it was time to get into their dresses and sparkly flip-flops. Amanda's friends from church had arrived, and Chase had just poked his head in the door to tell them to stay put while he got Paul out to the backyard. "Can't jinx a perfect marriage with one little peek before the ceremony," Chase teased.

Amanda turned to Rosemary. "It's happening."

"It is, dear." Rosemary took Amanda's hand in her own. "It is right."

"You sounded like Maeve just then. Thank you so much for being here. Meeting you, marrying Paul—so much has happened so fast, but it all feels so right."

A light tap at the door had Amanda scrambling to hide.

"It's just me," Tug said from the hall.

They all let out a sigh of relief. Rosemary let him in.

"My goodness." Tug patted his heart. "So much beauty in one room. It's my lucky day. How are you doing, Amanda?"

"Happy. Excited. Ready!"

"Good. Paul is ready too. The pastor is here. Everyone is downstairs. Chase just set the cake out. We're ready when you are."

"Let's do this." Her wide grin told the whole story.

"Jesse and I'll be back in a few minutes to get you," he said.

Rosemary fussed with a few tendrils of Amanda's hair in the clip. "I'm going to go get in my seat. I'm so happy for you. You look stunning. And, Hailey, you'll walk out first, as the maid of honor. Then Tug and Jesse will walk your mom up. Got it?"

"Yes, ma'am." She clung to a nosegay of five colorful roses that was a miniature of her mother's. It was tied with a trailing blue silk ribbon and captured all the colors of the sunset—white, pink, yellow, peach, and orange.

Rosemary passed Tug on the stairs on her way down.

"You look even more beautiful than the bride," Tug said with a twinkle in his eyes.

She swatted him. "I do not."

"You do to me."

She pecked him on the cheek. It was playful, but it had been an impulse. *Oops.* "Thank you for saying that. I'll save you a seat."

Tug glanced at his watch. "And we're right on time. See you in a couple of minutes."

Rosemary settled into her seat in the front row, where Tug would join her after walking Amanda down the aisle. The white folding chairs were arranged in pairs—three rows on each side—leaving a clear path down the center for the bride's grand entrance. Because no matter the size, every bride deserves those little touches.

The intimate setting made it even more special.

The pastor gave a nod, and soft organ music filled the air.

Hailey came out first, carrying her bouquet so tight her little hands looked pink, but her smile was wide. She took her spot next to the pastor.

Then those famous chords filled the backyard, and Tug and Jesse stepped out with Amanda between them.

Rosemary watched Paul catch his breath.

Paul, Tug, and Jesse wore khakis, light blue dress shirts, and bow ties.

Jesse gave his sister a thumbs-up as they walked, and Hailey waved back.

Tug, Jesse, and Amanda paused in front of the pastor. "Mom looks like a movie star," Jesse said to Hailey loud enough for everyone to hear.

Everyone laughed.

"Who gives this woman to be married to this man?" the pastor asked, chuckling.

"We do." Tug choked on the words.

Tug kissed Amanda on the cheek, and Paul shook Jesse's hand.

Tug then took the seat next to Rosemary. He patted her knee

and gave it a squeeze that felt as familiar as if they'd known each other forever.

Pastor Qualls, knowing the couple as he did, spoke briefly about how right these two were for each other and the beautiful family they made.

The vows were short, and when it came to "I do," both Jesse and Hailey were beaming.

The sun was lowering just as they'd planned.

Summer would soon become autumn. A season of change. Tug and Paul had strung fairy lights across the backyard over the last week and secretly set them all to come on at precisely 6:54. It would make for a dramatic transition into the evening. Amanda was going to be surprised. Like fireworks, only silent, it would take her breath away.

Rosemary glanced at her watch, then looked as the sky treated them to a glorious show of sunset colors. It was the perfect setting for two hearts to become one, surrounded by God's beautiful artwork.

Once the pastor pronounced them man and wife, Amanda took Hailey's hand, and Paul lifted Jesse onto his shoulders. They walked through the small aisle of special friends as the sky darkened and the lights came on across the backyard.

"That's how weddings are," Tug said. He clapped. "Beautiful. Meaningful."

"It was perfect."

Amanda stood next to the cake. "Tug and Rosemary have prepared a lovely meal for us. Dessert will be this scrumptious cake—everybody's favorite, chocolate inside. But I do have one favor to ask. The kids and I collected these shells." She lifted a bucket and shook it. "I've got some paint markers up here. One person is missing tonight. The dearest of all, Maeve. I know we all miss her. I . . ." She paused. "We want to include her on this very special day. So, in her honor, I'm asking you each to write a little wedding sentiment on a shell. I'm going to create a wind chime and hang it from the tree here with the Spanish moss that represents the trip Maeve and I took together. I'd like to hang it as a symbol of our love and appreciation for Maeve's role in bringing us together."

Everyone murmured agreement.

"So, let's eat!"

Tug and Rosemary flipped the lids on the chafing dishes and made sure everyone got what they needed. The coastal spread featured fresh tuna, flounder, crab cakes, and oysters fried and steamed, with side dishes ranging from buttery parsley potatoes, to grilled brussels sprouts, to Jesse's favorite mac and cheese. And no menu in this town would be complete without Tug's famous corn bread. It was simple sea fare perfect for this family affair.

Chase and Fisher helped pass around pitchers of sweet tea and pink lemonade.

After dinner, everyone pulled their chairs into a circle around the firepit. Beach towels served as blankets against the cooling evening temperatures until the fire warmed up.

Rosemary pulled a small card from her pocket and handed it to Tug.

"What's this?" He turned the unaddressed envelope over. "Is it for Amanda and Paul?"

"No," she said. "It's for you."

He looked pleasantly surprised. "Can I open it now?"

"I hoped you would."

He eyed her curiously as he slid his finger under the sealed edge of the envelope. He pulled out a card with a fancy monogrammed *P* on the front.

She watched him read the note, eager for his response. It

thanked him for helping her navigate through the last few weeks and being the recipe to her finding joy again.

He chuckled. "I'm your recipe, huh?"

"You are. There's more. Look on the back."

His mouth dropped open. "You're giving me the recipe for your Hawaiian pound cake? You said—"

"I know what I said." She swallowed her nerves. "You're that special to me. I have never shared the recipe with anyone until now."

"This is serious," Tug said quietly.

She couldn't quite read him. "Is that okay?"

"More than okay." He pressed his hand against his heart. "You are everything I never knew I needed."

"What's that mean?"

"Walk with me," he said.

She was still nervous. It had been a bold move, but she didn't want to hold back on anything any longer.

He stood and reached for her hand.

She placed her hand in his and let him lead her to the beach.

Tug knew this place by heart, and she knew she'd follow him anywhere. He stopped and looked back toward Maeve's old place. "It looks pretty from here, doesn't it?"

She turned. "It does. All the twinkle lights and the stars above."

"The way the music and waves sort of cancel each other out."

"Yeah, I hear it," she whispered. "Very soothing. And the laughter of my new friends and family in the distance. There is so much joy among them."

He stepped behind her and wrapped his arms around her, as he swayed softly. "I feel joy right here too."

"Me, too, Tug. We're on the same page," she said. "A lot has happened in a short time, hasn't it?"

"It has. Does it scare you?"

"At first it did. It was confusing more than scary," she said.

"Yeah. Me, too, but not so much now. It's exciting. I feel like a teenager. And those shells . . . I mean, yours was extra special. Mine was literally a call to action from Maeve. I think the timing of me finding it was incredible, but if you knew Maeve, that wouldn't surprise you. You would've loved her."

"She sounds wonderful."

"This—what I'm feeling—isn't about bucket lists, but I wouldn't mind living our lives from one bucket list item to the next," he said. "It's about wanting to continue to get to know each other and enjoy every day to its fullest."

"I'd really like that."

"So, we're trusting the light to lead us home, just like your shell said?"

"Yes. You feel like home, Tug."

"My heart is open, Rosemary. I think this is the beginning of the best years of my life."

She turned and faced him. "I can't wait to experience what is ahead of us."

"Even with all life has thrown at me lately, I have more hope than I've felt in years." He laced his fingers with hers. "Come on. Let's walk."

They walked silently along the beach. The moon seemed to follow them, lighting their path.

The waves were slow and steady, until a larger one surprised them, forcing them to scramble to get out of the way. Tug reached for her hand between a breathless laugh.

"Look." Rosemary pointed with her other hand toward a shadowy figure ahead.

Someone on the beach bent down to pick something up.

"Looks like they are collecting shells," he said.

"Maybe there's a message in one of theirs tonight," Rosemary said in delight.

"If there is, then we're witnessing another new beginning."

They chased each other up the beach, their playful banter trailing behind like the waves at their feet.

Out of breath, Tug tossed his head back. "I'm only focused on our beginning."

"Once upon a time . . ." She looked into his eyes, so blue even in the moonlight. She trusted the unspoken message in them.

"Let's decide on our first bucket list item to tackle," he said.

"Really? Right now?"

"Sure. Why wait? What do you want to do?"

"I'd do anything with you, Tug. It doesn't have to be a bucket list thing."

"How about we check off that climb up a lighthouse tomorrow afternoon?" he said. "We'll make a whole day of it."

"But you've already done that. That's my list item."

"I've never climbed a lighthouse with you. And anything with you is on my bucket list too."

There was an understanding in the air.

She'd thought her days of romance were long behind her, but Tug had reignited something within her. He had a way of making her feel cherished, seen, and youthful again. She smiled, a mix of anticipation and nervousness dancing in her chest.

The sound of the waves made the silence between them comfortable. Tug took her hand. "Rosemary," he said softly, "I don't think you know the struggle this past year has been for me. Then losing the diner . . . Without the comfort of you by my side, I don't even—"

"Tug, we all have those seasons." Rosemary's eyes blurred with unshed tears. "I'm just so thankful that this timing turned out to be so perfect, when in reality it looked like a crazy thing to make the trip to Whelk's Island in a hurricane. Despite all that, you've shown me it's never too late to find happiness and love."

He stepped closer, his free hand cupping her cheek. "May I?" he whispered, his breath warm against her skin.

Rosemary nodded, her heart pounding. "Yes, Tug."

Their lips met softly, a sweet, lingering kiss filled with new-found hope. Gentle and promising.

"That was really nice," she said.

"It was. And tomorrow we explore the lighthouse."

"I'm pretty sure there will be light in every day."

"To light the way forward. Come on. We have a wedding reception to get back to." They held hands and walked back toward the twinkle lights at the beach house. With each step, the rising sounds of happy times ahead filled their hearts.

Epilogue

A Few Months Later

TUG STEPPED OFF THE RESORT SHUTTLE AND TOOK A DEEP breath of crisp air on the frosty February evening. The two-hour trek even farther north from the Duluth airport hadn't sounded that long when he booked the trip, but added to the flight to get here, it had made for one long day.

He turned to help Rosemary down the steps, and she gave him a teasing smile. They stepped to the side to wait for their luggage as the other guests disembarked. A row of shiny, colorful golf carts were at the ready to transport guests to their cabins.

"This is so swanky," Rosemary said.

The resort even had a champagne toast on the shuttle for everyone to start the adventure.

"You know, Tug, when I started that whole bucket list thing, I never expected we'd actually get to do these things," she said. "Even as a Christmas present, it's extravagant. I still feel bad for just buying you that smoker."

"I love that smoker, but I hate to break it to you—I'd have been just as happy with a bag of beef jerky if you were the one giving it to me."

"You're silly."

"Besides, since I didn't rebuild the diner and am getting into the groove of this retirement thing, I wanted to celebrate. This is a splurge, but the way I look at it, it's my bonus for working all those years."

"You deserve it. I'm glad I'm here to enjoy it with you, but I still say you went above and beyond."

"Nothing is too above or beyond when it comes to you." He kissed her on the cheek. "It's the northern lights, baby! We'll only see them once. Besides, I wanted to make this extra special. You woke something in me with all that bucket-list talk, and I want to experience the aurora borealis with you. I think that discussion is when I knew, really knew, that I never wanted to be without you.

"And look at me." Tug spread his arms wide. "I'm over fifteen hundred miles from Whelk's Island. This is a first, even if we don't get lucky enough to experience the northern lights on this trip!"

"You're right. How's it feel to be so far from home?"

"Like the air is a little thin and missing something." He pretended to taste the air. "Mm-hmm. Salt. The air is missing salt."

Rosemary's eyes twinkled with mischief. "We'll trade the salt for the colorful lights. Seems fair enough."

He danced from foot to foot to stay warm. "I'm not sure our warmest beach clothes are going to be warm enough for this place."

"We'll snuggle."

"Yes, we will." He gave her a slow nod that made her giggle. He loved her laugh.

A young man named Ethan hooked the dolly with their luggage on it to the back of his golf cart, ready to take them to their cabin. The sun had set. The only light was the lanterns that lit the path.

Tug hadn't given Rosemary the complete lowdown on this

resort. He was excited to surprise her. Since there was no way to guarantee a northern lights experience, they were hedging the bet on satisfaction with a memorable list of amenities.

Each cabin lay nestled in a perfect spot, providing privacy while still being part of the larger community of eager northern lights–seeking resort guests.

The scent of grilled food wafted through the air, making their stomachs rumble. "It smells like someone is grilling out." Rosemary's nose twitched. "I'm starving."

"We know getting here is a trip in itself," Ethan said. "That's why we start these packages with a private dinner in your cabin upon arrival. Everything is waiting for you. I think you'll be very pleased with the food. We have one of the best chefs working here this winter."

"Wow," Rosemary mouthed.

"A full schedule of your visit and plans are outlined on the desk in your cabin. If you need to change it, just let us know. I see you'll be here for three nights, but actually tonight is the best chance to see the northern lights. NOAA is getting pretty good with these forecasts. I have an app on my phone to help me help you not miss a thing. Oh, and if you want I can call or text if they are out tonight, to be sure you're not sleeping through it."

"Yes," Tug and Rosemary said in unison.

Ethan grinned. "I'll take that as a yes. I know you're probably beat, but maybe put on a pot of coffee to be sure you're ready. If there's anything I can do for you on your visit, my card is on the counter. You can call me twenty-four seven." He deposited them at the cabin and carried in their bags.

"We're here, and isn't this the most adorable little cabin?" Rosemary walked around, touching things.

It was rustic yet luxurious at the same time. A kitchenette

and a stone fireplace in the middle, with bedrooms off each side.

But the real gem was outside—the open-air glamping setup. Cushy lounge chairs, thick blankets, and a clear view of the sky awaited them.

After unpacking, they sat down to the prepared meal, which was as wonderful as Ethan had promised.

Then they moved outside, scooched the two lounge chairs together, and settled into them, bundling up in the thick blankets provided. Tug's hand found Rosemary's.

"You don't think there are bears out here, do you?" she asked. "I don't think I'd like being attacked by a bear."

"I don't imagine it's on anyone's bucket list. Wouldn't they be hibernating?"

"Hope so. Do you think we'll really see the lights?" Rosemary asked, her voice a mix of hope and wonder.

Tug squeezed her hand. "I think we will."

They sat there in comfortable silence, scanning the sky. The stars twinkled brightly, a few shooting stars streaking across the expanse. Rosemary shifted to rest her head on Tug's shoulder.

Tug turned to look at her. "Life has a funny way of surprising us, doesn't it?"

"Mm-hmm. In a beautiful way." She took his hand, then all of the sudden pointed to the sky. "Look, Tug, I think I see something."

"I can see your breath in the crisp night air," he teased.

"I'm serious. See it. There's a faint shimmer of color rippling across the dark horizon."

He leaned in, wondering if his eyes were playing tricks. But it grew ever so slowly—brighter, bolder—until the sky came alive in the colors.

"I see it too." Tug whispered as if speaking louder might disrupt the fragile beauty above as the northern lights unfurled in a breathtaking display of green, pink, and purple.

"The colors twist and dance like ribbons in the wind." Rosemary tilted her head back, her gloved hand brushing Tug's.

He wrapped his hand around hers and squeezed it. The cold bit at his nose, but there was no place he'd rather be. This moment would be hard to surpass. "The colors move as if carried by a current."

Rosemary giggled. "All things lead back to the beach with you, don't they?"

"Maybe. But it's a nice place to be, especially with you."

She laid a soft kiss on his cheek. "It is."

They sat in quiet awe as the heavens painted a masterpiece just for them.

Captivated by the sky, she finally whispered, "It's incredible."

"Even better than incredible." Tug couldn't tell which glow was brighter—the one in the sky or the one blooming between them.

In silence, they watched until the lights began to fade, slowly retreating until the sky was once again filled with only stars. Tug and Rosemary stayed in their chairs, still holding hands, reluctant to leave the magic of the moment behind.

Eventually, they made their way back into the cabin, where the warmth of the fire welcomed them. They settled onto the couch, wrapped in a blanket, and sipped the hot cocoa that Tug had prepared earlier.

"You know," Rosemary said, leaning against Tug, "I think this might be the best night of my life."

Tug kissed the top of her head. "Mine too."

They sat there in contented silence, absorbed by the dancing flames.

"I have something for you," Tug said.

"You do?"

"This is what I think is missing." He reached into his pocket. Between his thumb and forefinger, he held a ring.

"Does this mean—"

"It means whatever you are ready for or want it to mean. Why not let the world know my intention to be there for you forever, every day forward?" He picked up her hand. "May I?"

"Of course, yes."

He slipped the ring on her finger.

Rosemary's hand shook. Softly she said, "'Life takes you to unexpected places. Trust the light to lead you home.'" She looked at him. "I had no idea what that quote meant when I found that shell. I do now. The light is love."

"Like I've never imagined," he said. "Do you love me too?"

"I do." She reached for his hands. "I know you've never married." Her voice was barely a whisper. Her eyes never left his. "Are you asking me to be your wife?"

"Please don't say no." His heart raced.

"Ask me," she said with a smile.

"I better do it right, if I'm going to do it." He looked into Rosemary's eyes, then took a knee. "You might have to help me up after this," he joked, though part of him knew it wasn't entirely untrue. He glanced at the ring already on her finger, the symbol of everything he wanted. "You're wearing the ring. Will you be my wife, Rosemary? My forever? My partner through every tide?"

Her eyes sparkled with that familiar warmth that had always drawn him in. "I'd be so honored to be your wife," she whispered, and before he could speak, she leaned down and kissed him.

He wrapped his arms around her, holding her close.

"This is it—the start of our forever." No grand speeches were needed, just the quiet understanding between them.

He kissed her again, slow and tender, feeling a youthful spark as he thought of the countless moments still waiting for them. They'd mark off the items on their bucket lists together, one by one, hand in hand.

Dear Reader,

Thank you for joining me for another visit to the fictional town of Whelk's Island. I imagine this town being somewhere along the southern end of the Outer Banks of North Carolina, where I've spent so much time over the years. As Virginia Beach natives, we flocked to North Carolina when the tourists flooded our beach. It's grown a lot over the years. More year-round residents and many more tourists, but still one of my favorite places.

If you've already read *The Shell Collector,* you've met Tug before. The owner of Tug's Diner and Maeve's dearest. *The Shell Collector* is the book of my heart, born following the loss of my husband in 2014 and, just five weeks later, my dear cousin Diane. She once told me the story about a friend of our family who walked the beach every morning. One day, while walking through the edge of the surf with something weighing heavy on her heart, she kicked up a shell. As she reached down to pick it up, she noticed a message written inside the shell. It was the perfect message to put her heart at ease that day. Long story short, that woman found a few other shells, but no one else found any, and no one knew who had written the notes. The day I lost my cousin, my first thought was, *I could use a bucket of those shells right now,* and that was etched into my grieving heart.

I was honored to have *The Shell Collector* adapted for the television screen, the first Fox Nation original movie and still streaming on Fox Nation. In that adaptation, Tug came to life just as I'd imagined. His love was deep, his actions honorable, and I knew I owed him a love story.

I hope Tug's love story in this special beach town is one that will linger in your heart.

And most importantly, because I'd hate for a tragic storm named Edwina to happen after I wrote about it, I want you to know that I intentionally chose a fictitious name. I concentrated on community pulling together to navigate the tragedy with grace, and among the rubble, it was so exciting to see love slip into the crevices of two lonely hearts.

With love,
Nancy

Readers Guide

1. How does the title, *To Light the Way Forward,* tie to the themes in this novel?

2. How did you feel about where Amanda and Paul were in their relationship as you began reading?

3. What was your first impression of Rosemary? Did you warm up to her quickly?

4. Tug left such a lasting impression in *The Shell Collector.* How did you feel about the possibility of him finding love?

5. The relationship between adult children and aging parents can be a delicate balance. Knowing when to intercede is tricky. Both Rosemary and Nina had good intentions, but they didn't always get it right. How so? What have you learned works best?

6. What lighthearted moments did you find particularly enjoyable?

7. Bucket lists come up as a way to focus on the future. How was this a special part of the story, and in what ways did it inspire you to consider things you might like to do?

8. What is your favorite quote from the book?

9. In what ways does the Whelk's Island story seem complete? What other stories are yet to be told on Whelk's Island?

Acknowledgments

This story came to me as I watched the television adaptation of *The Shell Collector* on Fox Nation. The actor who portrayed Tug brought that character to life just as he'd been in my heart and mind, and as I watched the scenes unfold between Tug and Maeve, I knew there had to be a story where Tug found love. Thank you, Jim Ewens of British Columbia, for the brilliant performance.

To my agent, Steve Laube, for guiding me through a season of change in my career as I grew in ways I'd never expected and for helping me through that difficult time so I could still tell stories that mattered.

To the entire team at WaterBrook, who continue to be such a beacon for this body of work. From idea to bookshelf, every team member brings such beauty to the process. And to my amazing editor, Jamie Lapeyrolerie, for embracing me and this idea for a second novel set on Whelk's Island and seeing the potential for a third. You've strengthened my skill set, nudging me to go that extra emotional distance, and I can never thank you enough for that. Thank you for every mentoring moment and the special touches you helped inspire in this story.

To Steve Harvey, who has no idea who the heck I am, but as I researched motivation and living your best life for this novel, I ran across his speech "Jump!" and it inspired me in such a special way. I hope everyone takes a minute to find it and listen to it. Thanks, Steve, for being you—spreading joy, laughs, and hope at every turn, something I try to do every day too.

Writing can be solitary, but having friends who are there during the process makes all the difference. The phone calls, months of no phone calls but knowing the support is there, and celebrating the wins together mean everything. To Sasha Summers, Lauren Ashwood, Karen Schaler, Lindsay Gibson, and Jenny Hale: Thank you all for moments you probably weren't aware of that helped me through the writing of this novel. But most of all, to Pam, who always helps me see the light that will lead me forward when I hit difficult times. Thank you for knowing when I need that.

And to my pastor, Charles Qualls, who is a fellow author, for his sermon that spoke directly to the scene that was still floating in my mind that Sunday morning in church. Thank you for letting me leverage your wisdom and kindness and pull bits of that sermon into this story. It was my pleasure to share your special touch with the world through a cameo character.

About the Author

USA Today and ECPA bestselling author Nancy Naigle whips up small-town love stories with a whole lot of heart. She began writing while juggling a successful career in finance and life on a seventy-six-acre farm. Now happily retired, this Virginia girl devotes her time to writing, antiquing, and spa days with friends.

Several of Nancy's novels have been adapted for television. You can find the complete list of movies and a free downloadable checklist of all her books in series order on her website, www.nancynaigle.com.

hose Who Have Lost Know the Value in Finding–and in Being Found

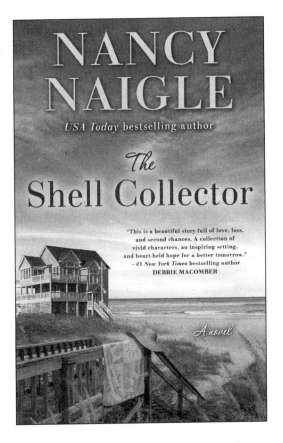

Single mother Amanda struggles to move on after her husband's death, heartbroken veteran Paul seeks meaning in work, and widow Maeve anchors the town in steadfast tradition. In this story of love and loss, friendships cross generations, while the smallest gifts from the heart lead to healing–and perhaps even love.

Learn more about Nancy's books at waterbrookmultnomah.com.

Three Months Can Change a Life– and Lead to Love

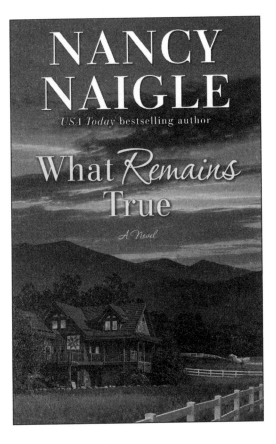

Successful executive Merry Anna Foster plans to be in Antler Creek for only three months. Budding rodeo star Adam Lockwood has no immediate plans to settle down. But when a little girl suddenly gets left in his care, both must reevaluate their well-laid plans–and listen to their hearts.

 **WATERBROOK**

Learn more about Nancy's books at waterbrookmultnomah.com.